Unicornado

Another
Phoebe and Her Unicorn Adventure

Complete Your Phoebe and Her Unicorn Collection

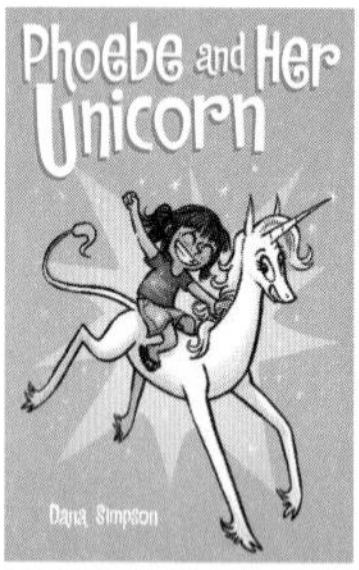
Phoebe and Her Unicorn
Dana Simpson

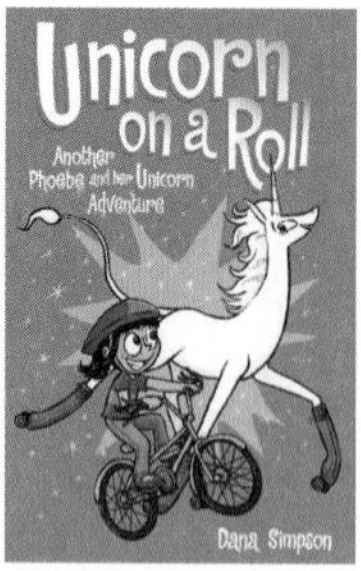
Unicorn on a Roll
Another Phoebe and Her Unicorn Adventure
Dana Simpson

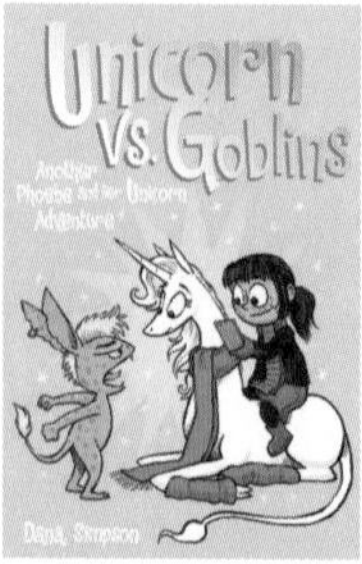
Unicorn vs. Goblins
Another Phoebe and Her Unicorn Adventure
Dana Simpson

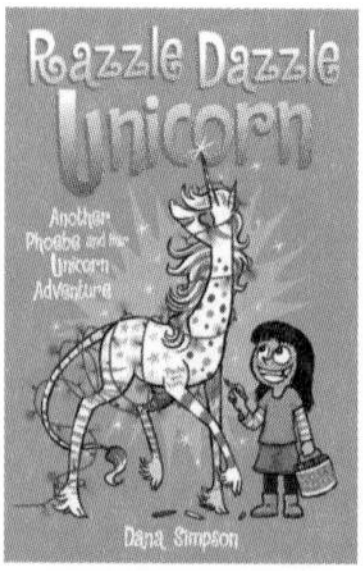
Razzle Dazzle Unicorn
Another Phoebe and Her Unicorn Adventure
Dana Simpson

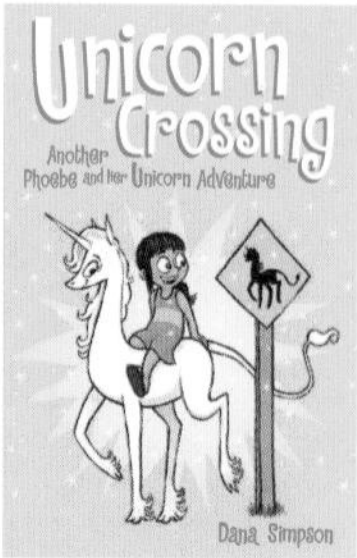
Unicorn Crossing
Another Phoebe and Her Unicorn Adventure
Dana Simpson

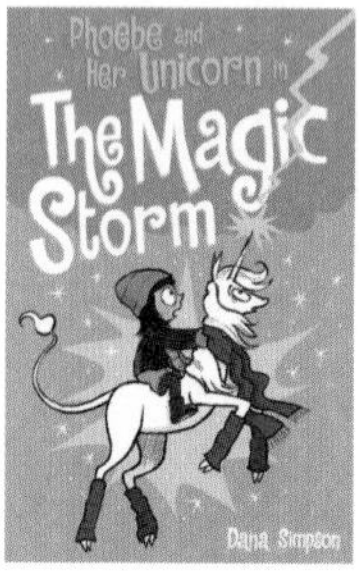
Phoebe and Her Unicorn in The Magic Storm
Dana Simpson

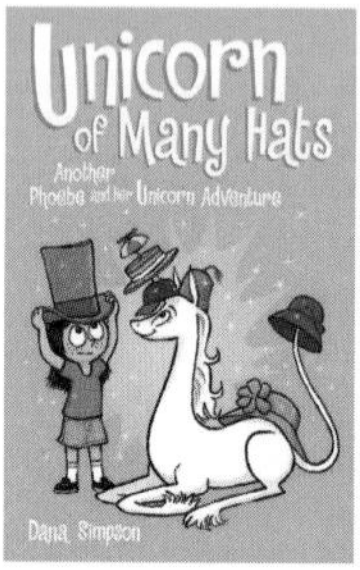
Unicorn of Many Hats
Another Phoebe and Her Unicorn Adventure
Dana Simpson

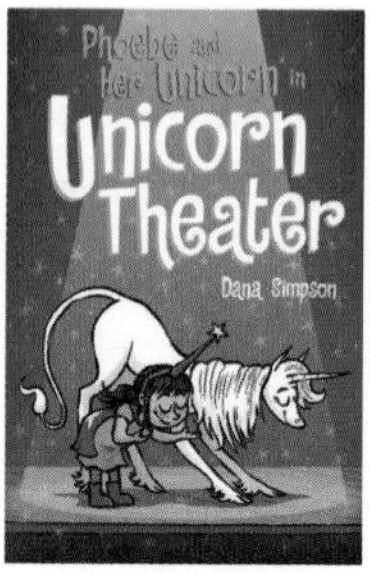
Phoebe and Her Unicorn in Unicorn Theater
Dana Simpson

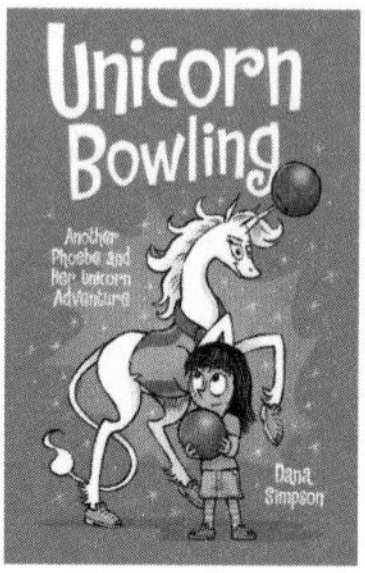
Unicorn Bowling
Another Phoebe and Her Unicorn Adventure
Dana Simpson

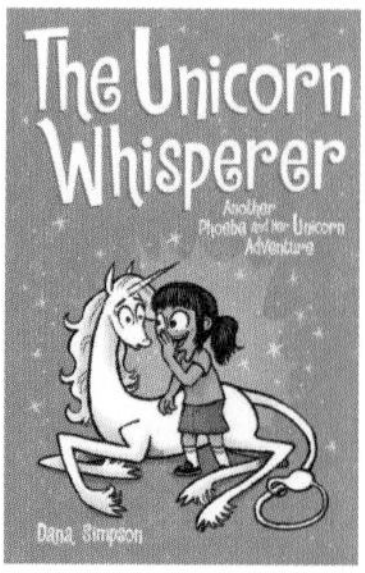
The Unicorn Whisperer
Another Phoebe and Her Unicorn Adventure
Dana Simpson

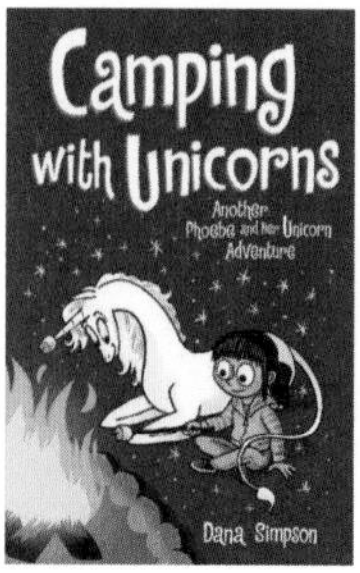
Camping with Unicorns
Another Phoebe and Her Unicorn Adventure
Dana Simpson

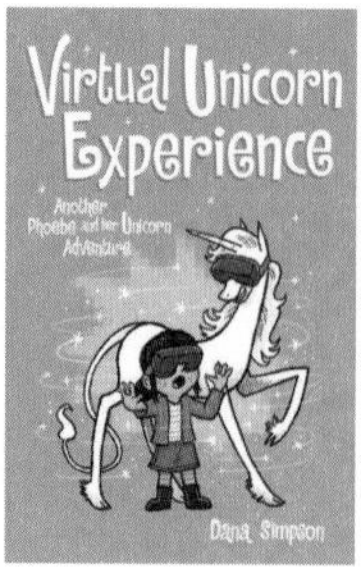
Virtual Unicorn Experience
Another Phoebe and Her Unicorn Adventure
Dana Simpson

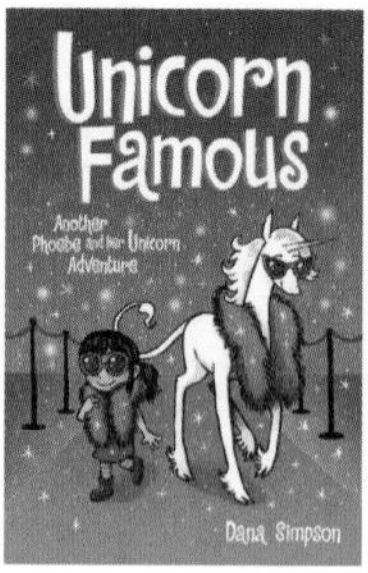
Unicorn Famous
Another Phoebe and Her Unicorn Adventure
Dana Simpson

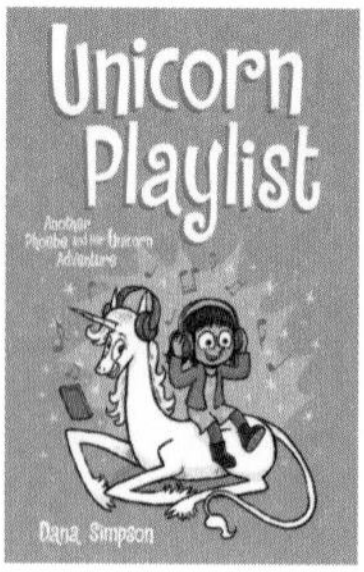
Unicorn Playlist
Another Phoebe and Her Unicorn Adventure
Dana Simpson

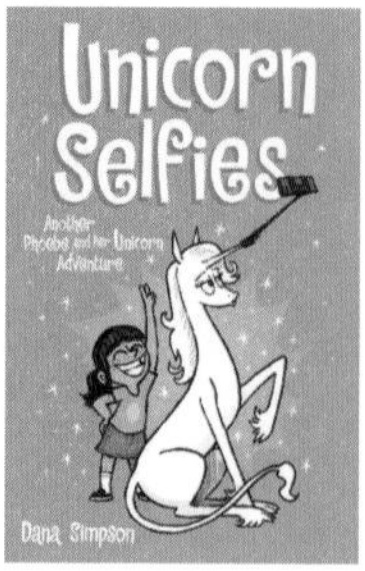
Unicorn Selfies
Another Phoebe and Her Unicorn Adventure
Dana Simpson

Unicornado
Another
Phoebe and Her Unicorn Adventure

Dana Simpson

Andrews McMeel
PUBLISHING®

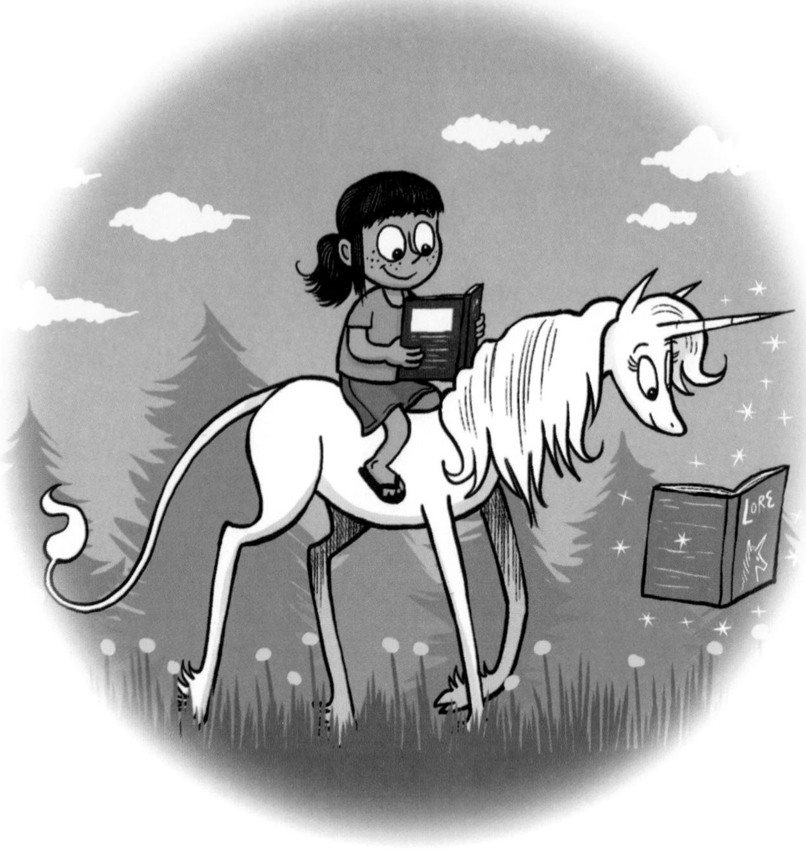
LORE

Hey, kids!

Check out the glossary starting on page 172
if you come across words you don't know.

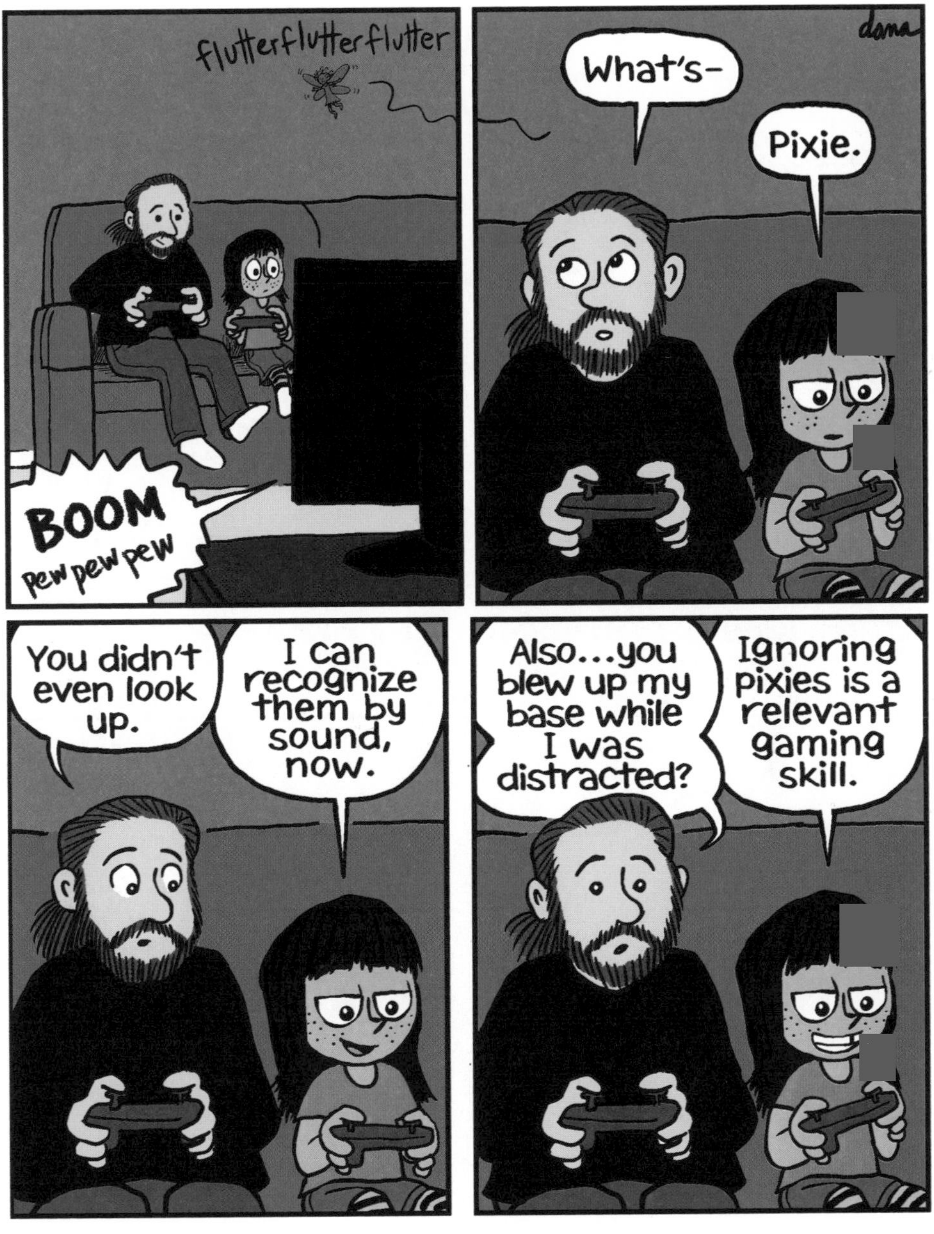
flutterflutterflutter
BOOM
pew pew pew
dana
What's-
Pixie.
You didn't even look up.
I can recognize them by sound, now.
Also...you blew up my base while I was distracted?
Ignoring pixies is a relevant gaming skill.

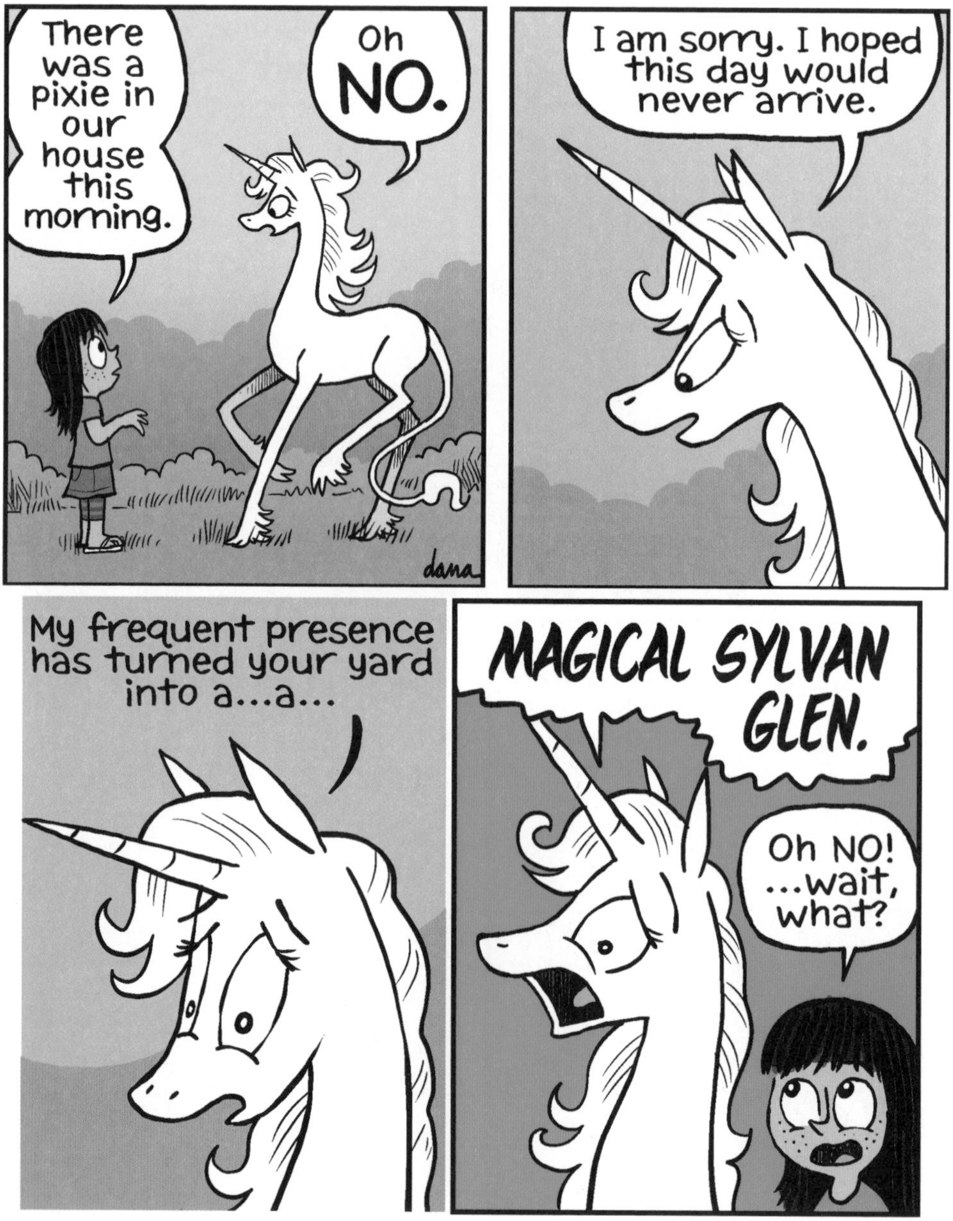
There was a pixie in our house this morning.
Oh NO.
I am sorry. I hoped this day would never arrive.
dana
My frequent presence has turned your yard into a...a...
MAGICAL SYLVAN GLEN.
Oh NO! ...wait, what?

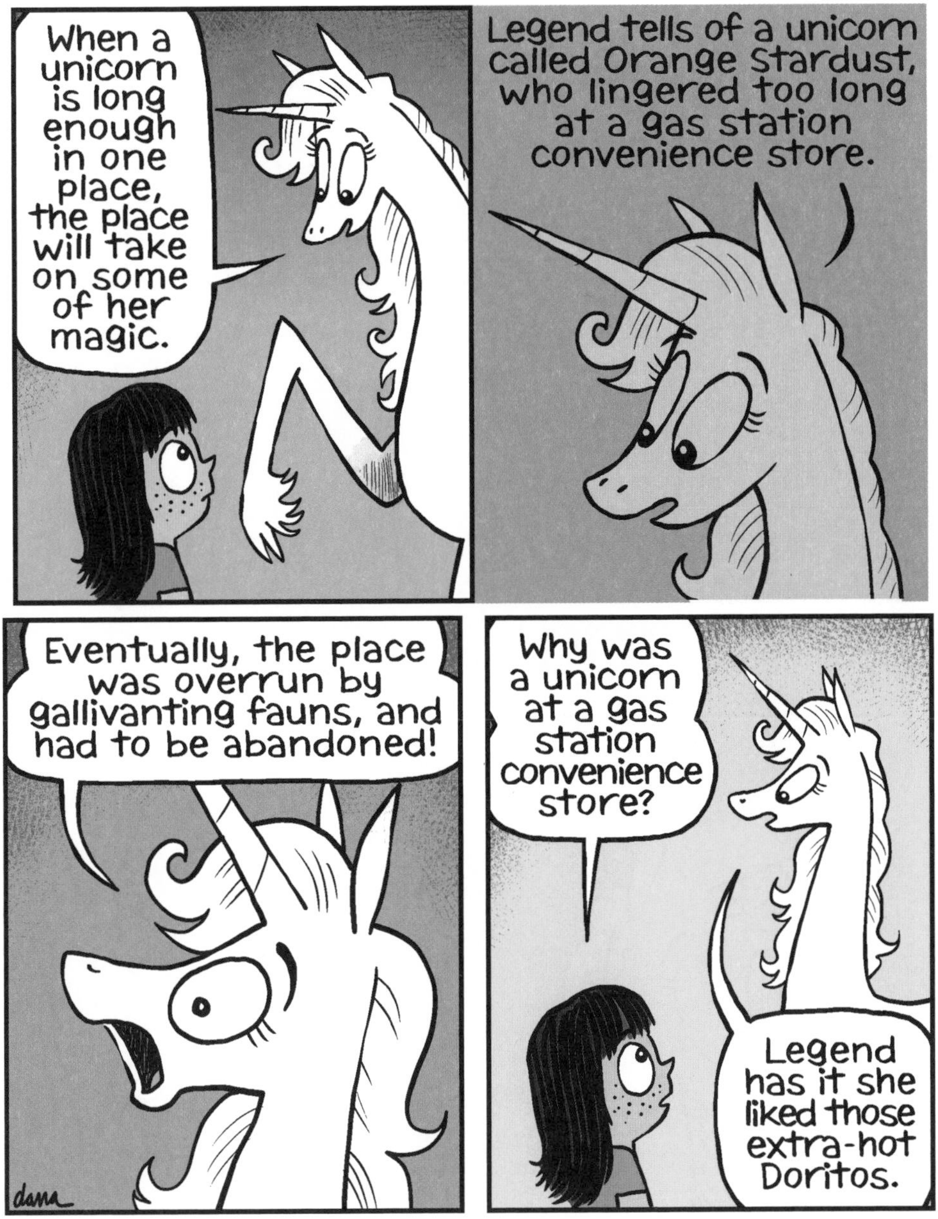
When a unicorn is long enough in one place, the place will take on some of her magic.
Legend tells of a unicorn called Orange Stardust, who lingered too long at a gas station convenience store.
Eventually, the place was overrun by gallivanting fauns, and had to be abandoned!
Why was a unicorn at a gas station convenience store?
Legend has it she liked those extra-hot Doritos.
dana

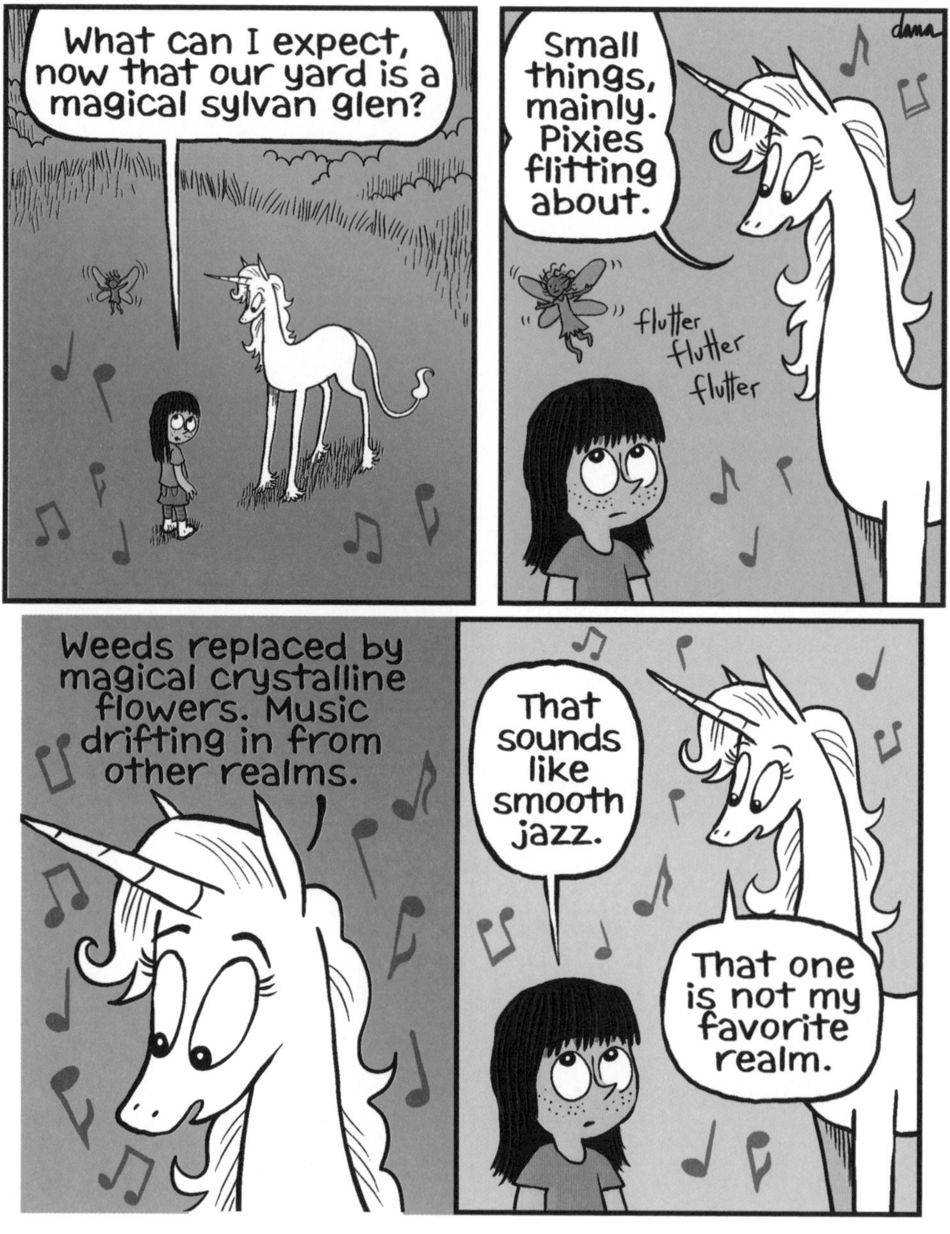
What can I expect, now that our yard is a magical sylvan glen?
Small things, mainly. Pixies flitting about.
flutter
flutter
flutter
Weeds replaced by magical crystalline flowers. Music drifting in from other realms.
That sounds like smooth jazz.
That one is not my favorite realm.

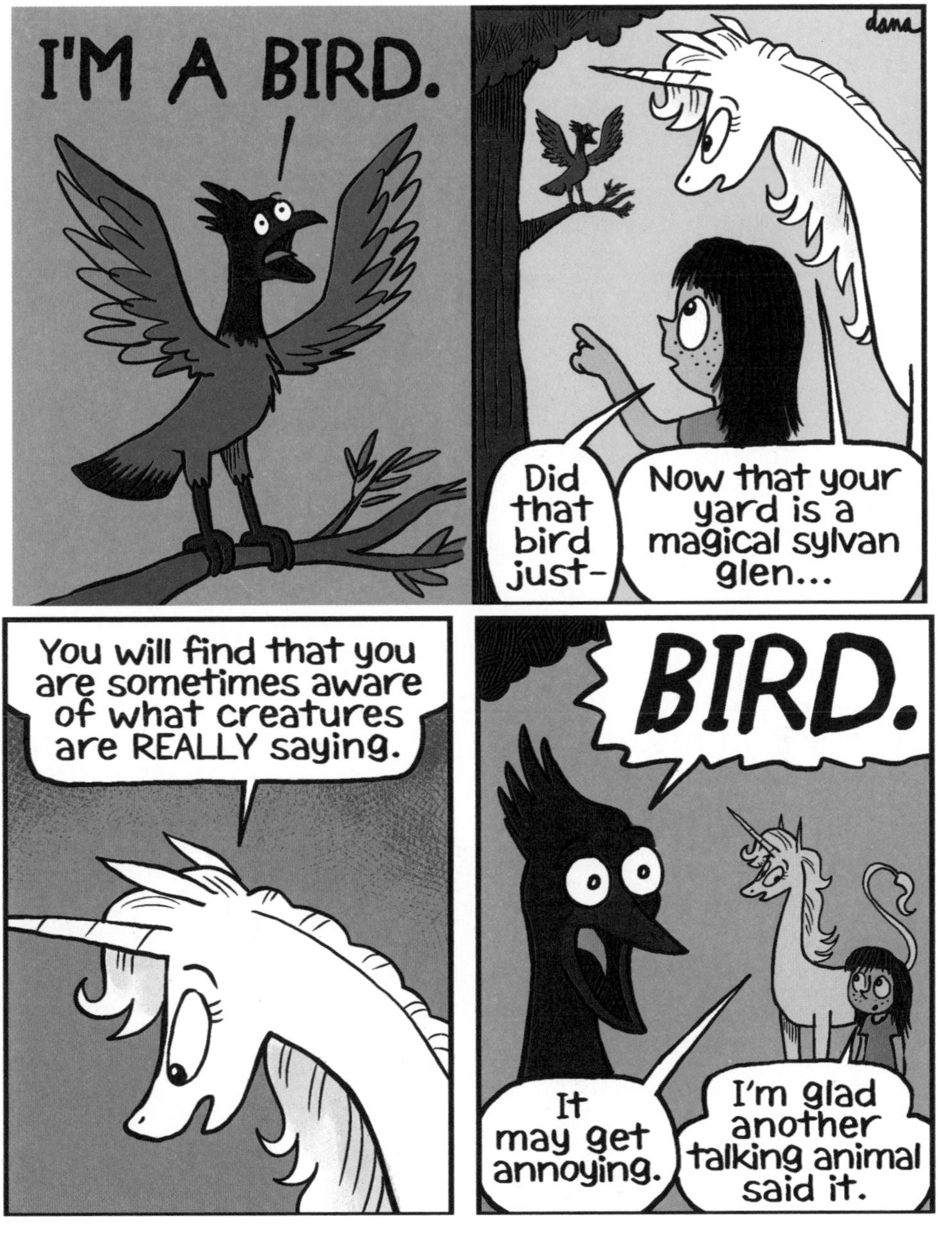

I'M A BIRD.
dana
Did that bird just-
Now that your yard is a magical sylvan glen...
You will find that you are sometimes aware of what creatures are REALLY saying.
BIRD.
It may get annoying.
I'm glad another talking animal said it.

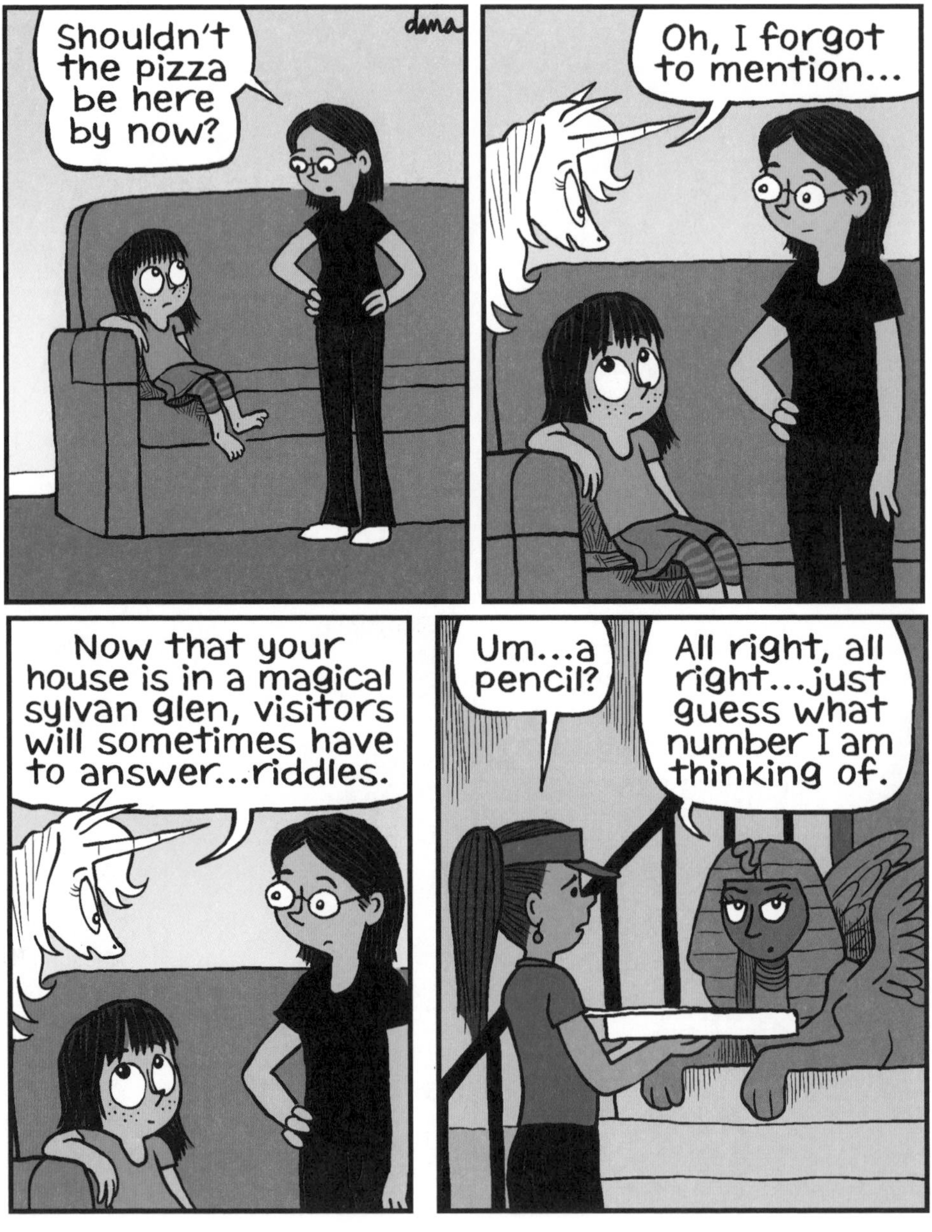
dana
Shouldn't the pizza be here by now?
Oh, I forgot to mention...
Now that your house is in a magical sylvan glen, visitors will sometimes have to answer...riddles.
Um...a pencil?
All right, all right...just guess what number I am thinking of.

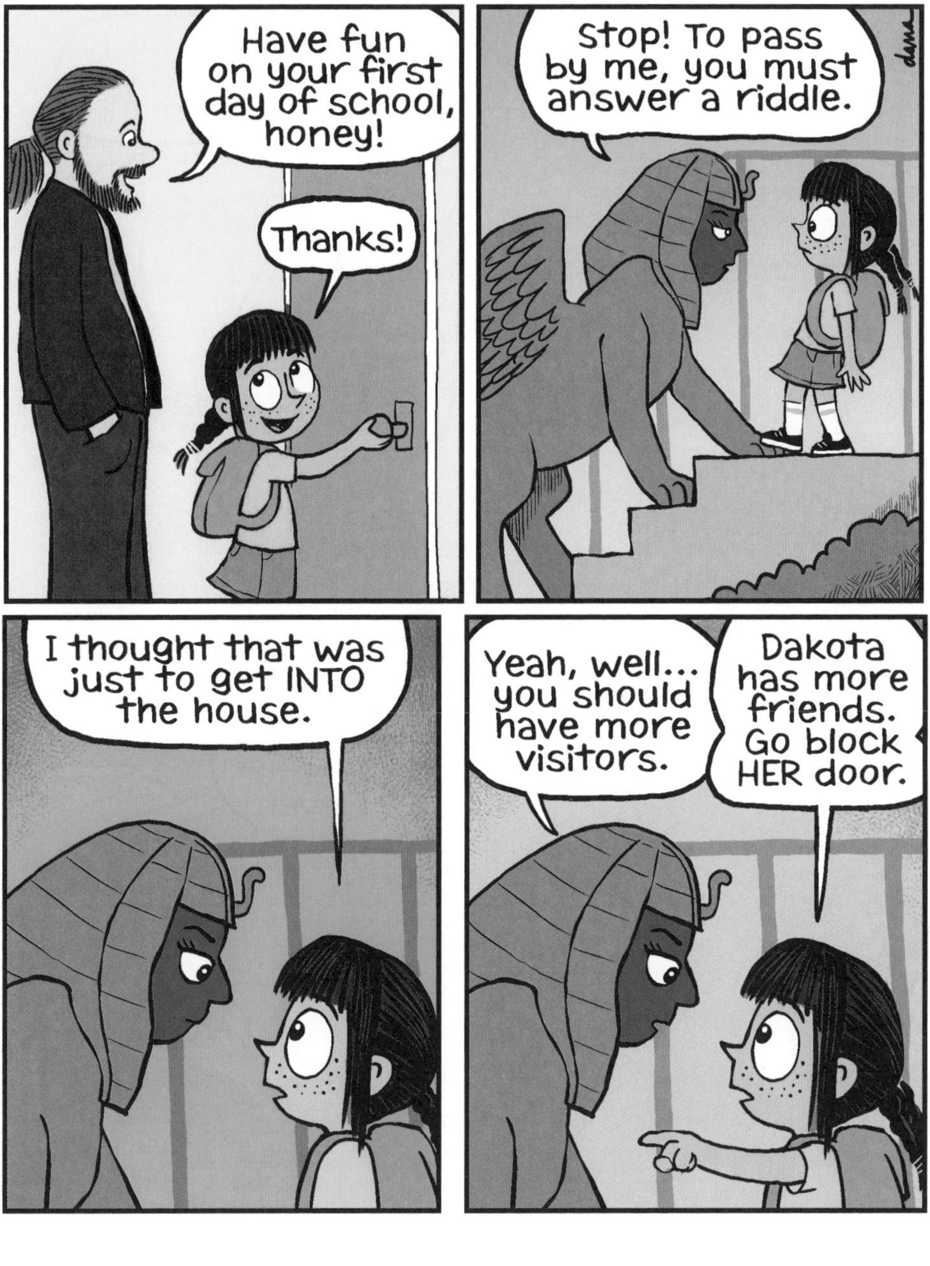
Have fun on your first day of school, honey!
Thanks!
Stop! To pass by me, you must answer a riddle.
I thought that was just to get INTO the house.
Yeah, well... you should have more visitors.
Dakota has more friends. Go block HER door.

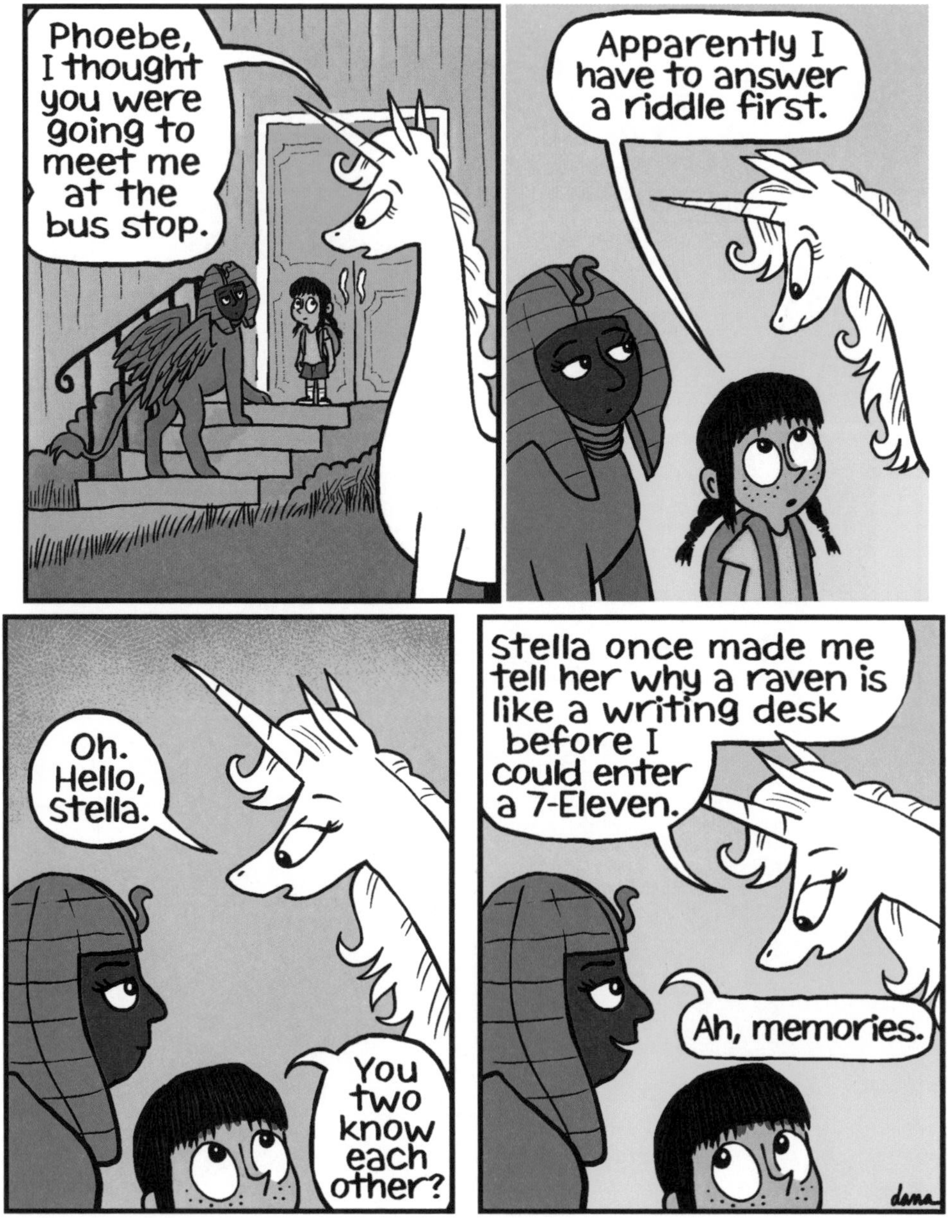
Phoebe, I thought you were going to meet me at the bus stop.
Apparently I have to answer a riddle first.
Oh. Hello, Stella.
You two know each other?
Stella once made me tell her why a raven is like a writing desk before I could enter a 7-Eleven.
Ah, memories.
dana

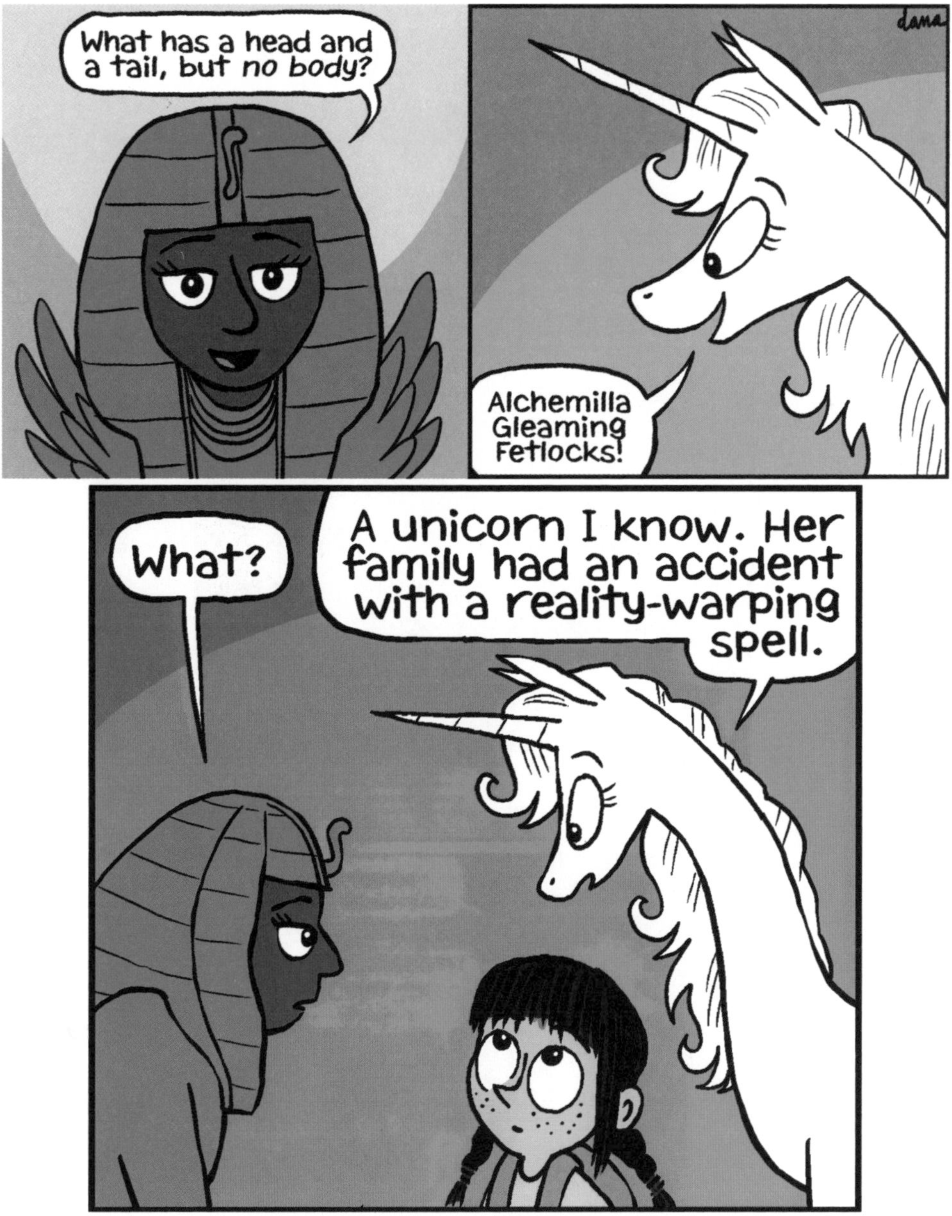
What has a head and a tail, but *no body?*
dana
Alchemilla Gleaming Fetlocks!
What?
A unicorn I know. Her family had an accident with a reality-warping spell.

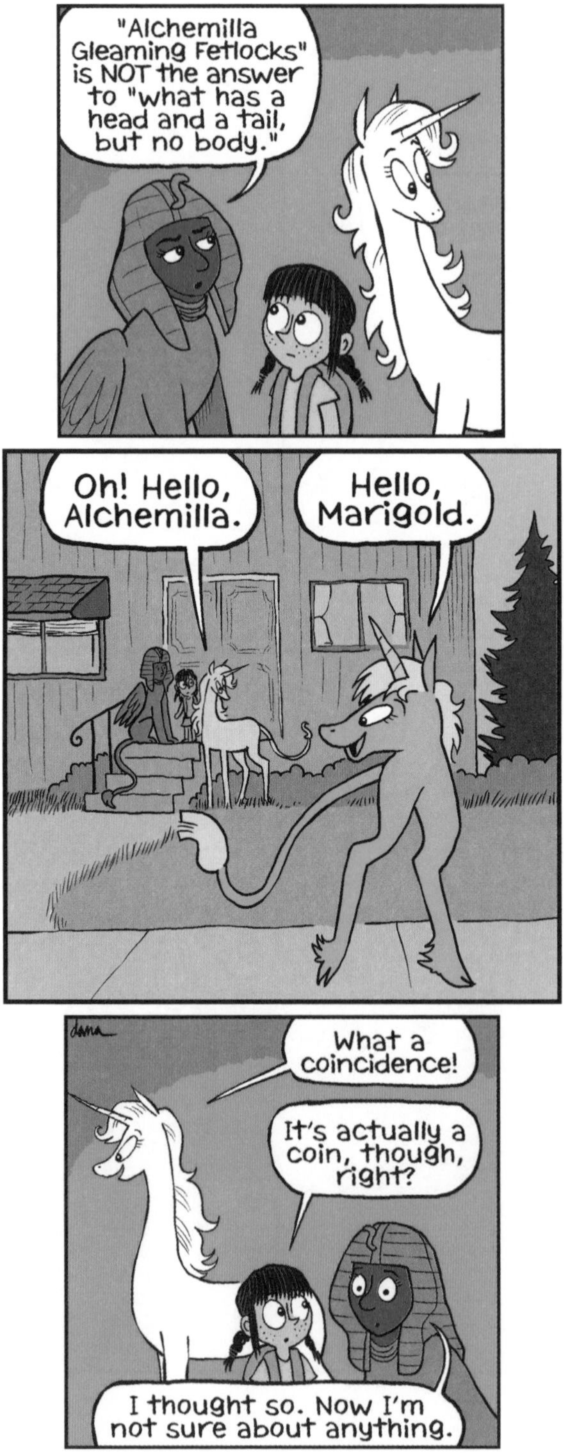
"Alchemilla Gleaming Fetlocks" is NOT the answer to "what has a head and a tail, but no body."
Oh! Hello, Alchemilla.
Hello, Marigold.
What a coincidence!
It's actually a coin, though, right?
I thought so. Now I'm not sure about anything.

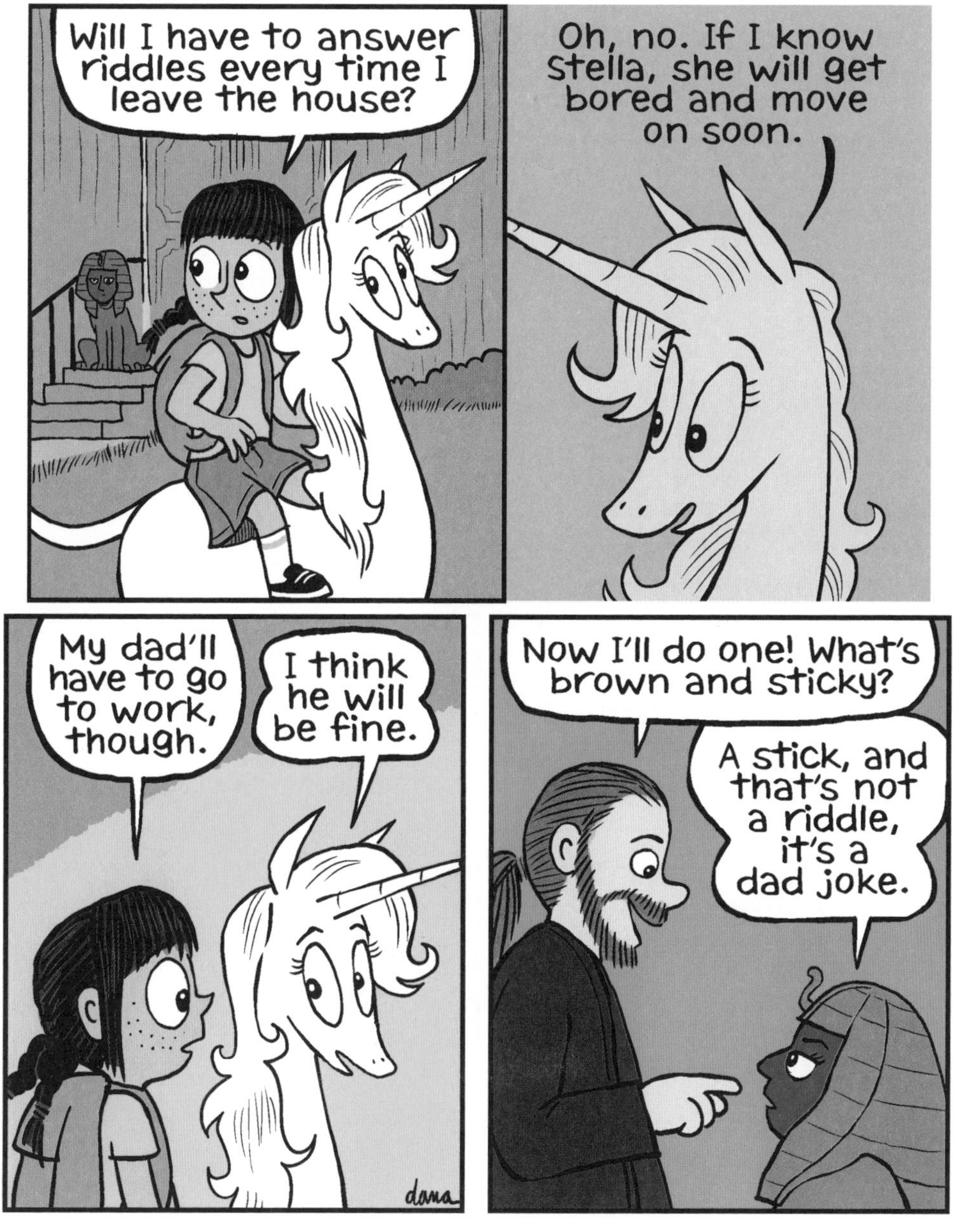
Will I have to answer riddles every time I leave the house?
Oh, no. If I know Stella, she will get bored and move on soon.
My dad'll have to go to work, though.
I think he will be fine.
Now I'll do one! What's brown and sticky?
A stick, and that's not a riddle, it's a dad joke.
dana

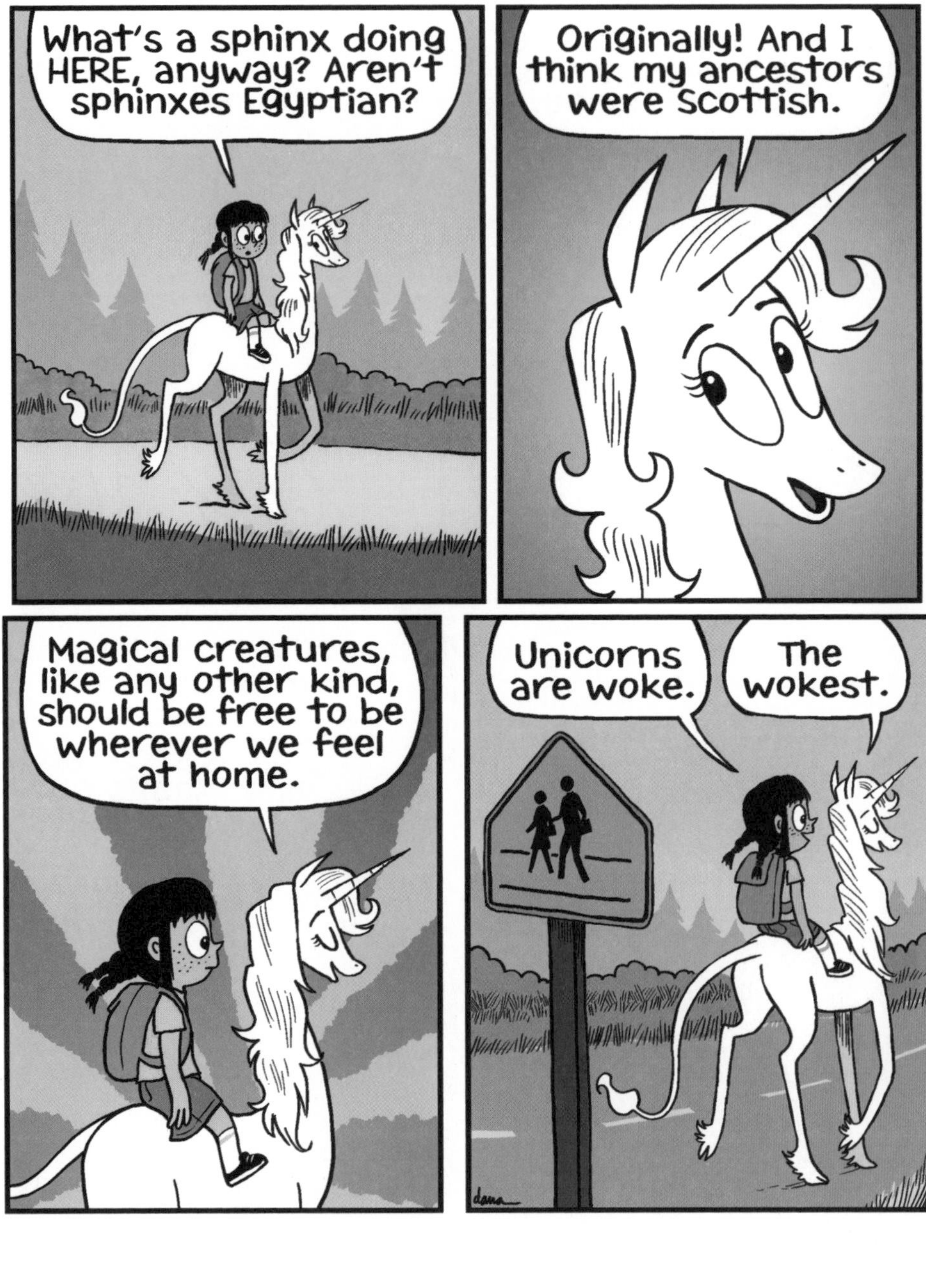
What's a sphinx doing HERE, anyway? Aren't sphinxes Egyptian?
Originally! And I think my ancestors were Scottish.
Magical creatures, like any other kind, should be free to be wherever we feel at home.
Unicorns are woke.
The wokest.

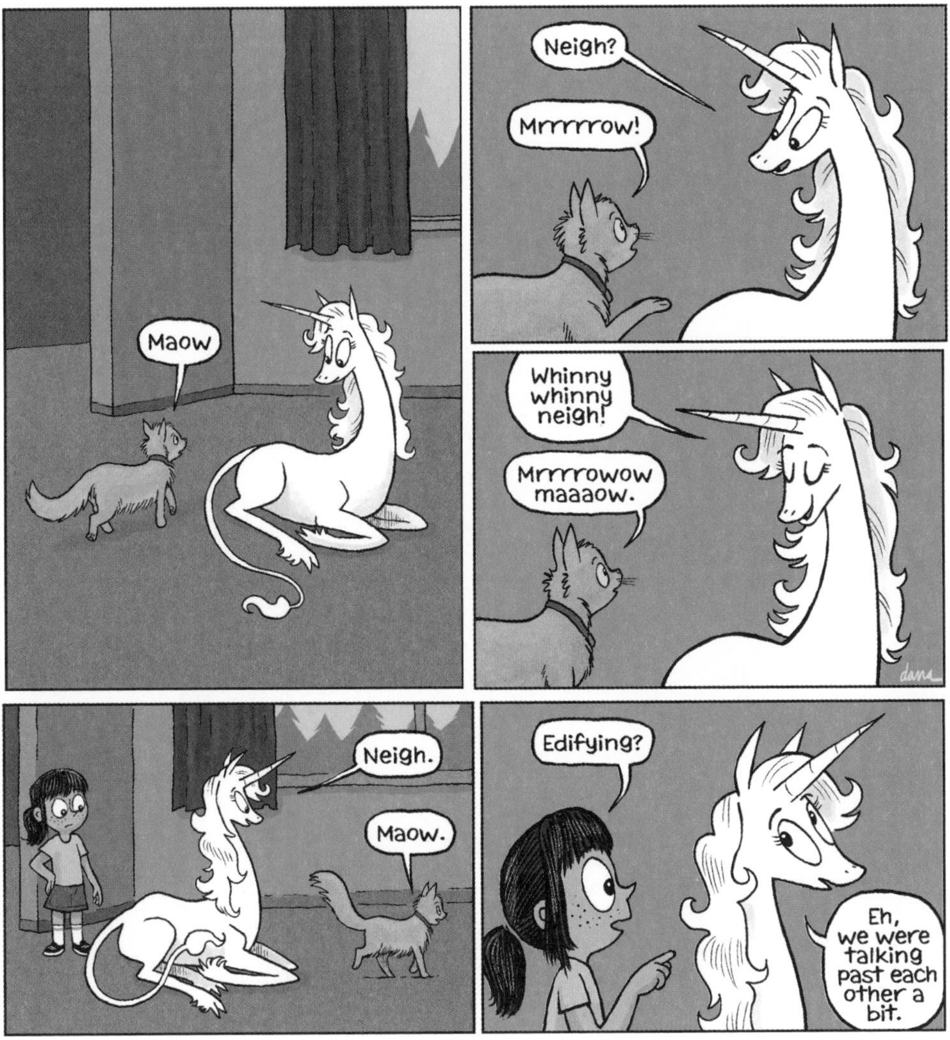
Maow
Neigh?
Mrrrrrow!
Whinny whinny neigh!
Mrrrrowow maaaow.
dana
Neigh.
Maow.
Edifying?
Eh, we were talking past each other a bit.

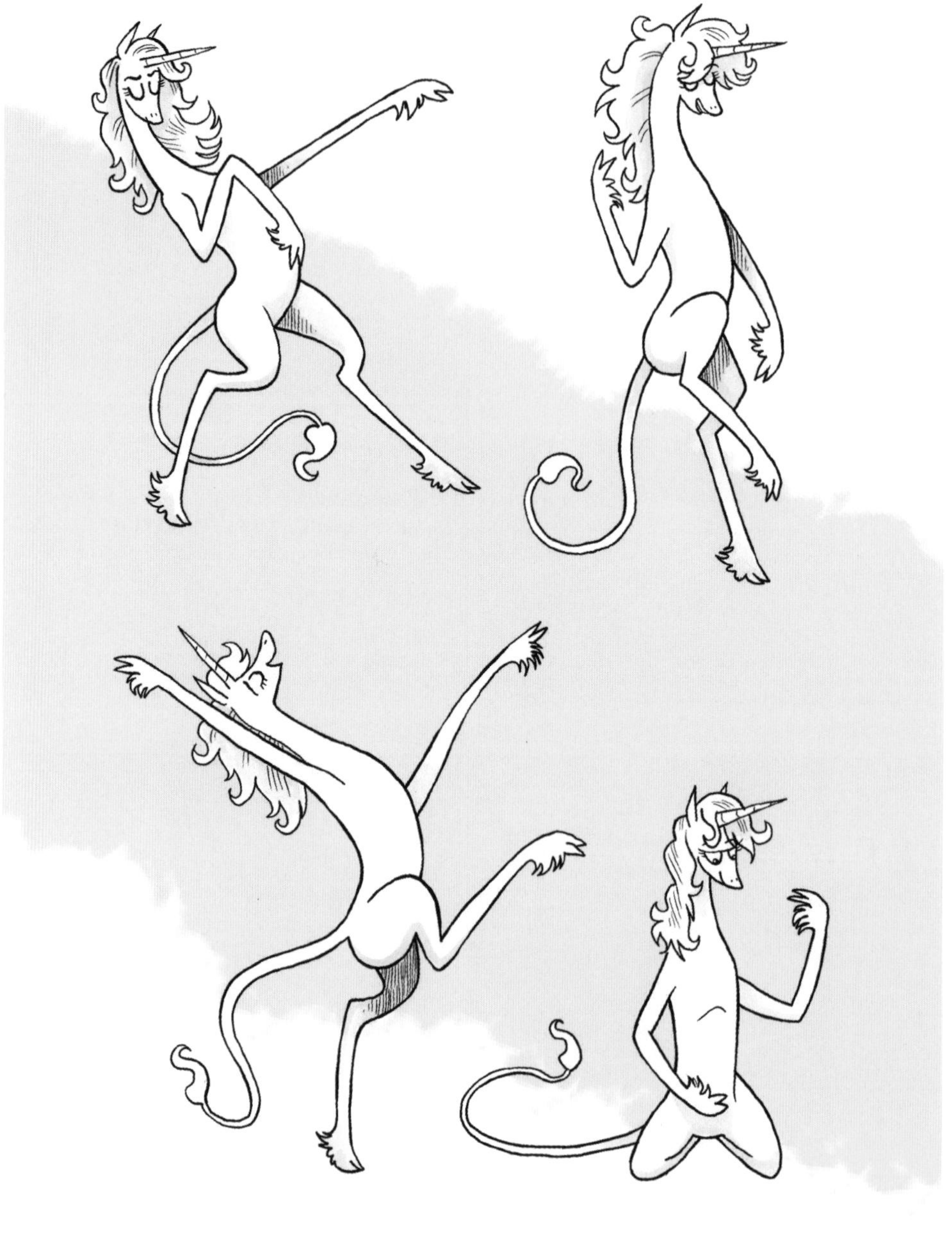

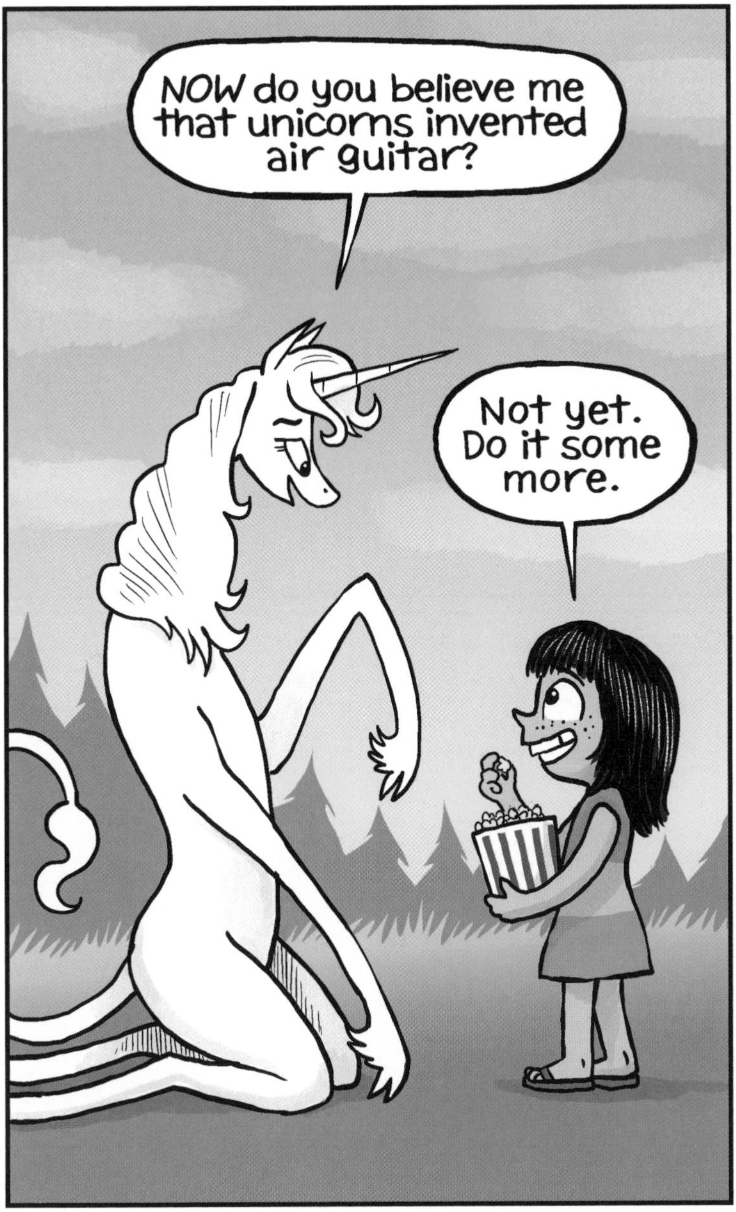
NOW do you believe me that unicorns invented air guitar?
Not yet. Do it some more.

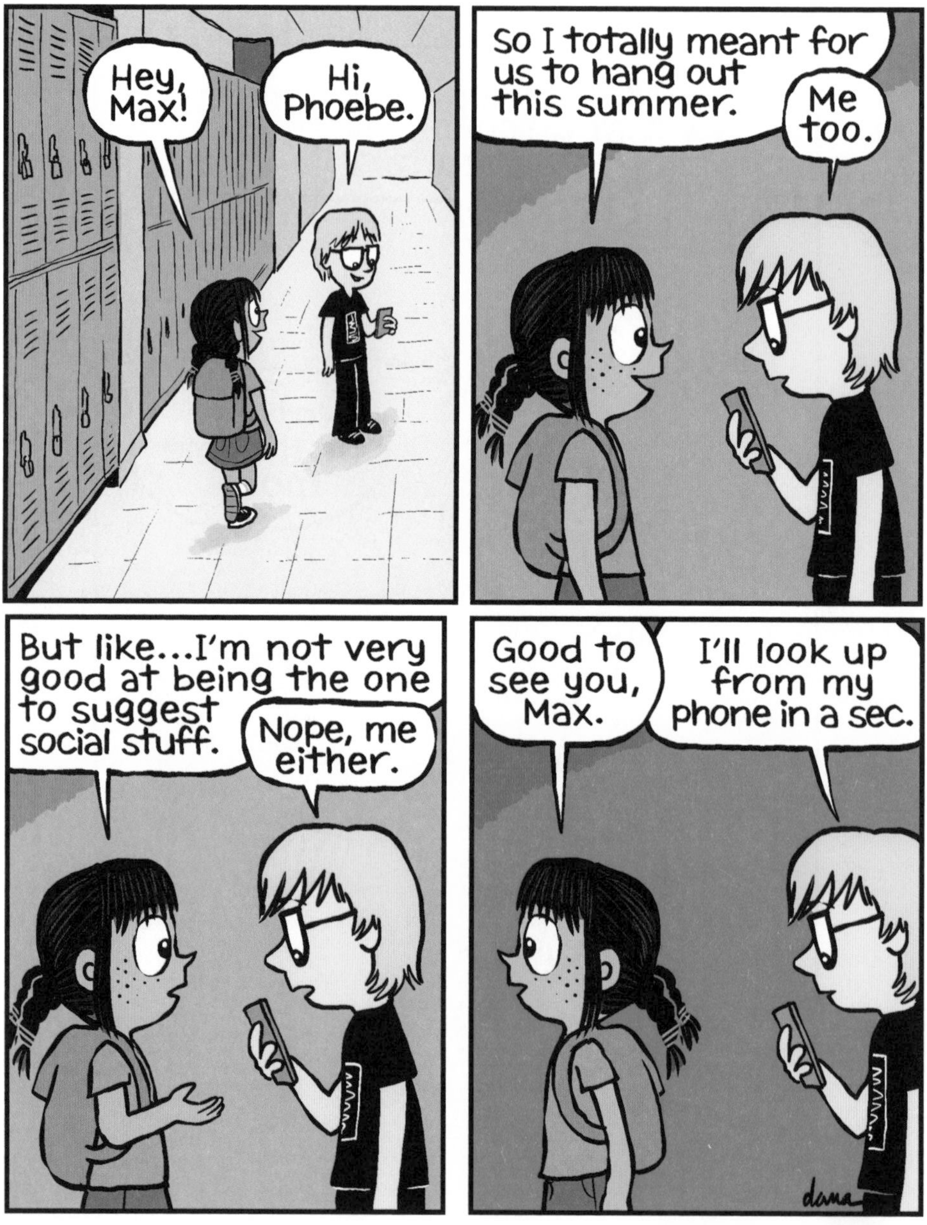
Hey, Max!
Hi, Phoebe.
So I totally meant for us to hang out this summer.
Me too.
But like...I'm not very good at being the one to suggest social stuff.
Nope, me either.
Good to see you, Max.
I'll look up from my phone in a sec.
dana

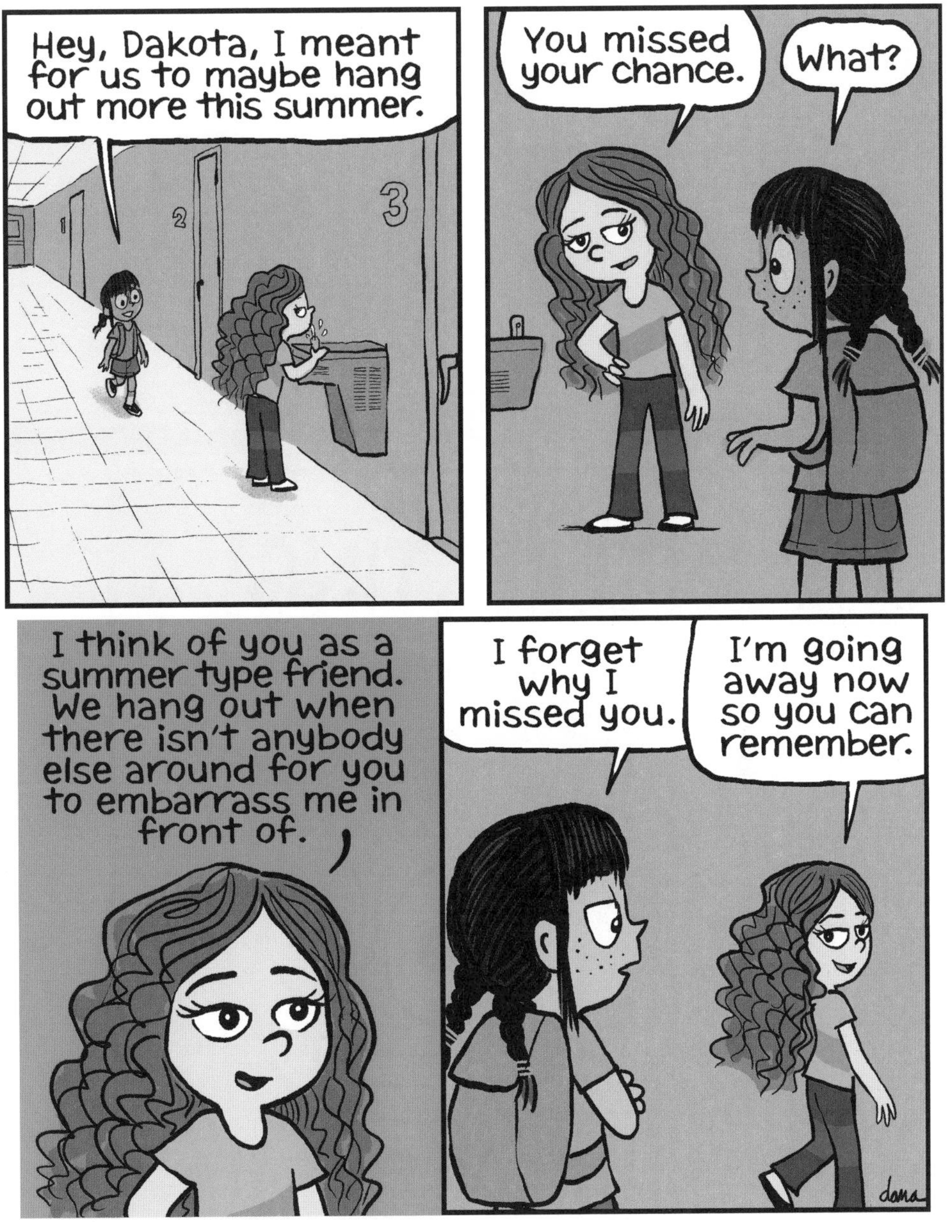
Hey, Dakota, I meant for us to maybe hang out more this summer.
3
2
1
You missed your chance.
What?
I think of you as a summer type friend. We hang out when there isn't anybody else around for you to embarrass me in front of.
I forget why I missed you.
I'm going away now so you can remember.
dana

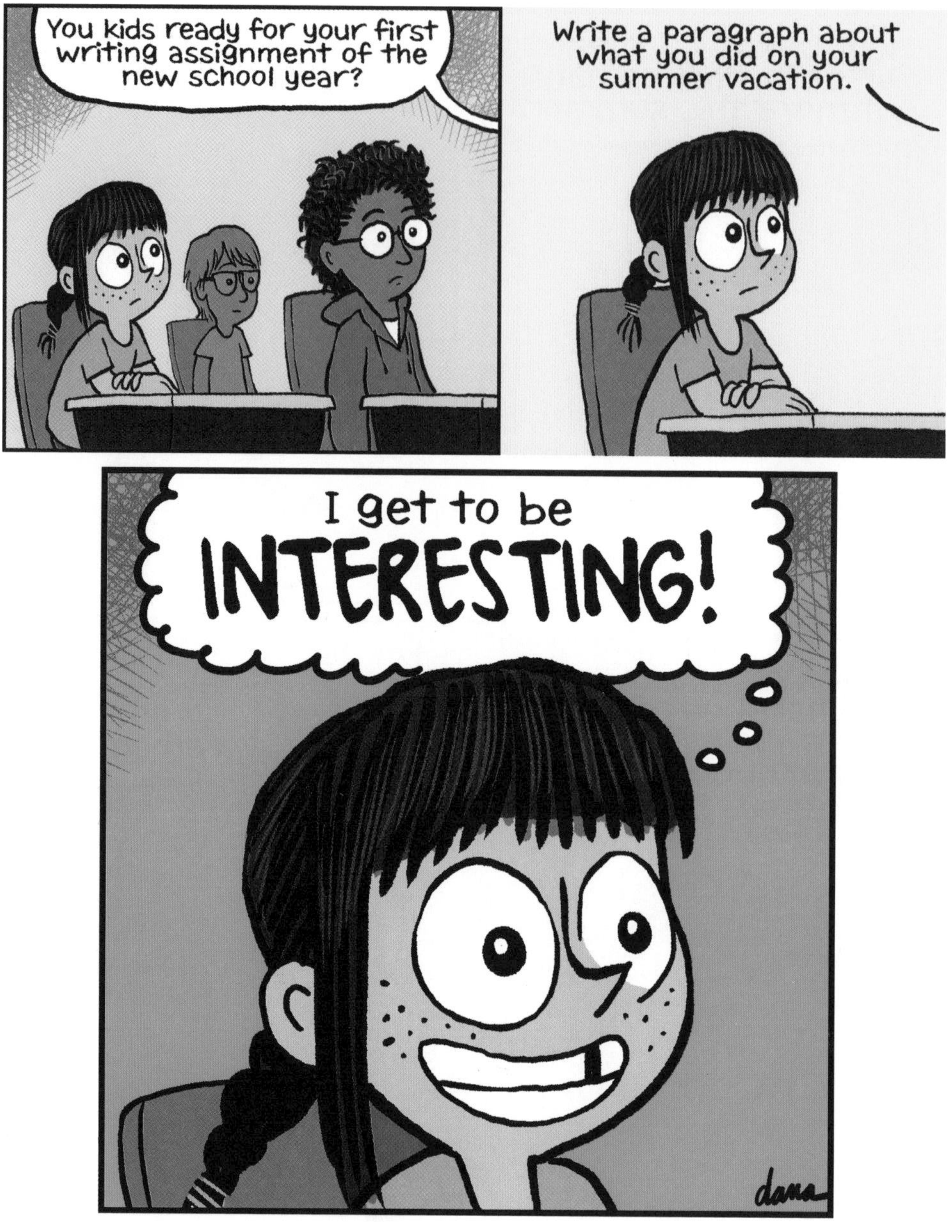
You kids ready for your first writing assignment of the new school year?
Write a paragraph about what you did on your summer vacation.
I get to be INTERESTING!
dana

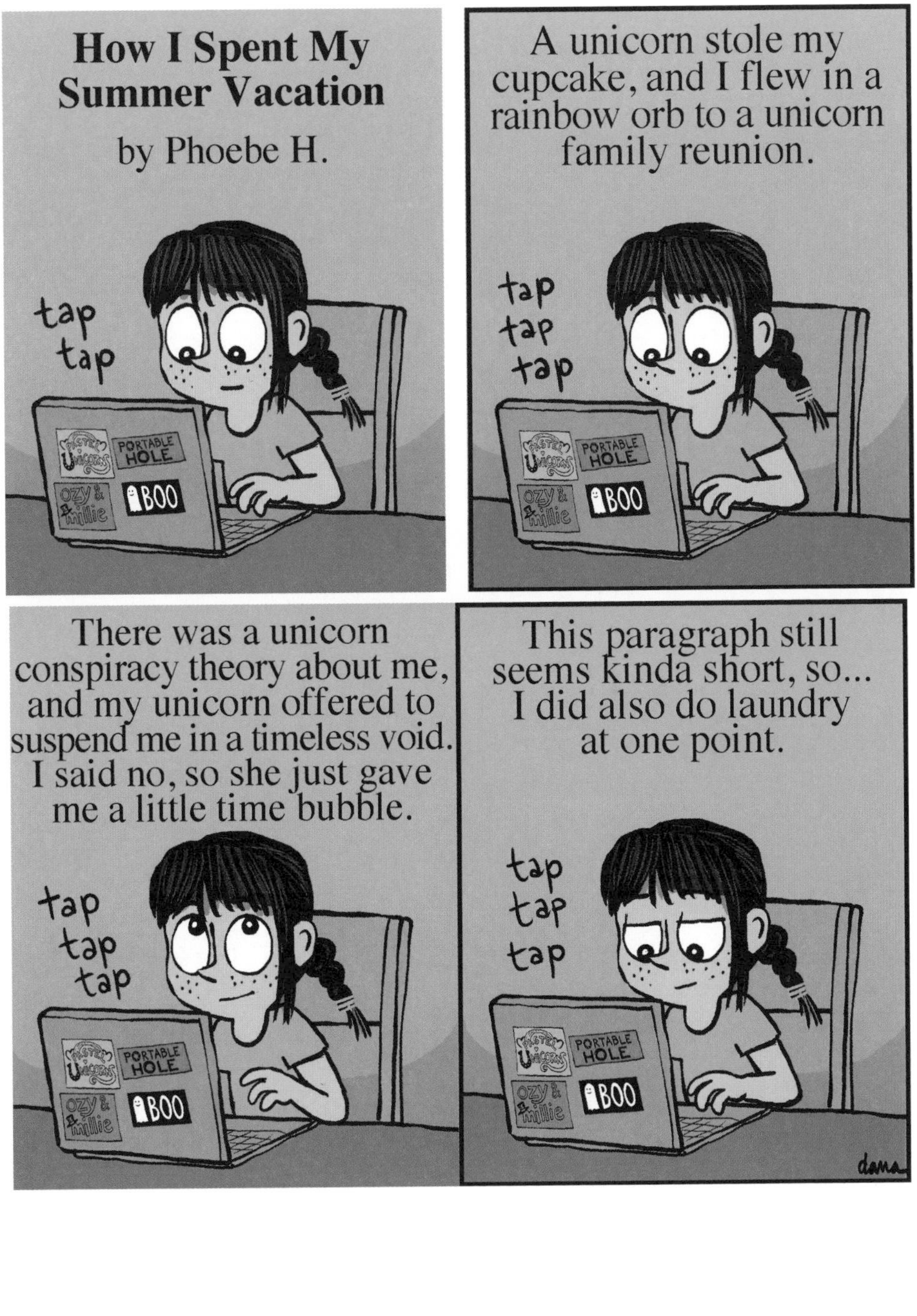
How I Spent My Summer Vacation
by Phoebe H.
tap tap
PORTABLE HOLE
BOO
A unicorn stole my cupcake, and I flew in a rainbow orb to a unicorn family reunion.
tap tap tap
There was a unicorn conspiracy theory about me, and my unicorn offered to suspend me in a timeless void. I said no, so she just gave me a little time bubble.
tap tap tap
This paragraph still seems kinda short, so... I did also do laundry at one point.
tap tap tap
dana

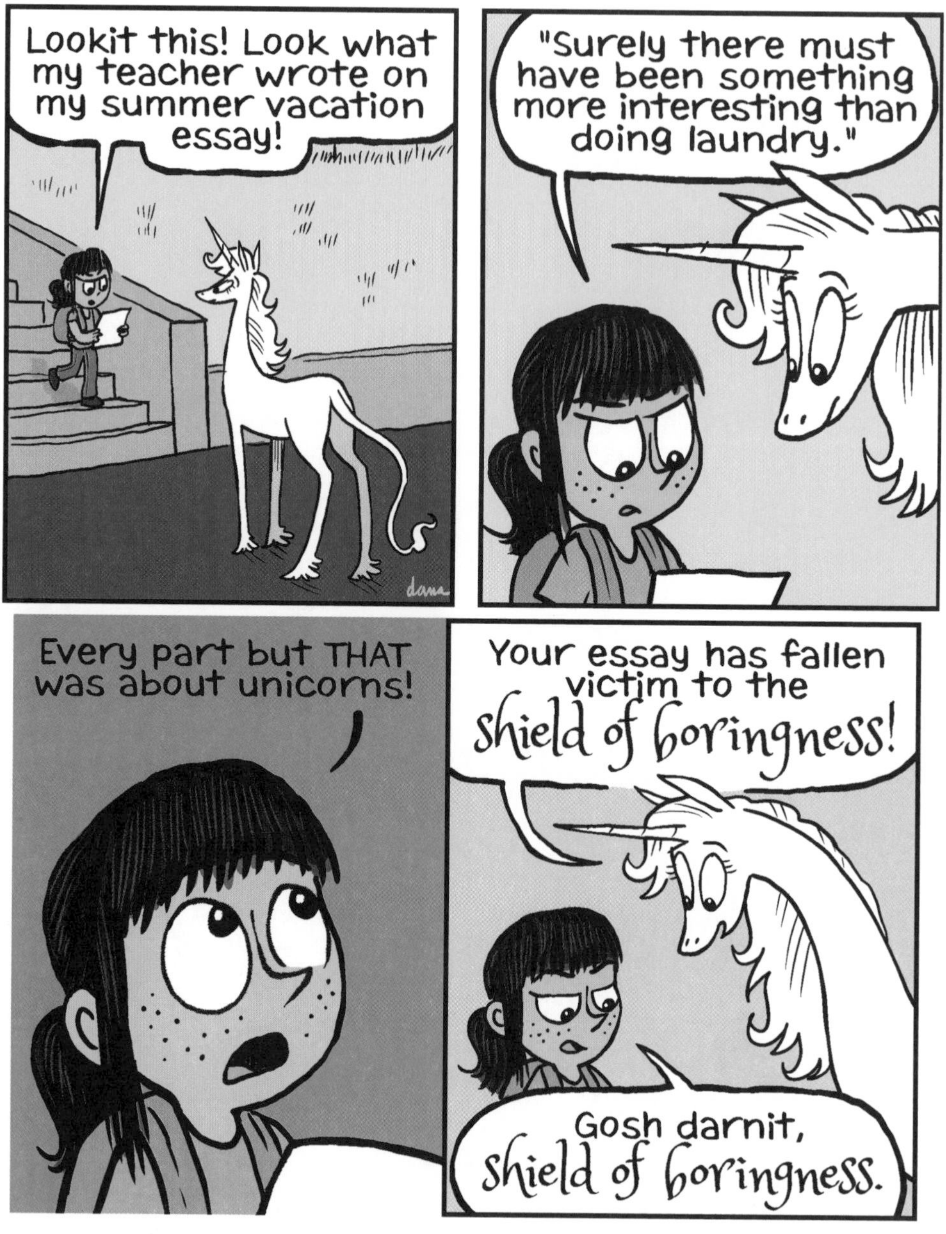
Lookit this! Look what my teacher wrote on my summer vacation essay!
"Surely there must have been something more interesting than doing laundry."
Every part but THAT was about unicorns!
Your essay has fallen victim to the Shield of Boringness!
Gosh darnit, Shield of Boringness.

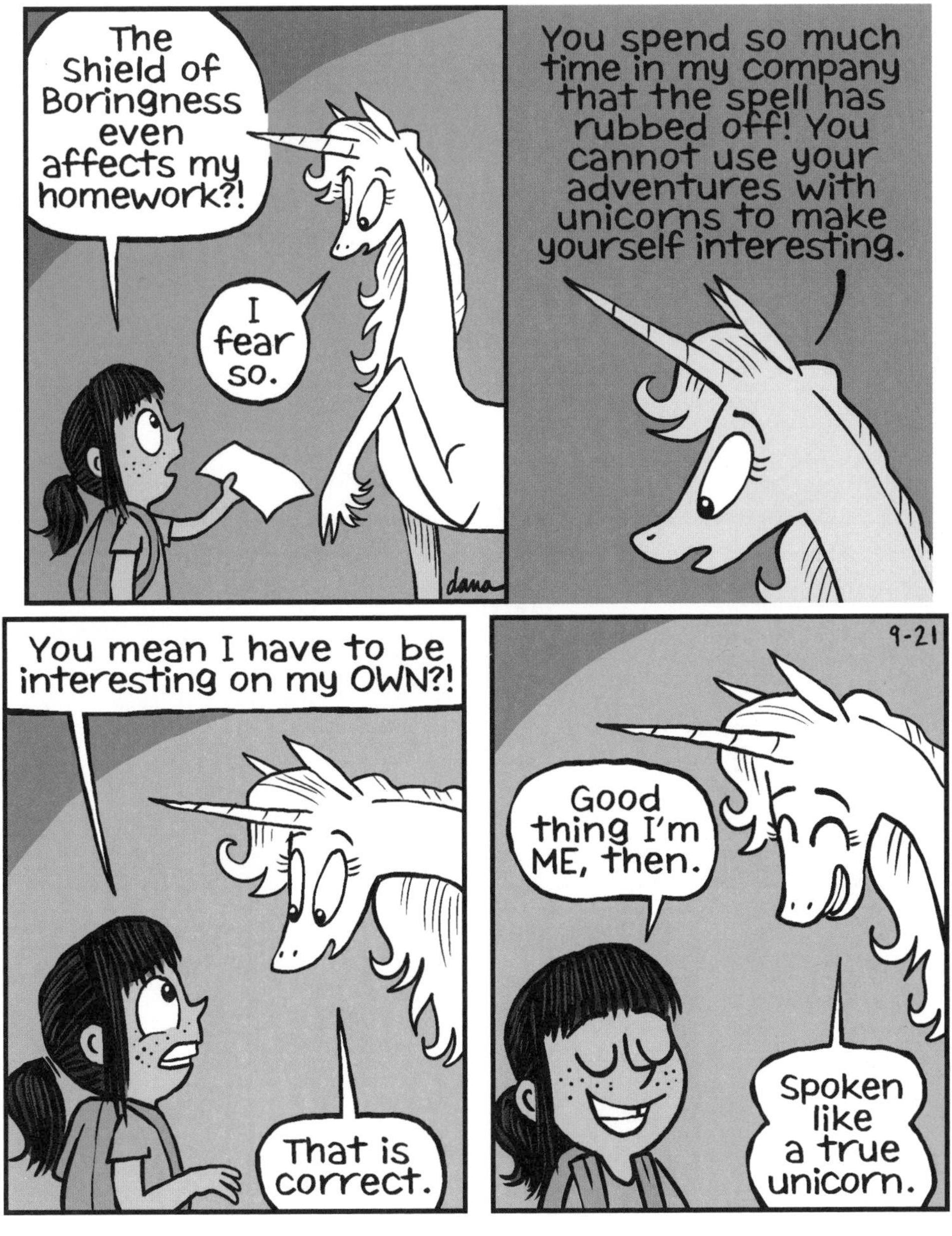
The Shield of Boringness even affects my homework?!
I fear so.
dana
You spend so much time in my company that the spell has rubbed off! You cannot use your adventures with unicorns to make yourself interesting.
You mean I have to be interesting on my OWN?!
That is correct.
9-21
Good thing I'm ME, then.
Spoken like a true unicorn.

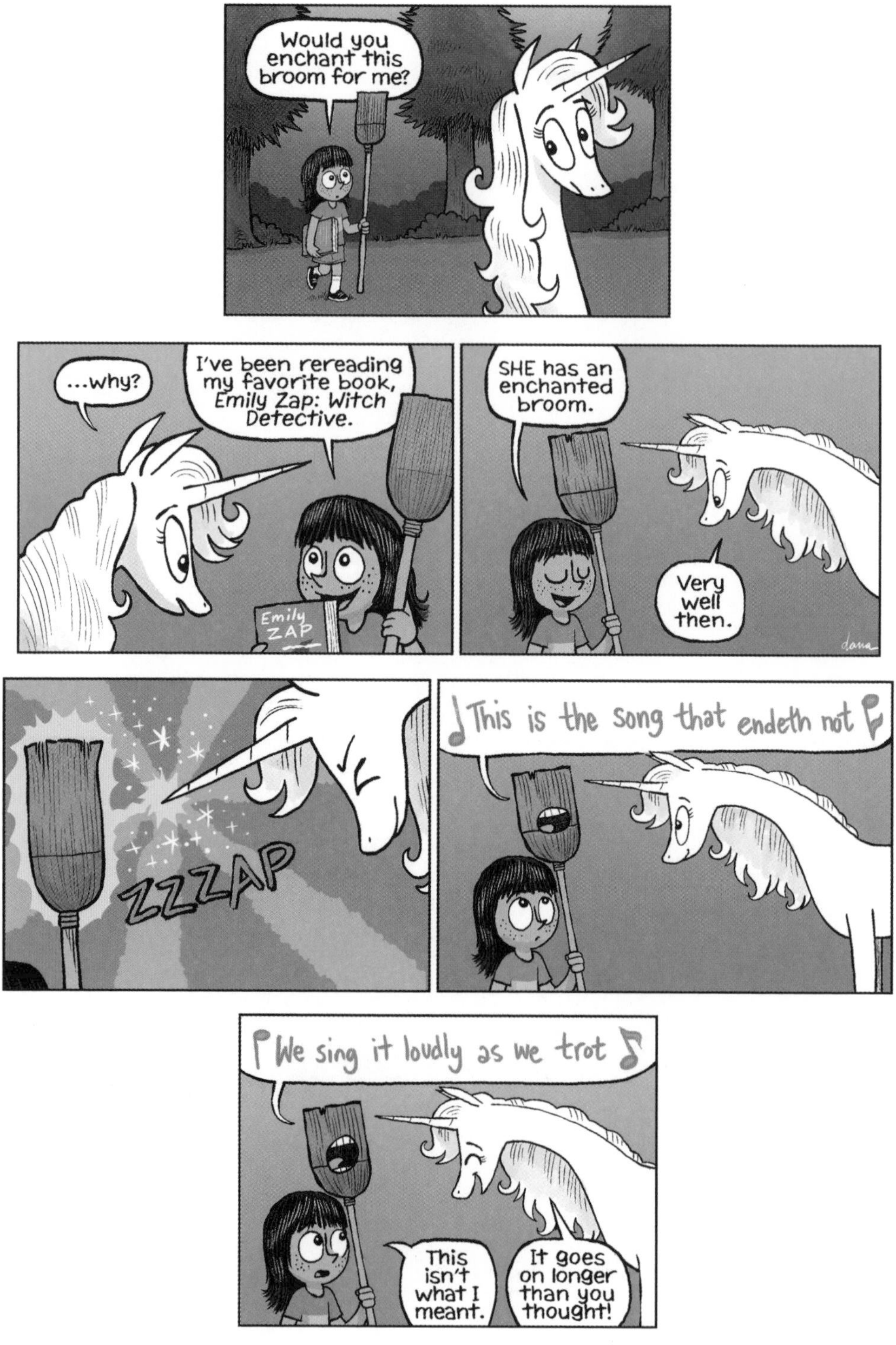
Would you enchant this broom for me?
...why?
I've been rereading my favorite book, Emily Zap: Witch Detective.
Emily ZAP
SHE has an enchanted broom.
Very well then.
dana
ZZZAP
This is the song that endeth not
We sing it loudly as we trot
This isn't what I meant.
It goes on longer than you thought!

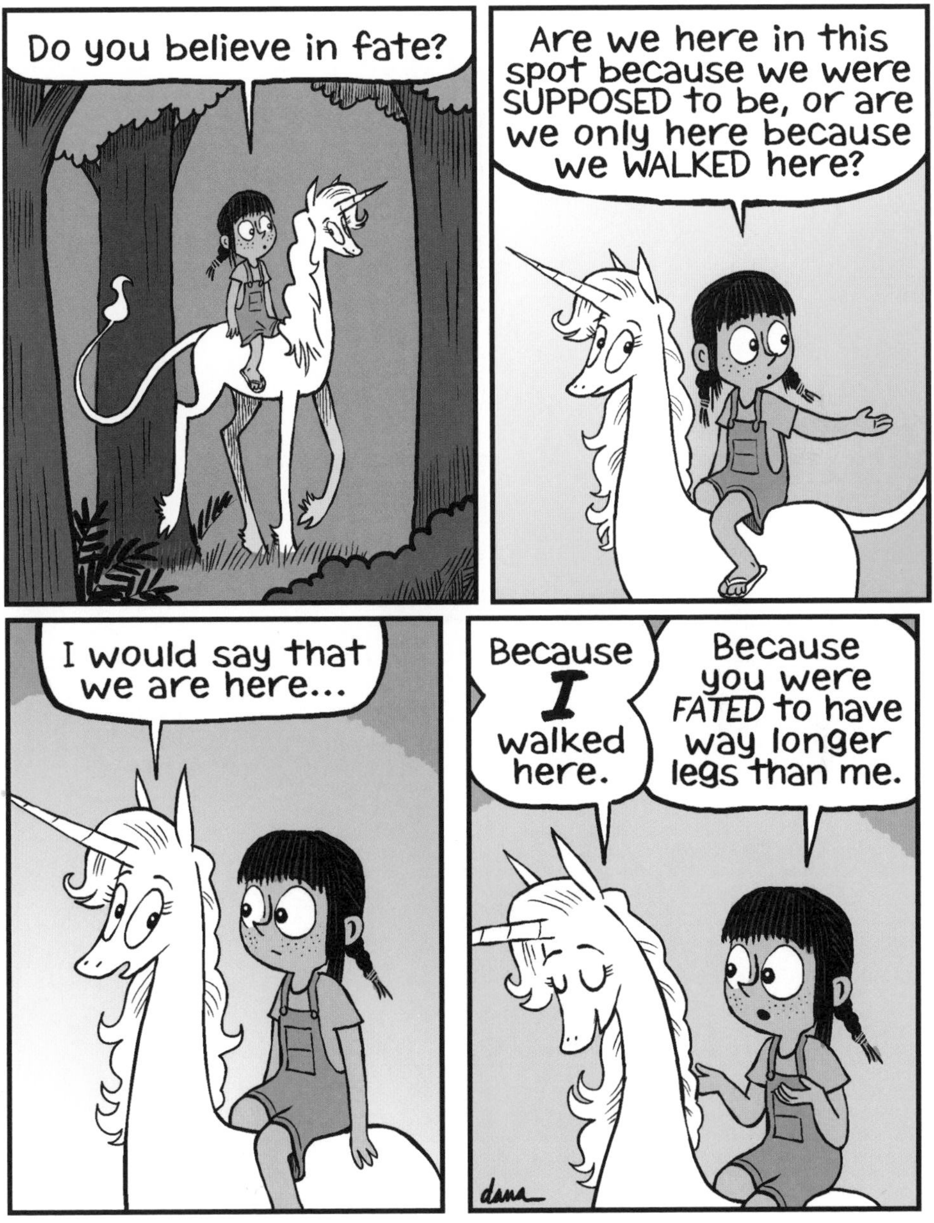
Do you believe in fate?
Are we here in this spot because we were SUPPOSED to be, or are we only here because we WALKED here?
I would say that we are here...
Because *I* walked here.
Because you were *FATED* to have way longer legs than me.
dana

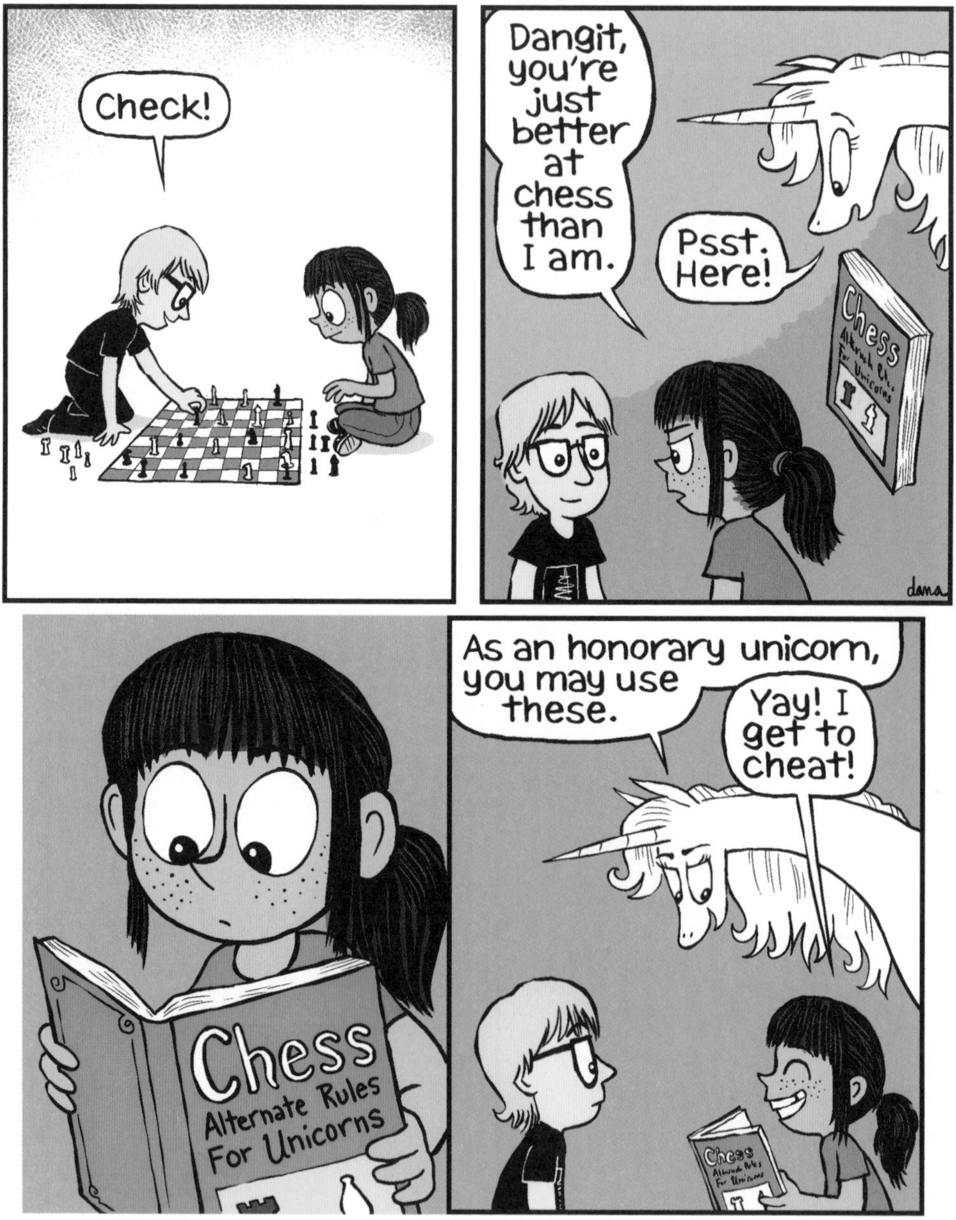
Check!
Dangit, you're just better at chess than I am.
Psst. Here!
Chess
Alternate Rules For Unicorns
dana
Chess
Alternate Rules For Unicorns
As an honorary unicorn, you may use these.
Yay! I get to cheat!

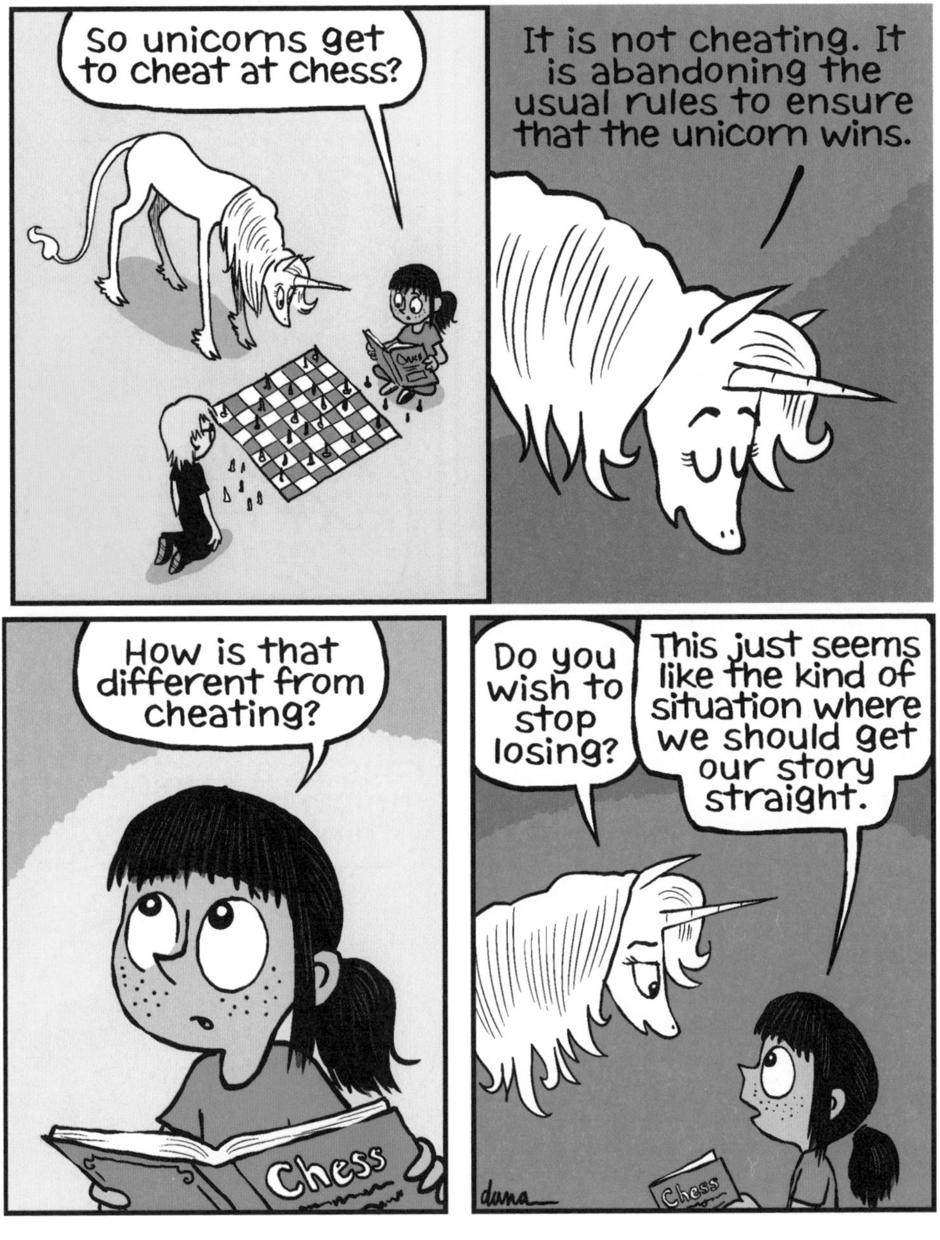
So unicorns get to cheat at chess?
Chess
It is not cheating. It is abandoning the usual rules to ensure that the unicorn wins.
How is that different from cheating?
Chess
Do you wish to stop losing?
This just seems like the kind of situation where we should get our story straight.
dana
Chess

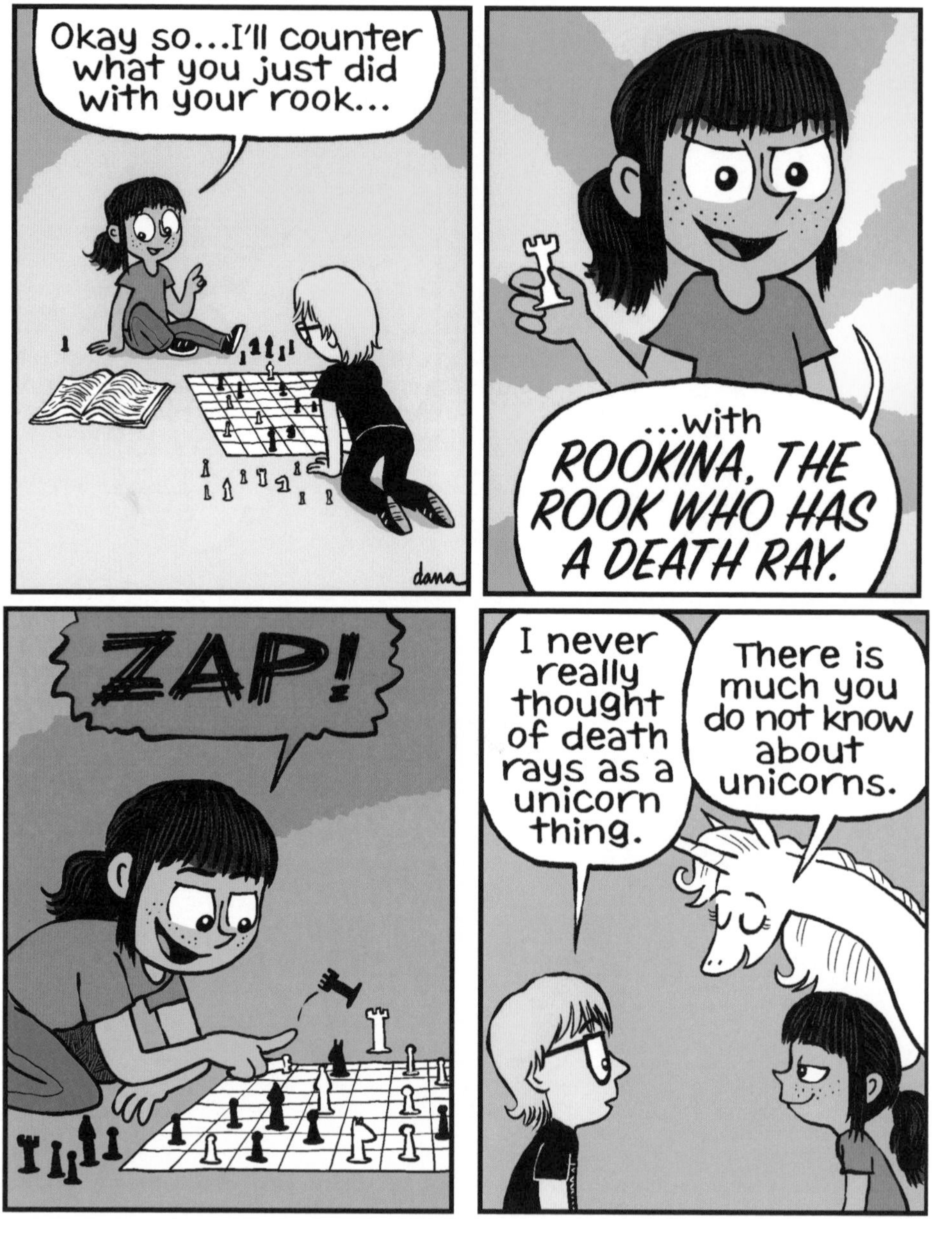
Okay so...I'll counter what you just did with your rook...
dana
...with ROOKINA, THE ROOK WHO HAS A DEATH RAY.
ZAP!
I never really thought of death rays as a unicorn thing.
There is much you do not know about unicorns.

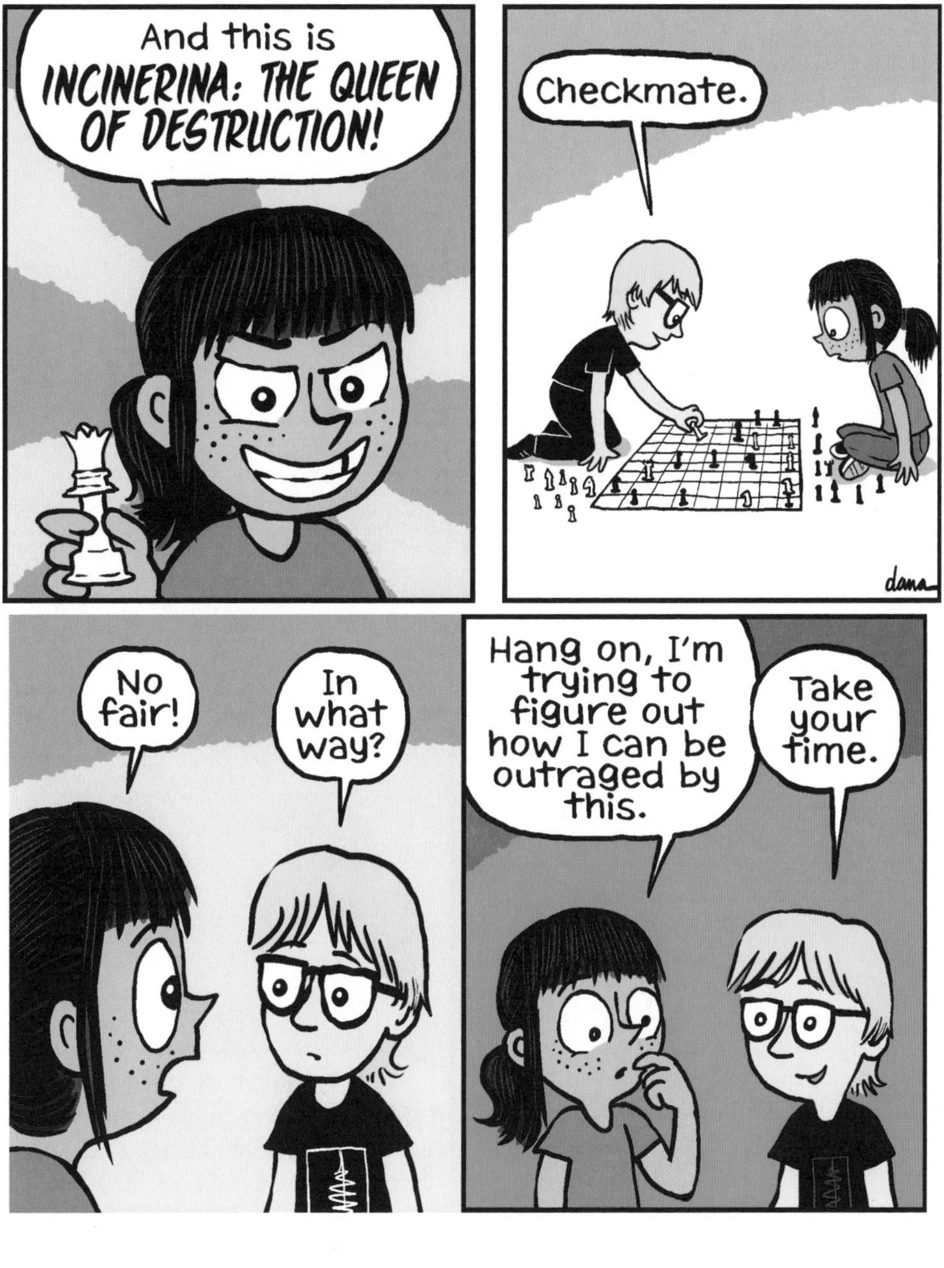

And this is INCINERINA: THE QUEEN OF DESTRUCTION!
Checkmate.
dana
No fair!
In what way?
Hang on, I'm trying to figure out how I can be outraged by this.
Take your time.

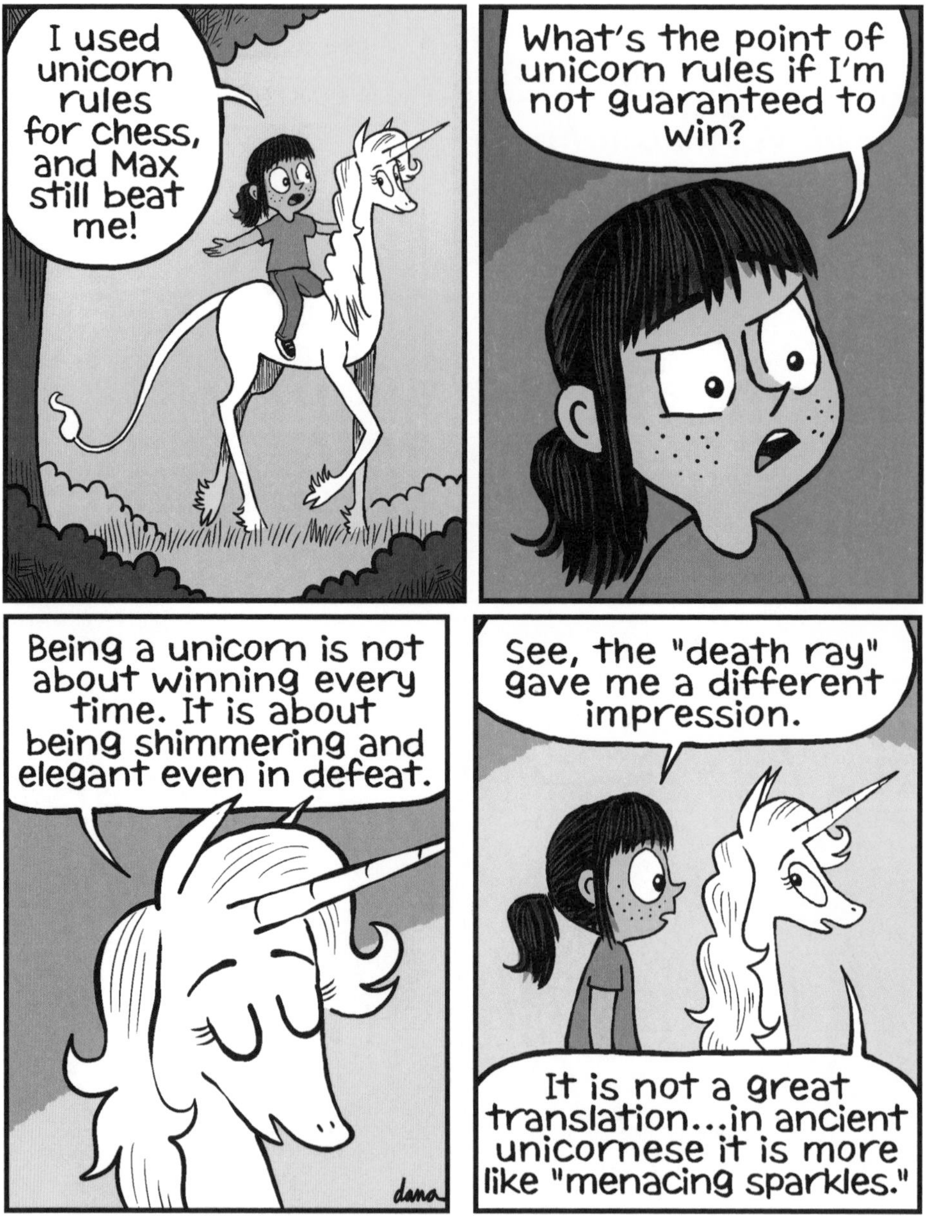
I used unicorn rules for chess, and Max still beat me!
What's the point of unicorn rules if I'm not guaranteed to win?
Being a unicorn is not about winning every time. It is about being shimmering and elegant even in defeat.
See, the "death ray" gave me a different impression.
It is not a great translation...in ancient unicornese it is more like "menacing sparkles."
dana

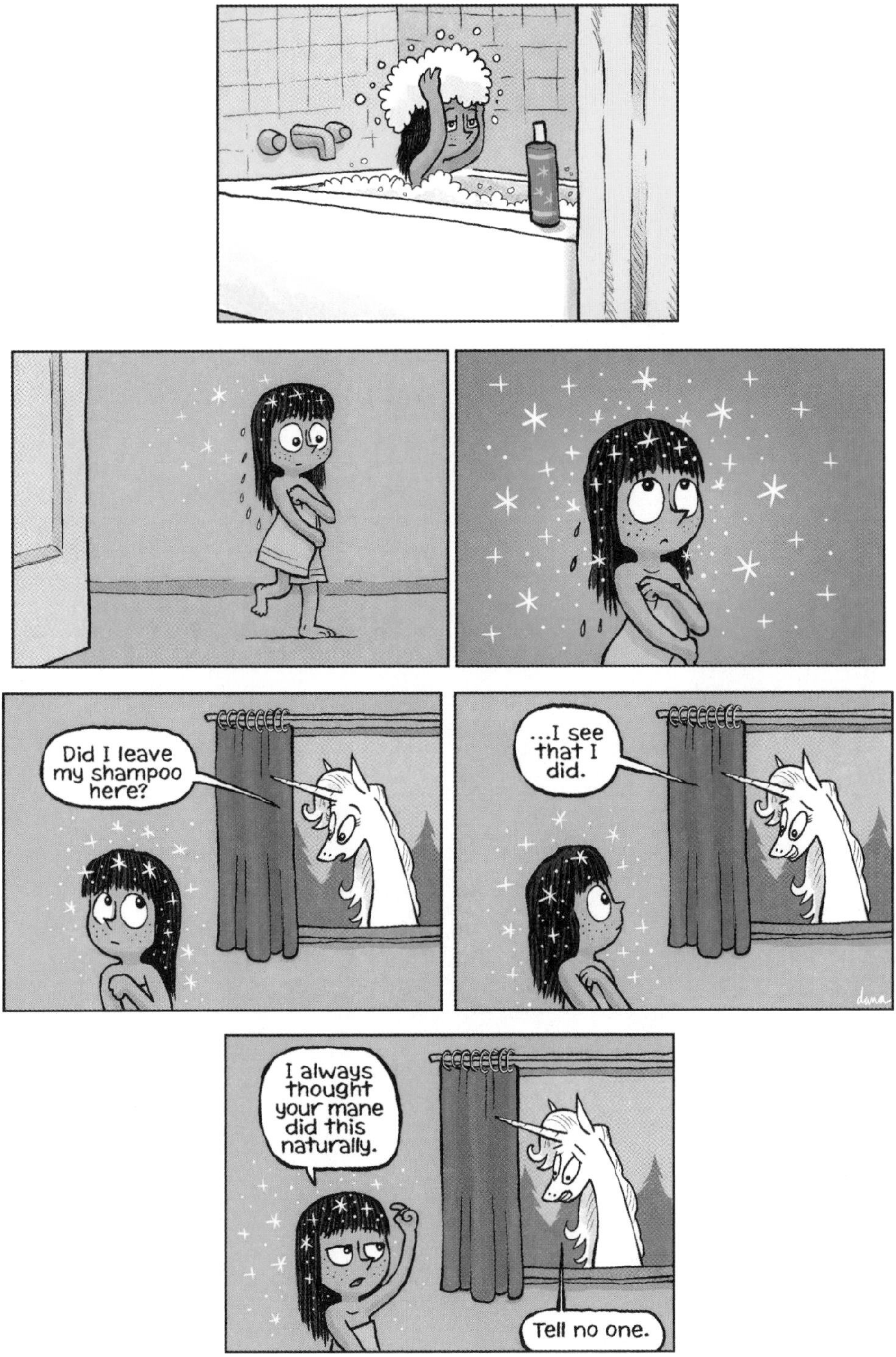
Did I leave my shampoo here?
...I see that I did.
I always thought your mane did this naturally.
Tell no one.

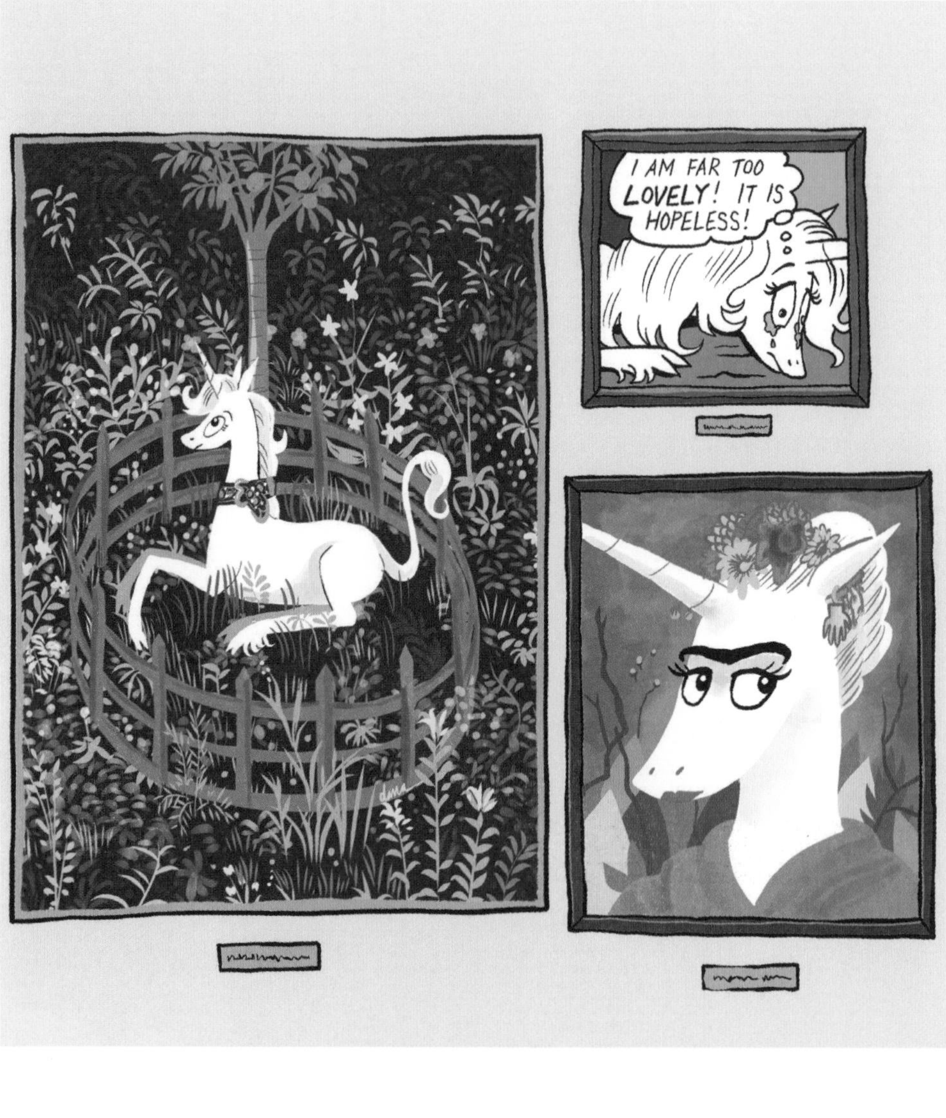
I AM FAR TOO LOVELY! IT IS HOPELESS!

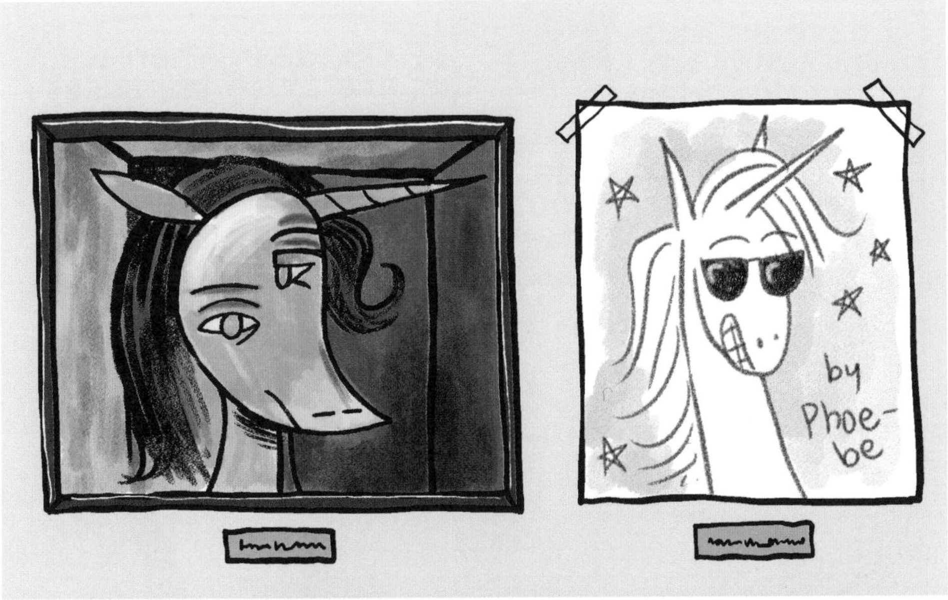
by
Phoe-
be

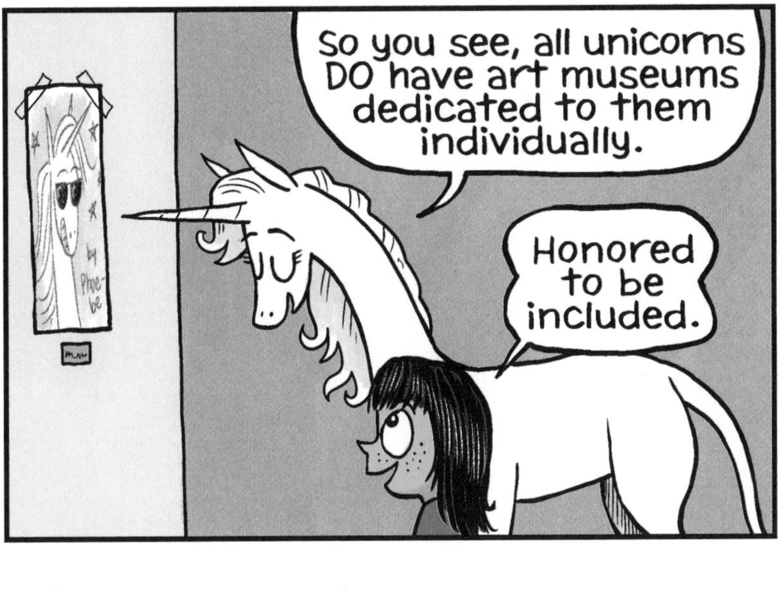
So you see, all unicorns DO have art museums dedicated to them individually.
Honored to be included.
by
Phoe-
be

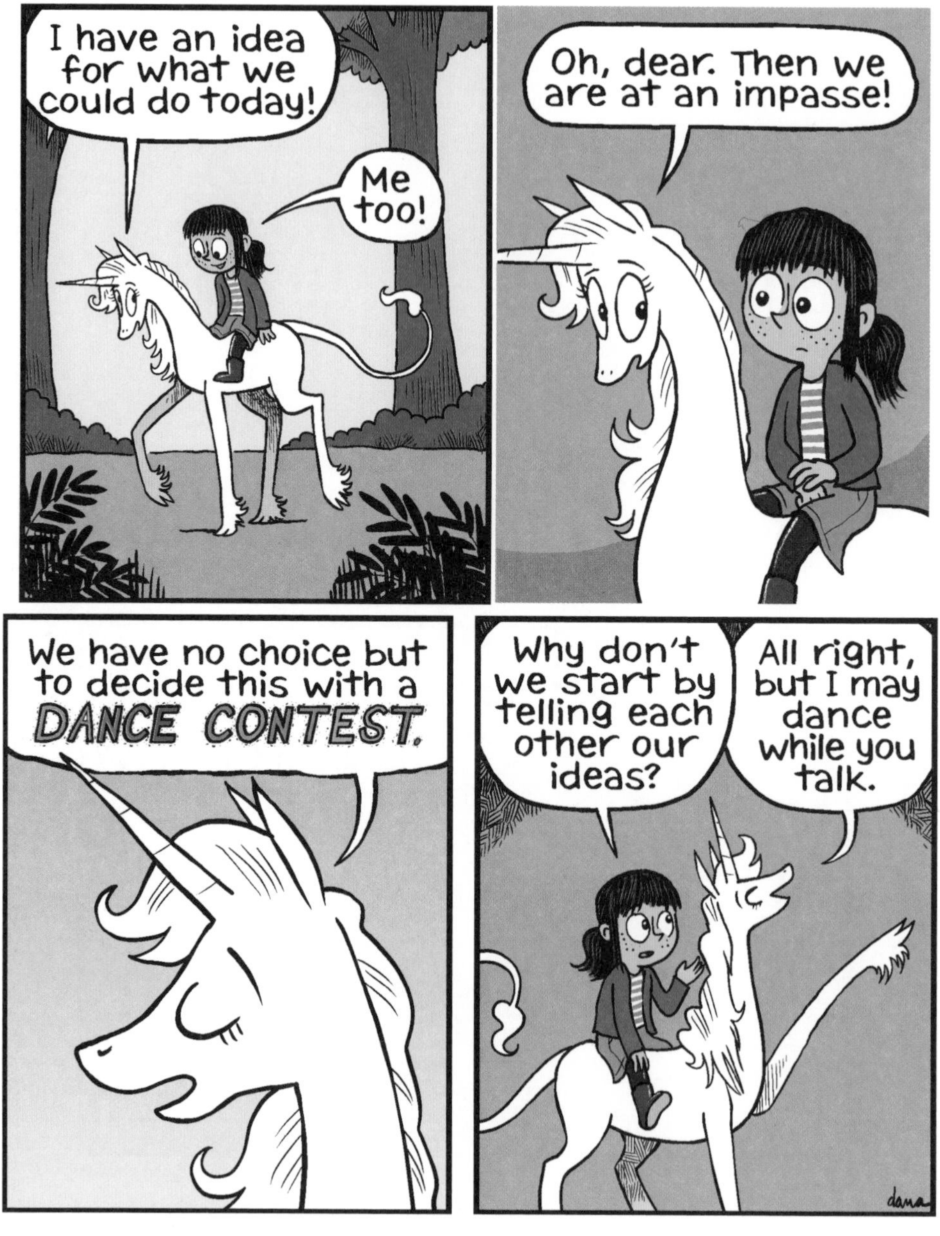
I have an idea for what we could do today!
Me too!
Oh, dear. Then we are at an impasse!
We have no choice but to decide this with a DANCE CONTEST.
Why don't we start by telling each other our ideas?
All right, but I may dance while you talk.
dana

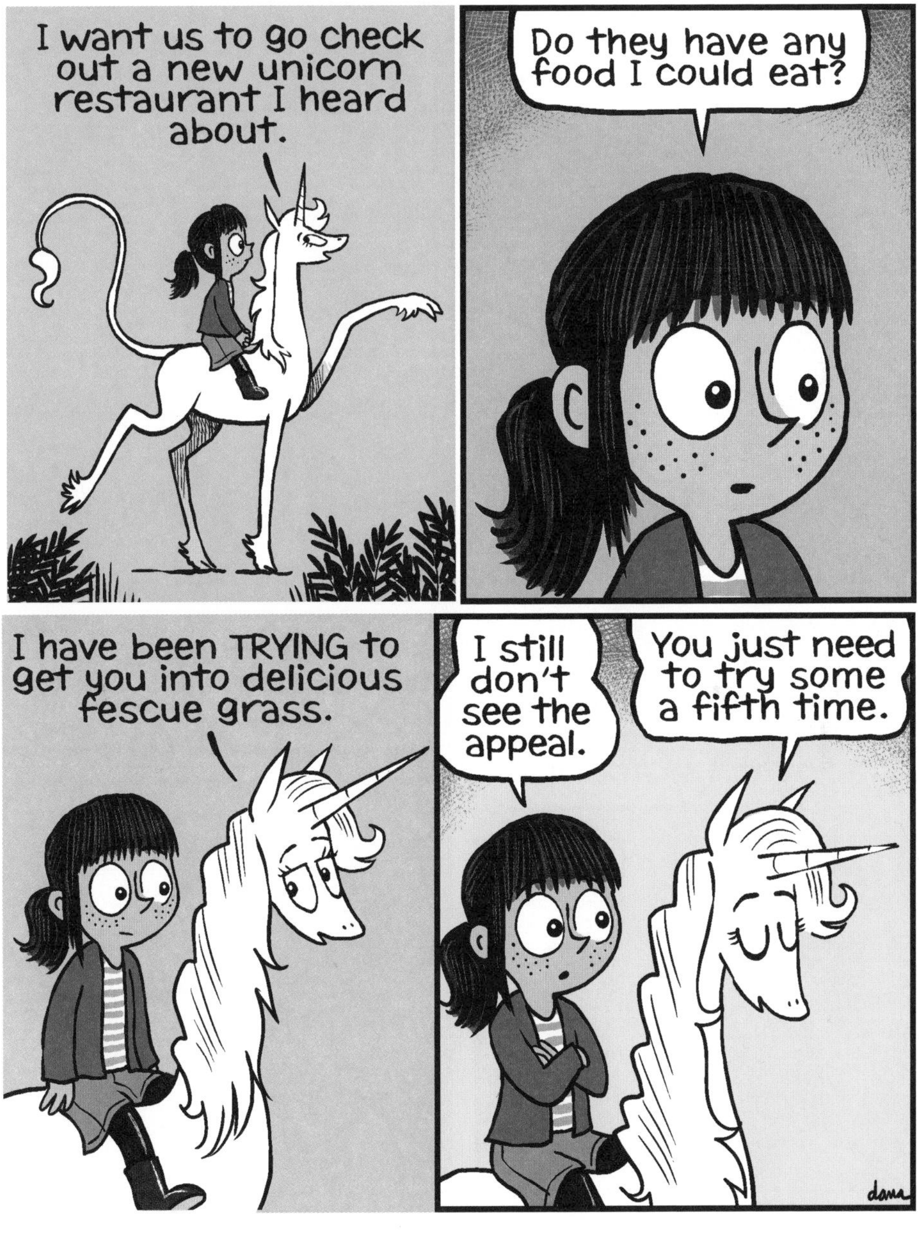
I want us to go check out a new unicorn restaurant I heard about.
Do they have any food I could eat?
I have been TRYING to get you into delicious fescue grass.
I still don't see the appeal.
You just need to try some a fifth time.
dana

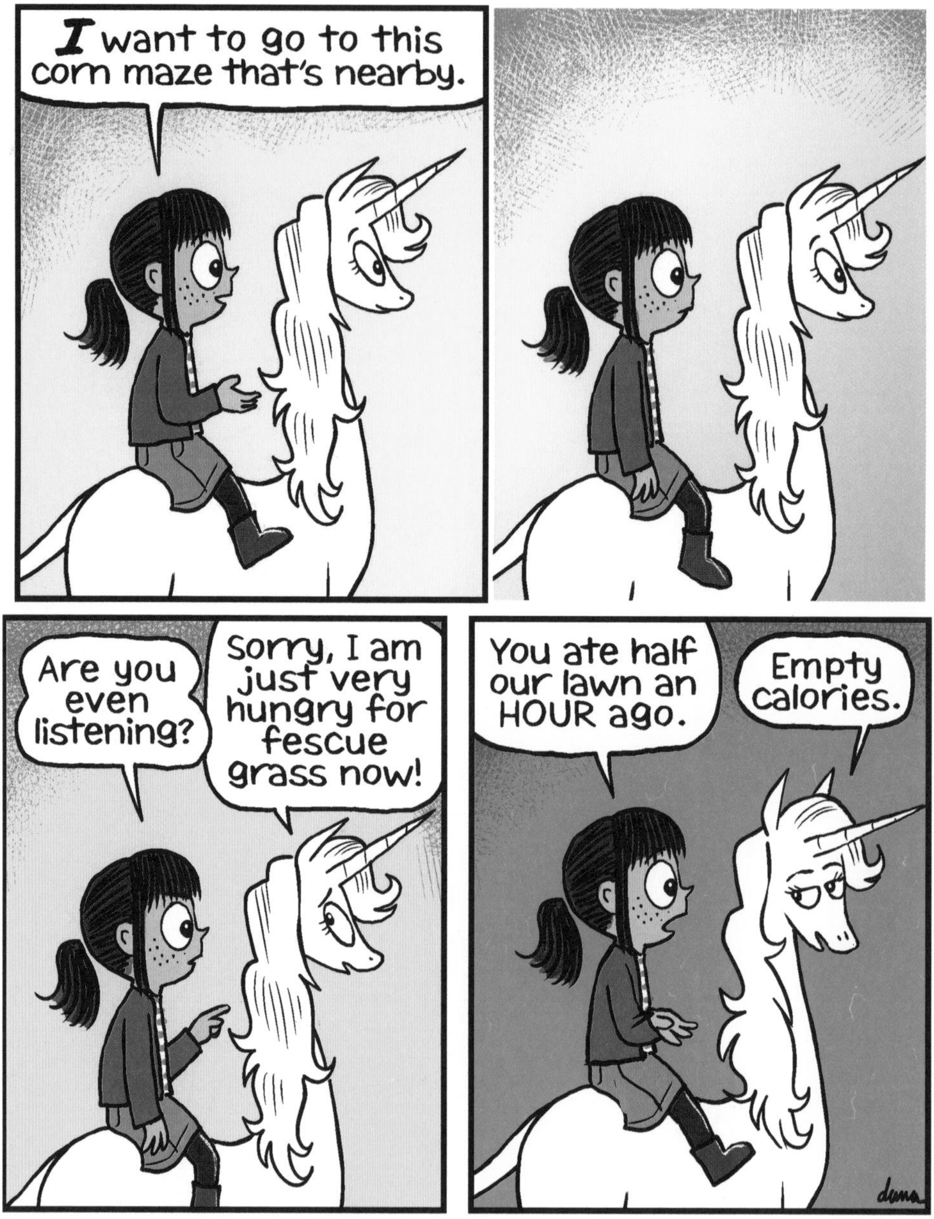
I want to go to this corn maze that's nearby.
Are you even listening?
Sorry, I am just very hungry for fescue grass now!
You ate half our lawn an HOUR ago.
Empty calories.

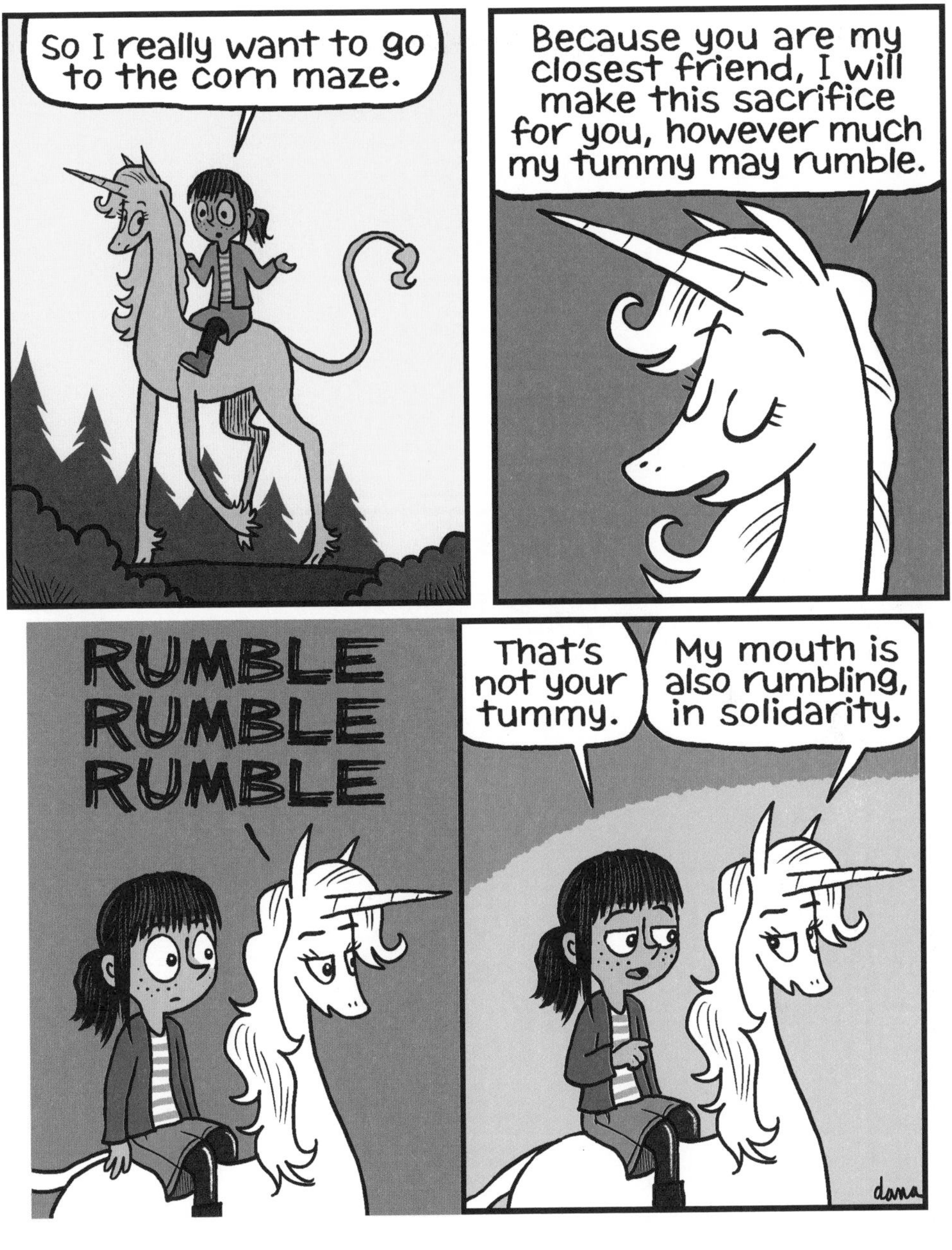
So I really want to go to the corn maze.
Because you are my closest friend, I will make this sacrifice for you, however much my tummy may rumble.
RUMBLE RUMBLE RUMBLE
That's not your tummy.
My mouth is also rumbling, in solidarity.
dana

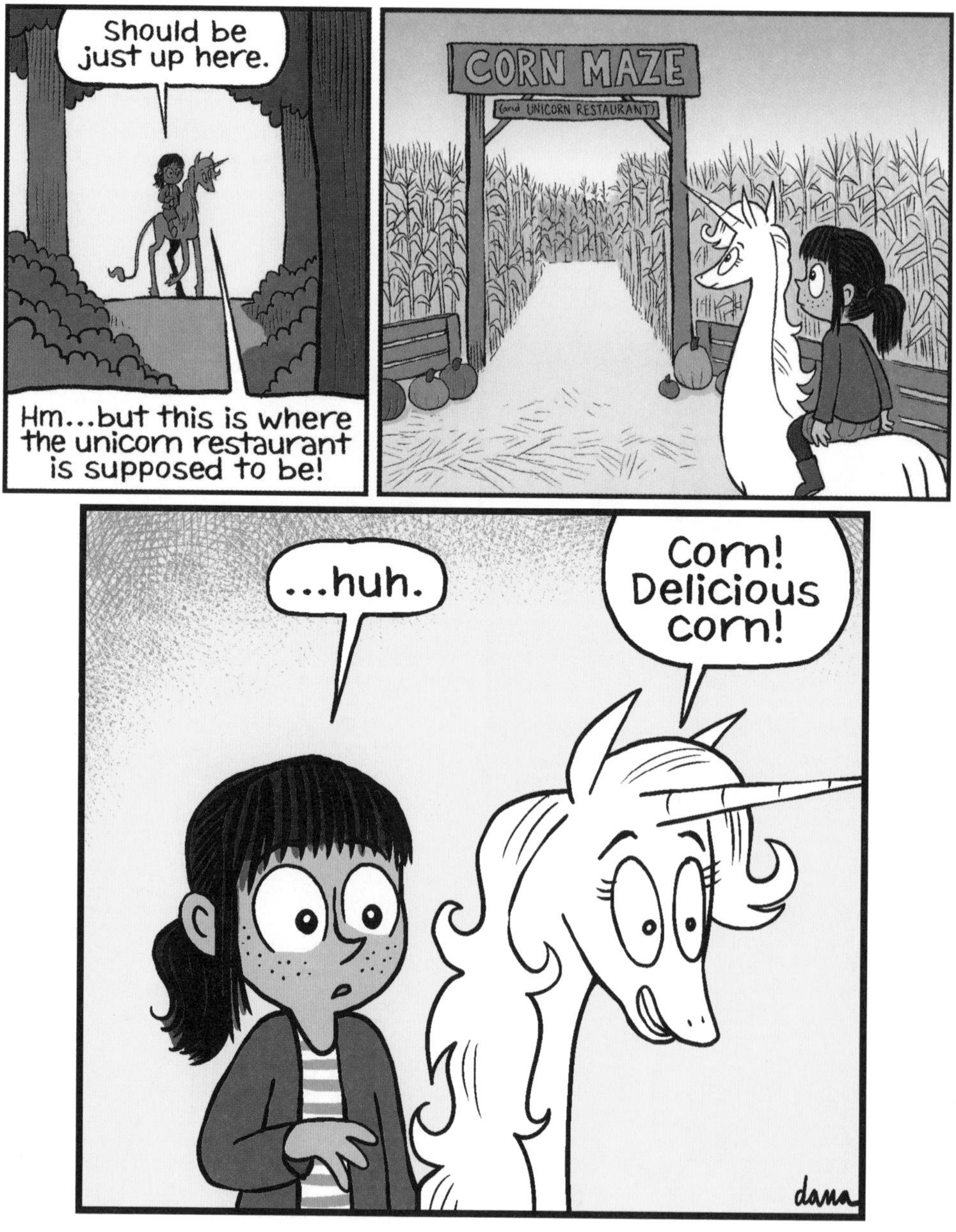
Should be just up here.
Hm...but this is where the unicorn restaurant is supposed to be!
CORN MAZE
(and UNICORN RESTAURANT)
...huh.
Corn! Delicious corn!
dana

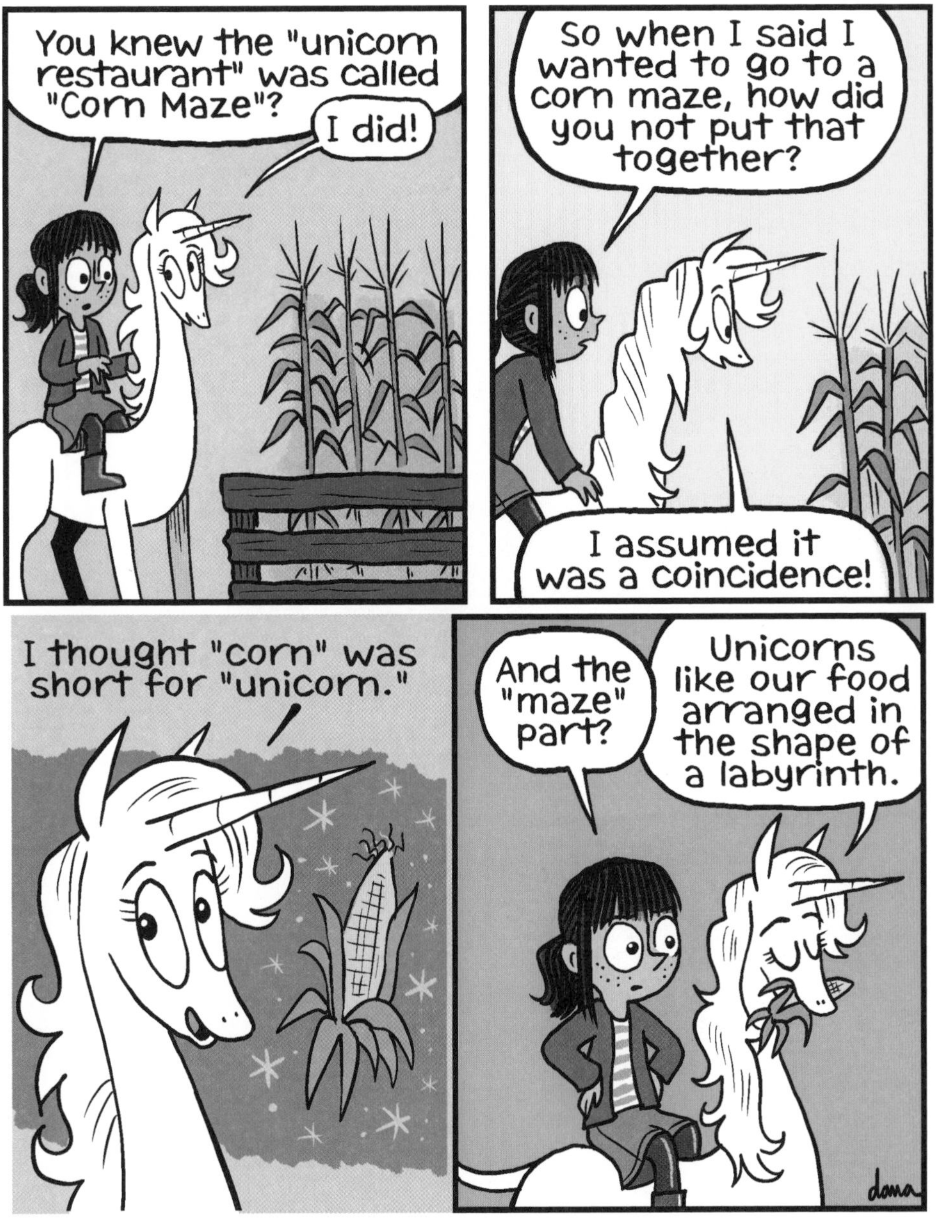
You knew the "unicorn restaurant" was called "Corn Maze"?
I did!
So when I said I wanted to go to a corn maze, how did you not put that together?
I assumed it was a coincidence!
I thought "corn" was short for "unicorn."
And the "maze" part?
Unicorns like our food arranged in the shape of a labyrinth.
dana

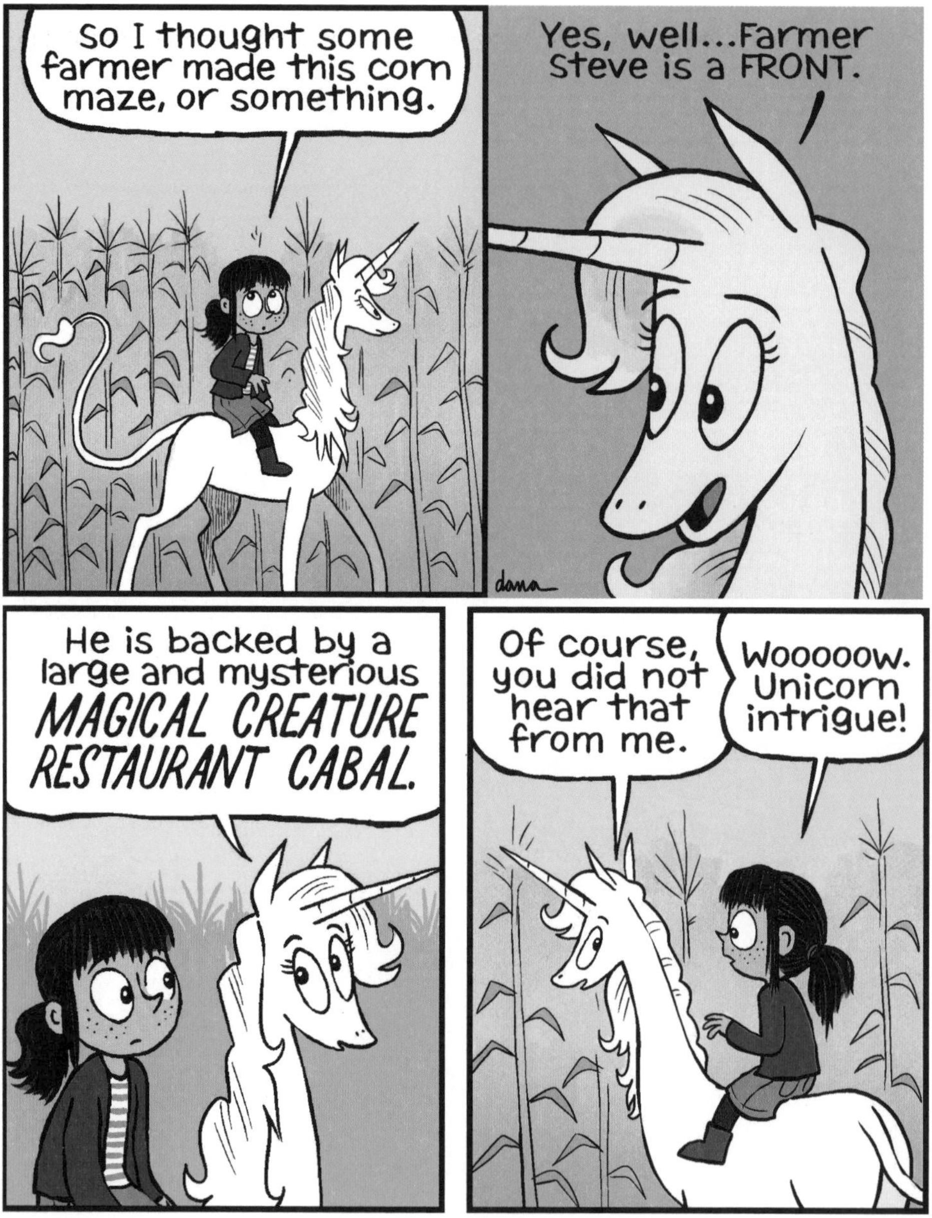
So I thought some farmer made this corn maze, or something.
Yes, well...Farmer Steve is a FRONT.
dana
He is backed by a large and mysterious MAGICAL CREATURE RESTAURANT CABAL.
Of course, you did not hear that from me.
Woooooow. Unicorn intrigue!

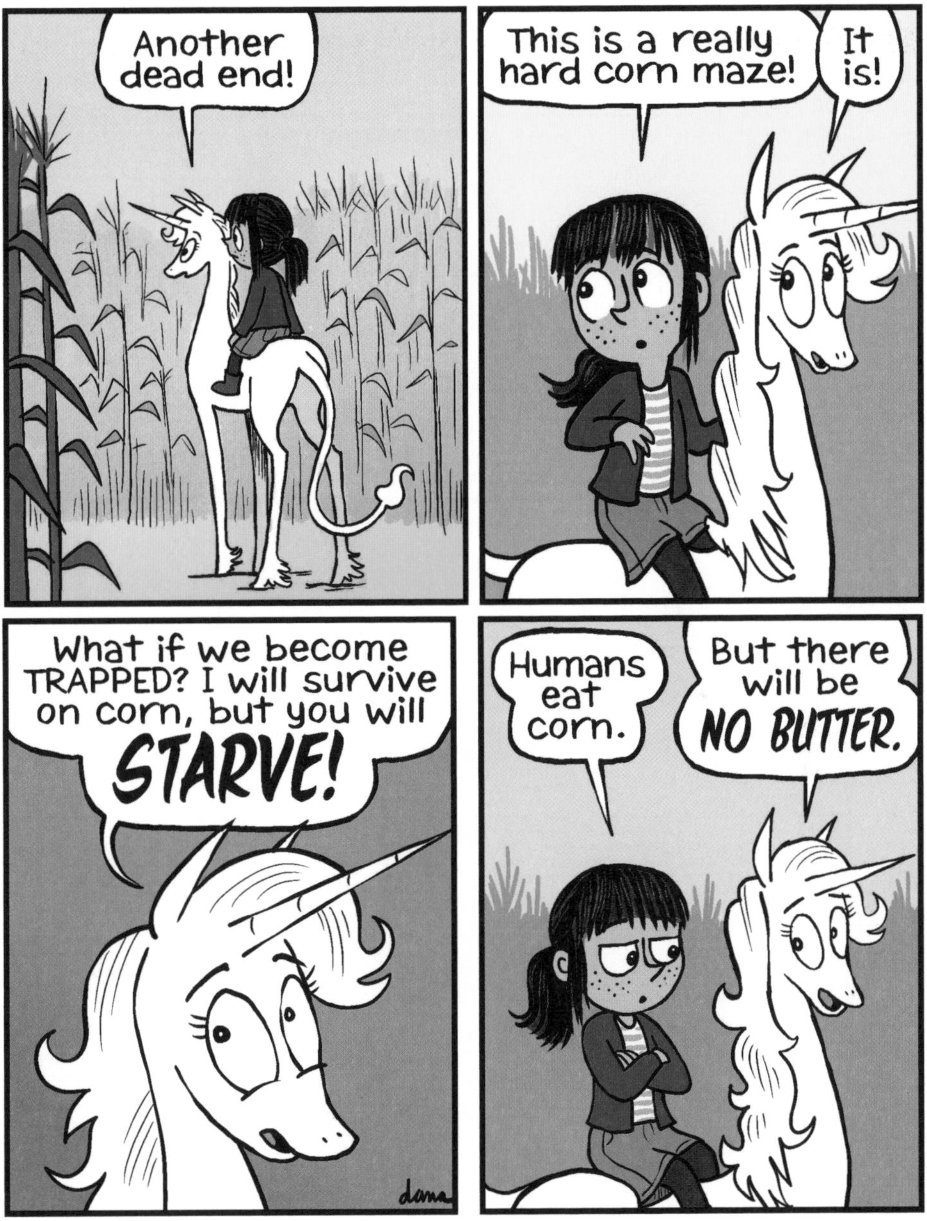
Another dead end!
This is a really hard corn maze!
It is!
What if we become TRAPPED? I will survive on corn, but you will STARVE!
Humans eat corn.
But there will be NO BUTTER.
dana

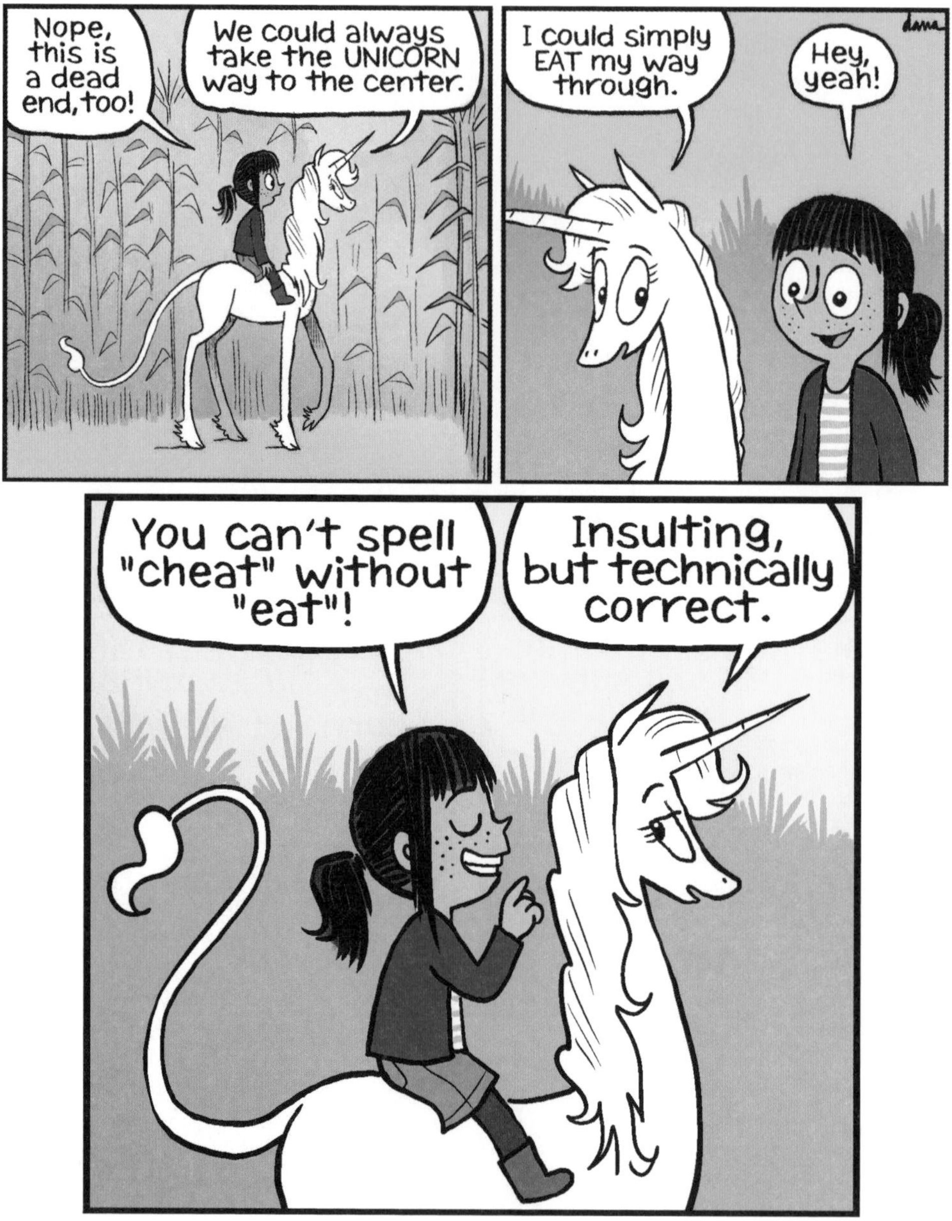
Nope, this is a dead end, too!
We could always take the UNICORN way to the center.
I could simply EAT my way through.
Hey, yeah!
You can't spell "cheat" without "eat"!
Insulting, but technically correct.

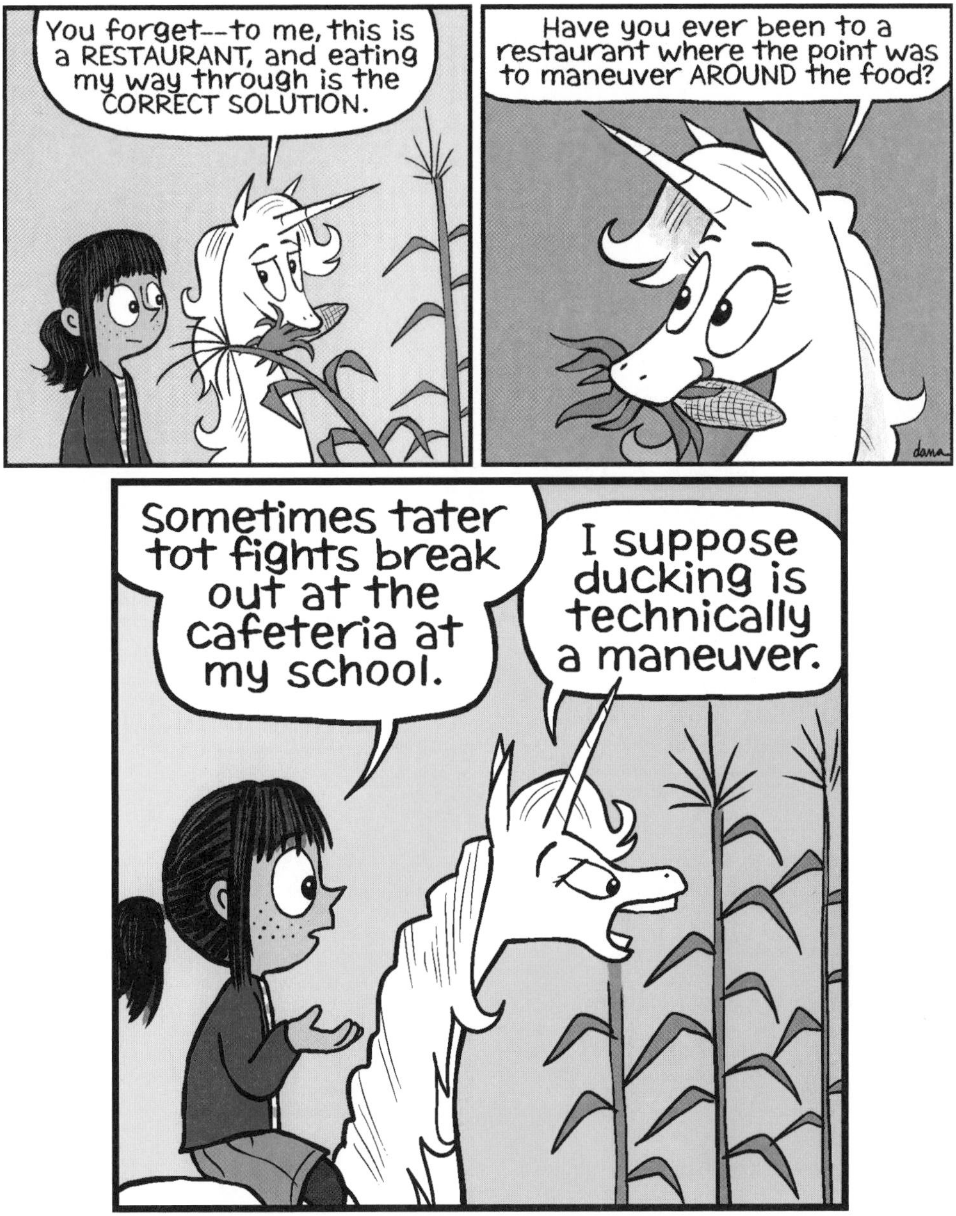
You forget--to me, this is a RESTAURANT, and eating my way through is the CORRECT SOLUTION.
Have you ever been to a restaurant where the point was to maneuver AROUND the food?
dana
Sometimes tater tot fights break out at the cafeteria at my school.
I suppose ducking is technically a maneuver.

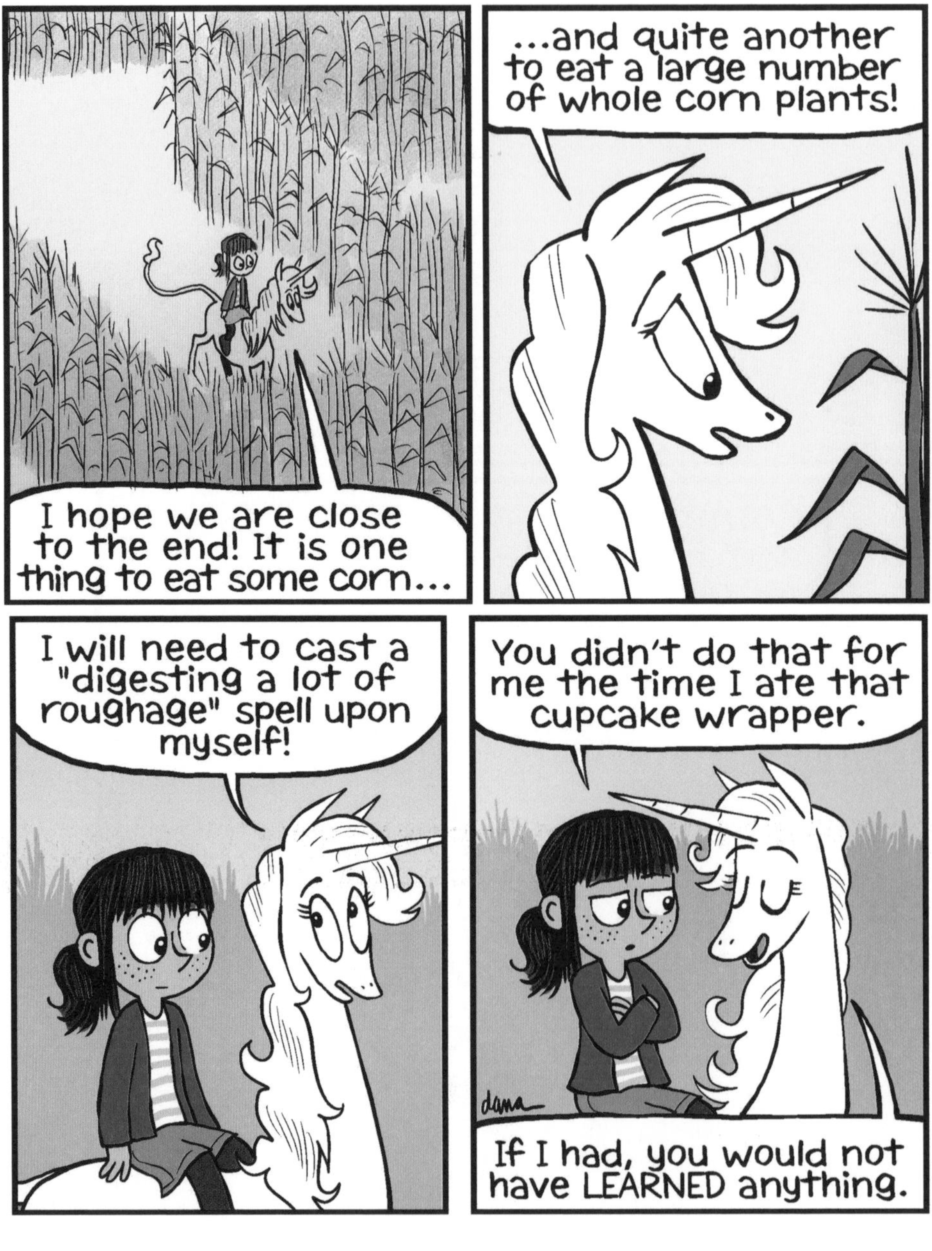
I hope we are close to the end! It is one thing to eat some corn...
...and quite another to eat a large number of whole corn plants!
I will need to cast a "digesting a lot of roughage" spell upon myself!
You didn't do that for me the time I ate that cupcake wrapper.
If I had, you would not have LEARNED anything.
dana

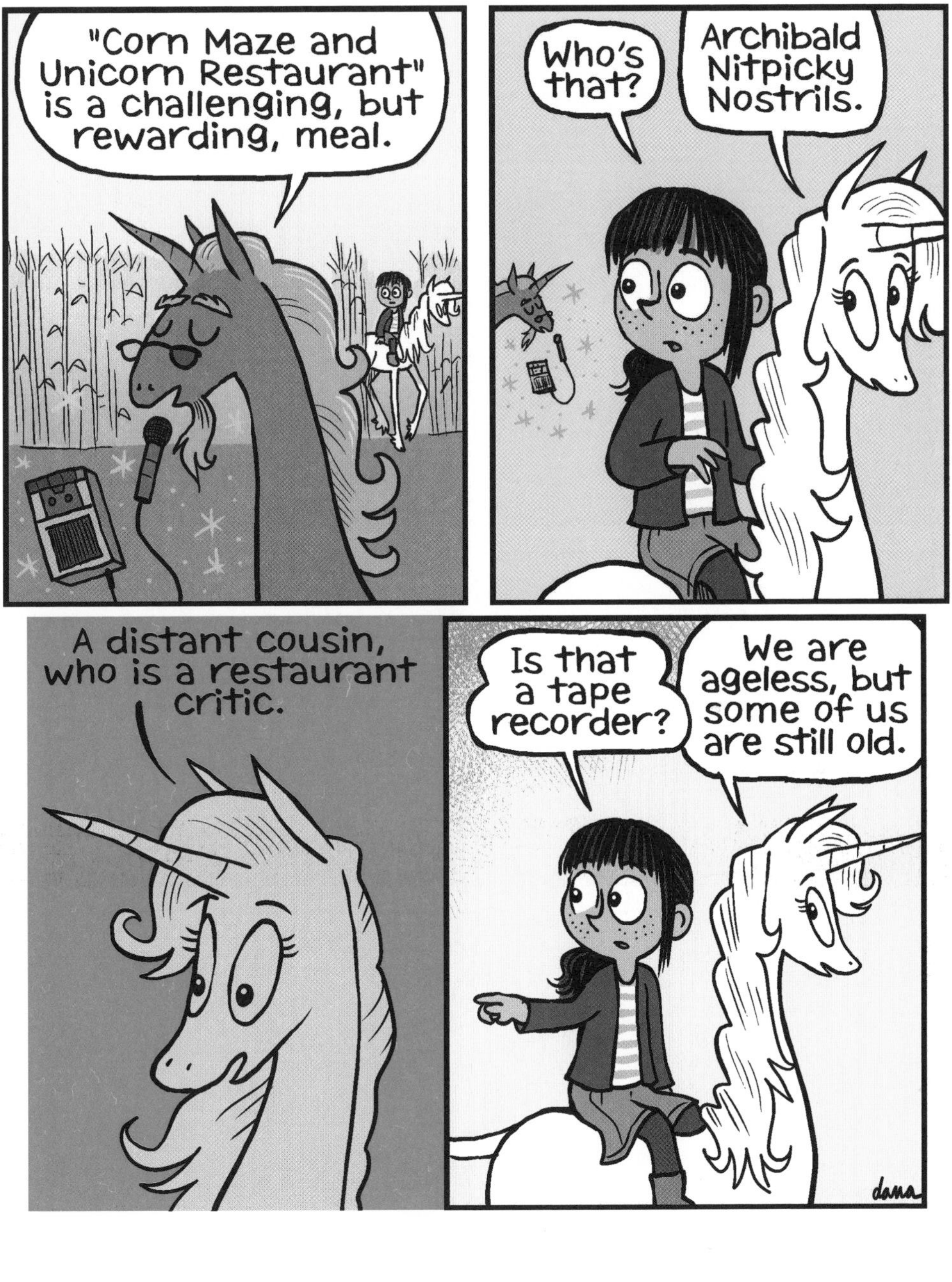
"Corn Maze and Unicorn Restaurant" is a challenging, but rewarding, meal.
Who's that?
Archibald Nitpicky Nostrils.
A distant cousin, who is a restaurant critic.
Is that a tape recorder?
We are ageless, but some of us are still old.
dana

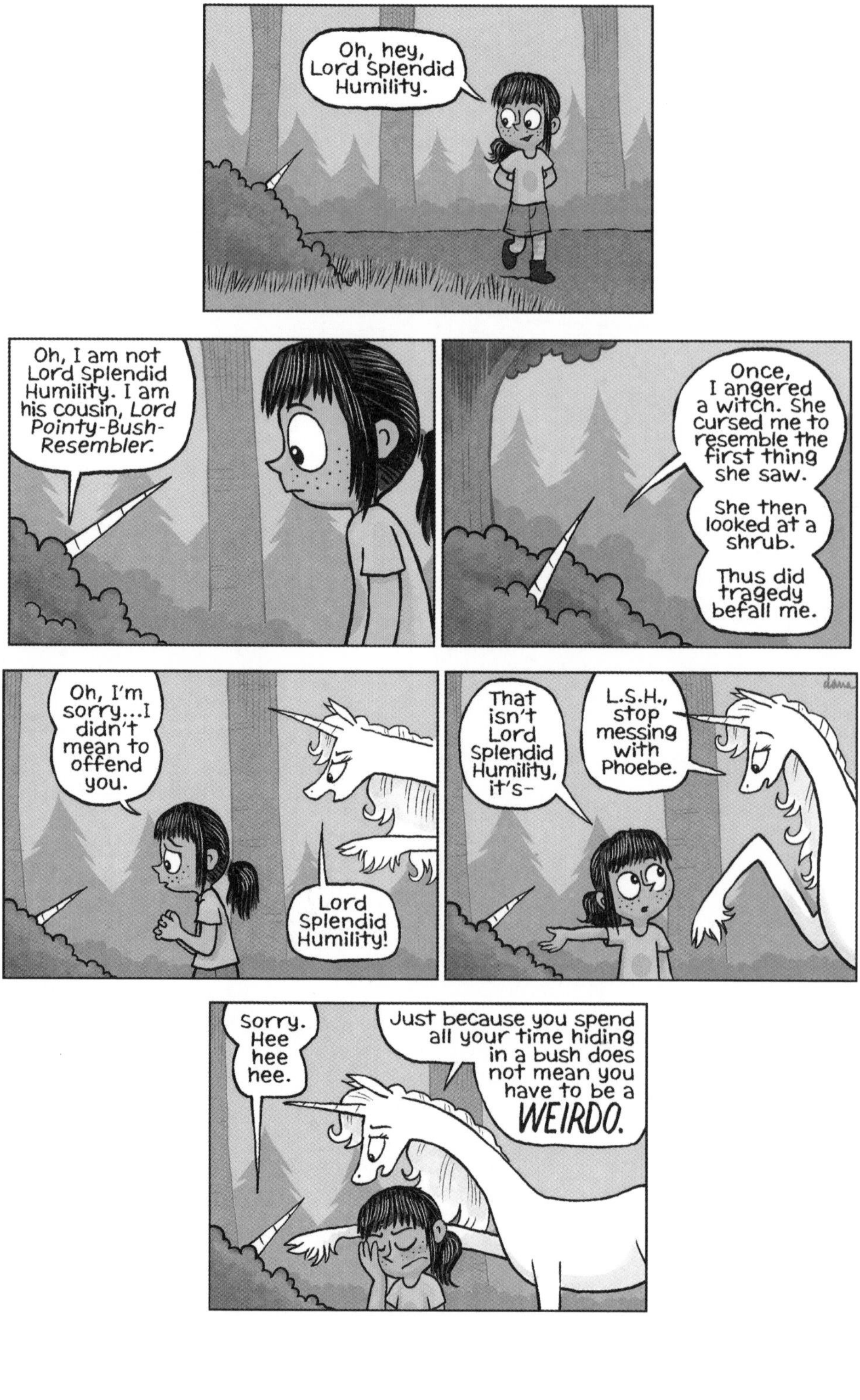
Oh, hey, Lord Splendid Humility.
Oh, I am not Lord Splendid Humility. I am his cousin, *Lord Pointy-Bush-Resembler.*
Once, I angered a witch. She cursed me to resemble the first thing she saw.
She then looked at a shrub.
Thus did tragedy befall me.
Oh, I'm sorry...I didn't mean to offend you.
Lord Splendid Humility!
That isn't Lord Splendid Humility, it's-
L.S.H., stop messing with Phoebe.
Sorry. Hee hee hee.
Just because you spend all your time hiding in a bush does not mean you have to be a WEIRDO.

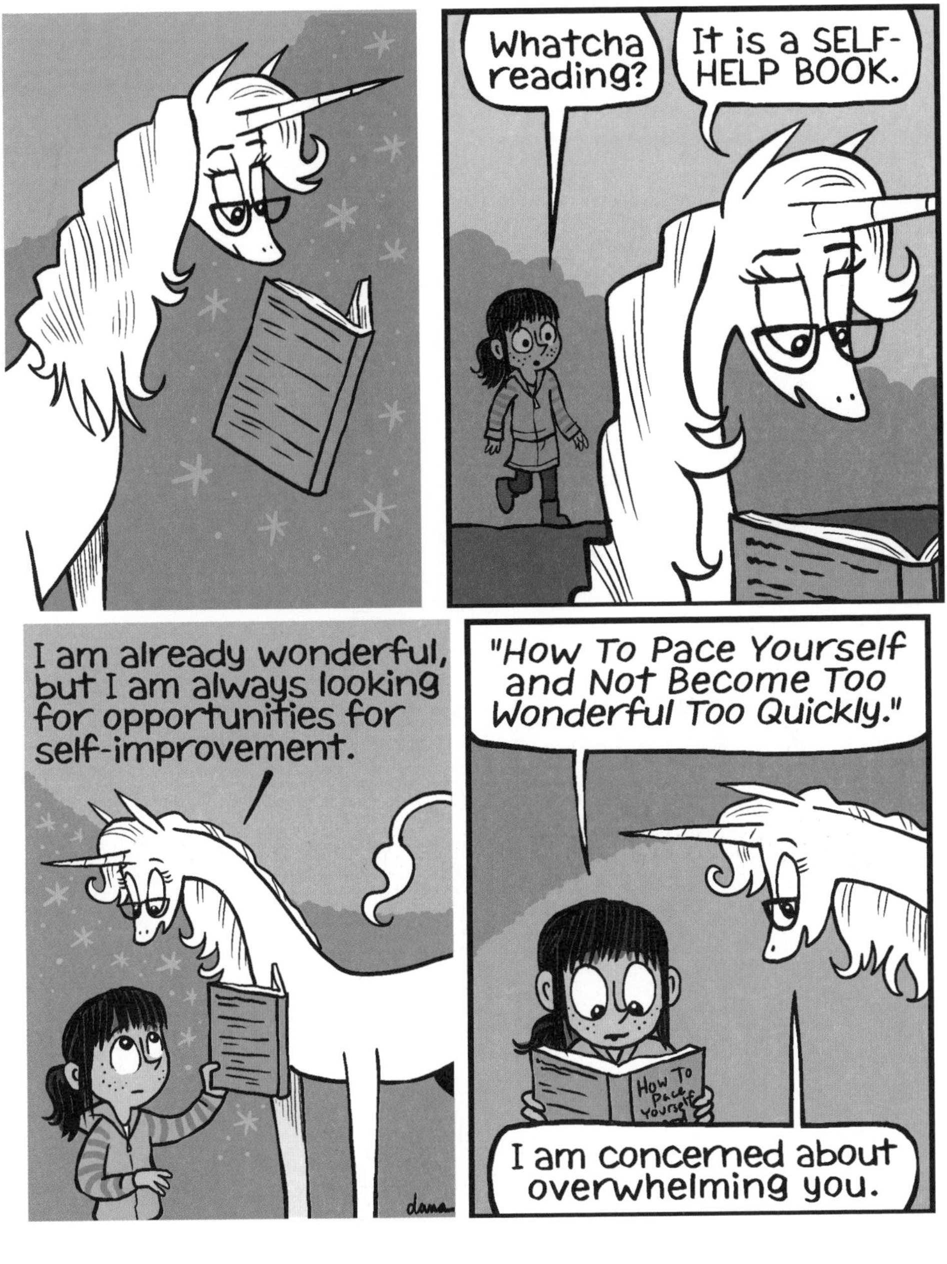
Whatcha reading?
It is a SELF-HELP BOOK.
I am already wonderful, but I am always looking for opportunities for self-improvement.
"How To Pace Yourself and Not Become Too Wonderful Too Quickly."
How To Pace Yourself
I am concerned about overwhelming you.
dana

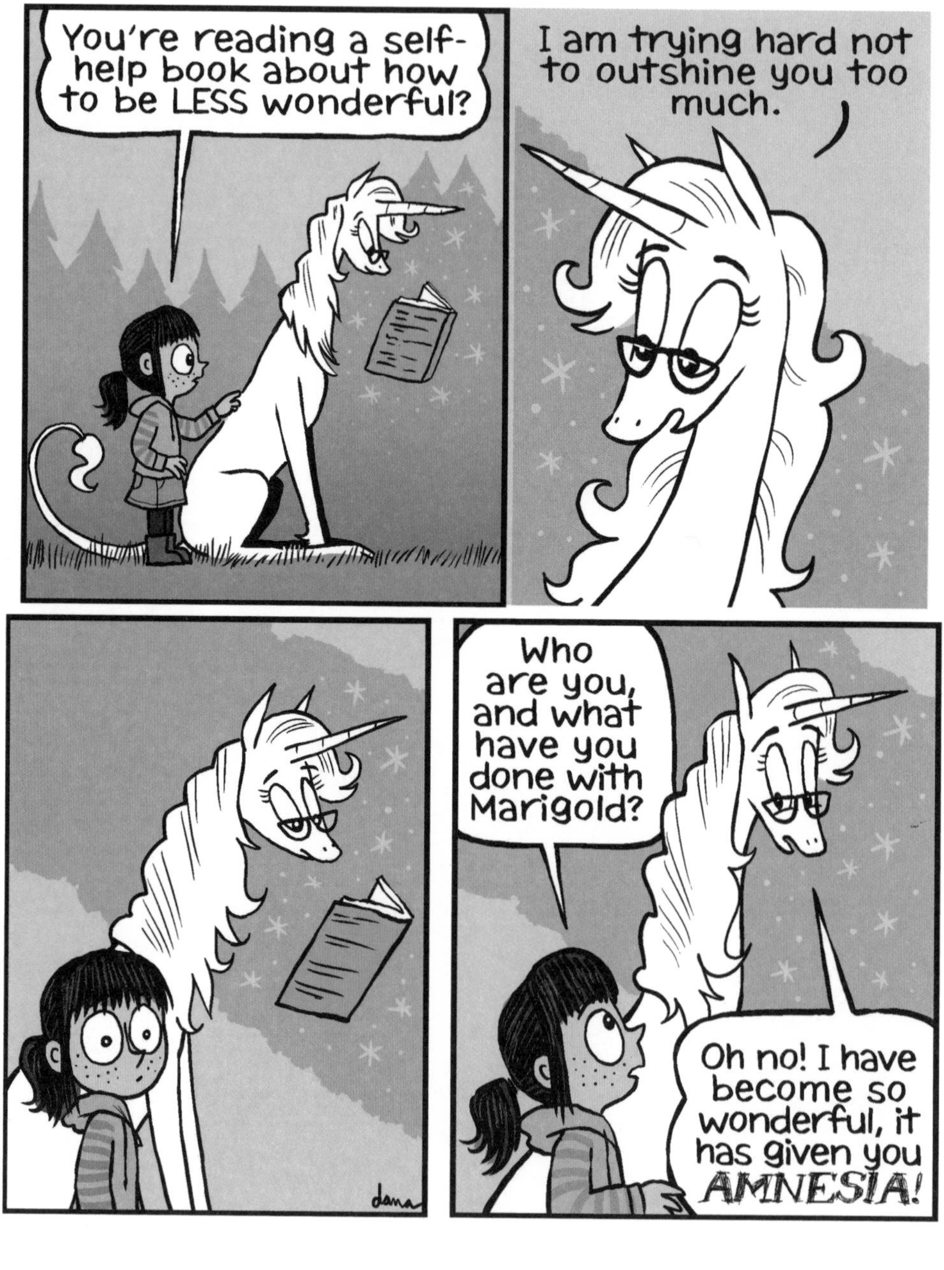
You're reading a self-help book about how to be LESS wonderful?
I am trying hard not to outshine you too much.
Who are you, and what have you done with Marigold?
Oh no! I have become so wonderful, it has given you AMNESIA!
dana

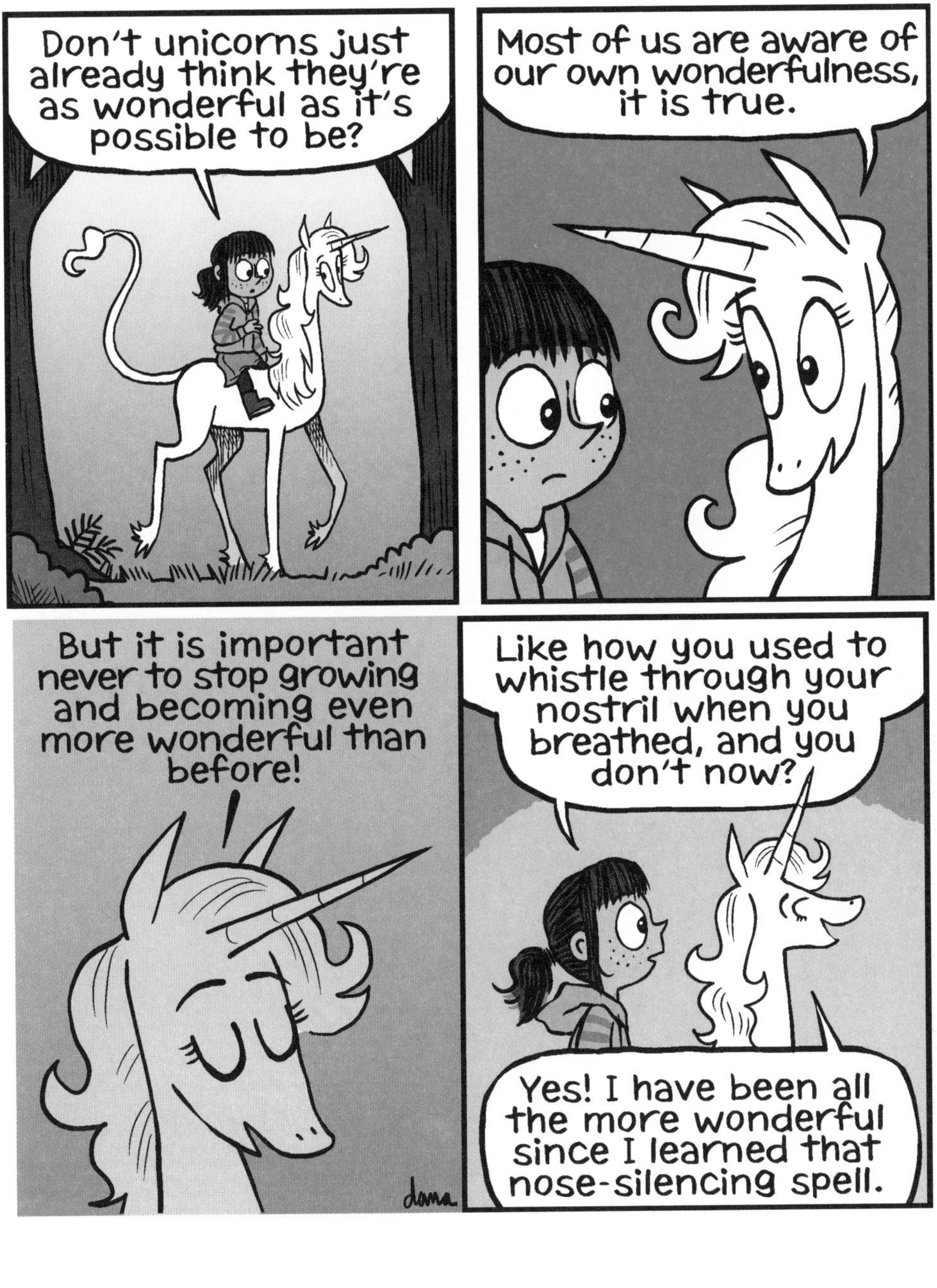
Don't unicorns just already think they're as wonderful as it's possible to be?
Most of us are aware of our own wonderfulness, it is true.
But it is important never to stop growing and becoming even more wonderful than before!
Like how you used to whistle through your nostril when you breathed, and you don't now?
Yes! I have been all the more wonderful since I learned that nose-silencing spell.
dana

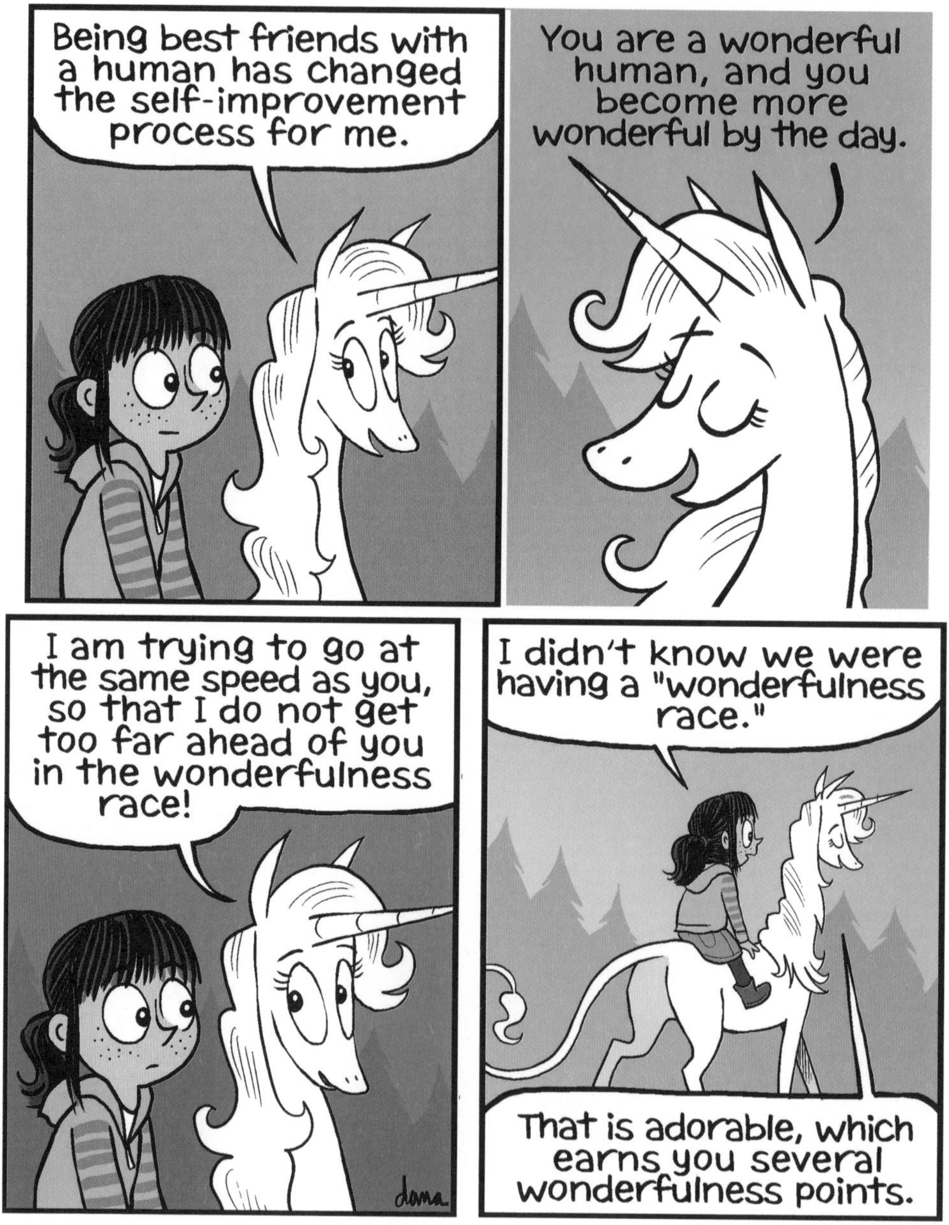
Being best friends with a human has changed the self-improvement process for me.
You are a wonderful human, and you become more wonderful by the day.
I am trying to go at the same speed as you, so that I do not get too far ahead of you in the wonderfulness race!
I didn't know we were having a "wonderfulness race."
That is adorable, which earns you several wonderfulness points.
dana

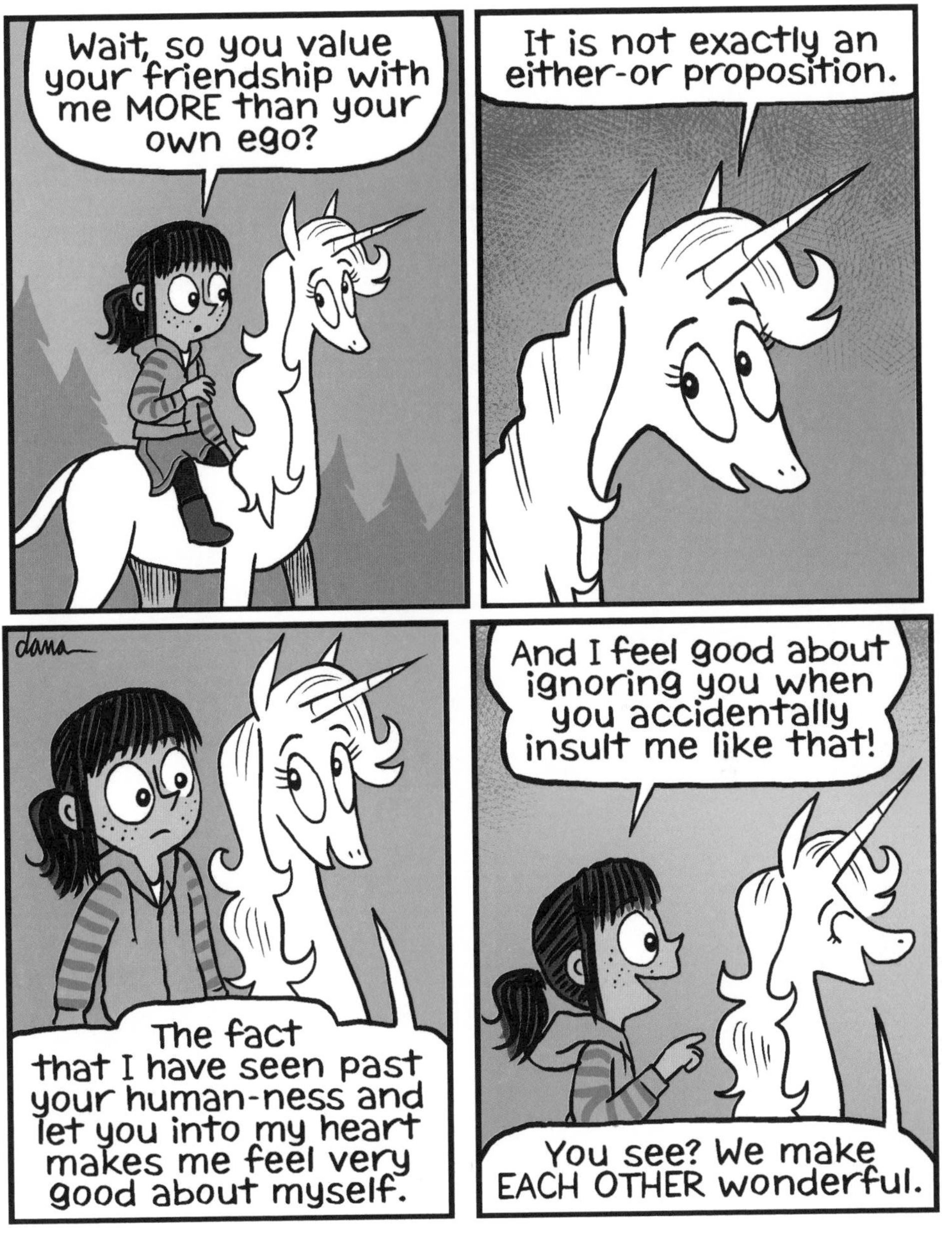
Wait, so you value your friendship with me MORE than your own ego?
It is not exactly an either-or proposition.
dana
The fact that I have seen past your human-ness and let you into my heart makes me feel very good about myself.
And I feel good about ignoring you when you accidentally insult me like that!
You see? We make EACH OTHER wonderful.

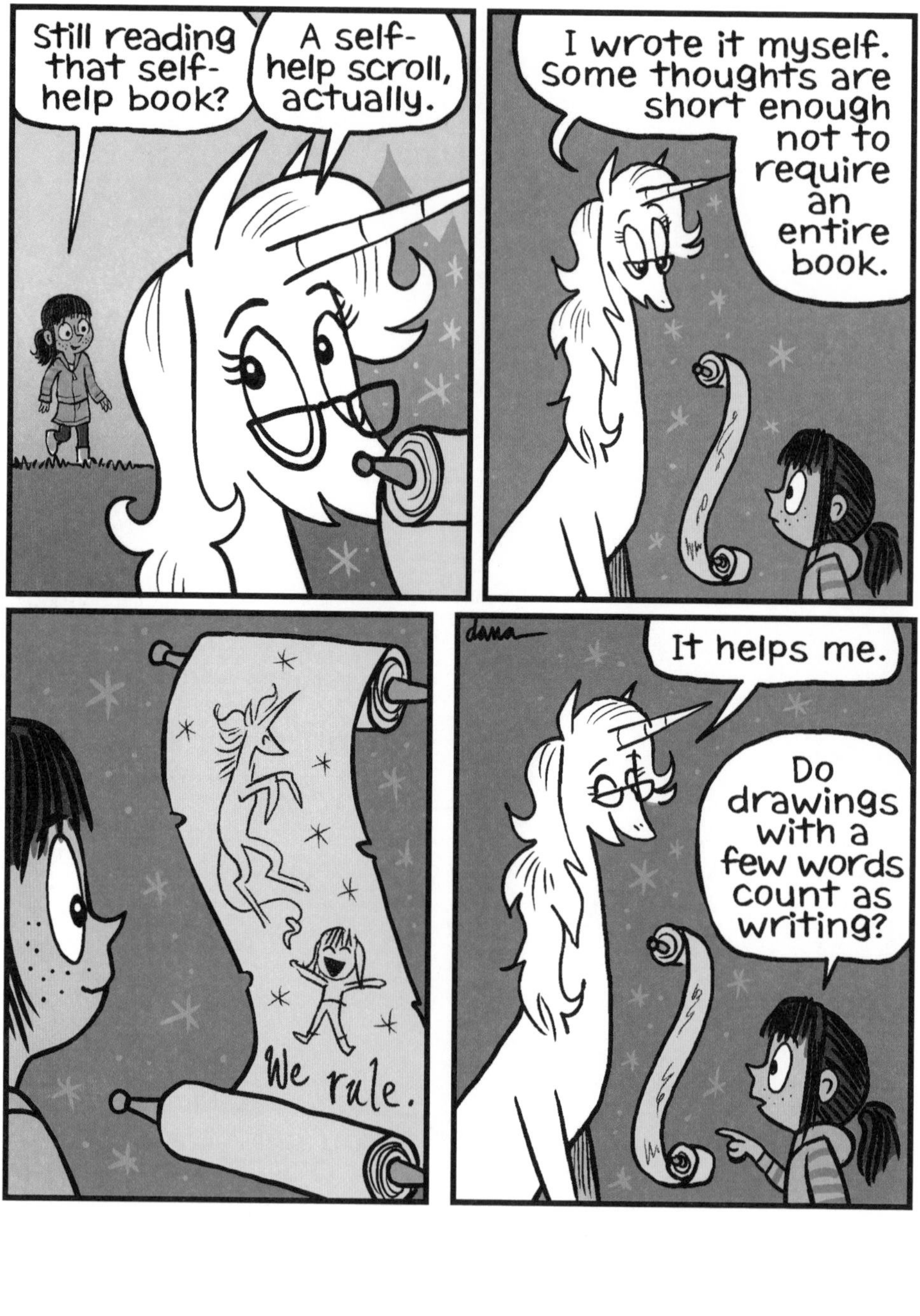
Still reading that self-help book?
A self-help scroll, actually.
I wrote it myself. Some thoughts are short enough not to require an entire book.
We rule.
dana
It helps me.
Do drawings with a few words count as writing?

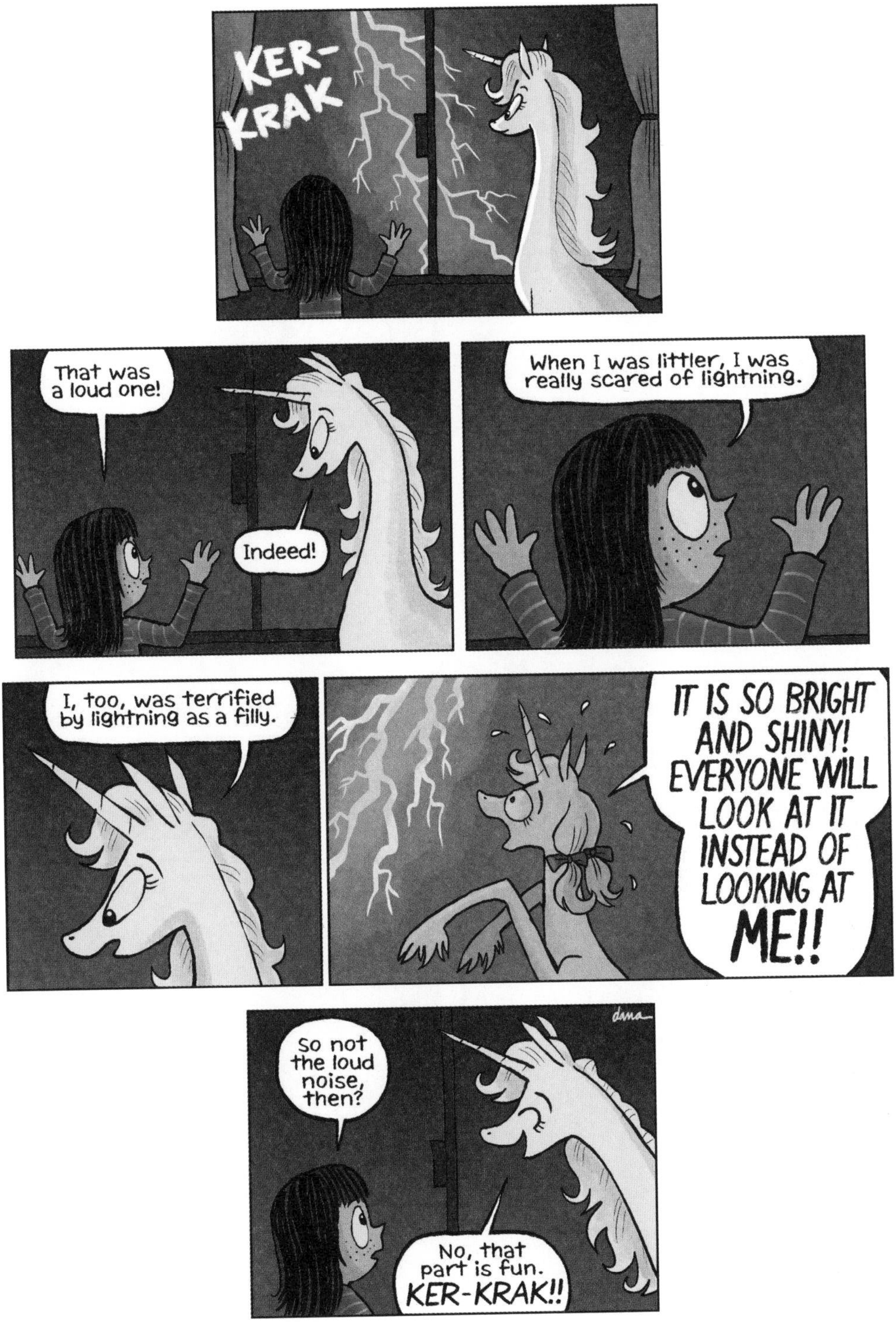
KER-KRAK
That was a loud one!
Indeed!
When I was littler, I was really scared of lightning.
I, too, was terrified by lightning as a filly.
IT IS SO BRIGHT AND SHINY! EVERYONE WILL LOOK AT IT INSTEAD OF LOOKING AT ME!!
So not the loud noise, then?
No, that part is fun. KER-KRAK!!

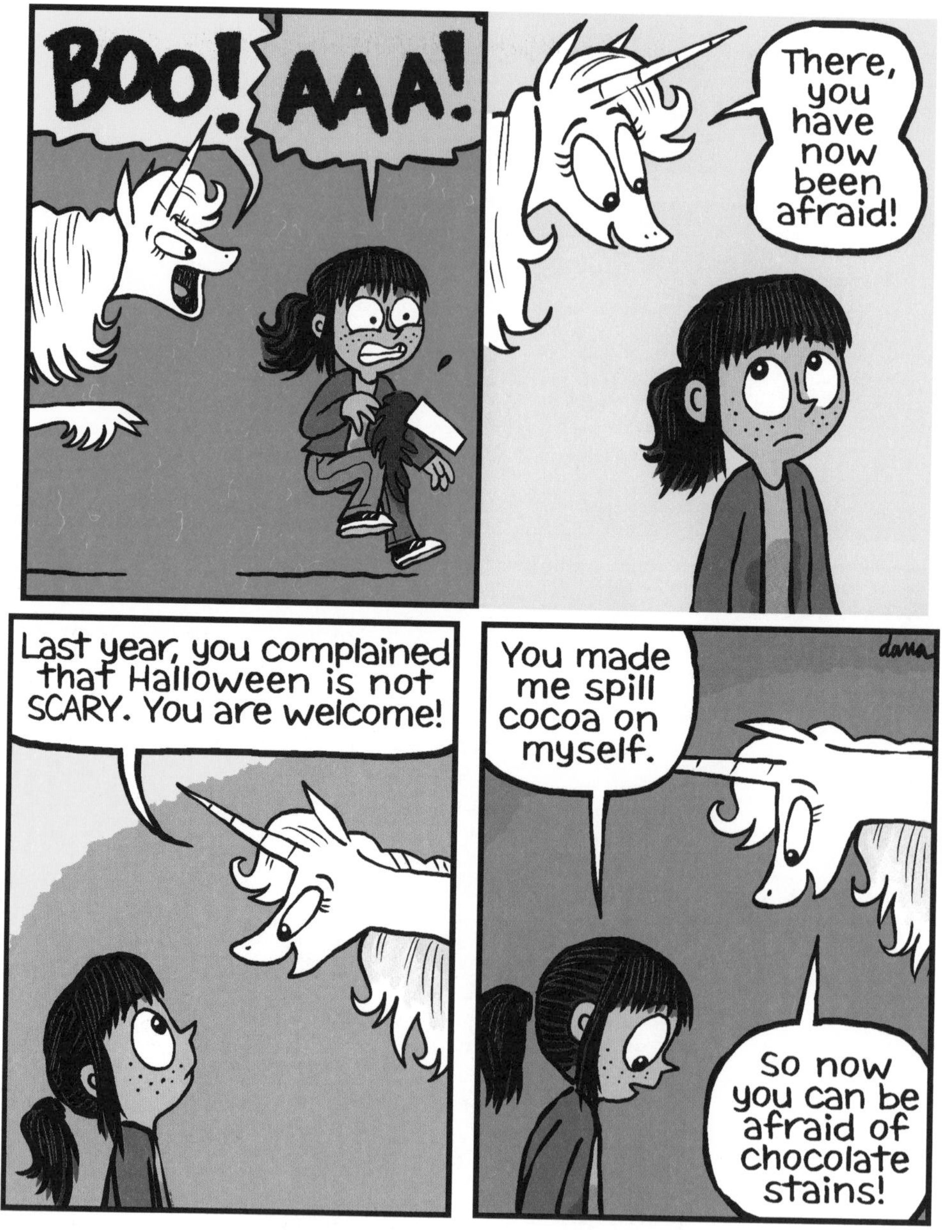
BOO!
AAA!
There, you have now been afraid!
Last year, you complained that Halloween is not SCARY. You are welcome!
You made me spill cocoa on myself.
So now you can be afraid of chocolate stains!
dana

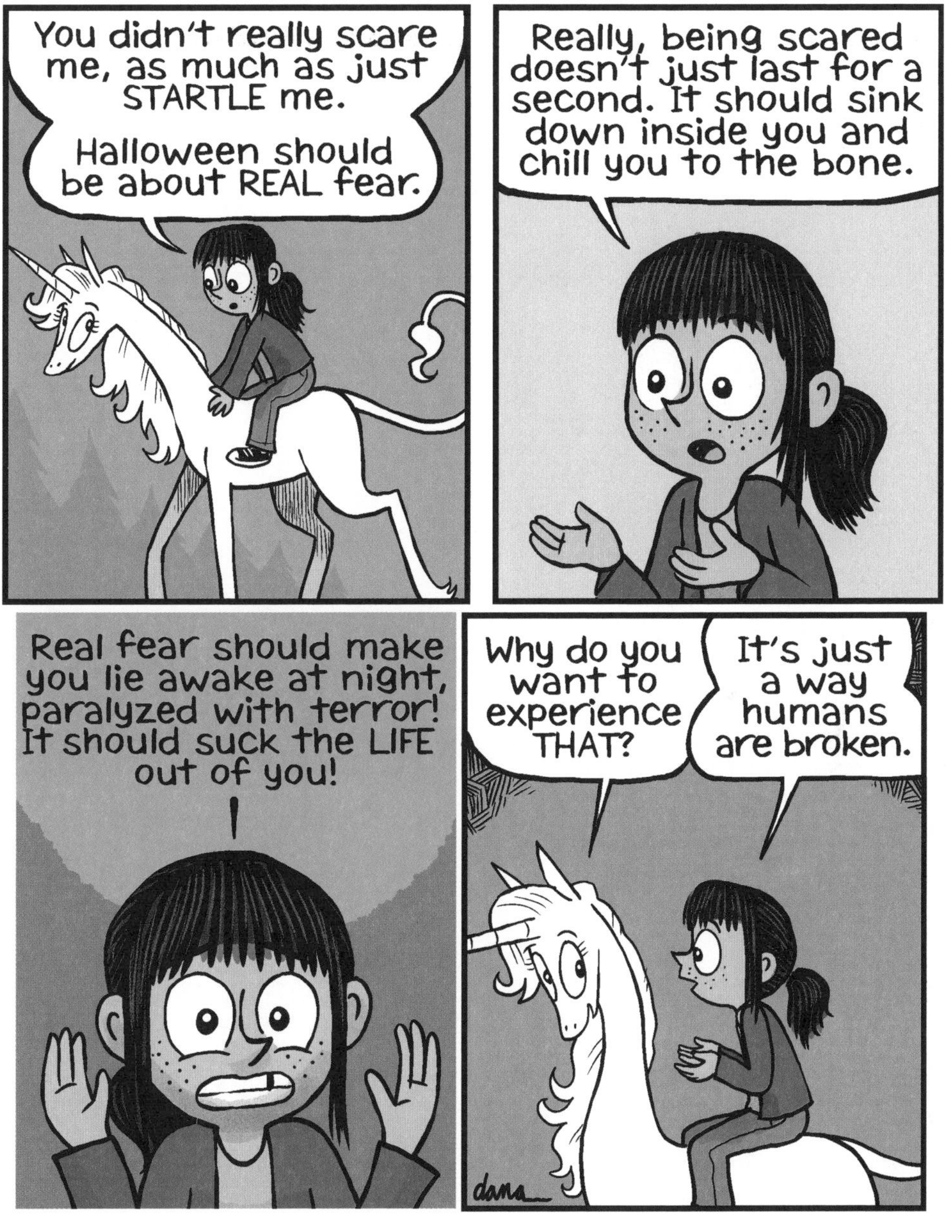

You didn't really scare me, as much as just STARTLE me.
Halloween should be about REAL fear.
Really, being scared doesn't just last for a second. It should sink down inside you and chill you to the bone.
Real fear should make you lie awake at night, paralyzed with terror! It should suck the LIFE out of you!
Why do you want to experience THAT?
It's just a way humans are broken.
dana

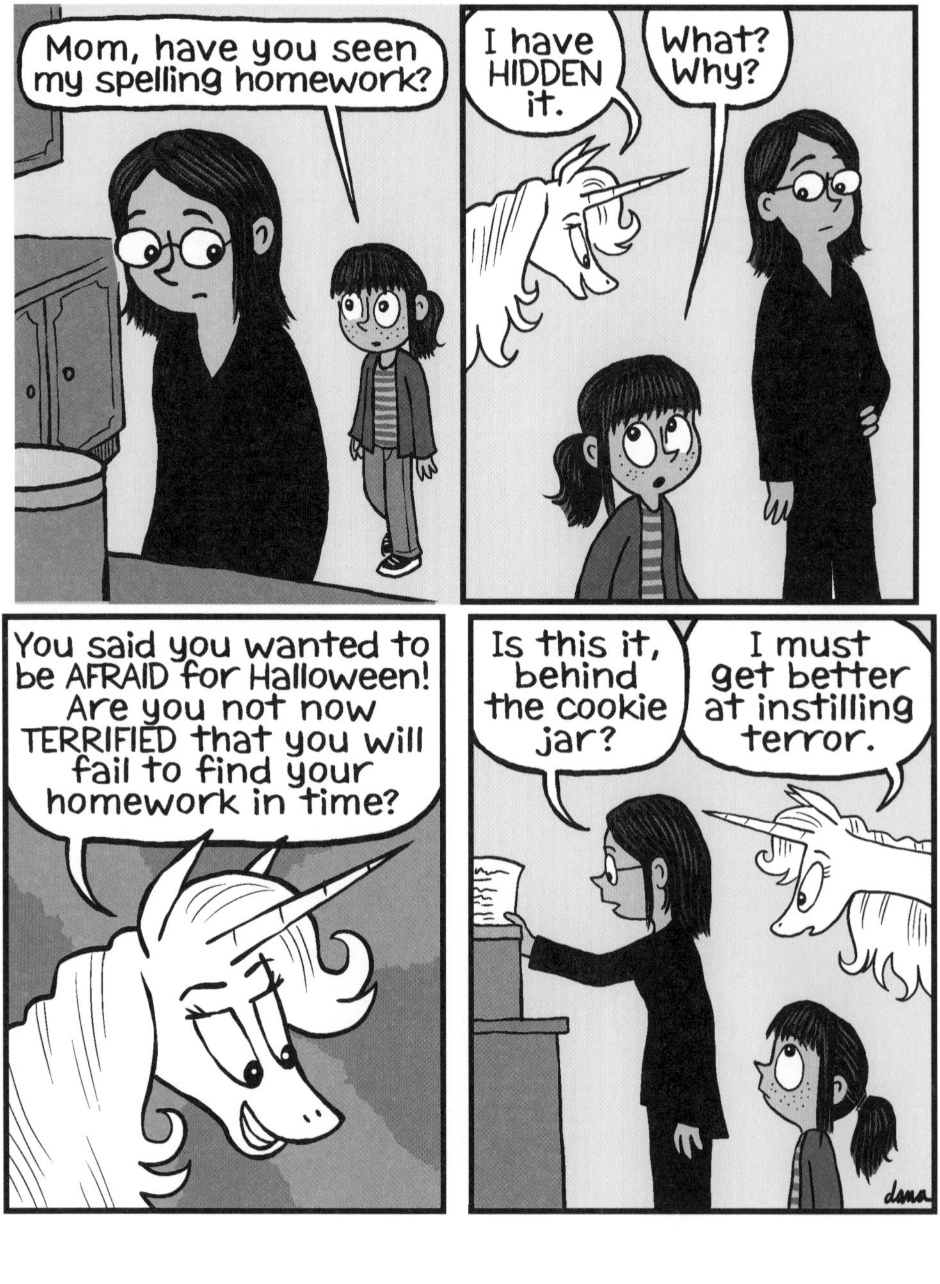
Mom, have you seen my spelling homework?
I have HIDDEN it.
What? Why?
You said you wanted to be AFRAID for Halloween! Are you not now TERRIFIED that you will fail to find your homework in time?
Is this it, behind the cookie jar?
I must get better at instilling terror.
dana

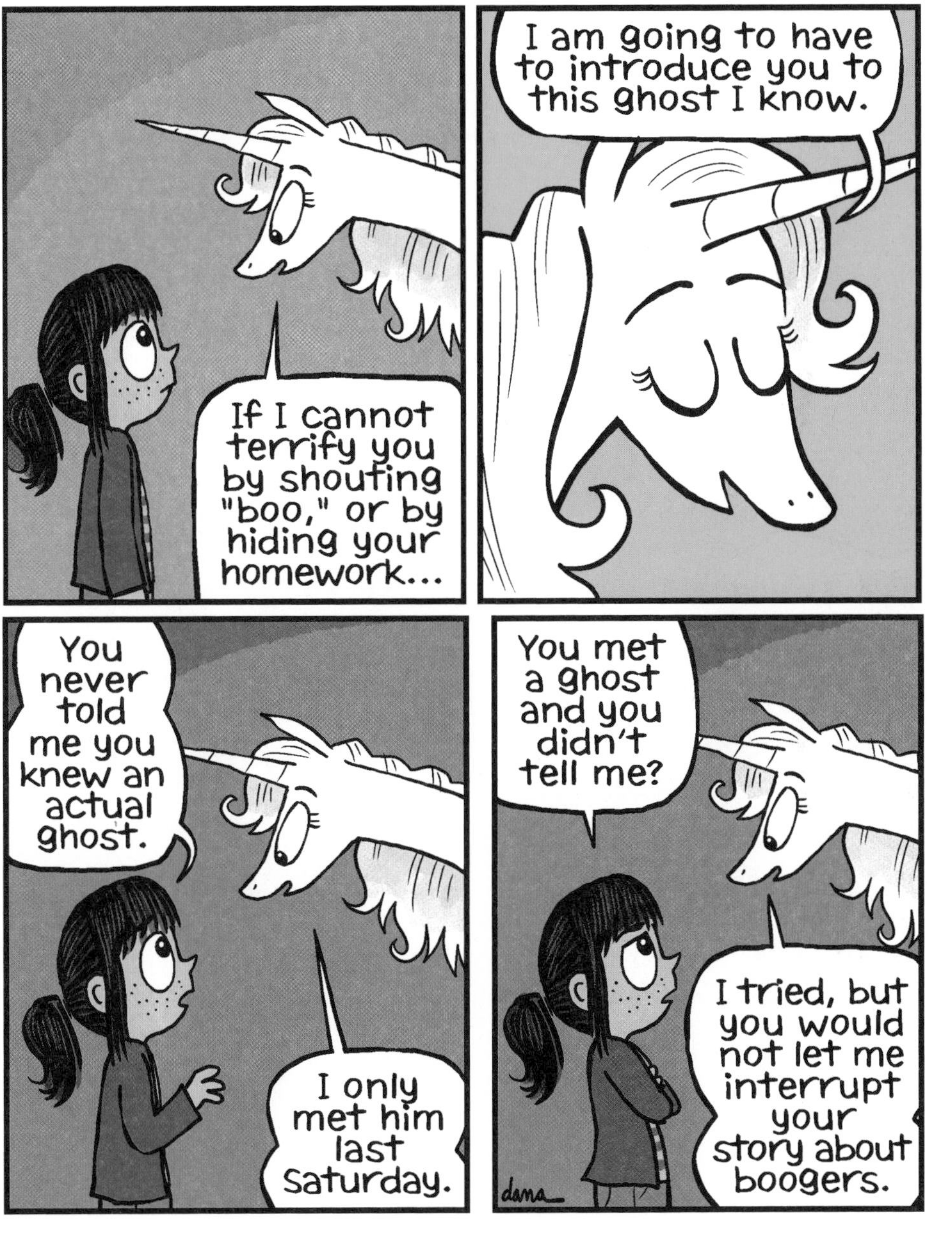
If I cannot terrify you by shouting "boo," or by hiding your homework...
I am going to have to introduce you to this ghost I know.
You never told me you knew an actual ghost.
I only met him last Saturday.
You met a ghost and you didn't tell me?
I tried, but you would not let me interrupt your story about boogers.
dana

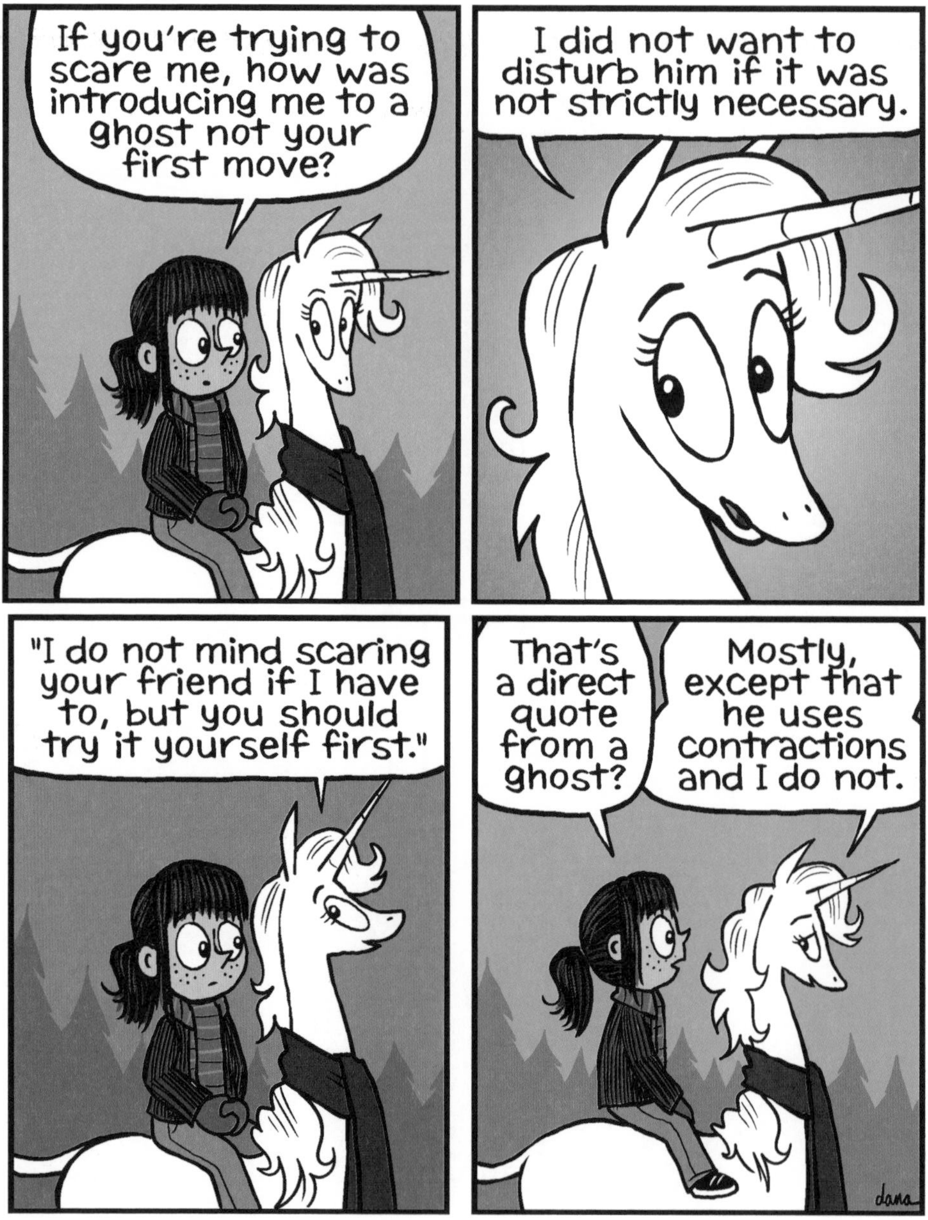
If you're trying to scare me, how was introducing me to a ghost not your first move?
I did not want to disturb him if it was not strictly necessary.
"I do not mind scaring your friend if I have to, but you should try it yourself first."
That's a direct quote from a ghost?
Mostly, except that he uses contractions and I do not.
dana

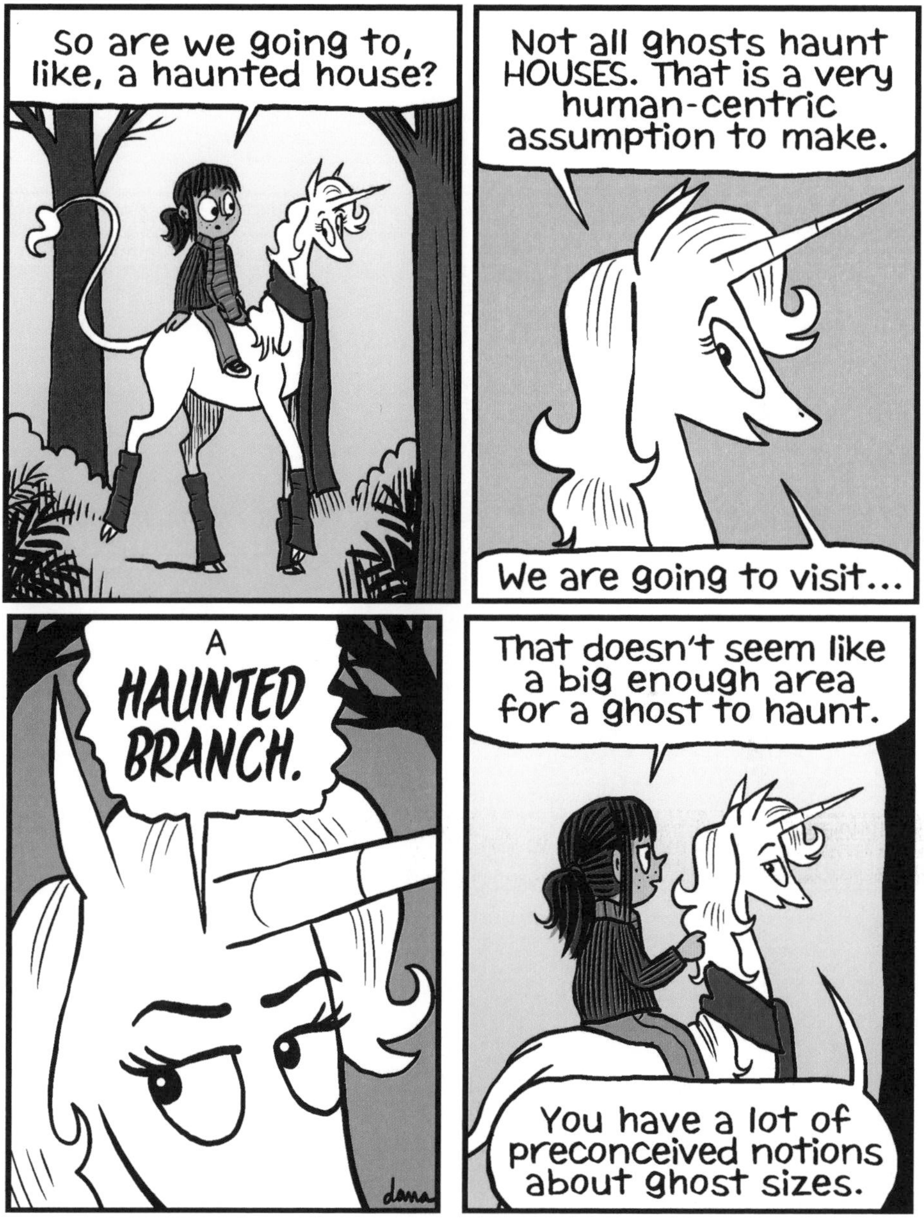
So are we going to, like, a haunted house?
Not all ghosts haunt HOUSES. That is a very human-centric assumption to make.
We are going to visit...
A HAUNTED BRANCH.
That doesn't seem like a big enough area for a ghost to haunt.
You have a lot of preconceived notions about ghost sizes.
dana

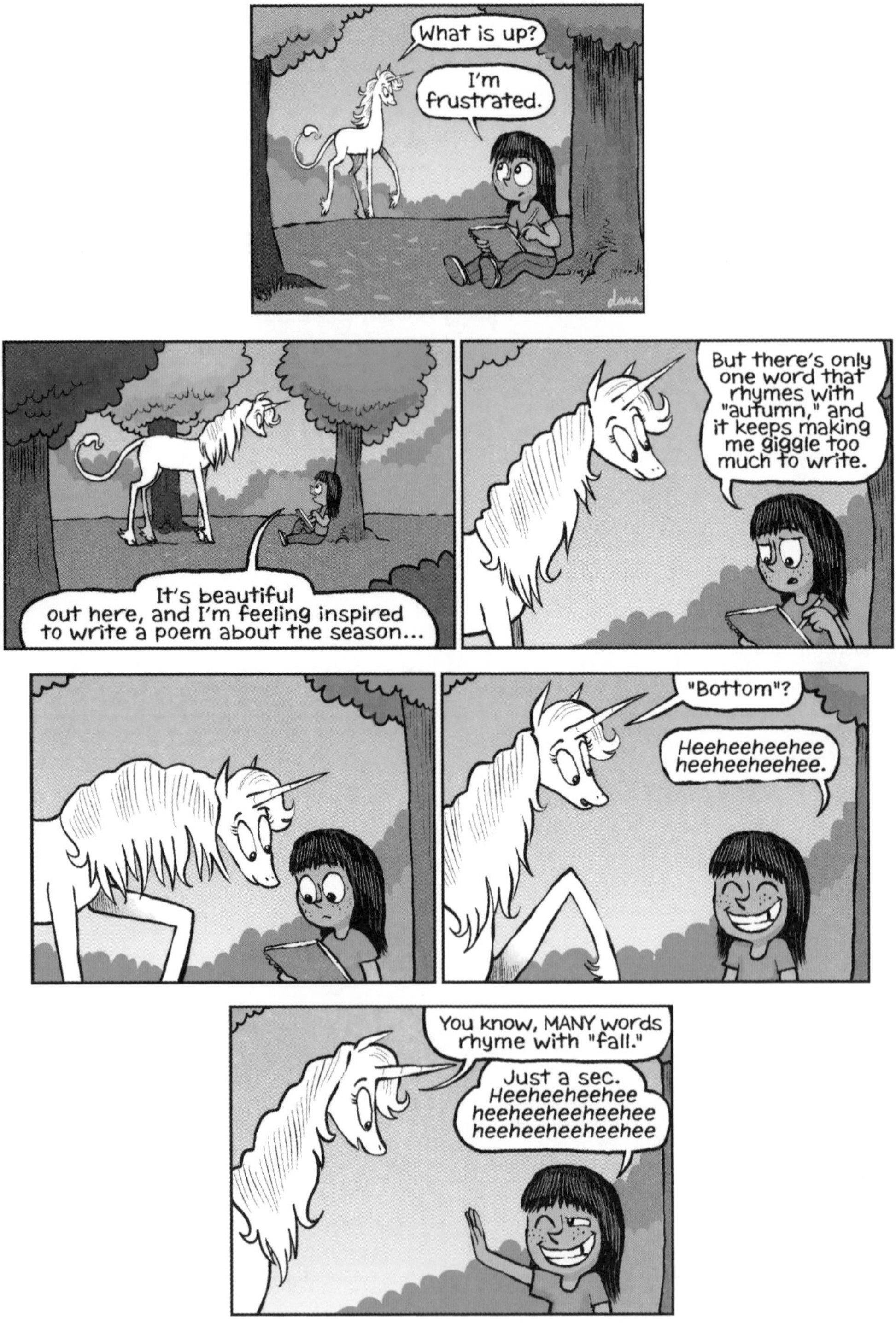
What is up?
I'm frustrated.
It's beautiful out here, and I'm feeling inspired to write a poem about the season...
But there's only one word that rhymes with "autumn," and it keeps making me giggle too much to write.
"Bottom"?
Heeheeheehee heeheeheehee.
You know, MANY words rhyme with "fall."
Just a sec. Heeheeheehee heeheeheeheehee heeheeheeheehee

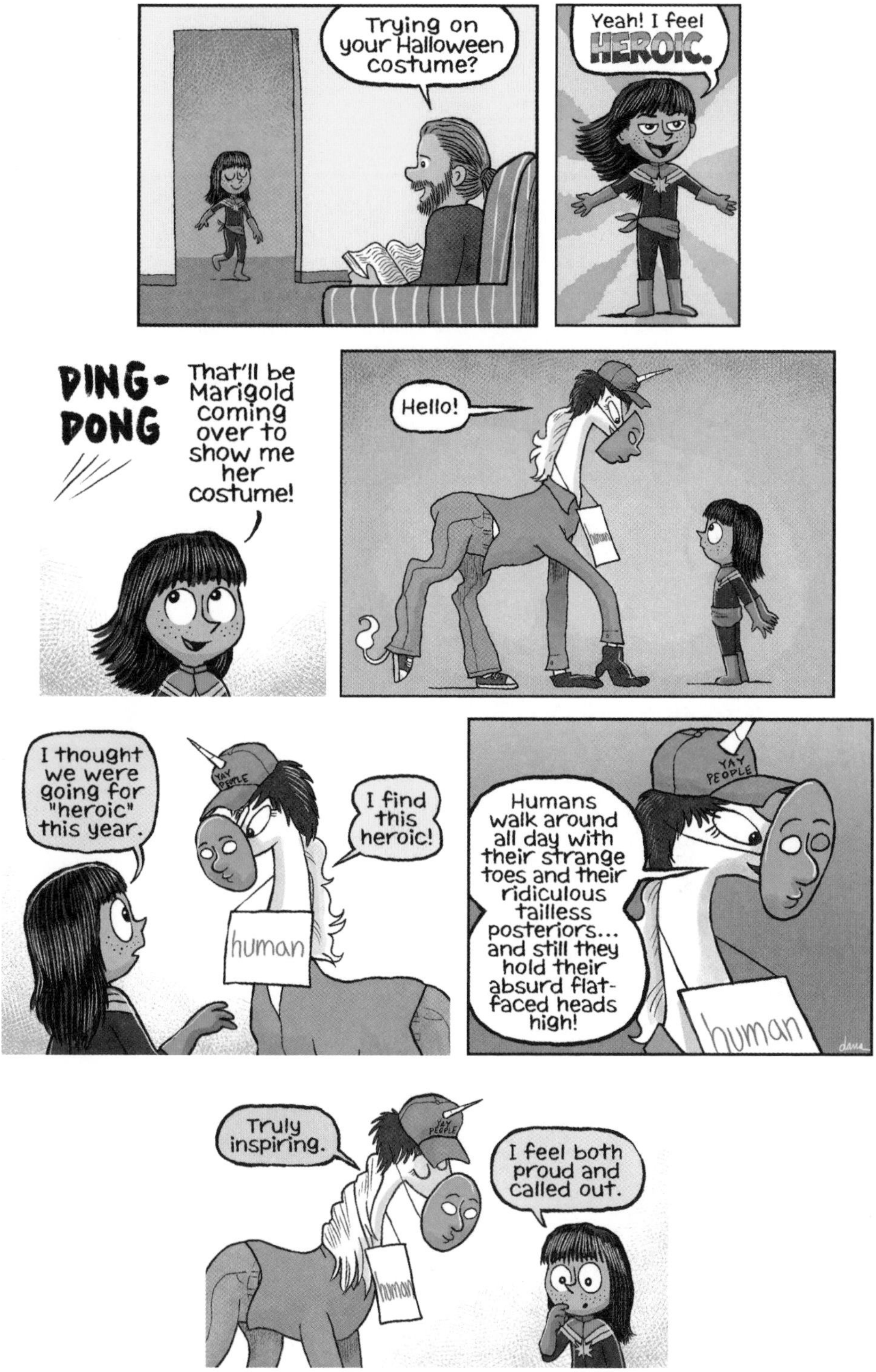
Trying on your Halloween costume?
Yeah! I feel HEROIC.
DING-DONG
That'll be Marigold coming over to show me her costume!
Hello!
I thought we were going for "heroic" this year.
YAY PEOPLE
I find this heroic!
human
YAY PEOPLE
Humans walk around all day with their strange toes and their ridiculous tailless posteriors... and still they hold their absurd flat-faced heads high!
human
Truly inspiring.
I feel both proud and called out.
human

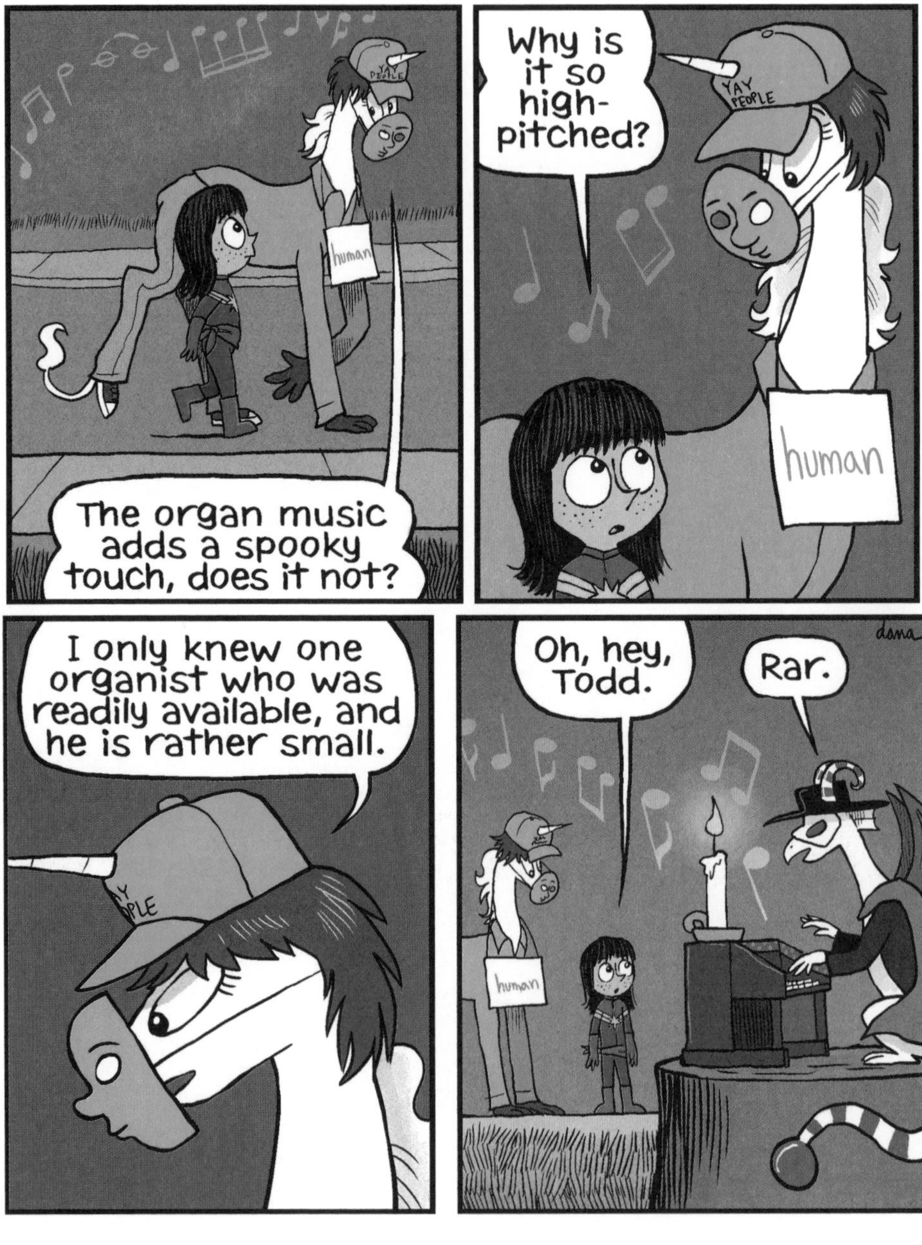
The organ music adds a spooky touch, does it not?
Why is it so high-pitched?
human
I only knew one organist who was readily available, and he is rather small.
Oh, hey, Todd.
Rar.
human
dana

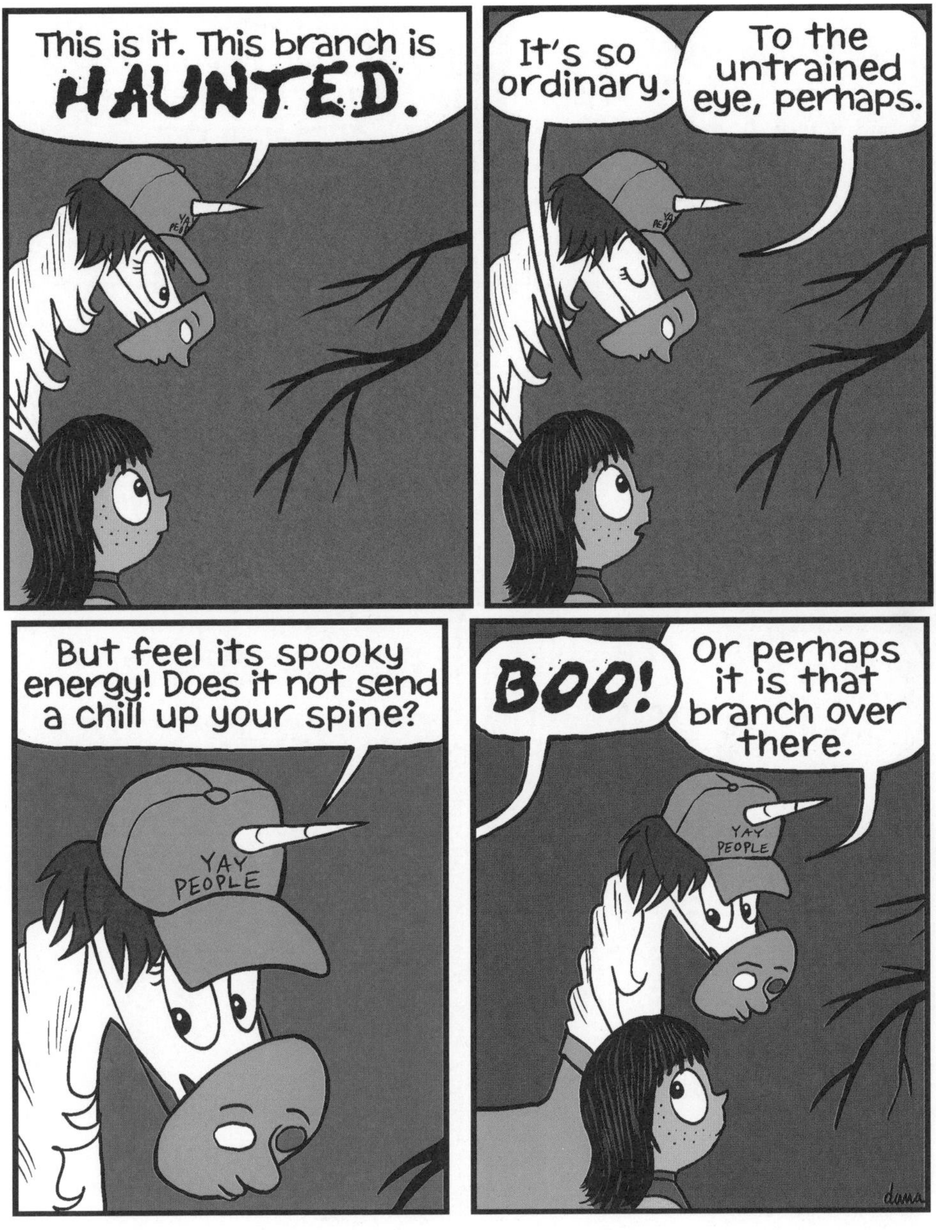
This is it. This branch is HAUNTED.
It's so ordinary.
To the untrained eye, perhaps.
But feel its spooky energy! Does it not send a chill up your spine?
YAY PEOPLE
BOO!
Or perhaps it is that branch over there.
YAY PEOPLE
dana

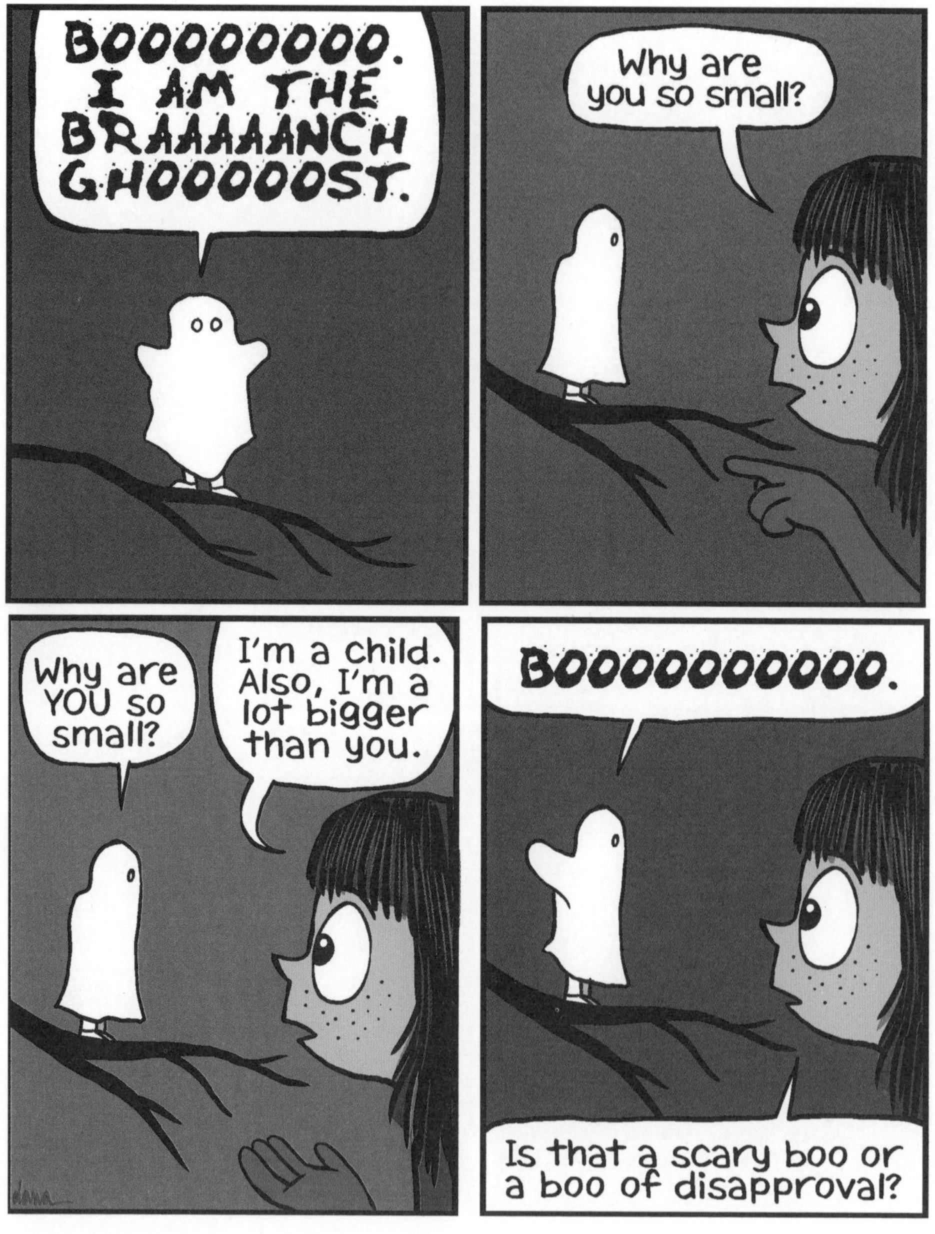
BOOOOOOOO. I AM THE BRAAAAANCH GHOOOOOST.
Why are you so small?
Why are YOU so small?
I'm a child. Also, I'm a lot bigger than you.
BOOOOOOOOOOO.
Is that a scary boo or a boo of disapproval?

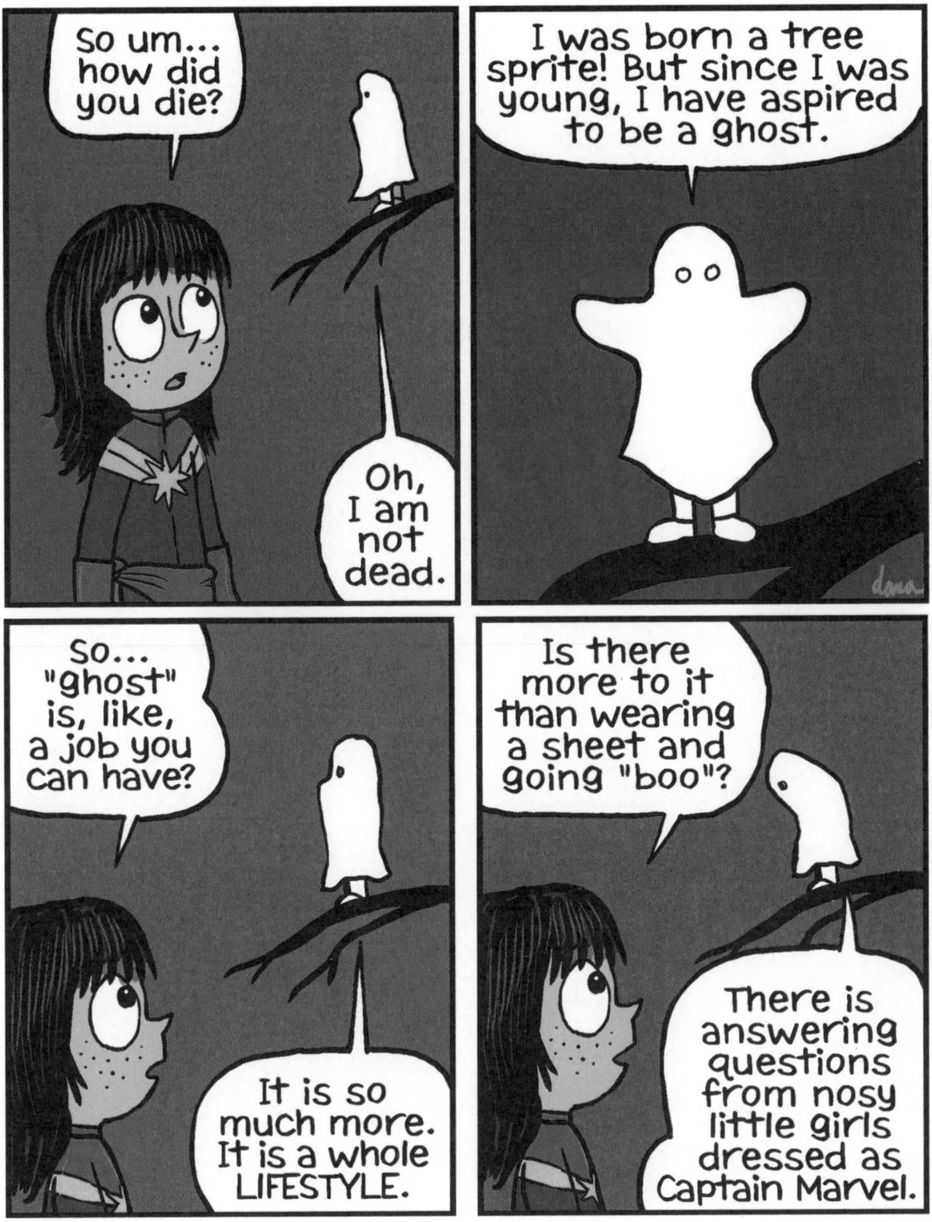

So um... how did you die?
Oh, I am not dead.
I was born a tree sprite! But since I was young, I have aspired to be a ghost.
So... "ghost" is, like, a job you can have?
It is so much more. It is a whole LIFESTYLE.
Is there more to it than wearing a sheet and going "boo"?
There is answering questions from nosy little girls dressed as Captain Marvel.

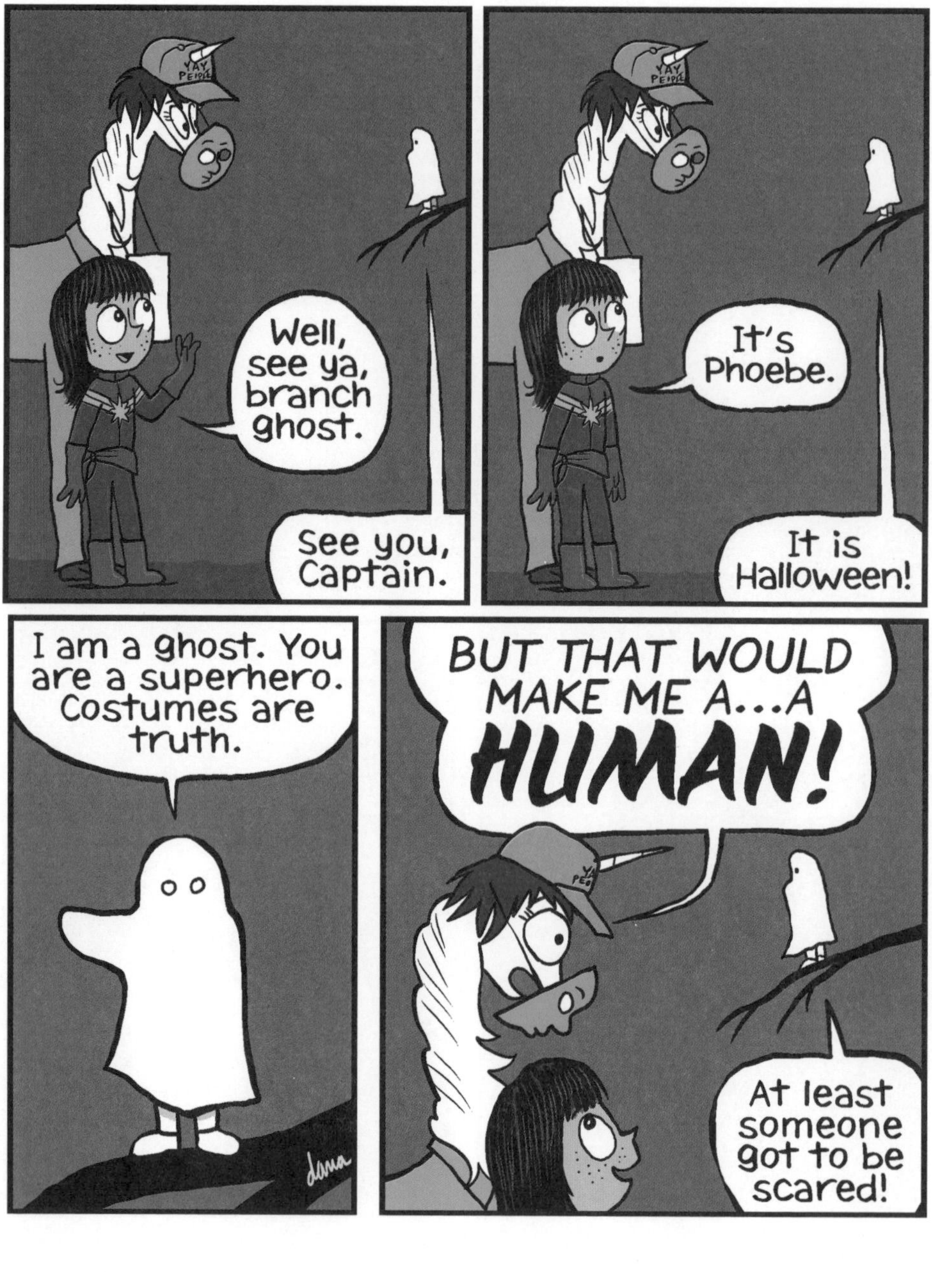
Well, see ya, branch ghost.
See you, Captain.
It's Phoebe.
It is Halloween!
I am a ghost. You are a superhero. Costumes are truth.
BUT THAT WOULD MAKE ME A...A HUMAN!
At least someone got to be scared!

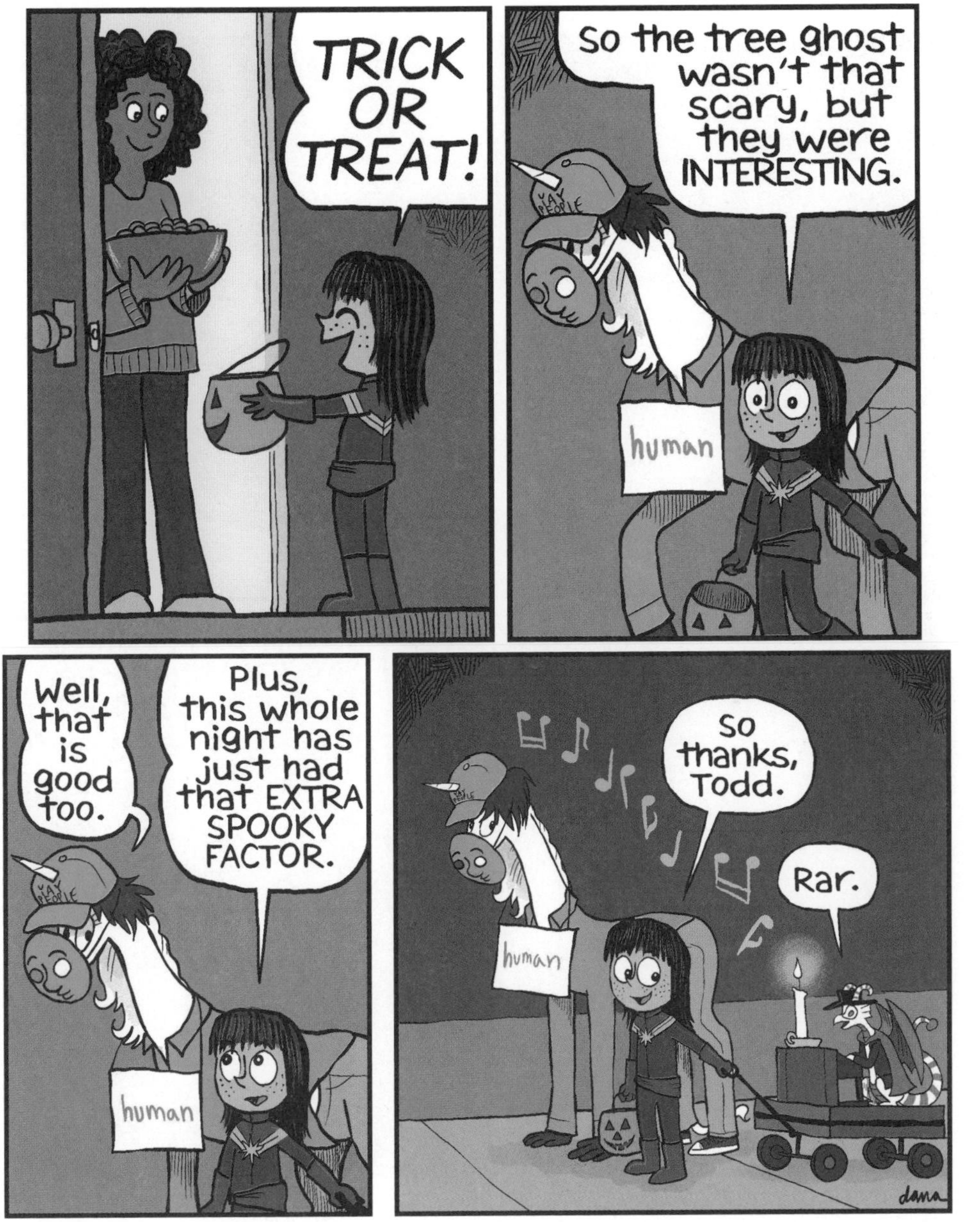
TRICK OR TREAT!
So the tree ghost wasn't that scary, but they were INTERESTING.
YAY PEOPLE
human
Well, that is good too.
Plus, this whole night has just had that EXTRA SPOOKY FACTOR.
YAY PEOPLE
human
So thanks, Todd.
Rar.
human
dana

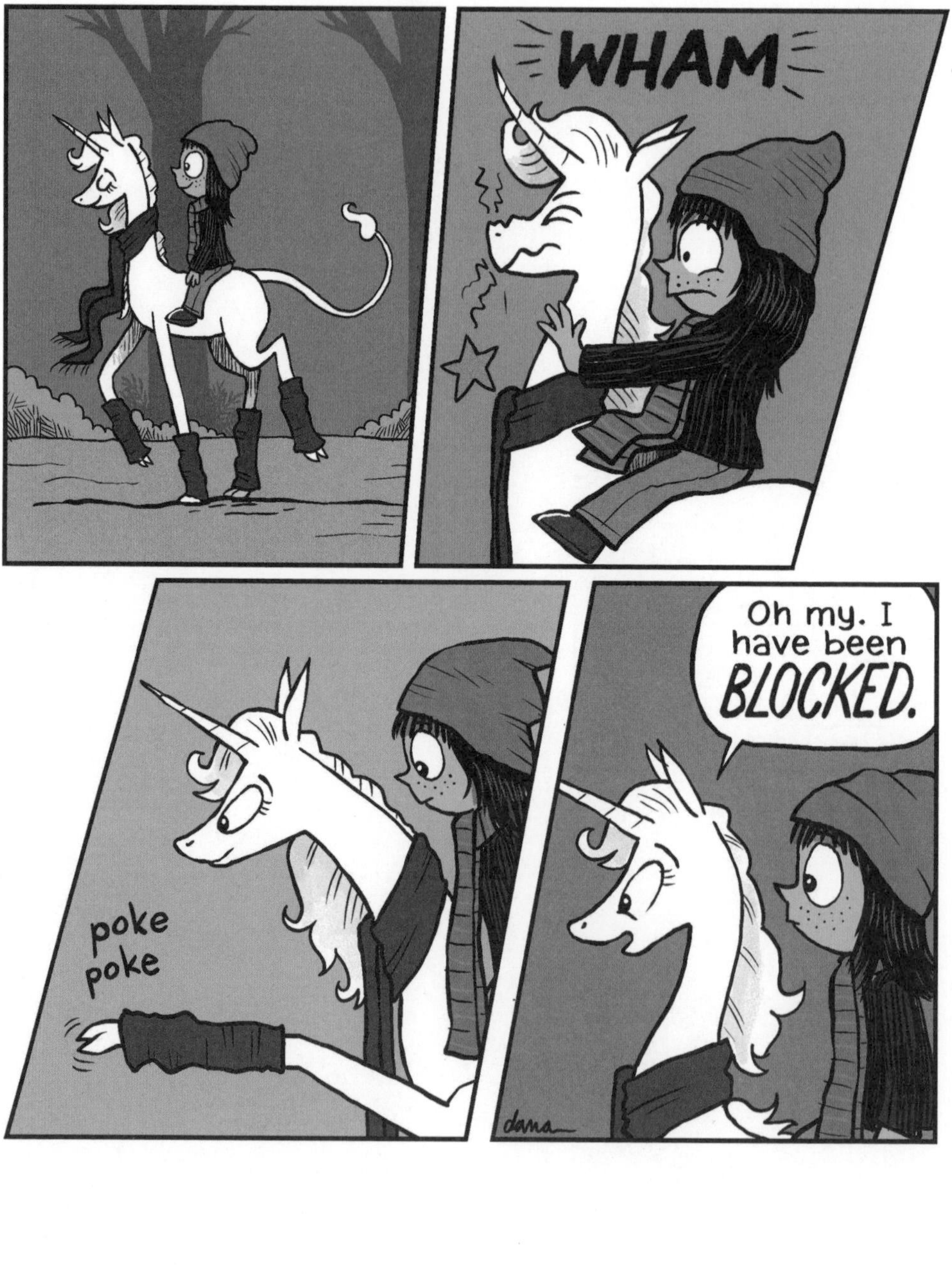
WHAM
poke
poke
Oh my. I have been BLOCKED.
dana

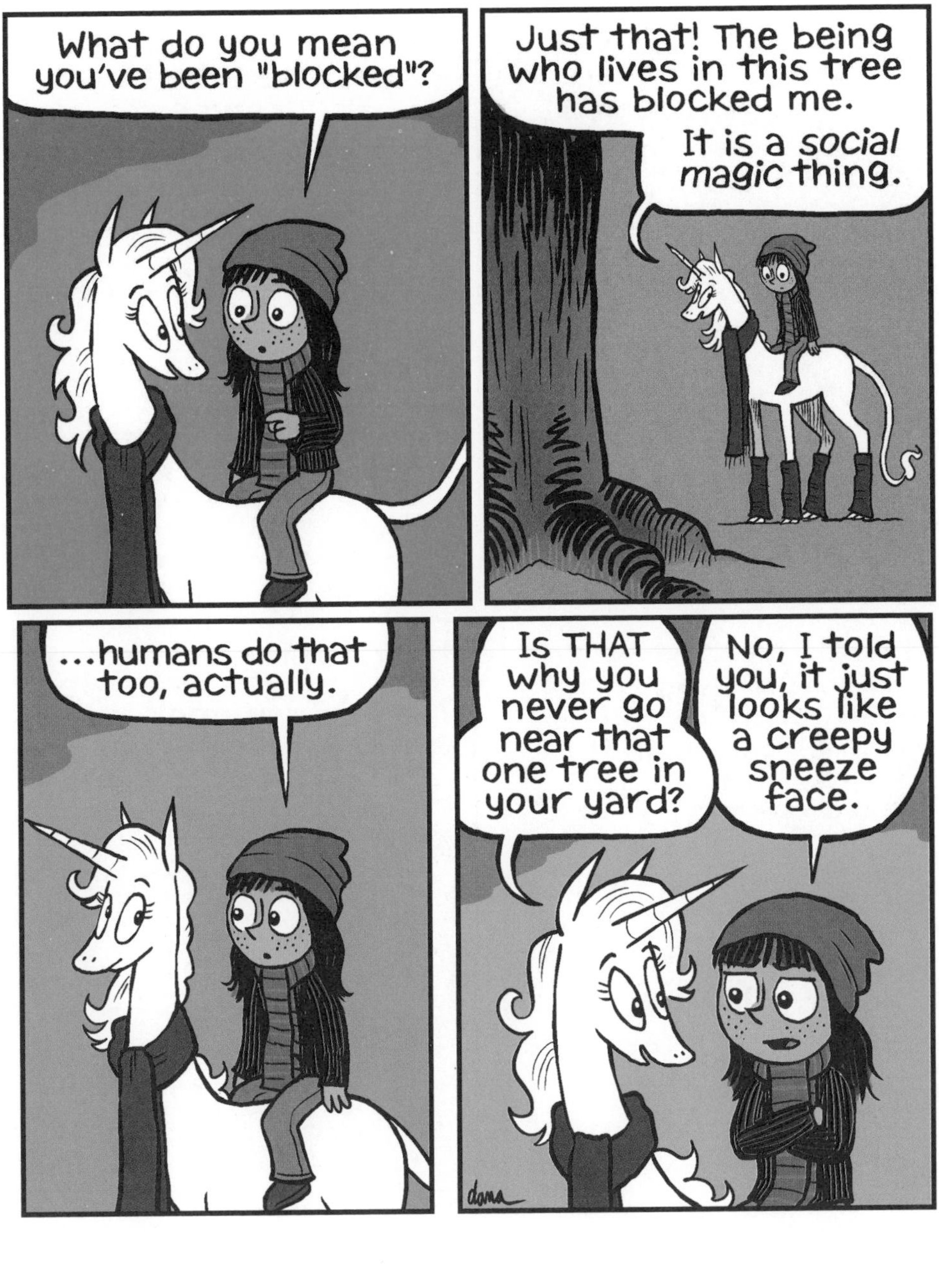
What do you mean you've been "blocked"?
Just that! The being who lives in this tree has blocked me.
It is a *social magic* thing.
...humans do that too, actually.
Is THAT why you never go near that one tree in your yard?
No, I told you, it just looks like a creepy sneeze face.
dana

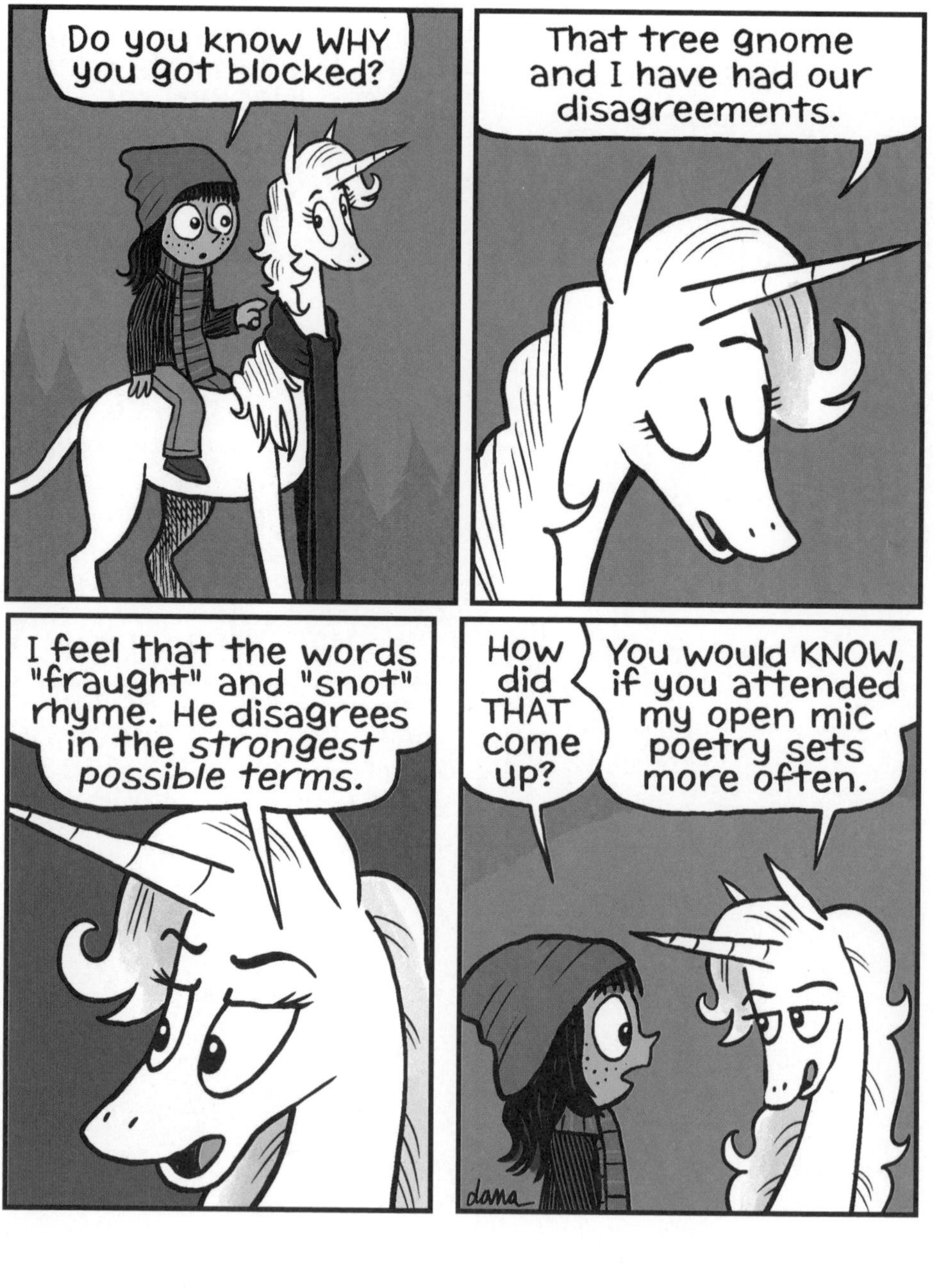
Do you know WHY you got blocked?
That tree gnome and I have had our disagreements.
I feel that the words "fraught" and "snot" rhyme. He disagrees in the *strongest possible terms.*
How did THAT come up?
You would KNOW, if you attended my open mic poetry sets more often.
dana

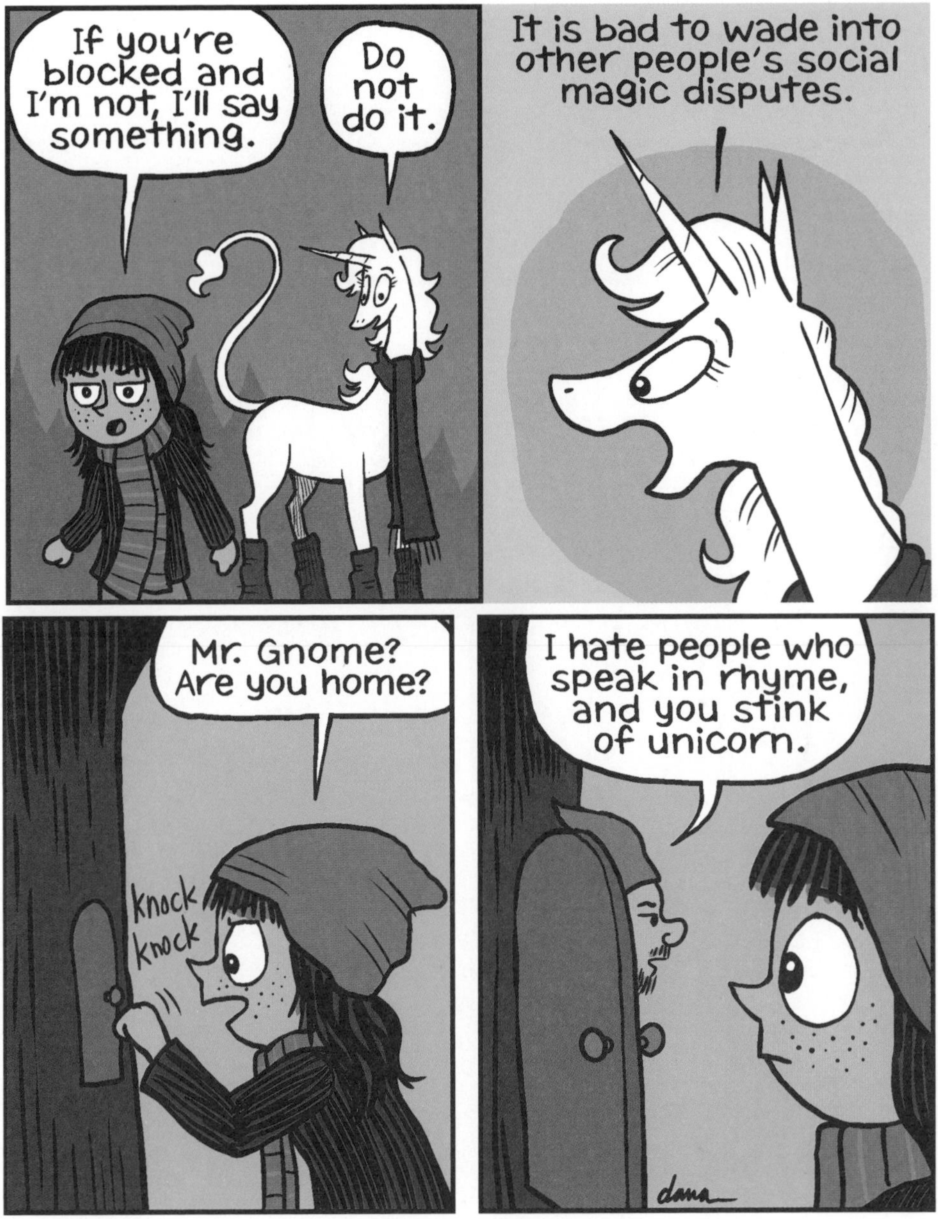
If you're blocked and I'm not, I'll say something.
Do not do it.
It is bad to wade into other people's social magic disputes.
Mr. Gnome? Are you home?
knock knock
I hate people who speak in rhyme, and you stink of unicorn.
dana

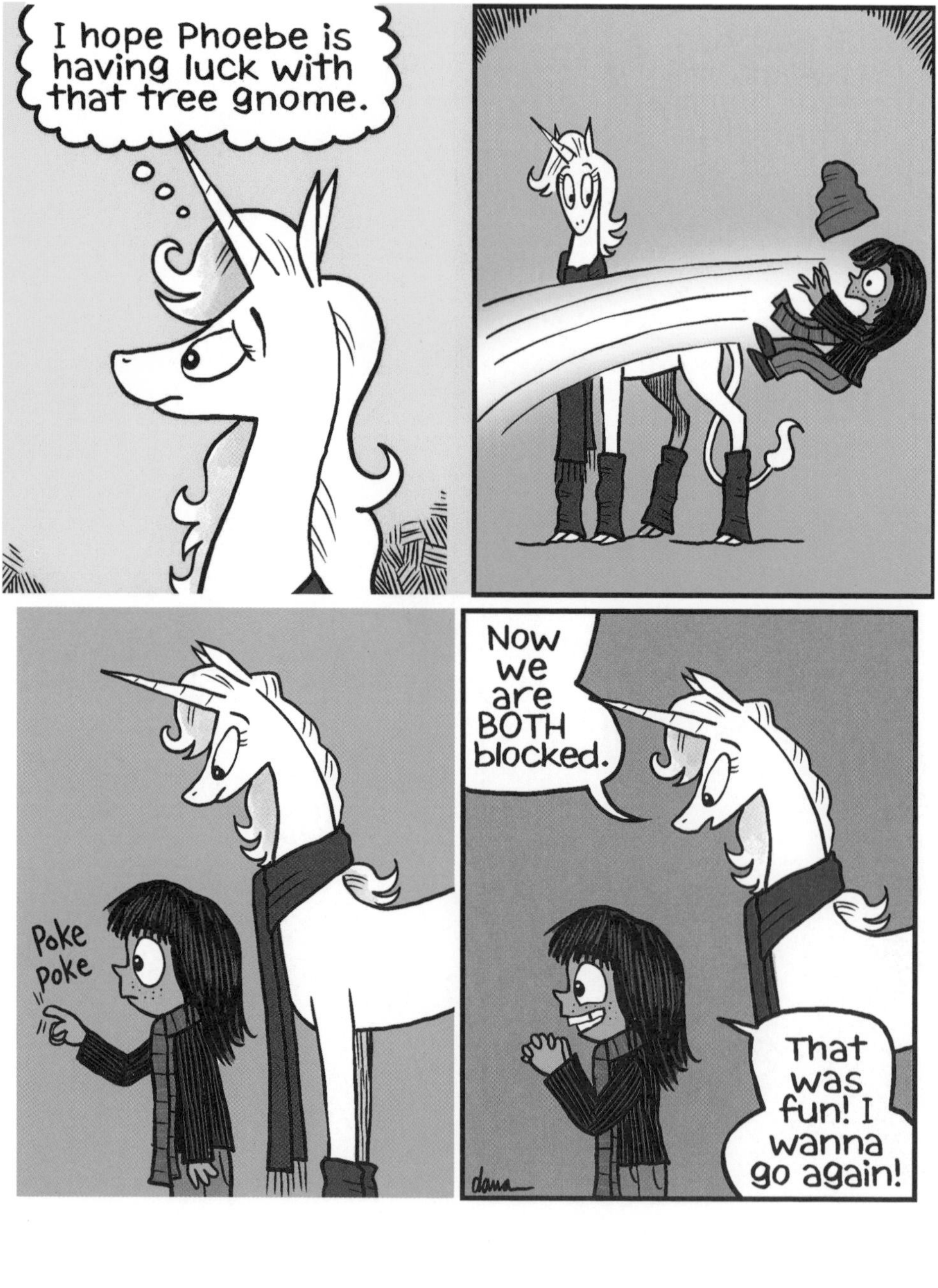
I hope Phoebe is having luck with that tree gnome.
Poke poke
Now we are BOTH blocked.
That was fun! I wanna go again!
dana

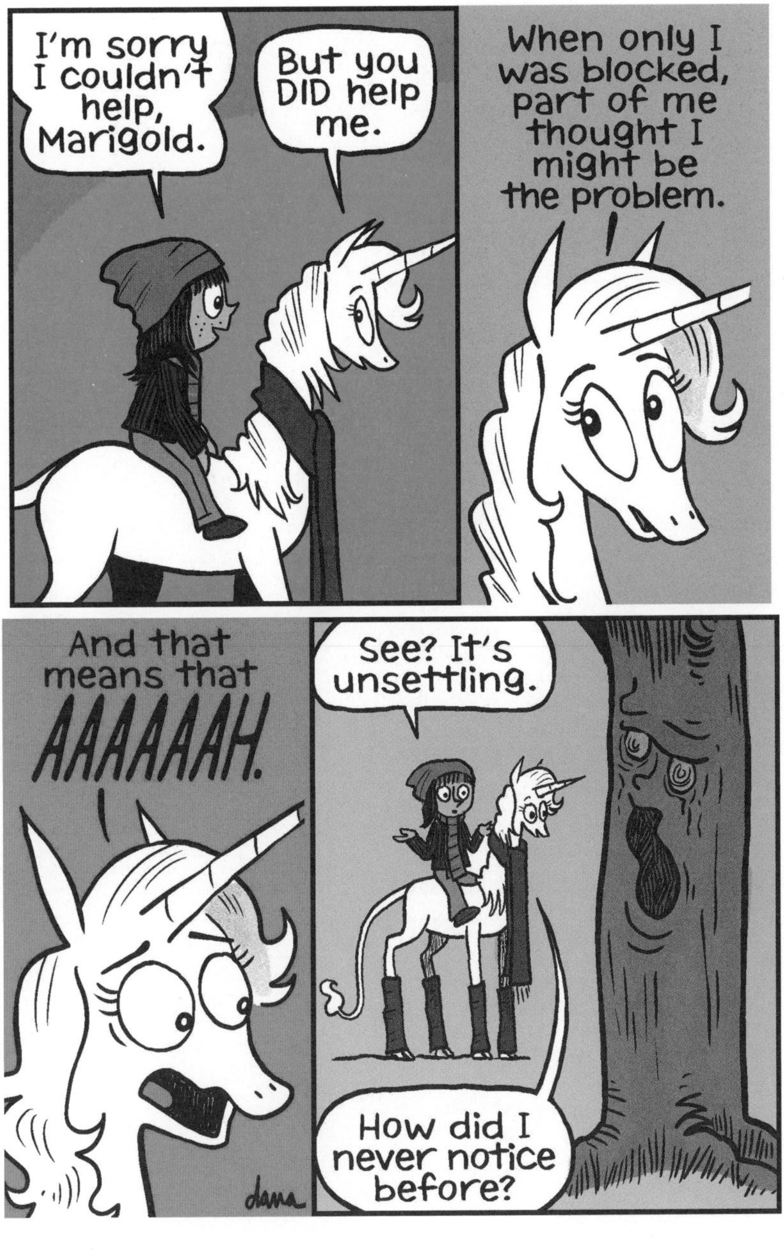
I'm sorry I couldn't help, Marigold.
But you DID help me.
When only I was blocked, part of me thought I might be the problem.
And that means that
AAAAAAH.
See? It's unsettling.
How did I never notice before?
dana

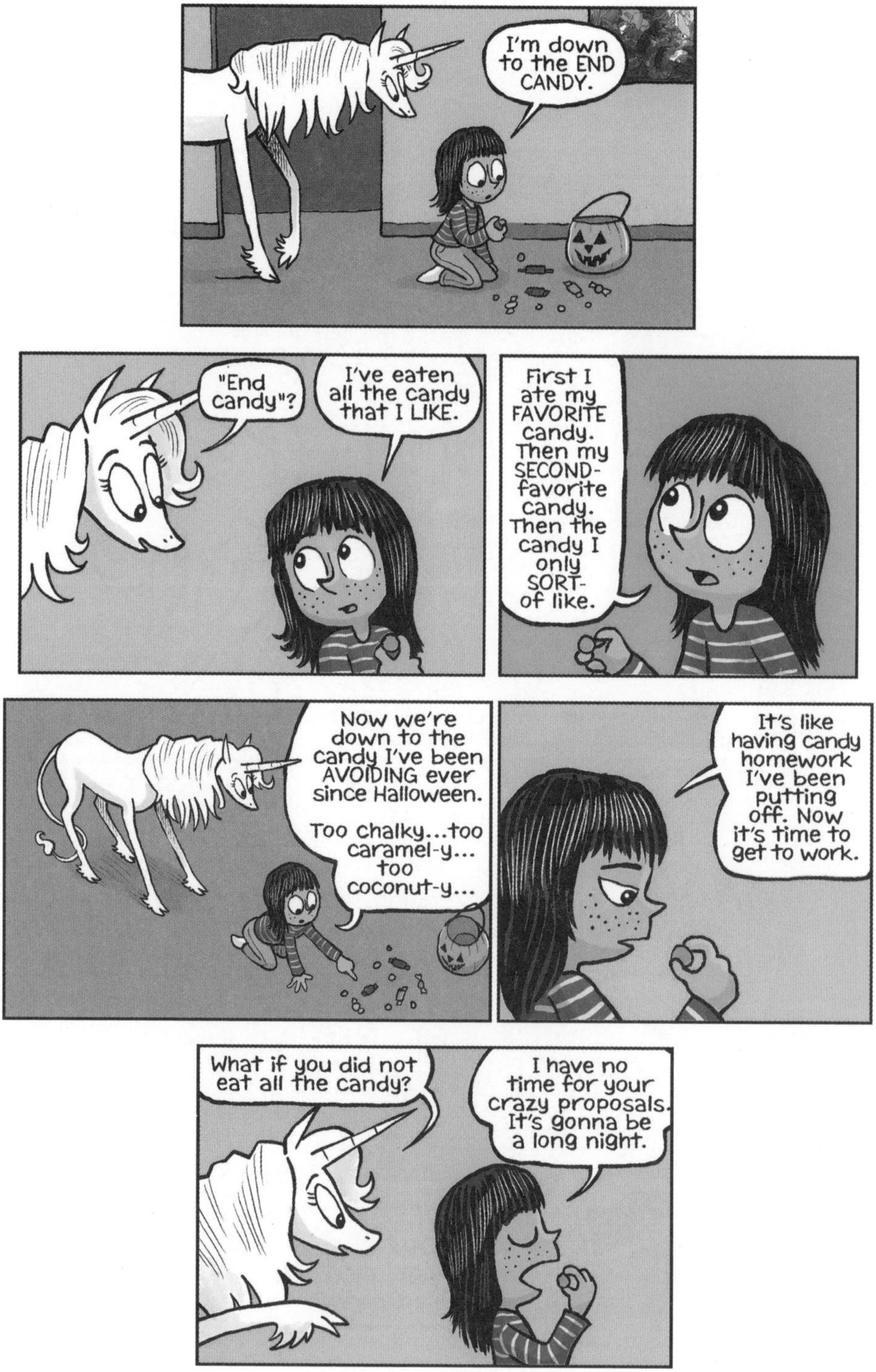
I'm down to the END CANDY.
"End candy"?
I've eaten all the candy that I LIKE.
First I ate my FAVORITE candy. Then my SECOND-favorite candy. Then the candy I only SORT-of like.
Now we're down to the candy I've been AVOIDING ever since Halloween.
Too chalky...too caramel-y...too coconut-y...
It's like having candy homework I've been putting off. Now it's time to get to work.
What if you did not eat all the candy?
I have no time for your crazy proposals. It's gonna be a long night.

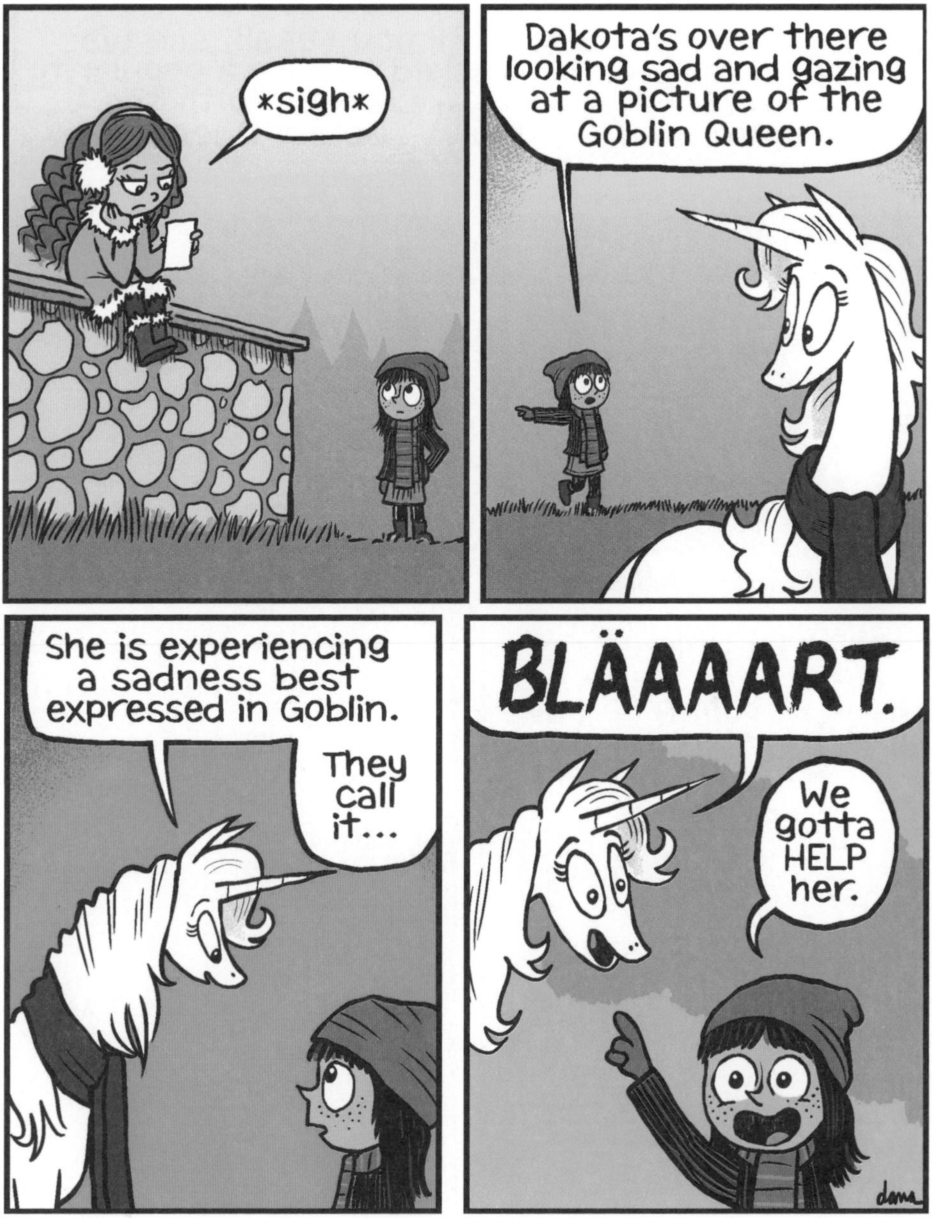
sigh
Dakota's over there looking sad and gazing at a picture of the Goblin Queen.
She is experiencing a sadness best expressed in Goblin.
They call it...
BLÄAAART.
We gotta HELP her.

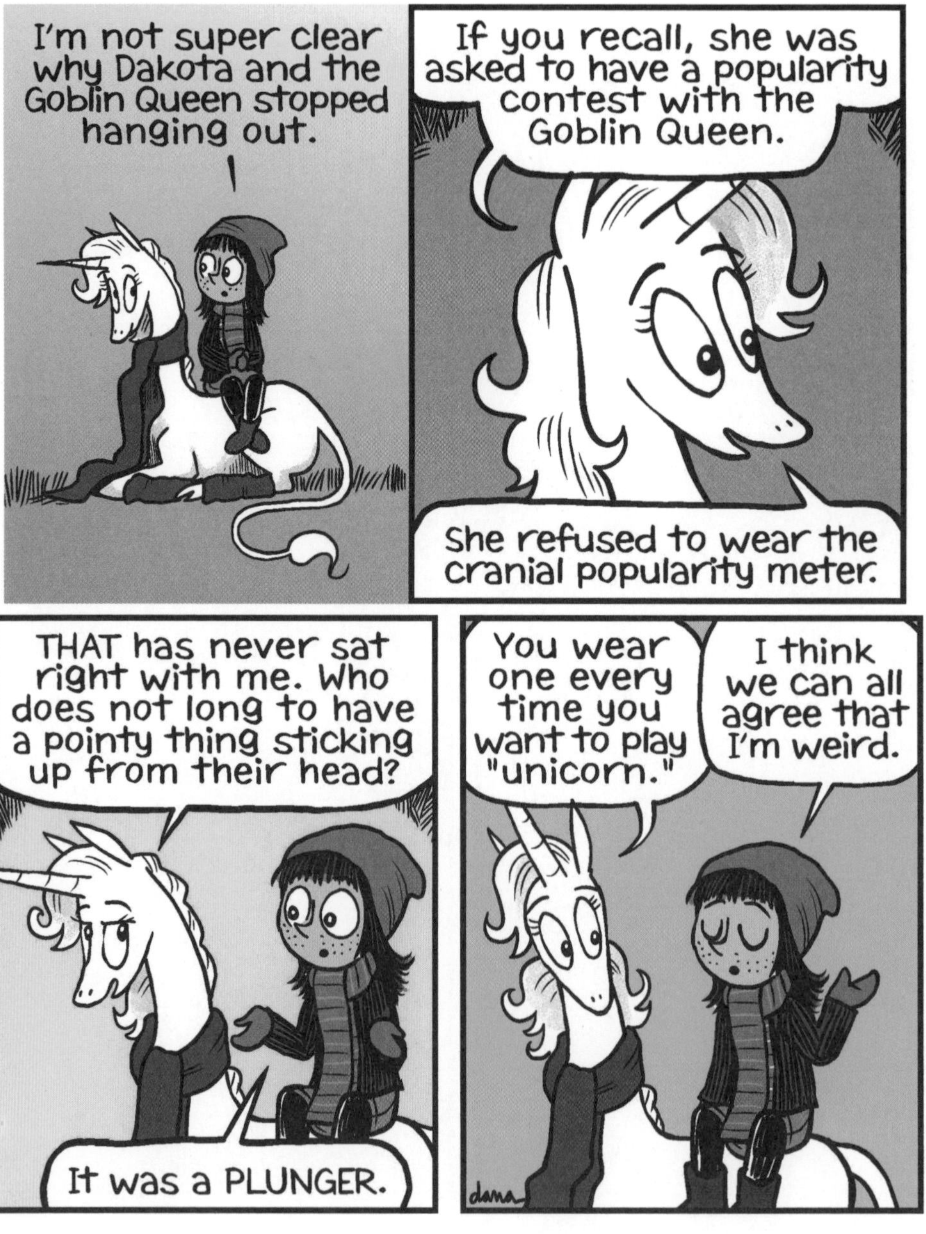
I'm not super clear why Dakota and the Goblin Queen stopped hanging out.
If you recall, she was asked to have a popularity contest with the Goblin Queen.
She refused to wear the cranial popularity meter.
THAT has never sat right with me. Who does not long to have a pointy thing sticking up from their head?
It was a PLUNGER.
You wear one every time you want to play "unicorn."
I think we can all agree that I'm weird.
dana

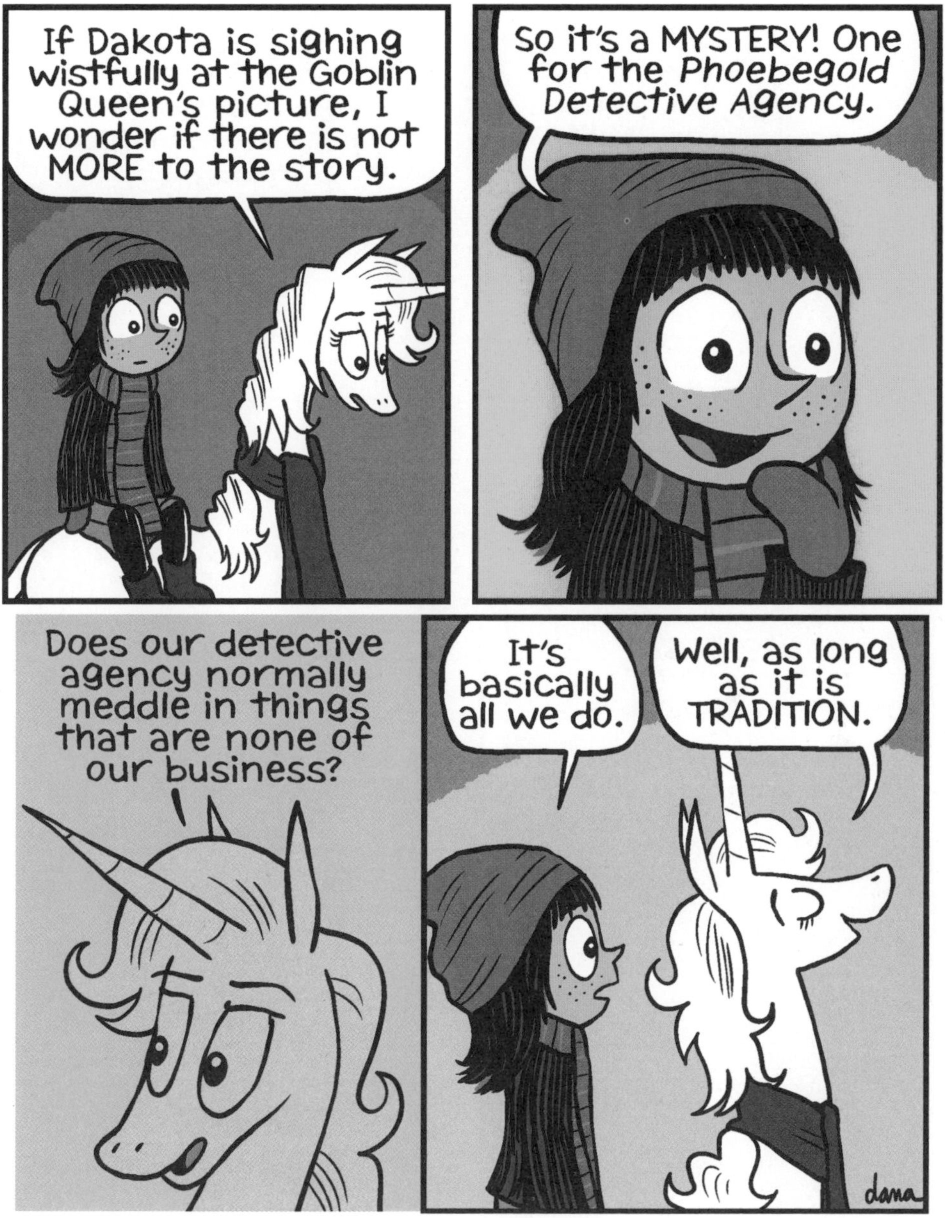
If Dakota is sighing wistfully at the Goblin Queen's picture, I wonder if there is not MORE to the story.
So it's a MYSTERY! One for the Phoebegold Detective Agency.
Does our detective agency normally meddle in things that are none of our business?
It's basically all we do.
Well, as long as it is TRADITION.
dana

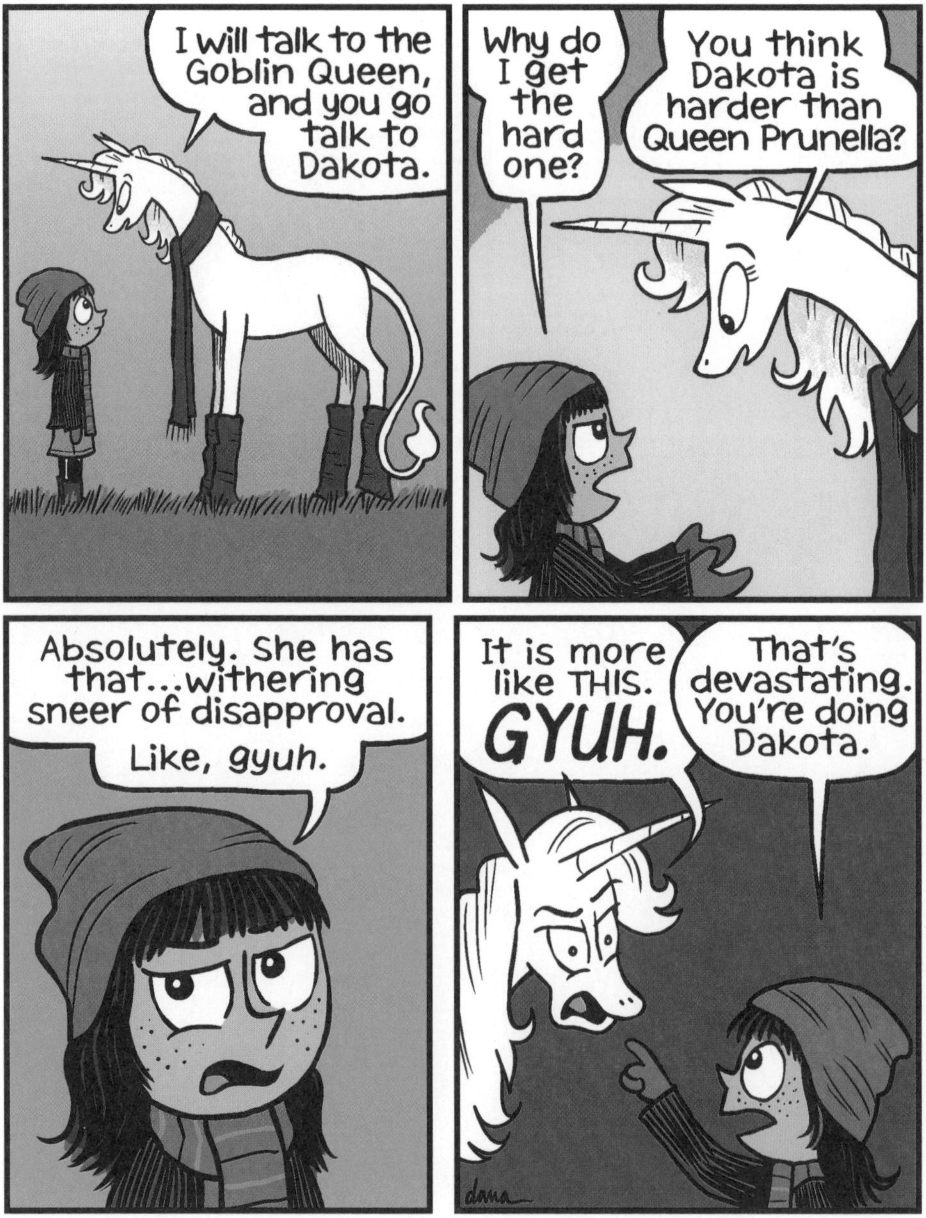
I will talk to the Goblin Queen, and you go talk to Dakota.
Why do I get the hard one?
You think Dakota is harder than Queen Prunella?
Absolutely. She has that...withering sneer of disapproval.
Like, *gyuh*.
It is more like THIS. **GYUH.**
That's devastating. You're doing Dakota.
dana

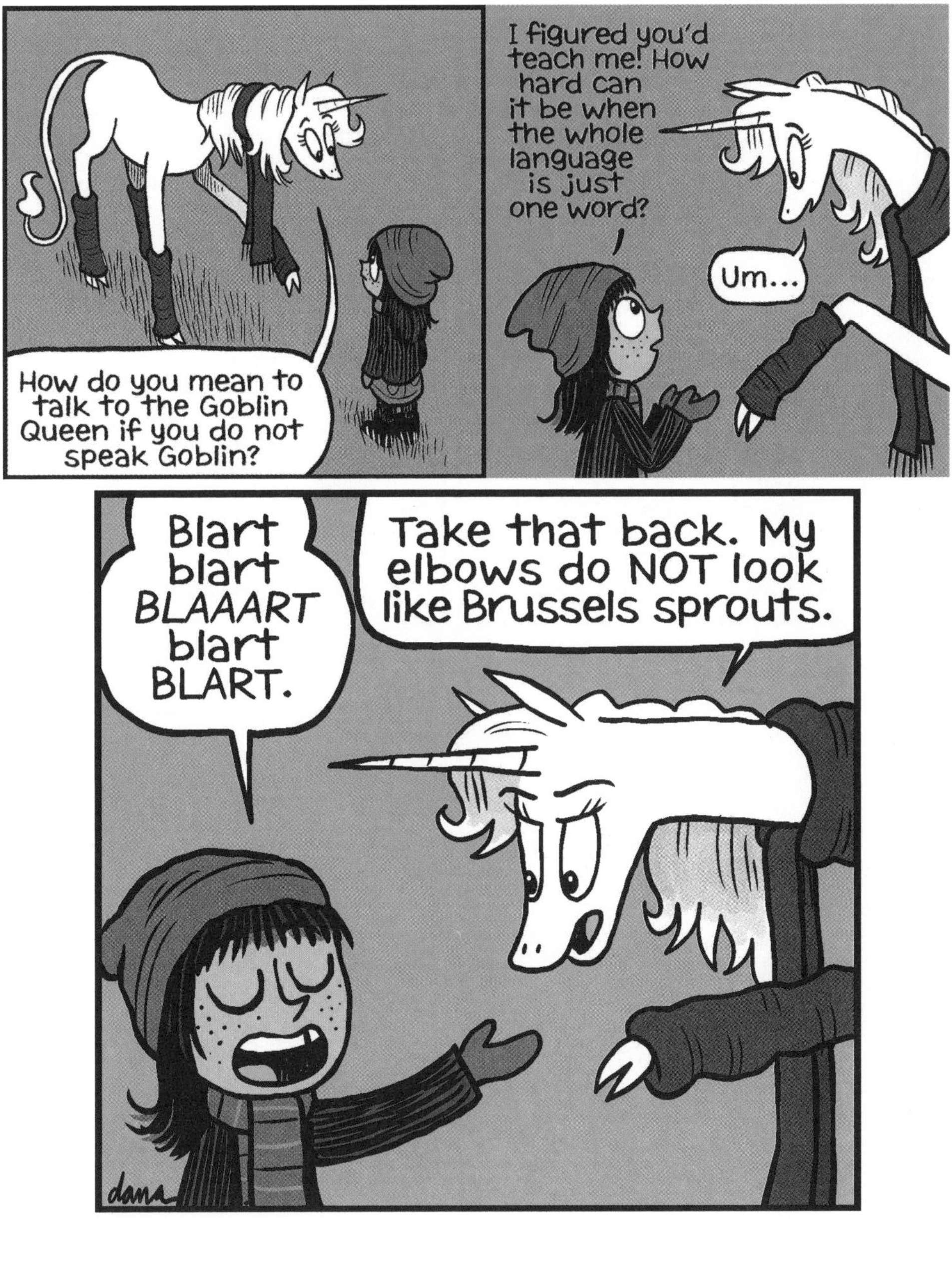
How do you mean to talk to the Goblin Queen if you do not speak Goblin?
I figured you'd teach me! How hard can it be when the whole language is just one word?
Um...
Blart blart BLAAART blart BLART.
Take that back. My elbows do NOT look like Brussels sprouts.
dana

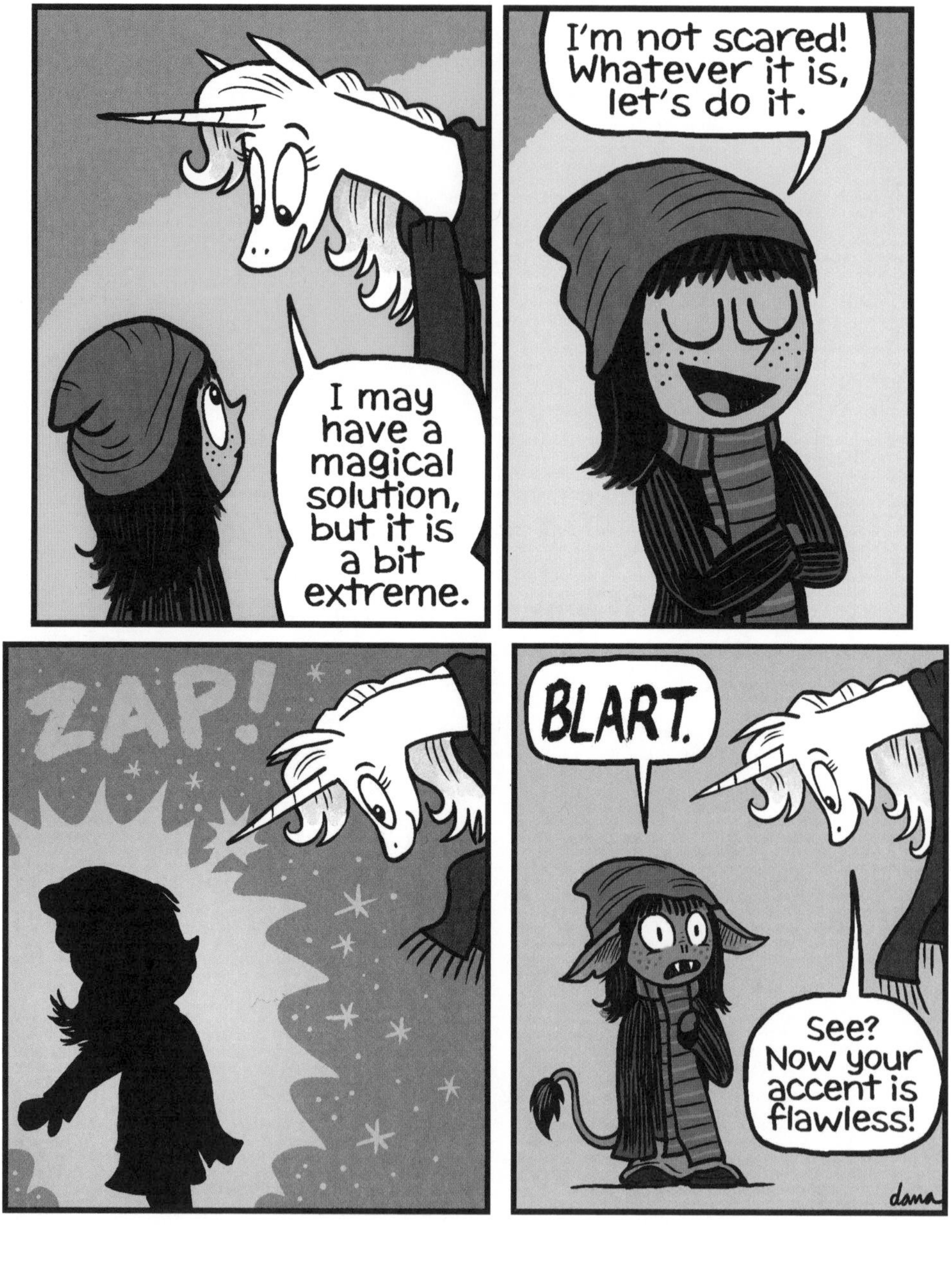
I may have a magical solution, but it is a bit extreme.
I'm not scared! Whatever it is, let's do it.
ZAP!
BLART.
See? Now your accent is flawless!
dana

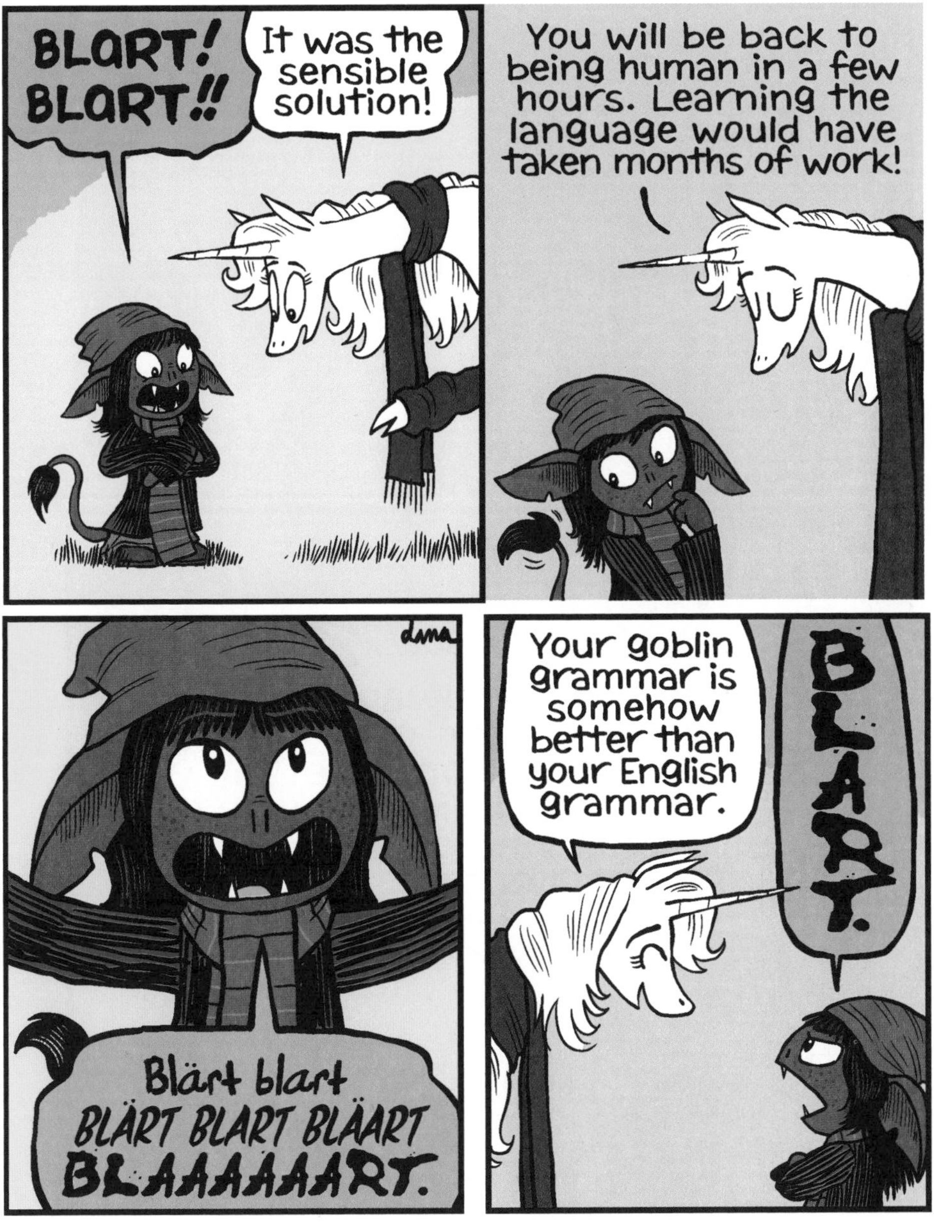
BLART! BLART!!
It was the sensible solution!
You will be back to being human in a few hours. Learning the language would have taken months of work!
Blärt blart BLÄRT BLART BLÄART BLAAAAAART.
Your goblin grammar is somehow better than your English grammar.
BLART.

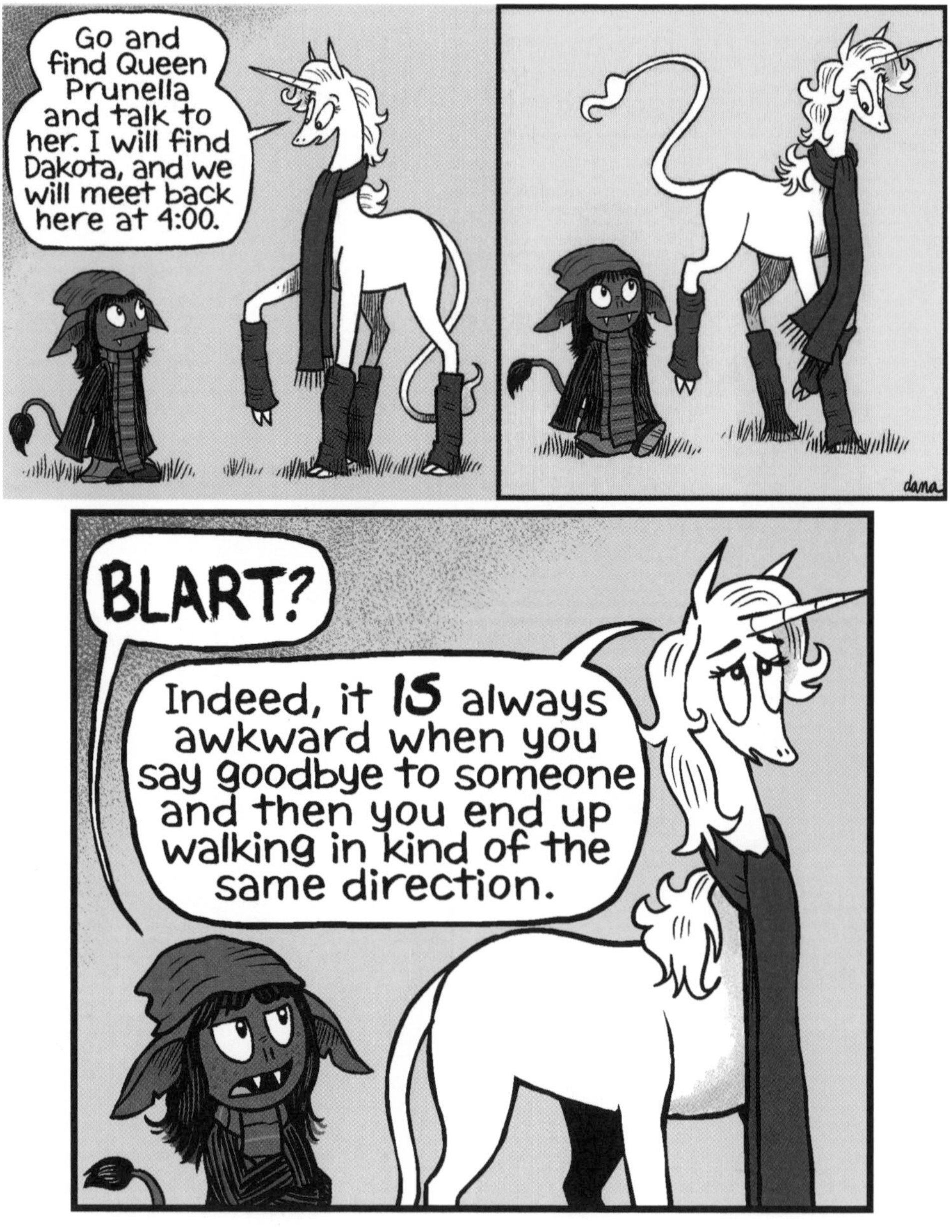

Go and find Queen Prunella and talk to her. I will find Dakota, and we will meet back here at 4:00.
dana
BLART?
Indeed, it IS always awkward when you say goodbye to someone and then you end up walking in kind of the same direction.

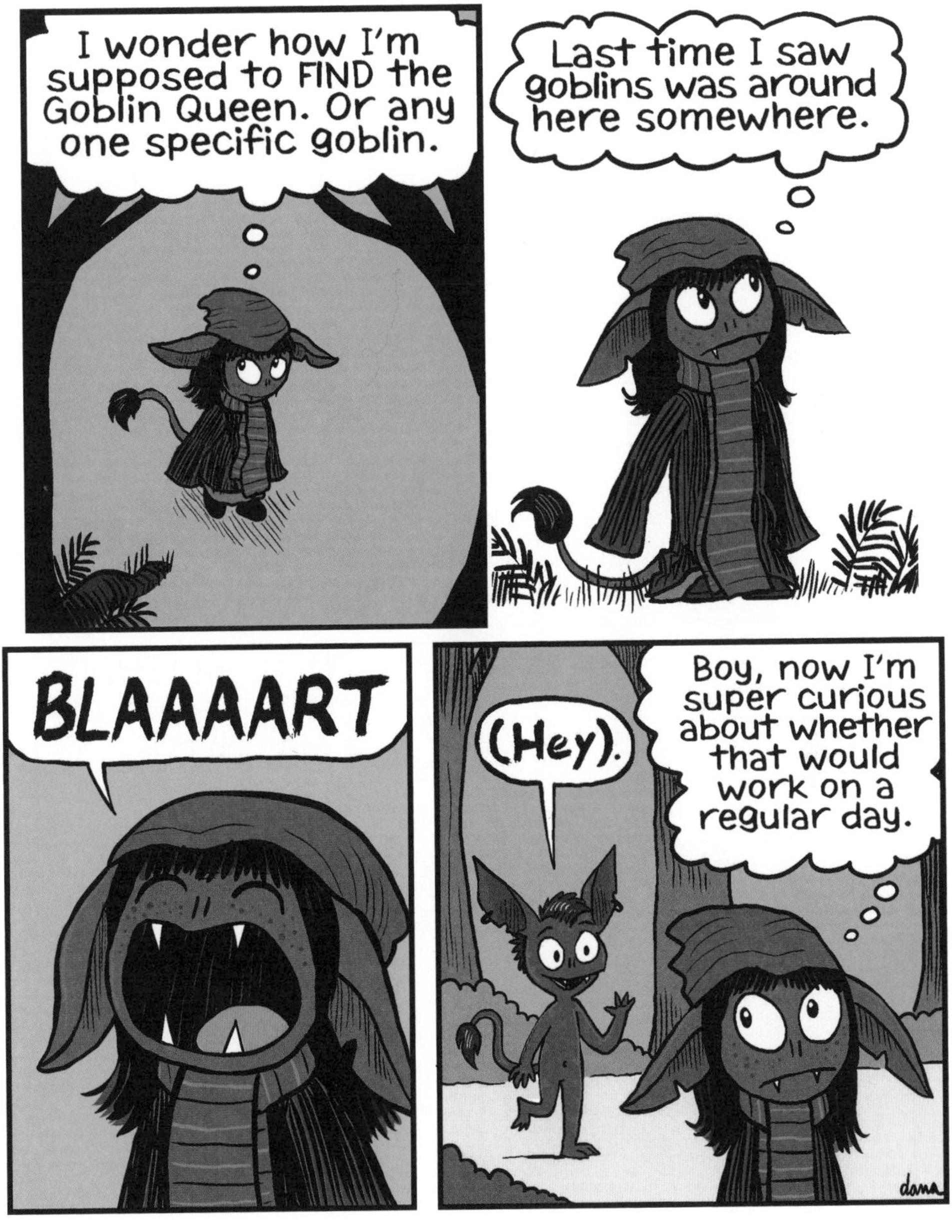
I wonder how I'm supposed to FIND the Goblin Queen. Or any one specific goblin.
Last time I saw goblins was around here somewhere.
BLAAAART
(Hey).
Boy, now I'm super curious about whether that would work on a regular day.
dana

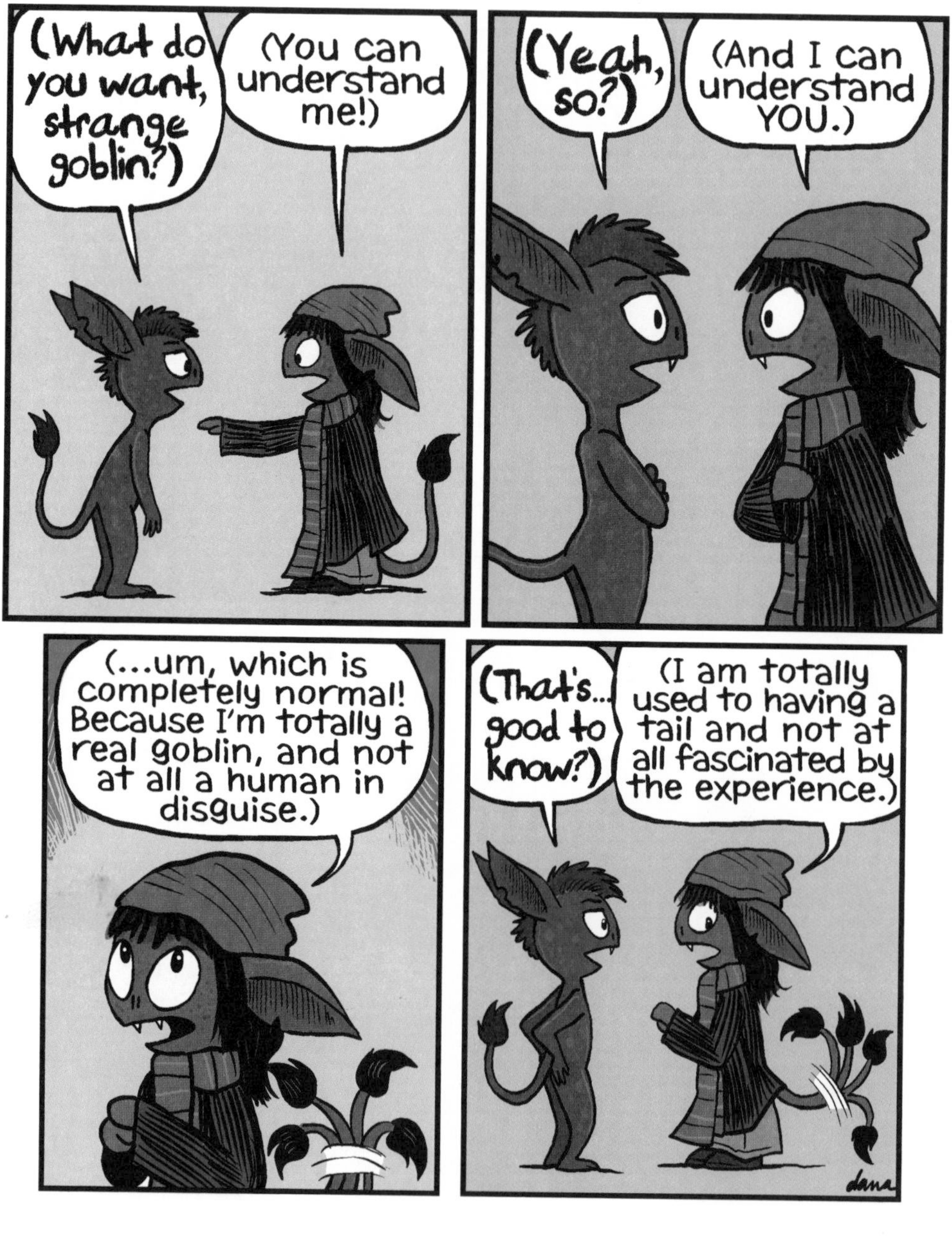
(What do you want, strange goblin?)
(You can understand me!)
(Yeah, so?)
(And I can understand YOU.)
(...um, which is completely normal! Because I'm totally a real goblin, and not at all a human in disguise.)
(That's... good to know?)
(I am totally used to having a tail and not at all fascinated by the experience.)
dana

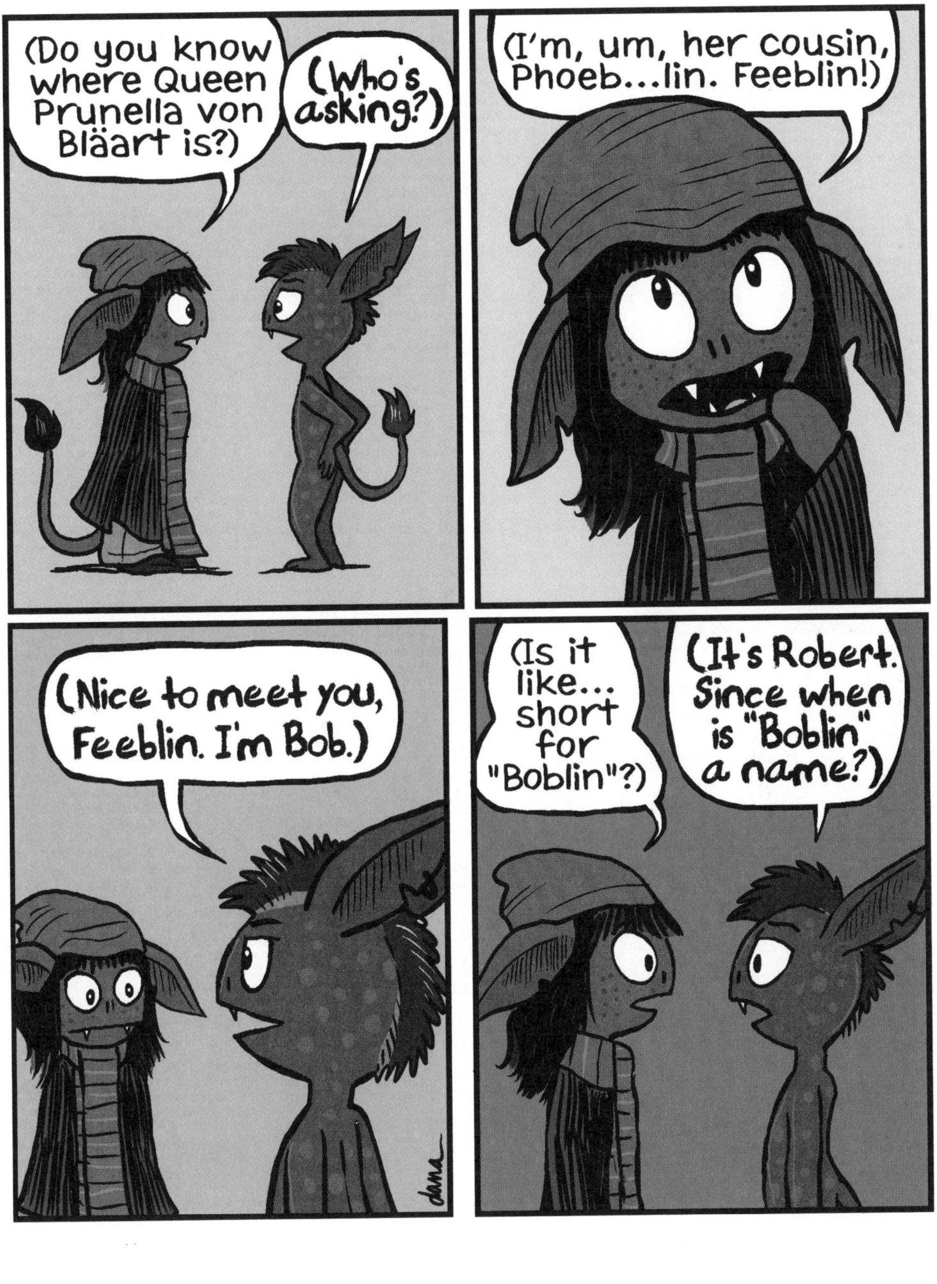
(Do you know where Queen Prunella von Bläart is?)
(Who's asking?)
(I'm, um, her cousin, Phoeb...lin. Feeblin!)
(Nice to meet you, Feeblin. I'm Bob.)
dana
(Is it like... short for "Boblin"?)
(It's Robert. Since when is "Boblin" a name?)

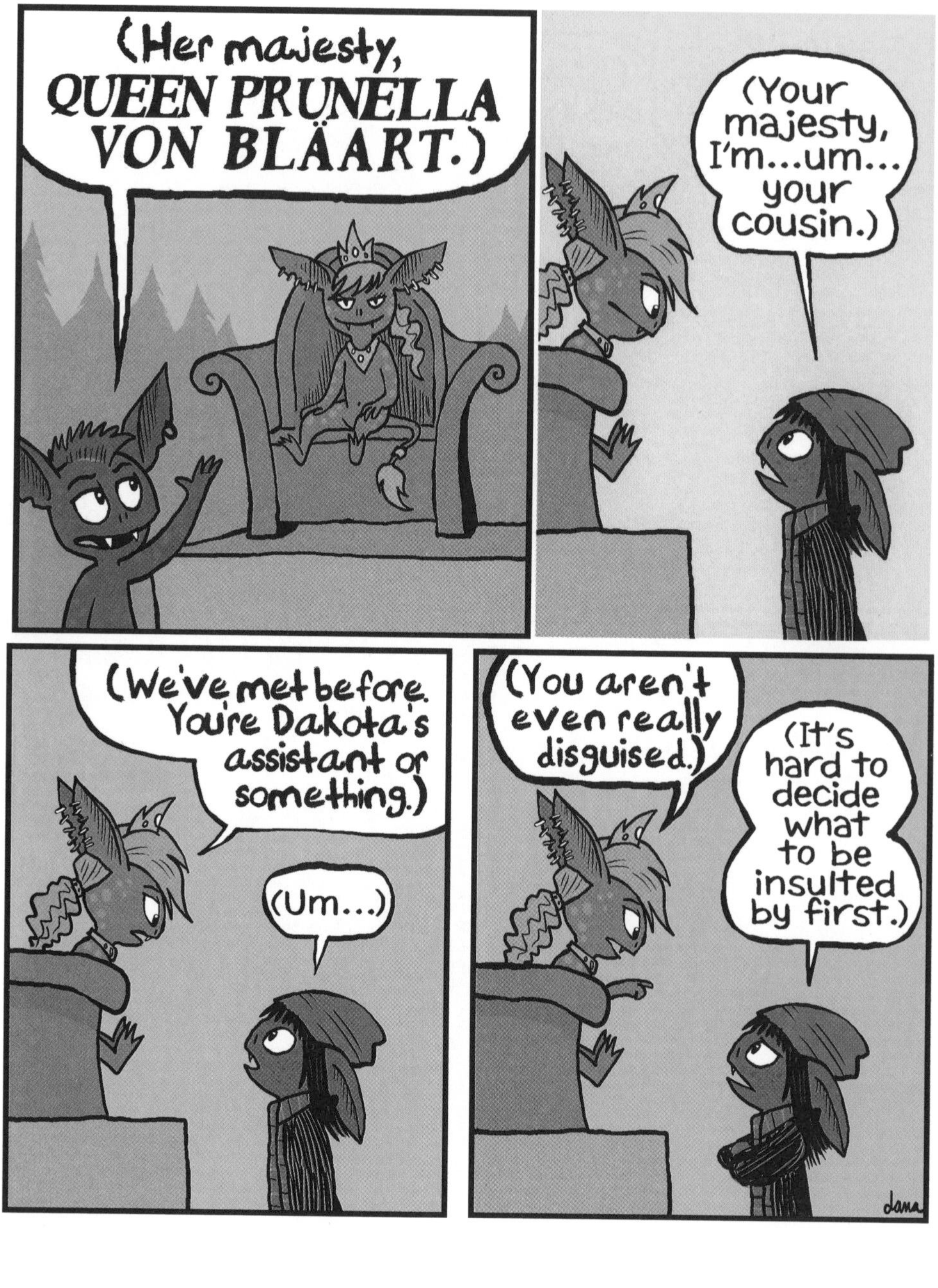
(Her majesty, QUEEN PRUNELLA VON BLÄART.)
(Your majesty, I'm...um... your cousin.)
(We've met before. You're Dakota's assistant or something.)
(Um...)
(You aren't even really disguised.)
(It's hard to decide what to be insulted by first.)
dana

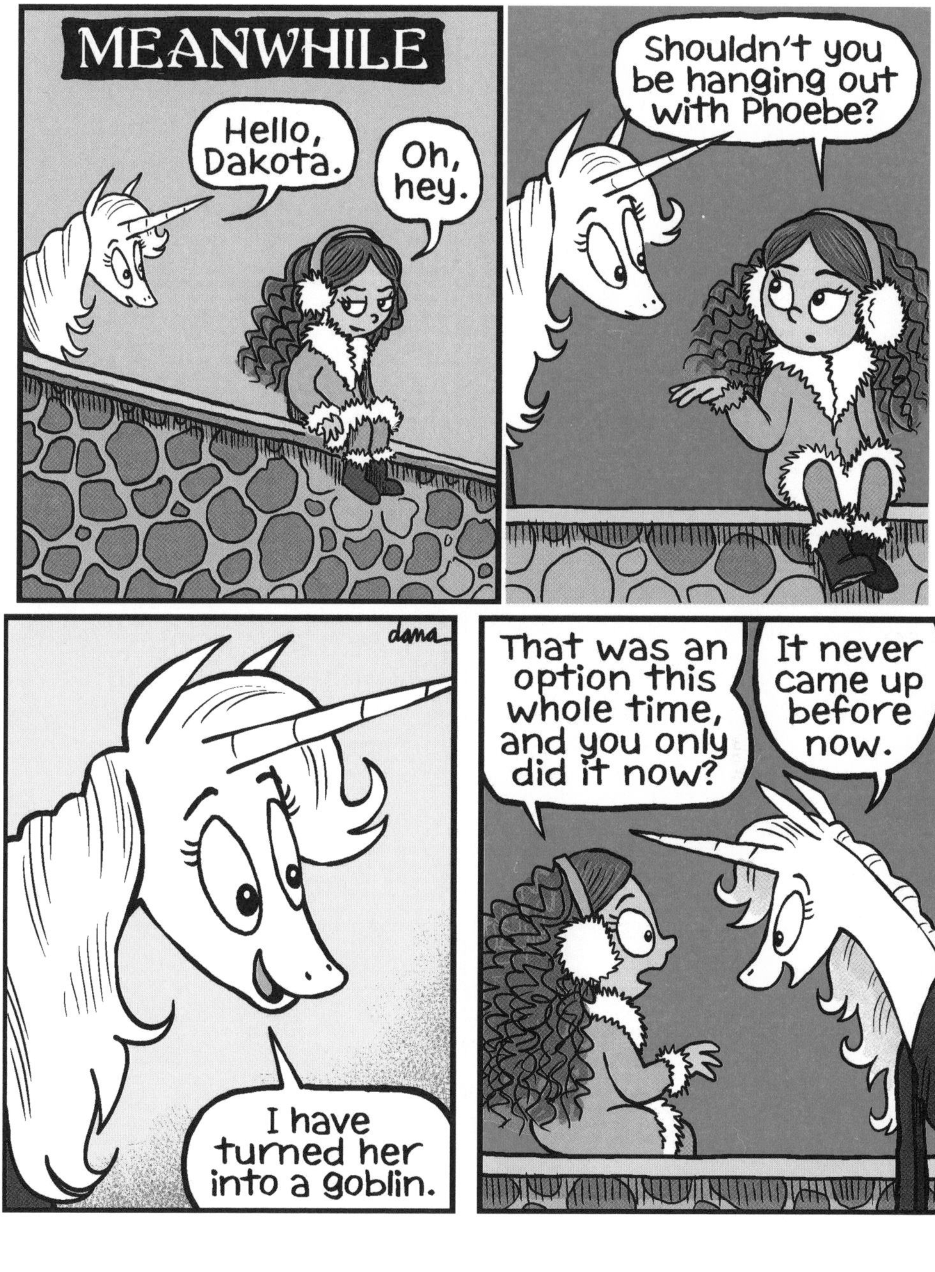
MEANWHILE
Hello, Dakota.
Oh, hey.
Shouldn't you be hanging out with Phoebe?
dana
I have turned her into a goblin.
That was an option this whole time, and you only did it now?
It never came up before now.

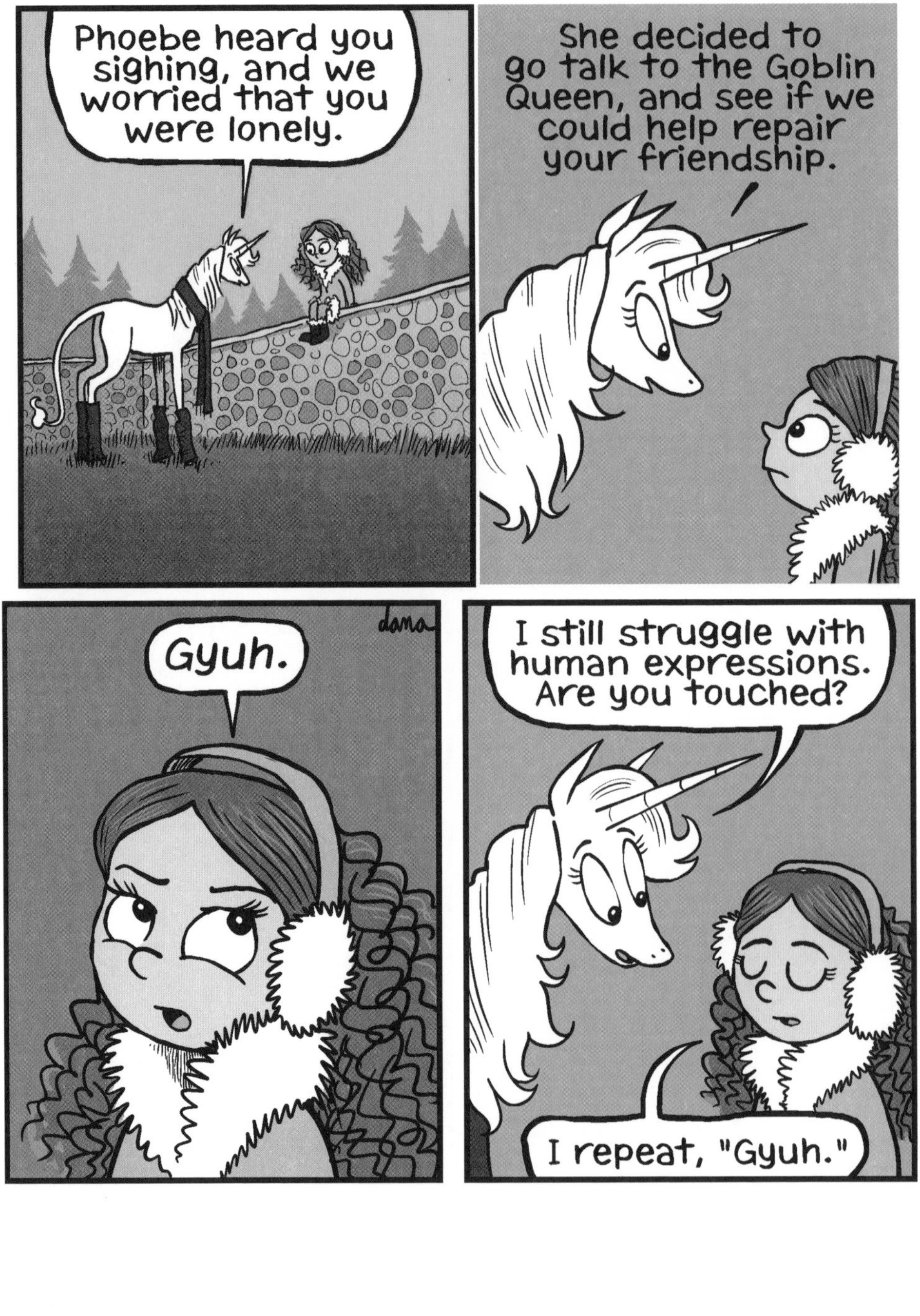
Phoebe heard you sighing, and we worried that you were lonely.
She decided to go talk to the Goblin Queen, and see if we could help repair your friendship.
Gyuh.
dana
I still struggle with human expressions. Are you touched?
I repeat, "Gyuh."

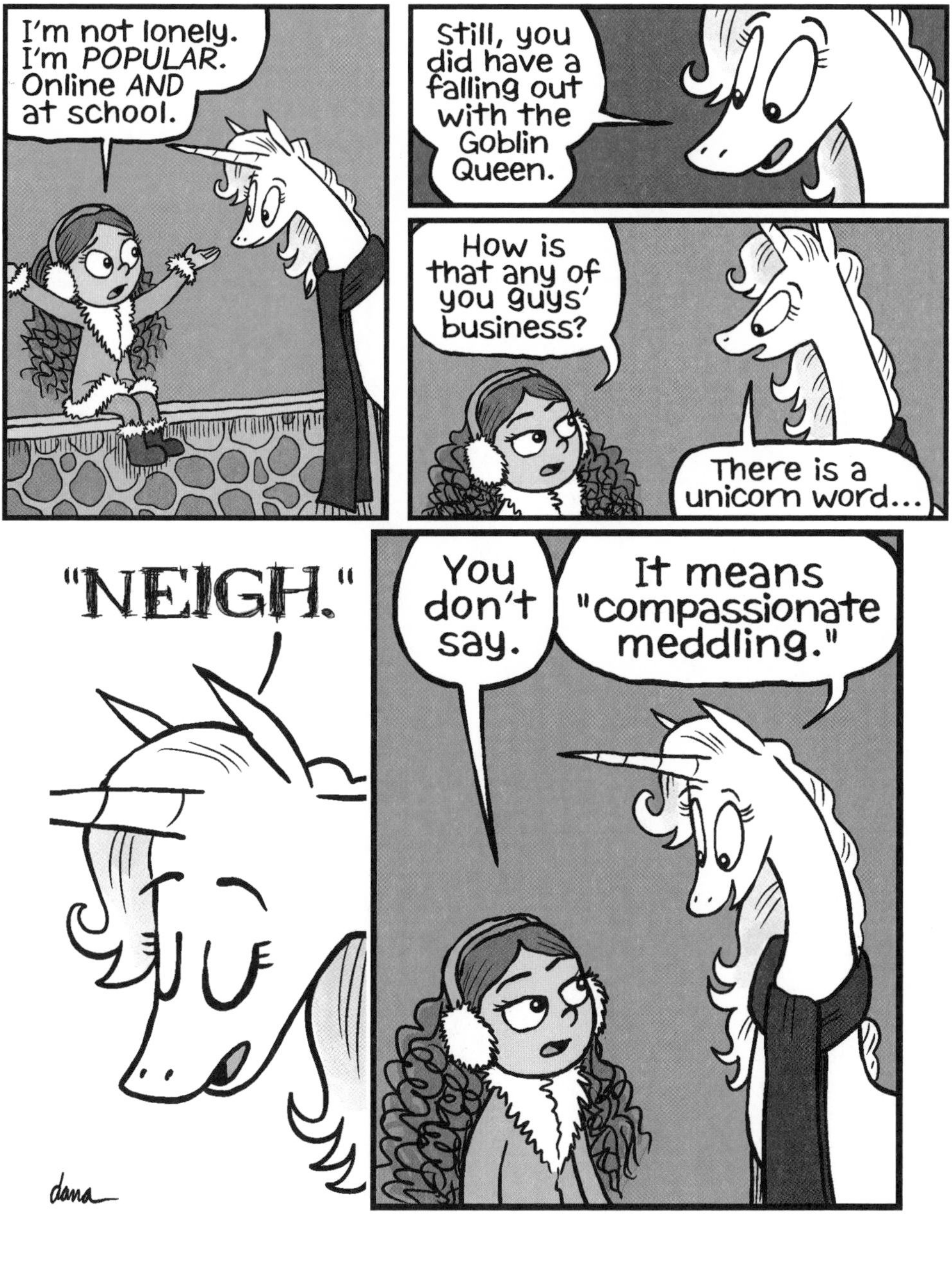
I'm not lonely. I'm POPULAR. Online AND at school.
Still, you did have a falling out with the Goblin Queen.
How is that any of you guys' business?
There is a unicorn word...
"NEIGH."
It means "compassionate meddling."
You don't say.
dana

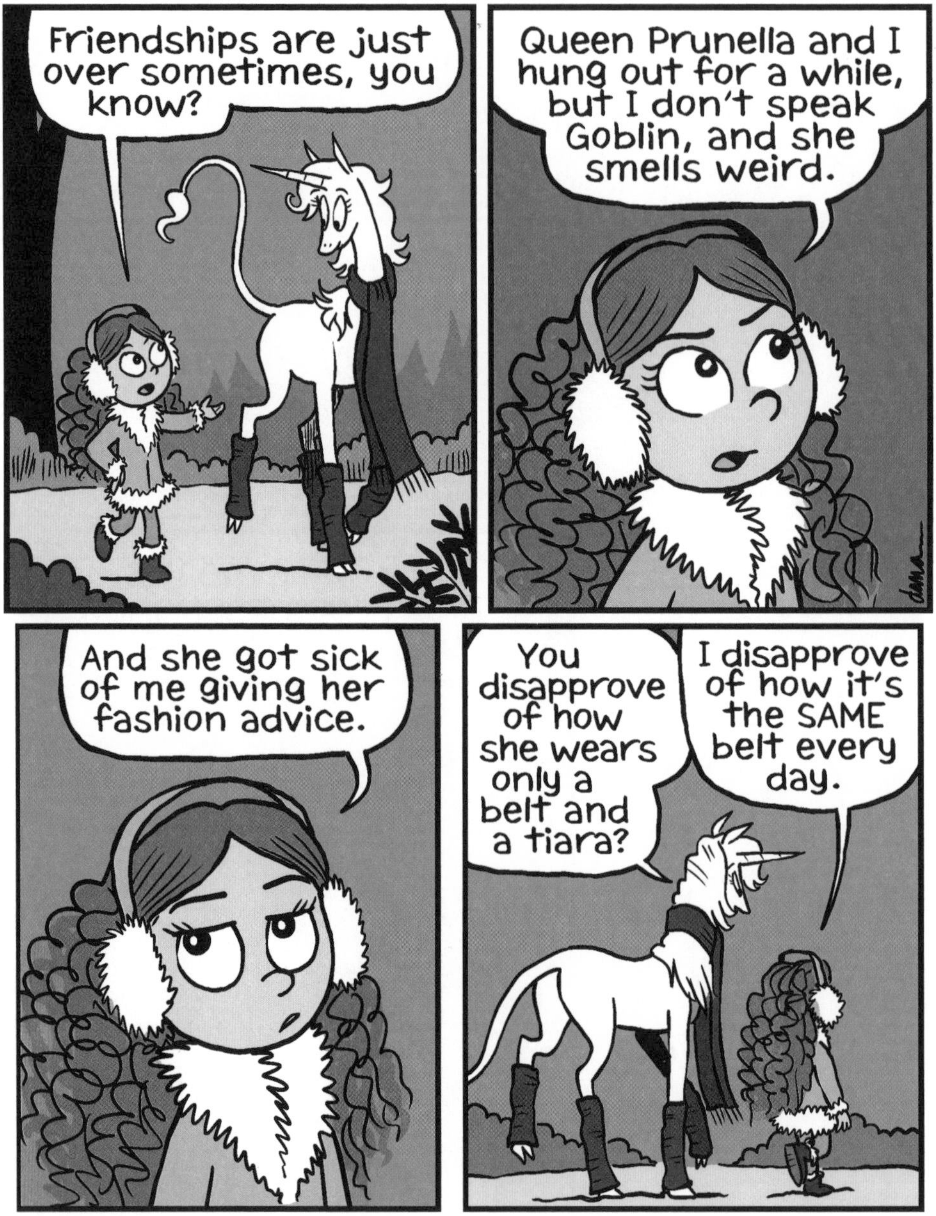
Friendships are just over sometimes, you know?
Queen Prunella and I hung out for a while, but I don't speak Goblin, and she smells weird.
dana
And she got sick of me giving her fashion advice.
You disapprove of how she wears only a belt and a tiara?
I disapprove of how it's the SAME belt every day.

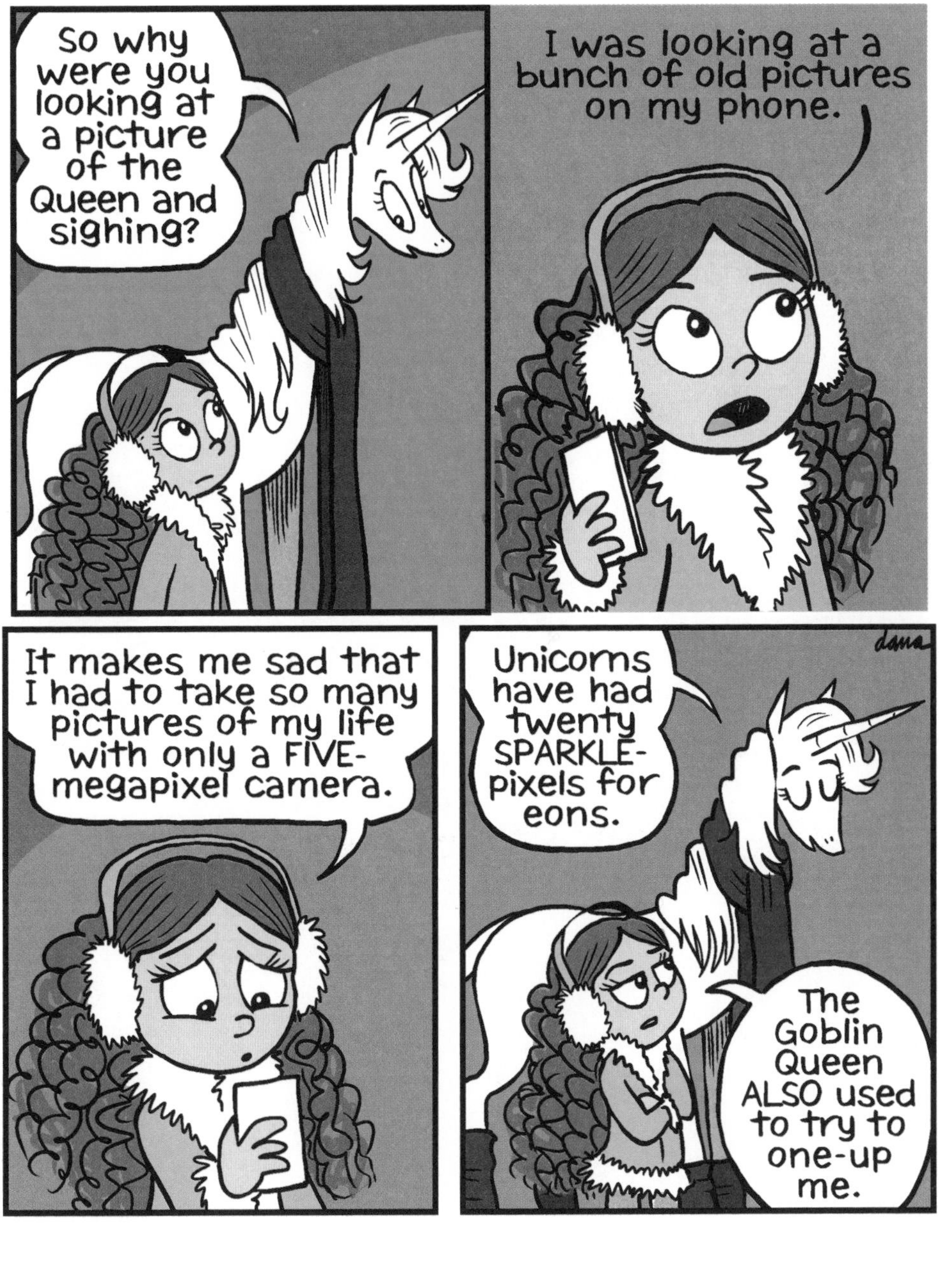
So why were you looking at a picture of the Queen and sighing?
I was looking at a bunch of old pictures on my phone.
It makes me sad that I had to take so many pictures of my life with only a FIVE-megapixel camera.
dana
Unicorns have had twenty SPARKLE-pixels for eons.
The Goblin Queen ALSO used to try to one-up me.

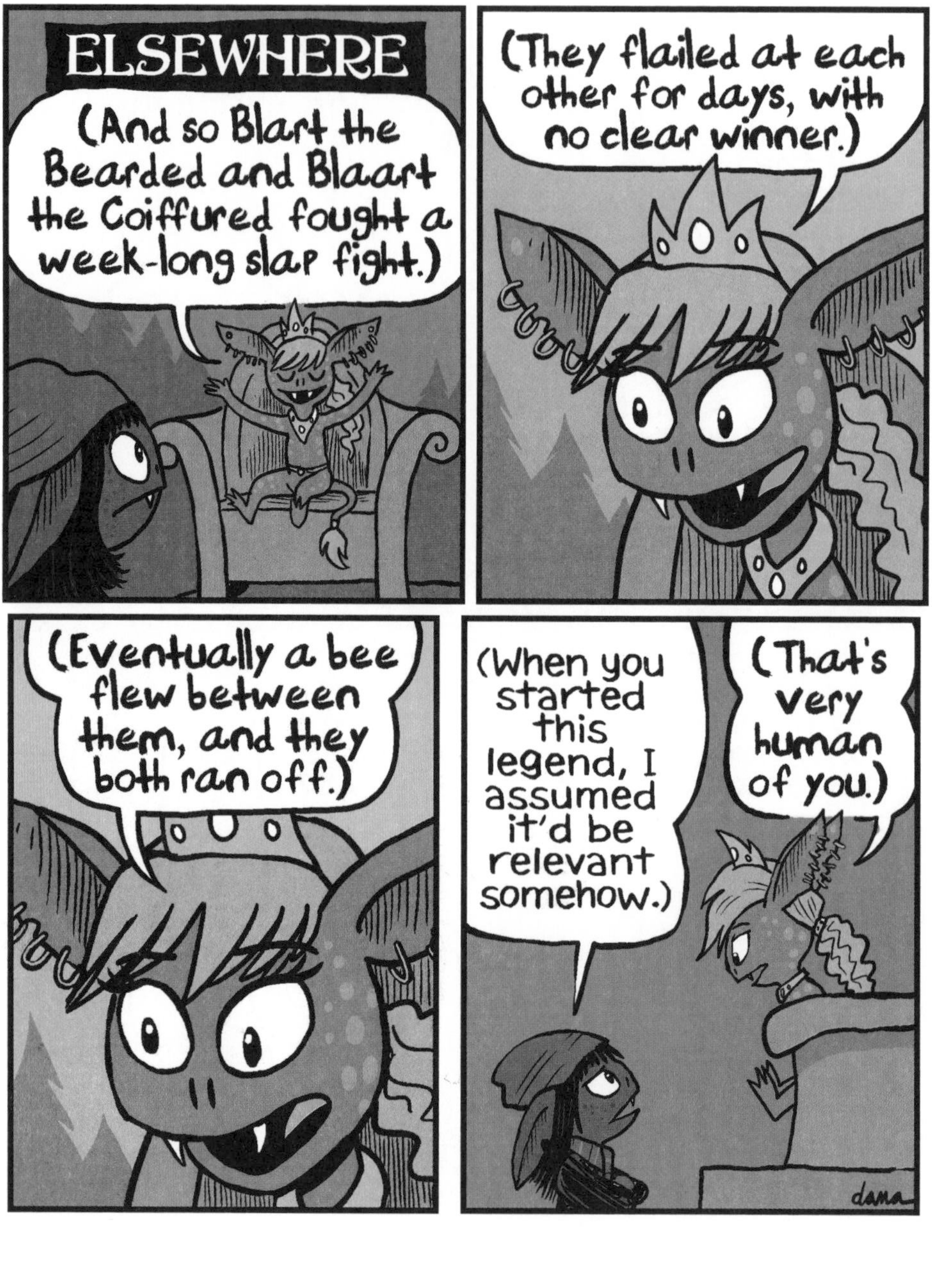
ELSEWHERE
(And so Blart the Bearded and Blaart the Coiffured fought a week-long slap fight.)
(They flailed at each other for days, with no clear winner.)
(Eventually a bee flew between them, and they both ran off.)
(When you started this legend, I assumed it'd be relevant somehow.)
(That's very human of you.)
dana

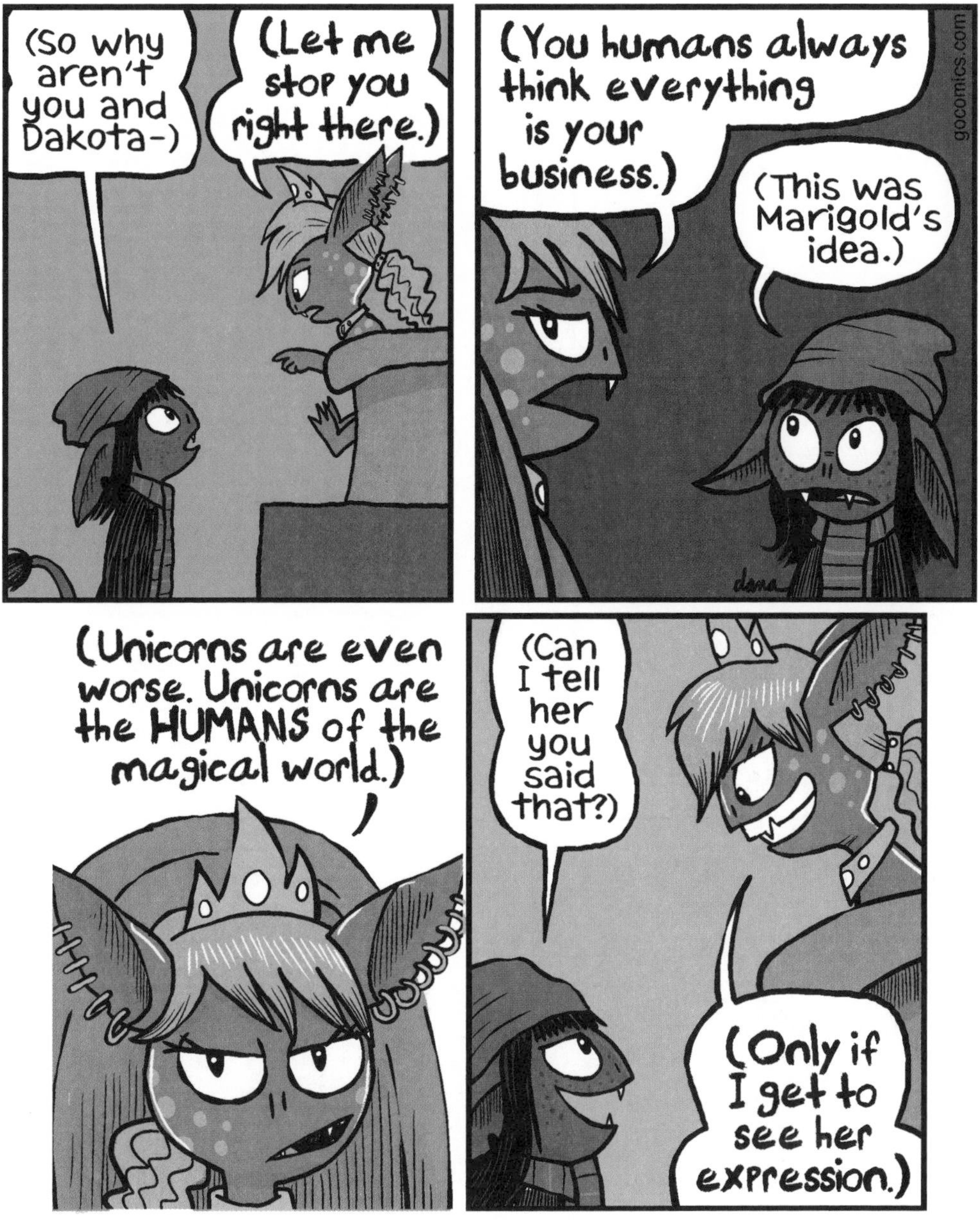
(So why aren't you and Dakota-)
(Let me stop you right there.)
(You humans always think everything is your business.)
(This was Marigold's idea.)
gocomics.com
dana
(Unicorns are even worse. Unicorns are the HUMANS of the magical world.)
(Can I tell her you said that?)
(Only if I get to see her expression.)

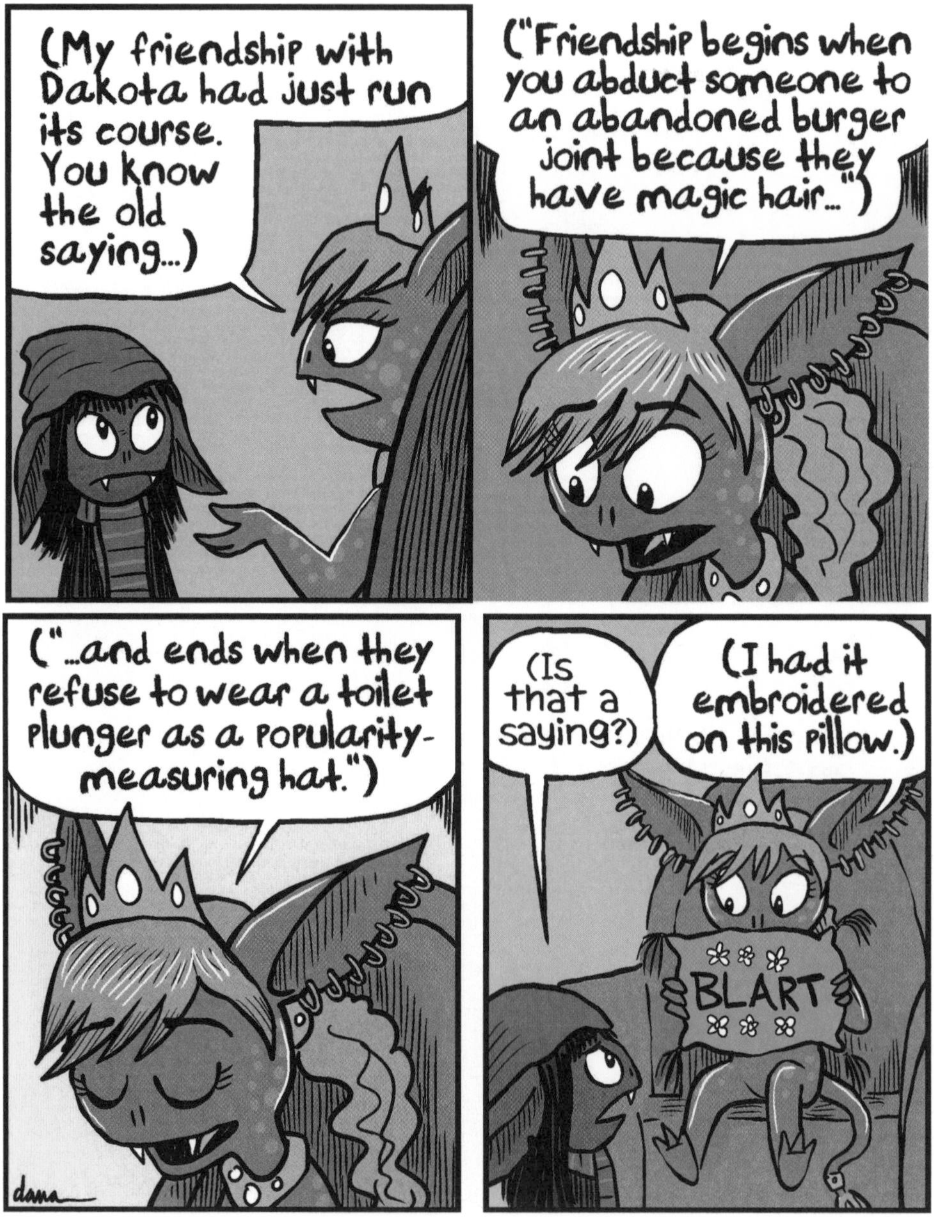
(My friendship with Dakota had just run its course. You know the old saying...)
("Friendship begins when you abduct someone to an abandoned burger joint because they have magic hair...")
("...and ends when they refuse to wear a toilet plunger as a popularity-measuring hat.")
(Is that a saying?)
(I had it embroidered on this pillow.)
BLART
dana

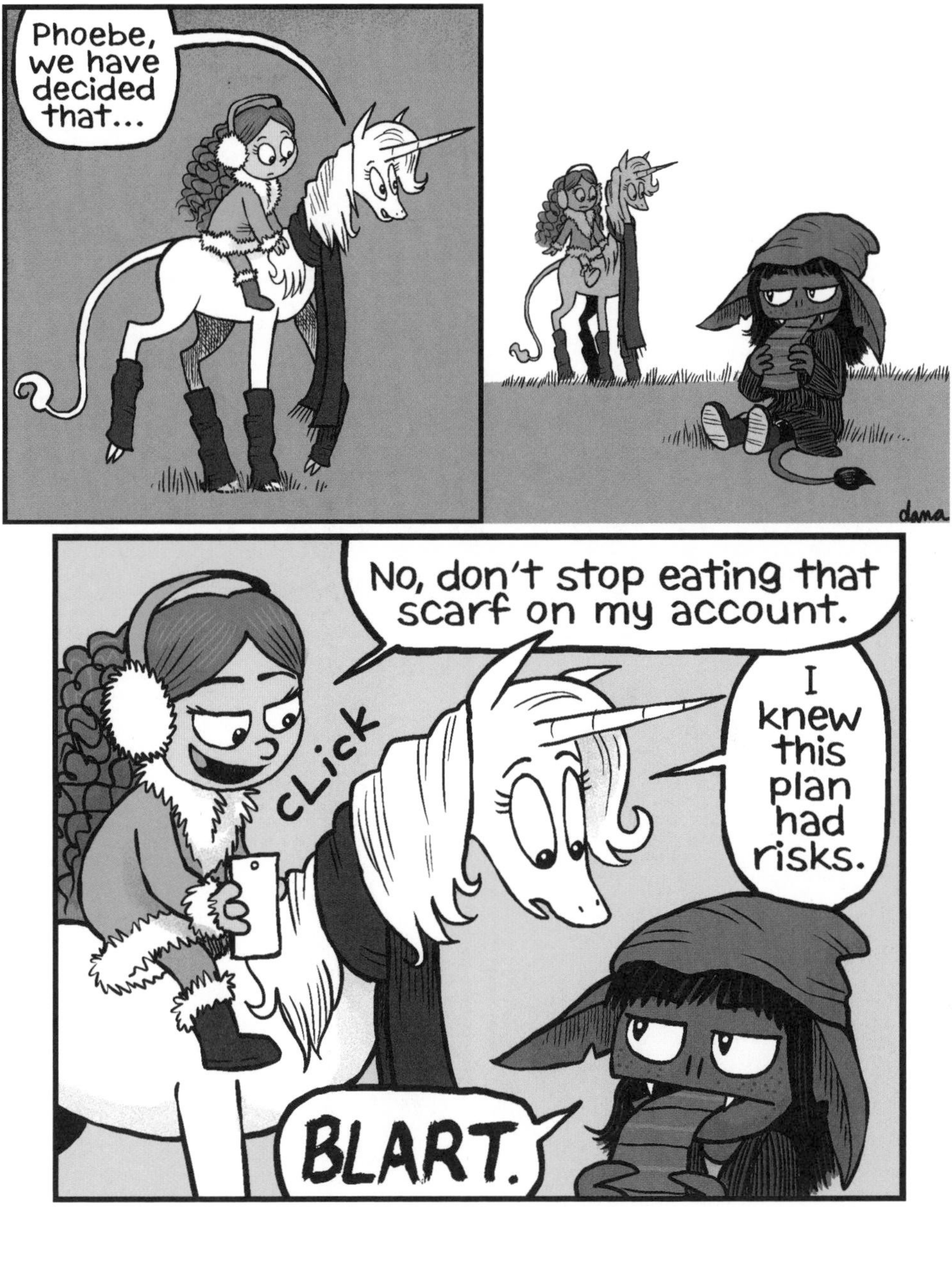
Phoebe, we have decided that...
No, don't stop eating that scarf on my account.
CLick
I knew this plan had risks.
BLART.
dana

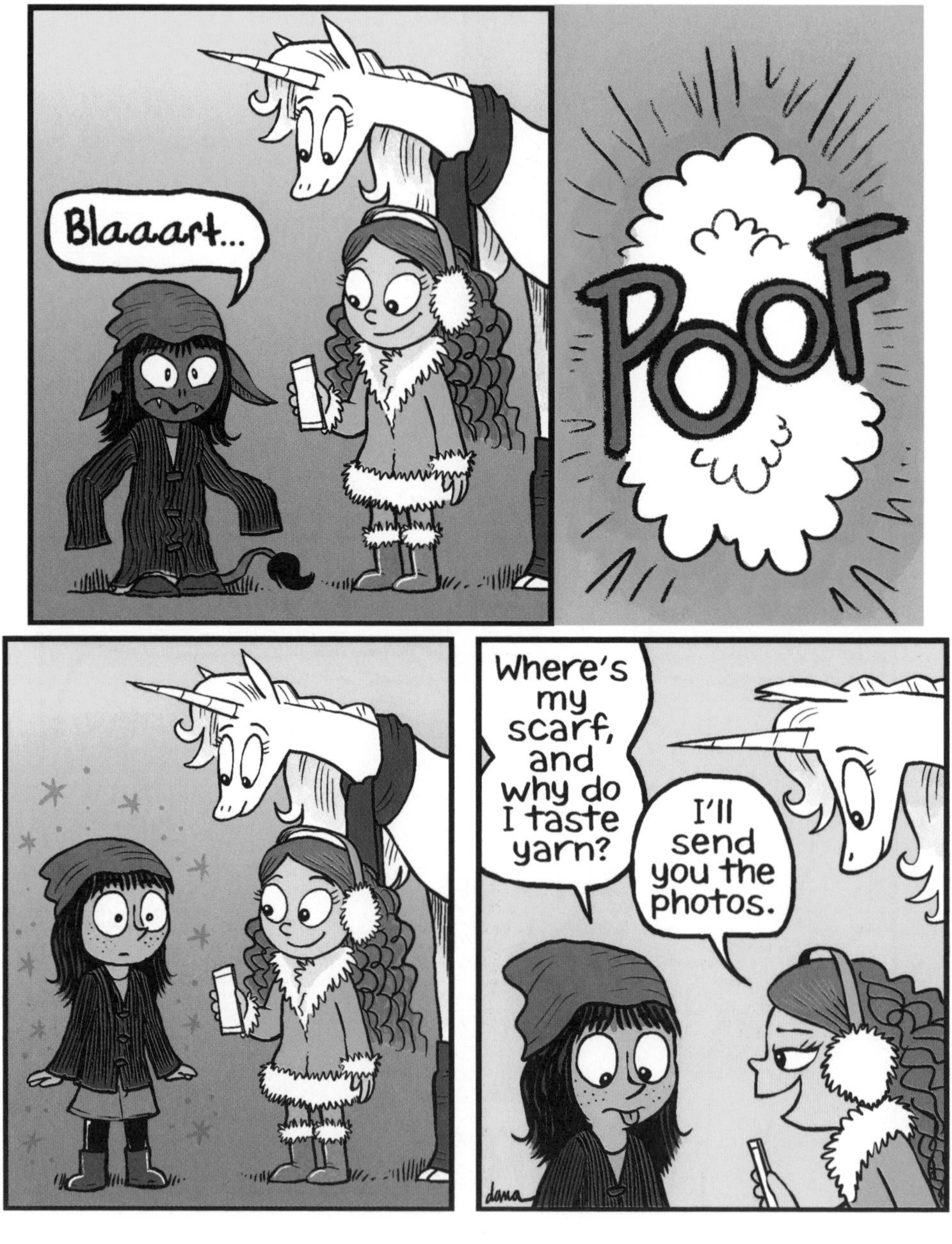
Blaaart...
POOF
Where's my scarf, and why do I taste yarn?
I'll send you the photos.
dana

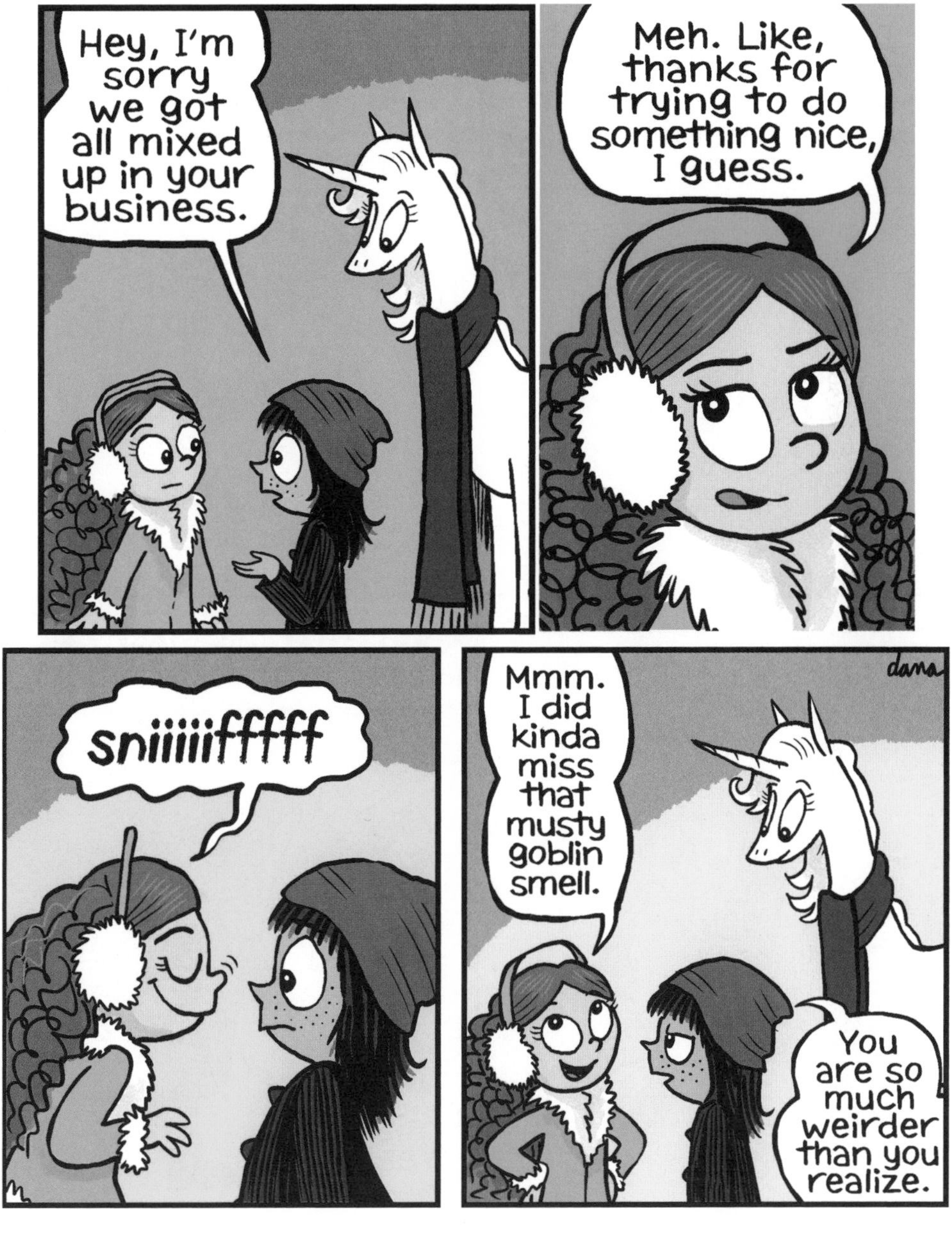
Hey, I'm sorry we got all mixed up in your business.
Meh. Like, thanks for trying to do something nice, I guess.
sniiiiifffff
Mmm. I did kinda miss that musty goblin smell.
You are so much weirder than you realize.
dana

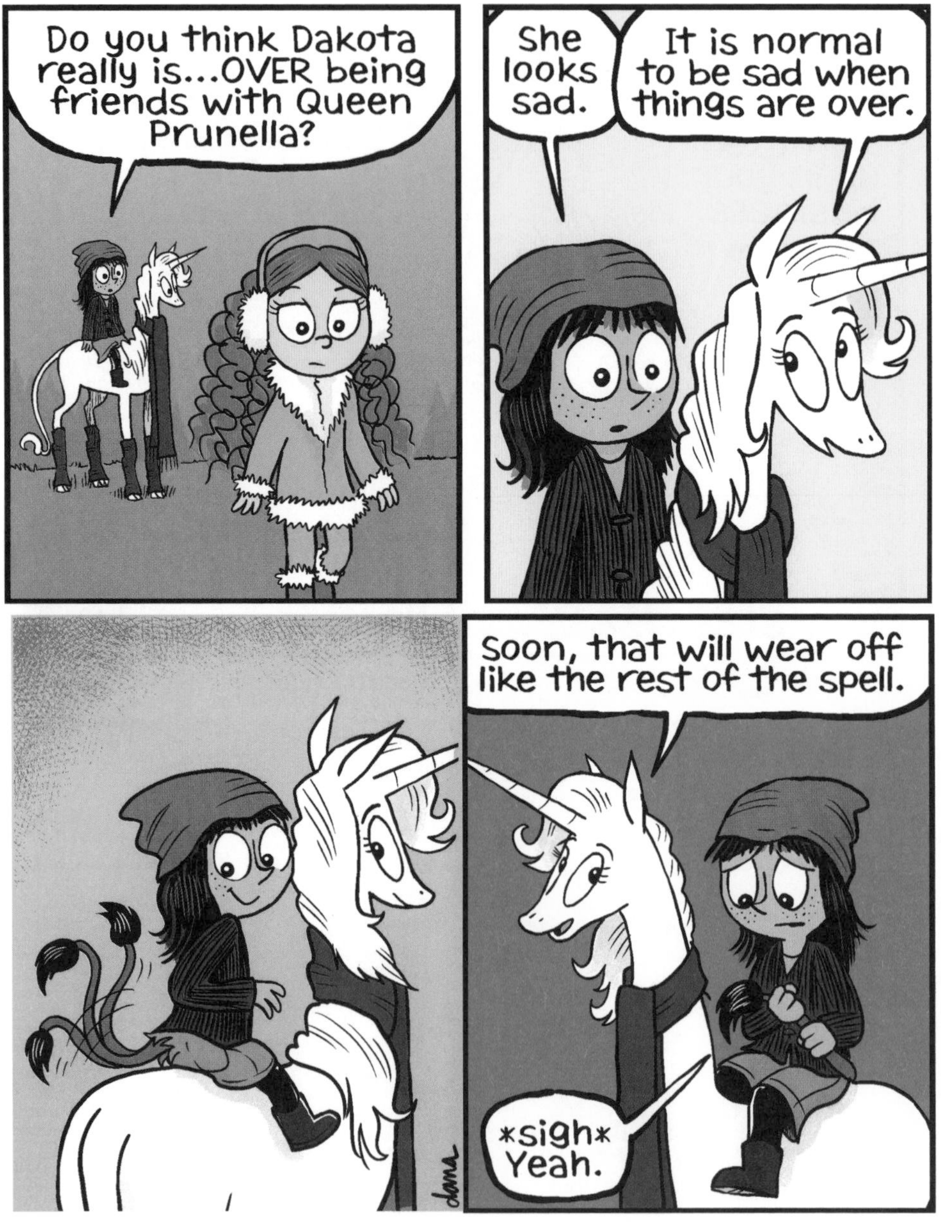
Do you think Dakota really is...OVER being friends with Queen Prunella?
She looks sad.
It is normal to be sad when things are over.
Soon, that will wear off like the rest of the spell.
sigh Yeah.

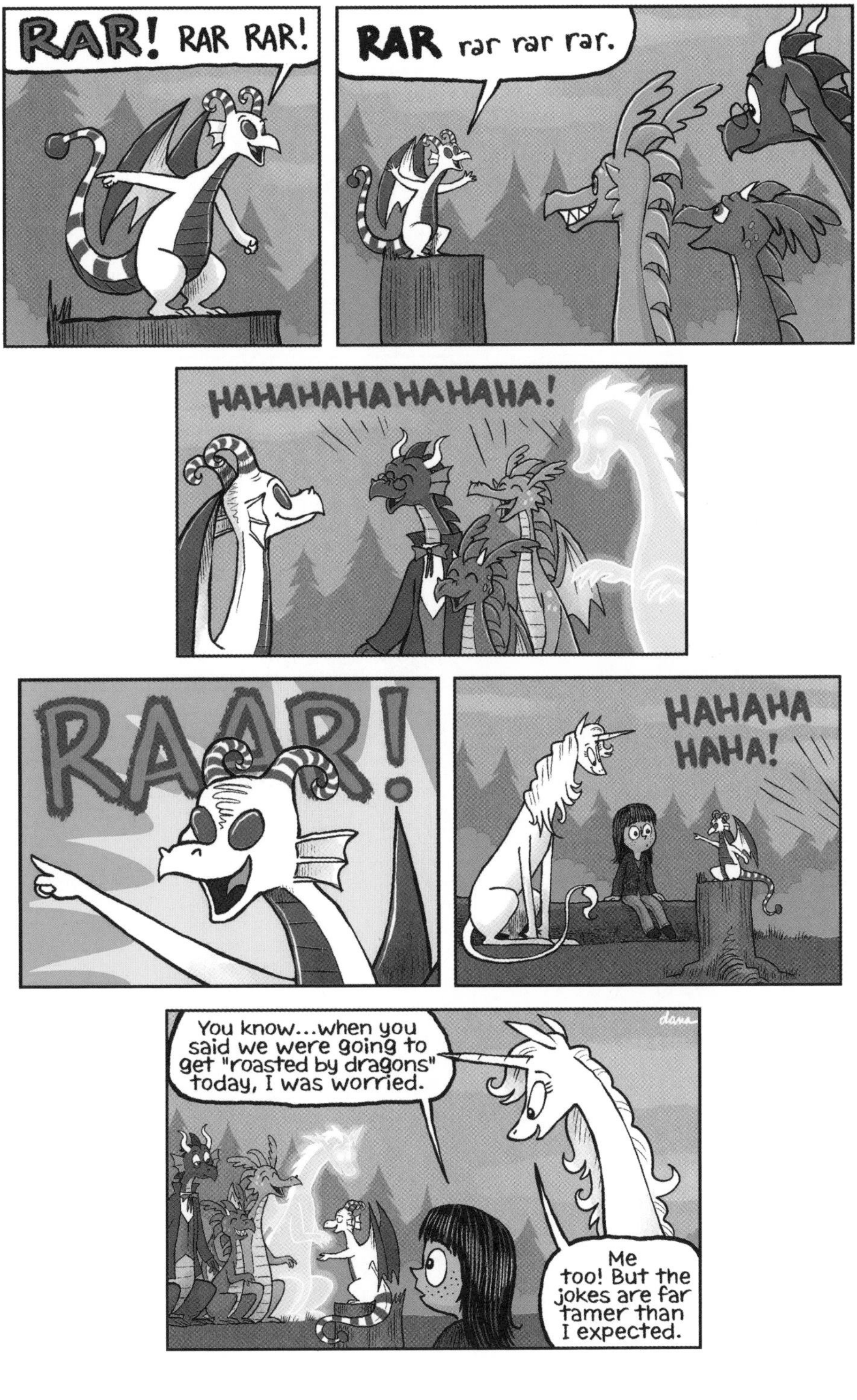
RAR! RAR RAR!
RAR rar rar rar.
HAHAHAHAHAHAHA!
RAAR!
HAHAHA HAHA!
dana
You know...when you said we were going to get "roasted by dragons" today, I was worried.
Me too! But the jokes are far tamer than I expected.

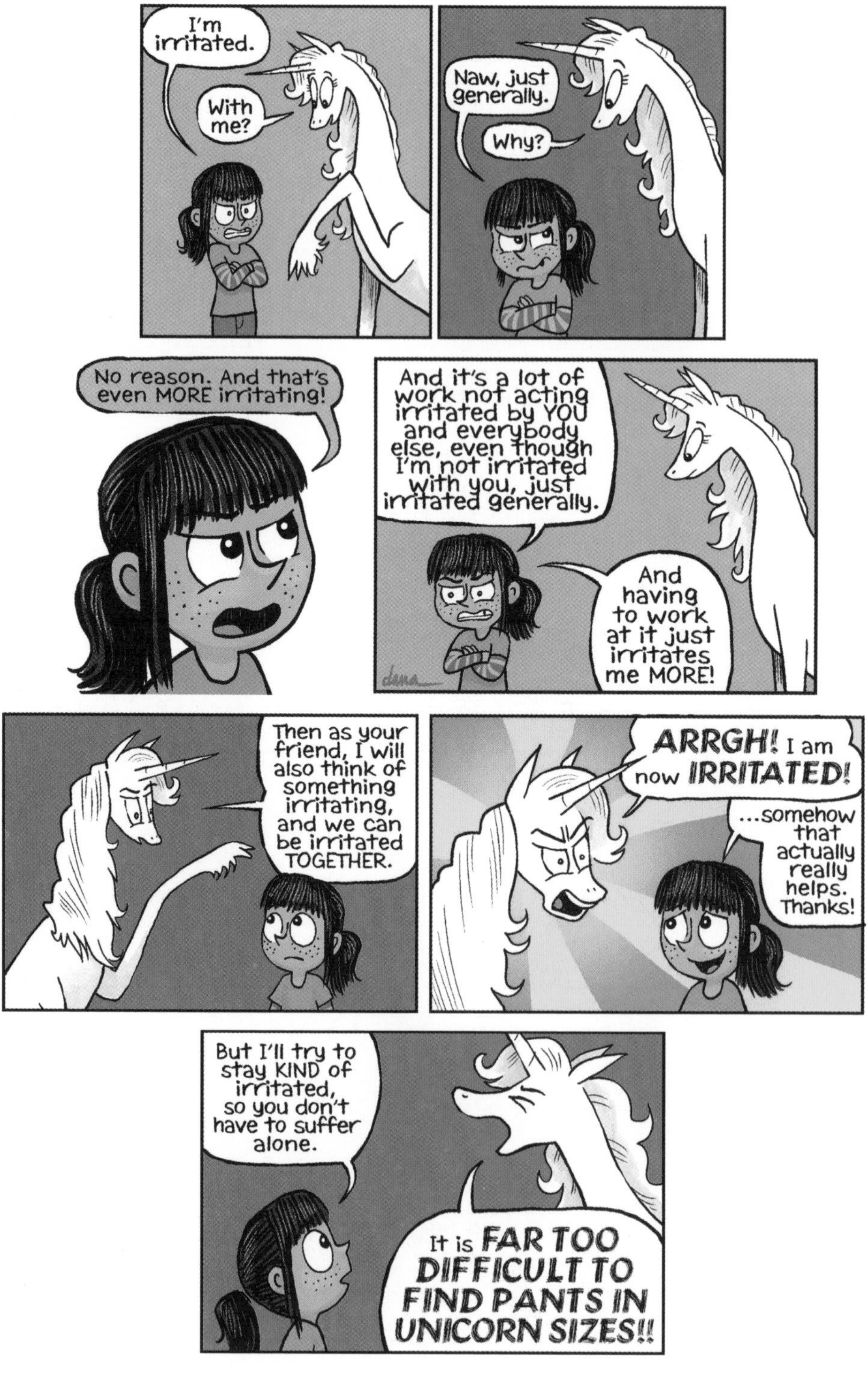
I'm irritated.
With me?
Naw, just generally.
Why?
No reason. And that's even MORE irritating!
And it's a lot of work not acting irritated by YOU and everybody else, even though I'm not irritated with you, just irritated generally.
And having to work at it just irritates me MORE!
dana
Then as your friend, I will also think of something irritating, and we can be irritated TOGETHER.
ARRGH! I am now IRRITATED!
...somehow that actually really helps. Thanks!
But I'll try to stay KIND of irritated, so you don't have to suffer alone.
It is FAR TOO DIFFICULT TO FIND PANTS IN UNICORN SIZES!!

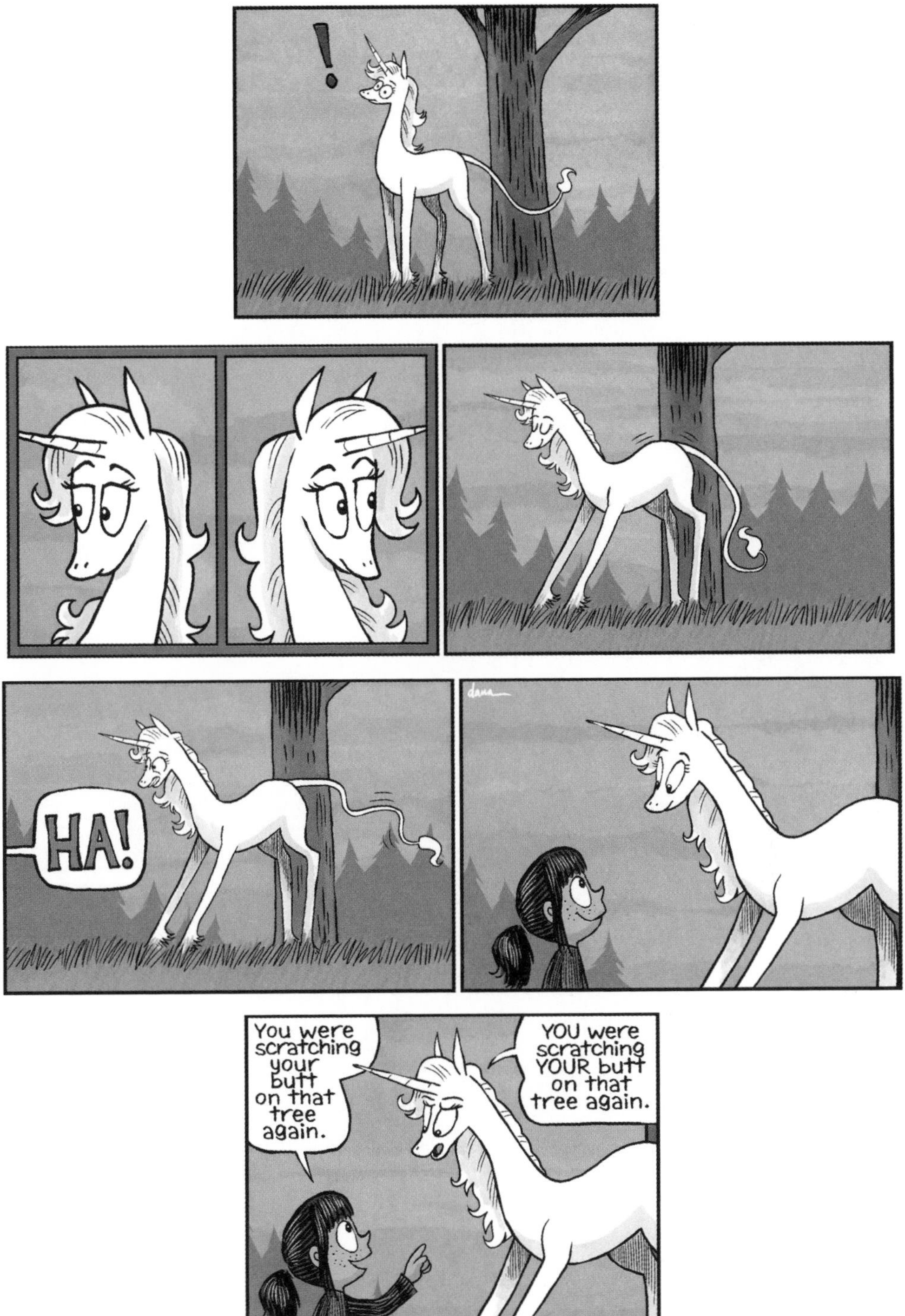
!
HA!
dana
You were scratching your butt on that tree again.
YOU were scratching YOUR butt on that tree again.

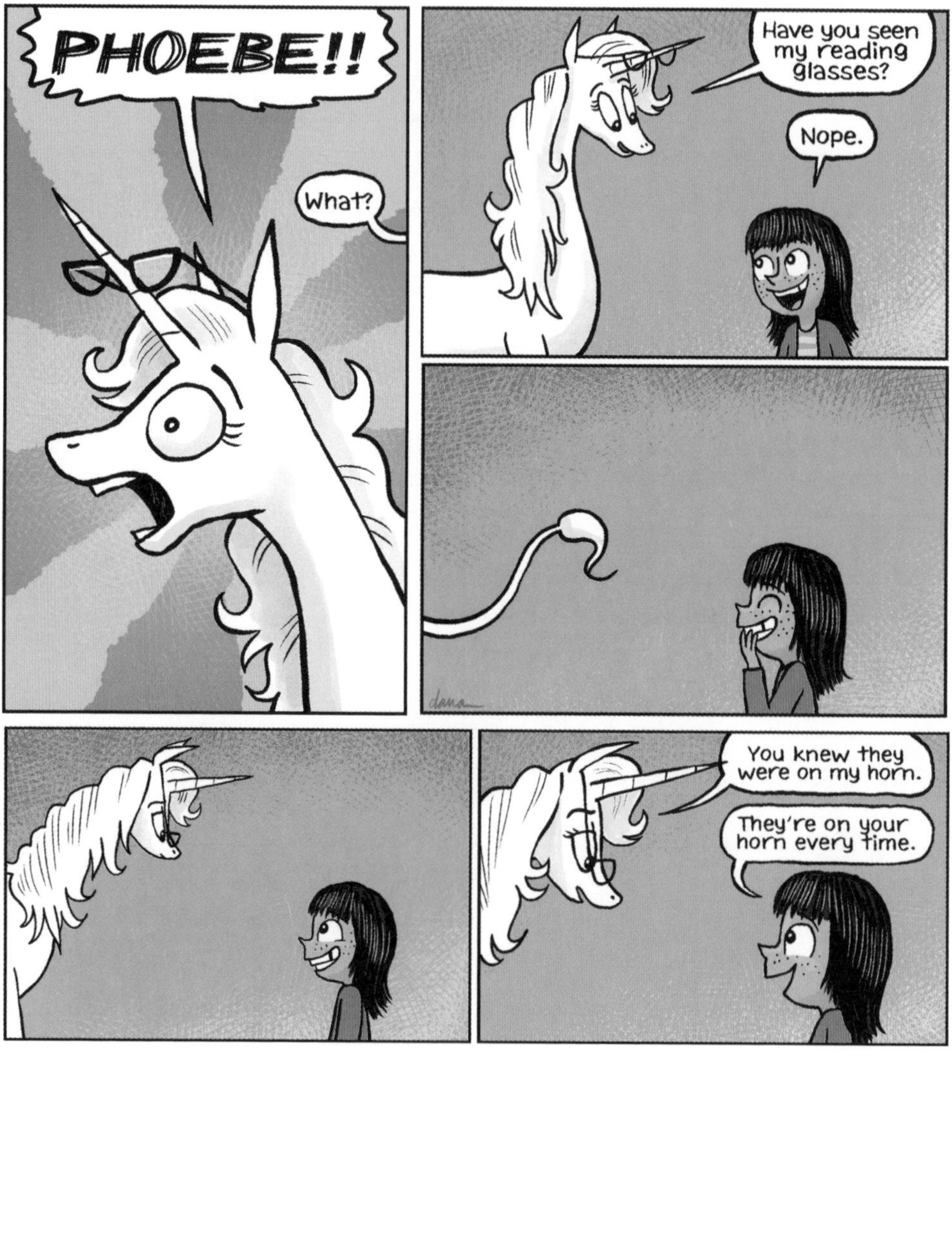
PHOEBE!!
What?
Have you seen my reading glasses?
Nope.
You knew they were on my horn.
They're on your horn every time.

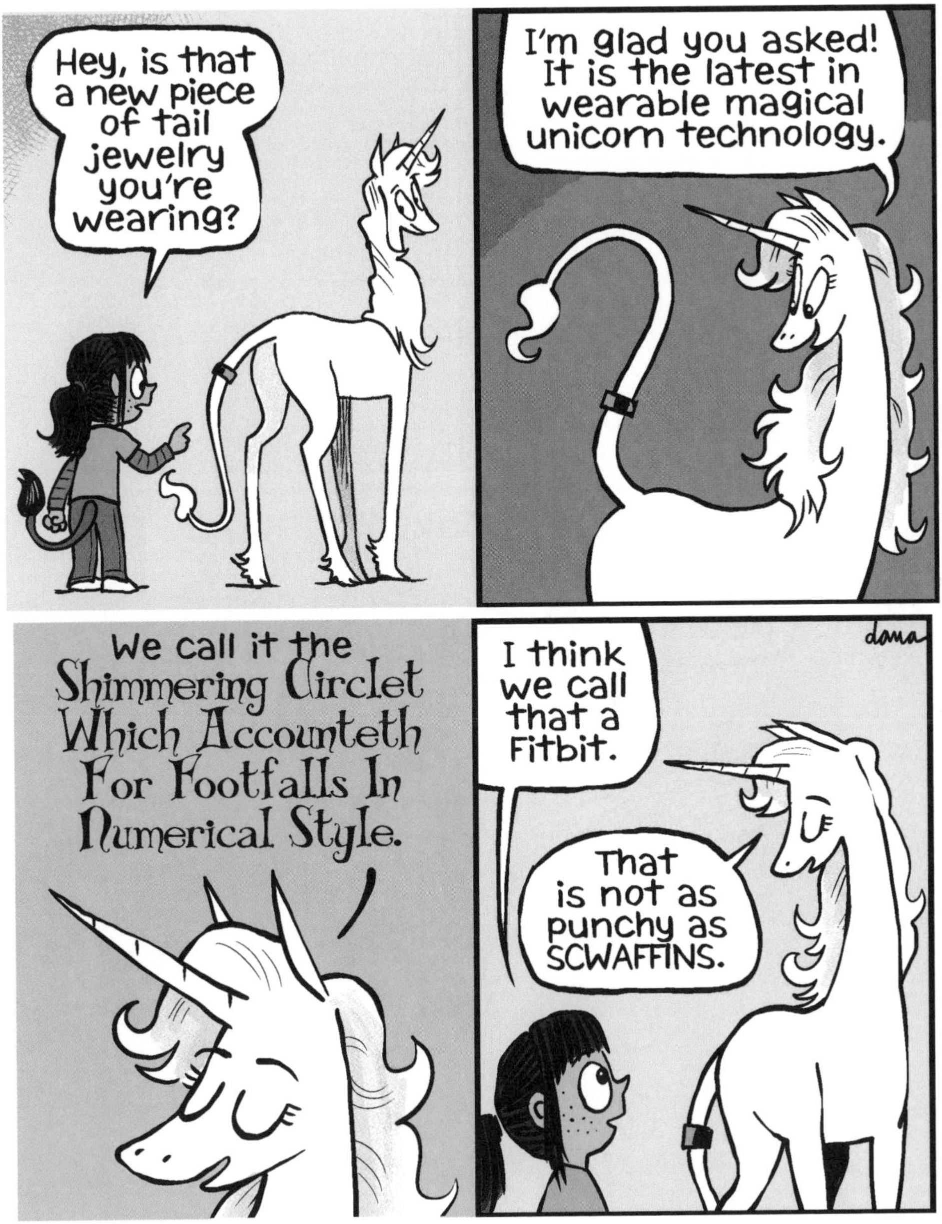
Hey, is that a new piece of tail jewelry you're wearing?
I'm glad you asked! It is the latest in wearable magical unicorn technology.
We call it the Shimmering Circlet Which Accounteth For Footfalls In Numerical Style.
I think we call that a Fitbit.
That is not as punchy as SCWAFFINS.
dana

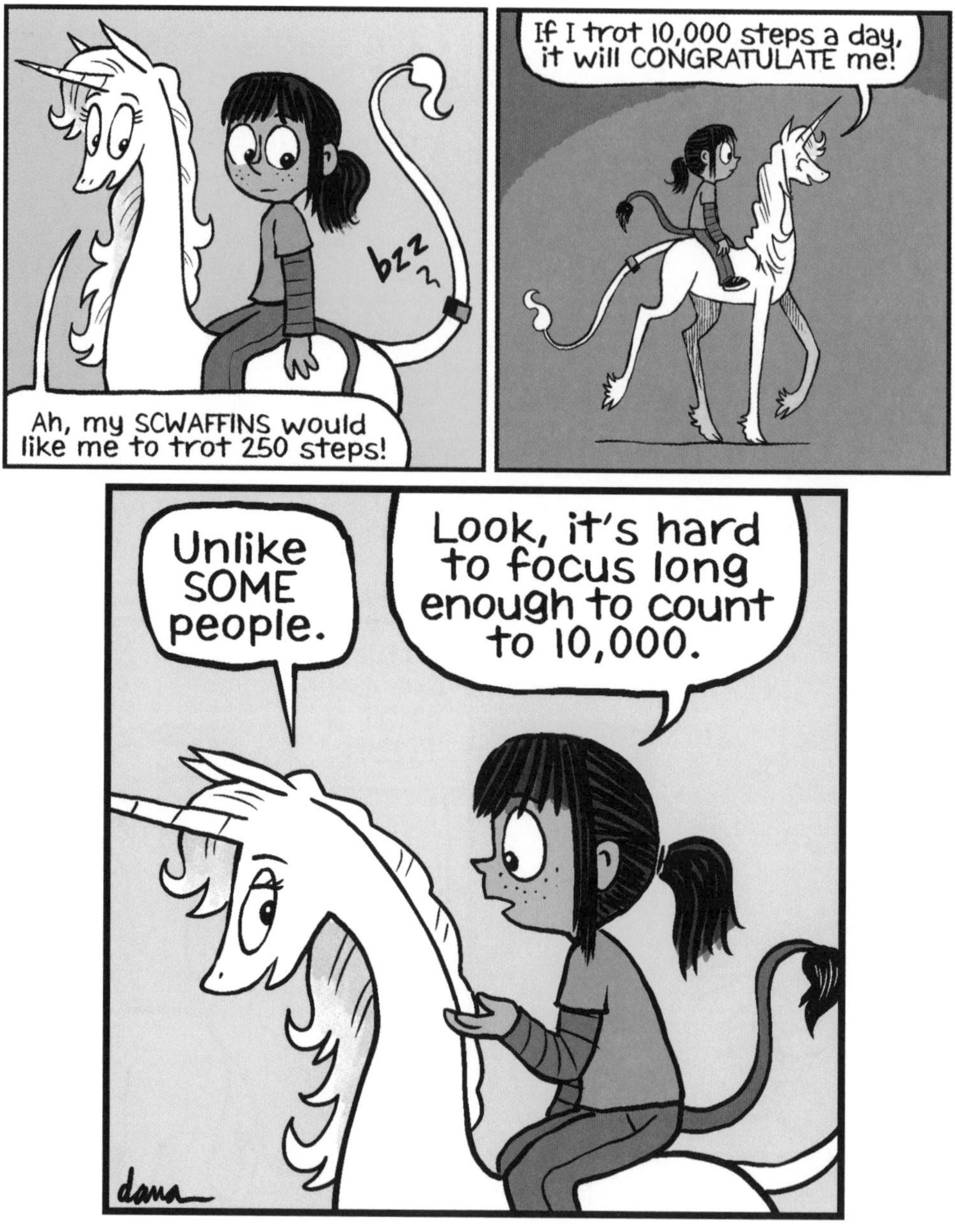
Ah, my SCWAFFINS would like me to trot 250 steps!
bzz
If I trot 10,000 steps a day, it will CONGRATULATE me!
Look, it's hard to focus long enough to count to 10,000.
Unlike SOME people.
dana

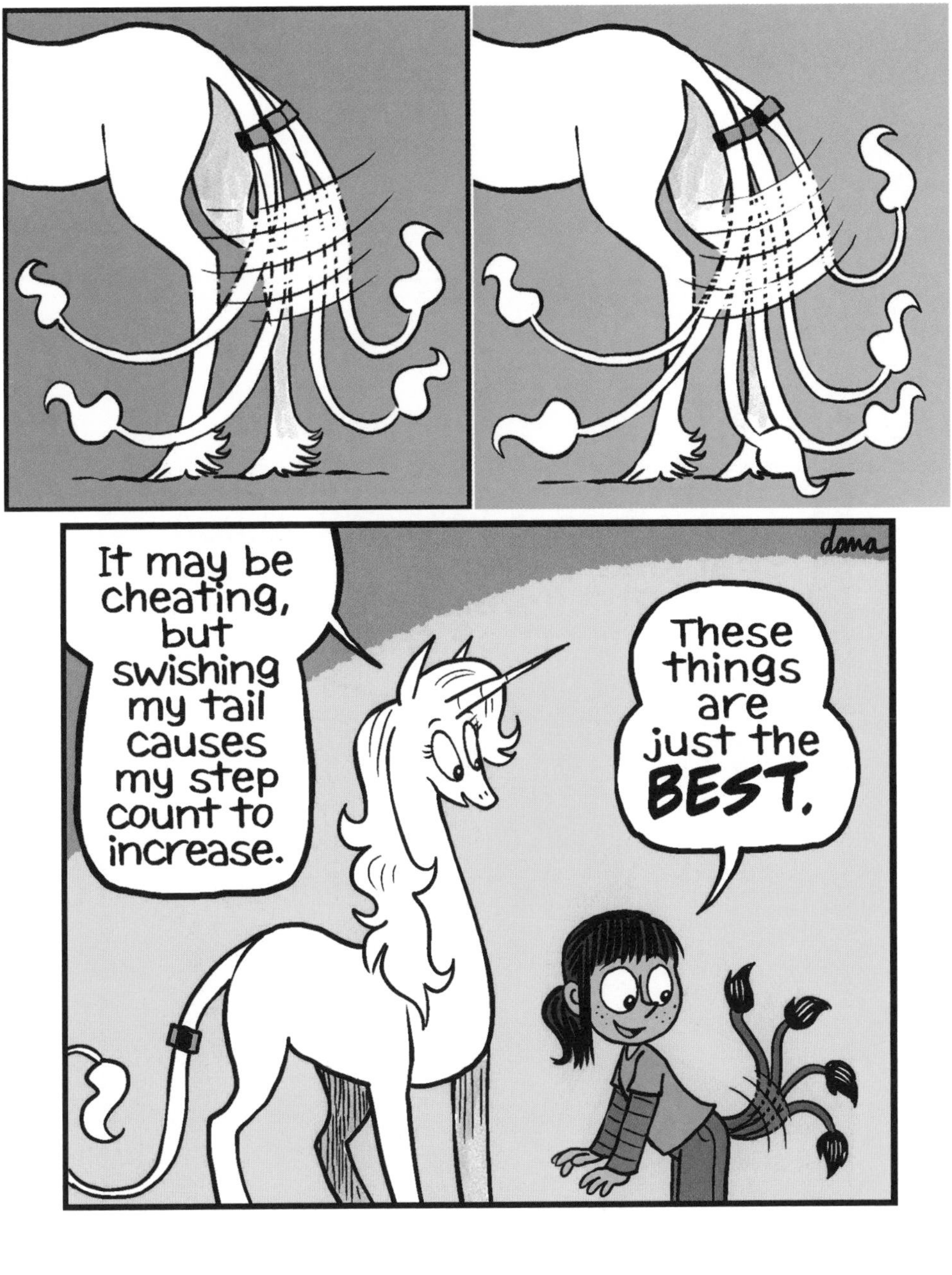

dana
It may be cheating, but swishing my tail causes my step count to increase.
These things are just the BEST.

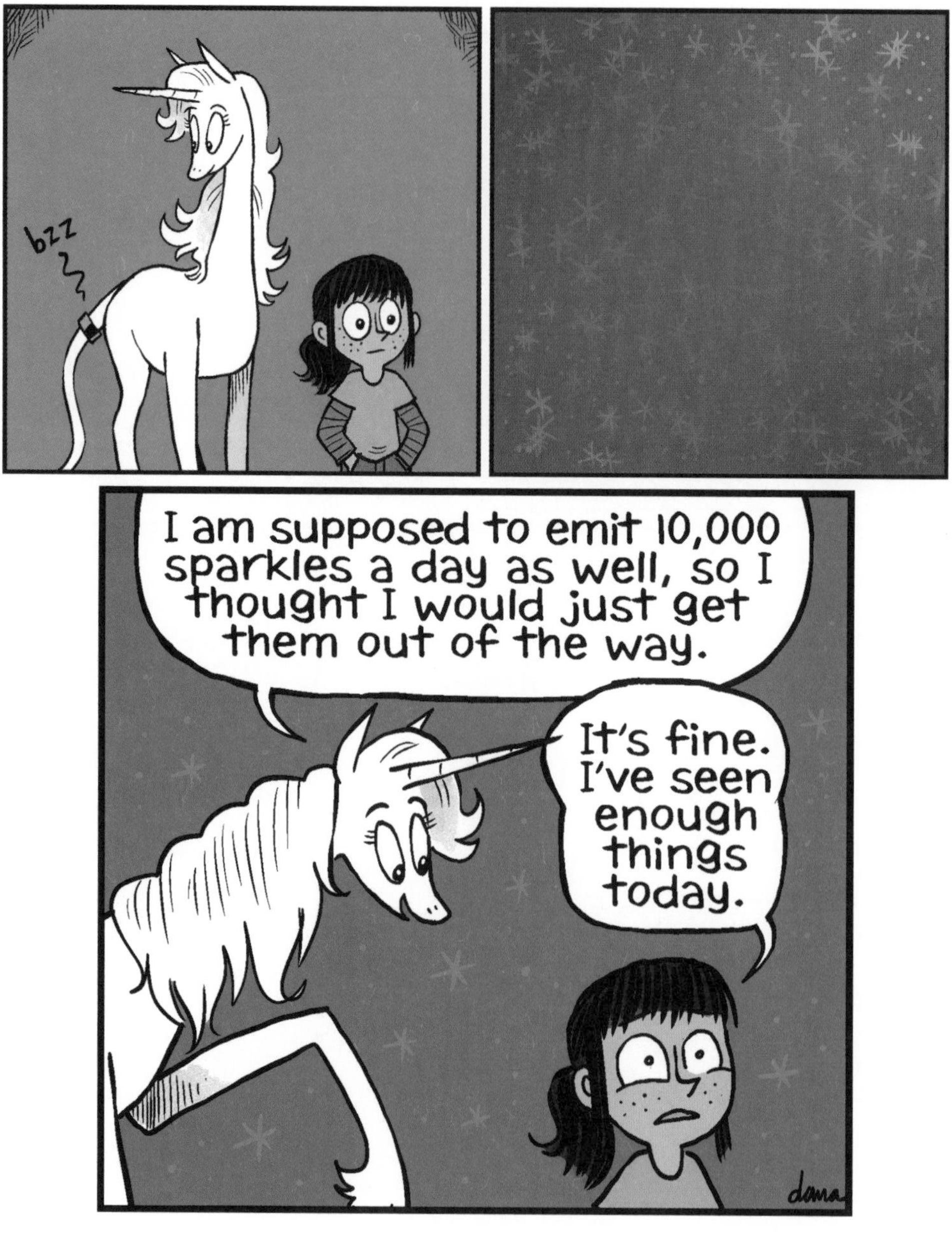
bzz
I am supposed to emit 10,000 sparkles a day as well, so I thought I would just get them out of the way.
It's fine. I've seen enough things today.
dana

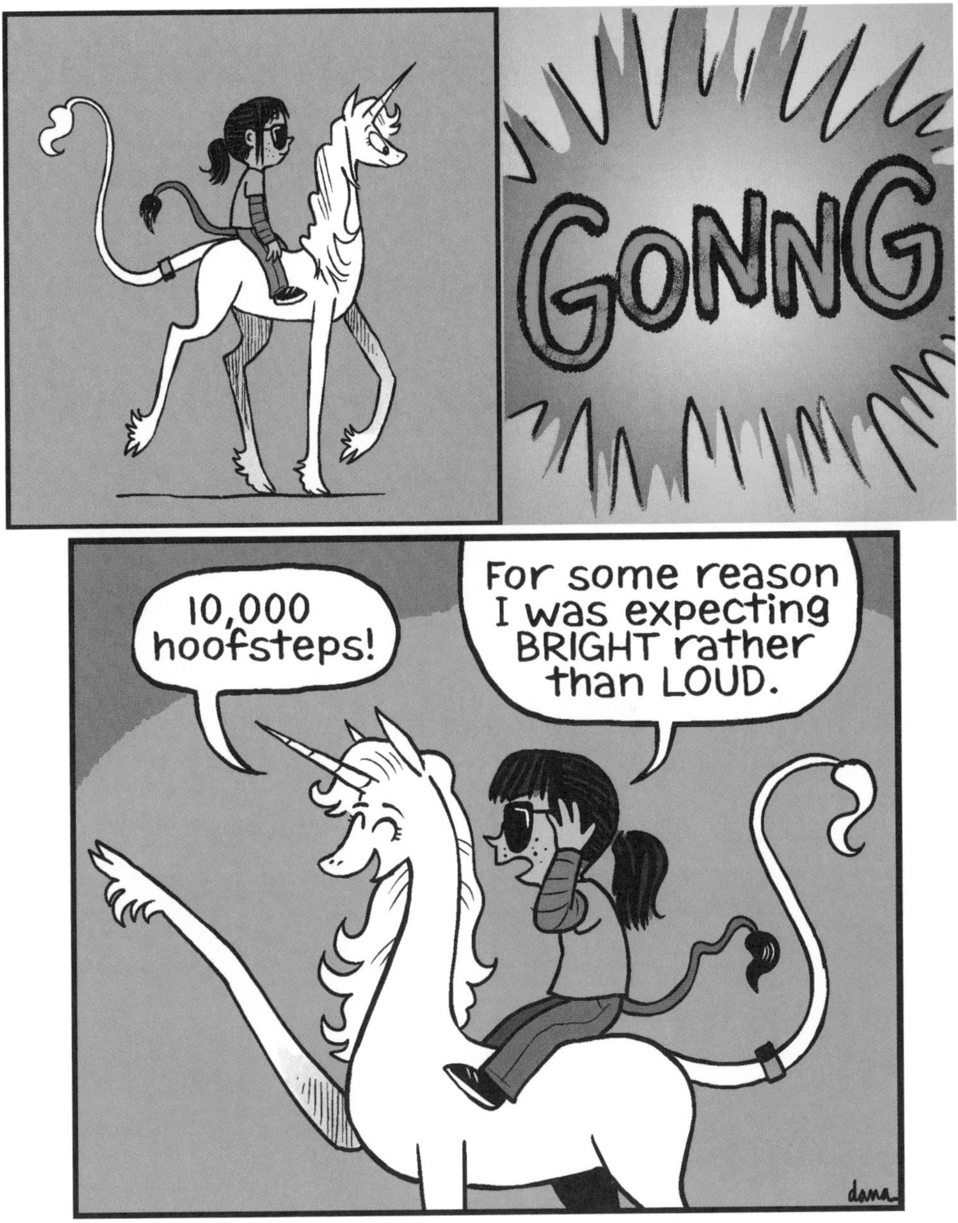
GONNG
10,000 hoofsteps!
For some reason I was expecting BRIGHT rather than LOUD.
dana

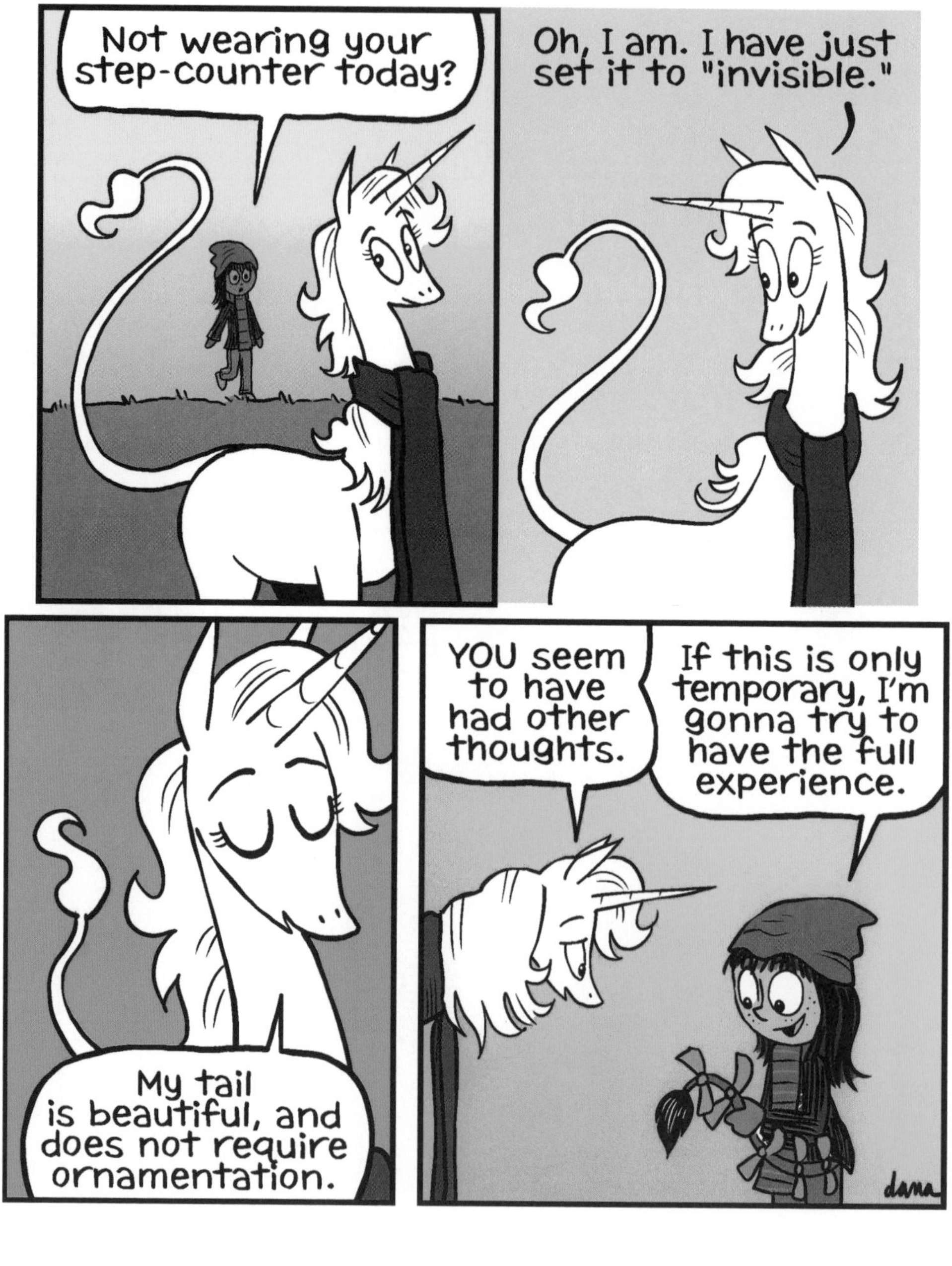
Not wearing your step-counter today?
Oh, I am. I have just set it to "invisible."
My tail is beautiful, and does not require ornamentation.
YOU seem to have had other thoughts.
If this is only temporary, I'm gonna try to have the full experience.
dana

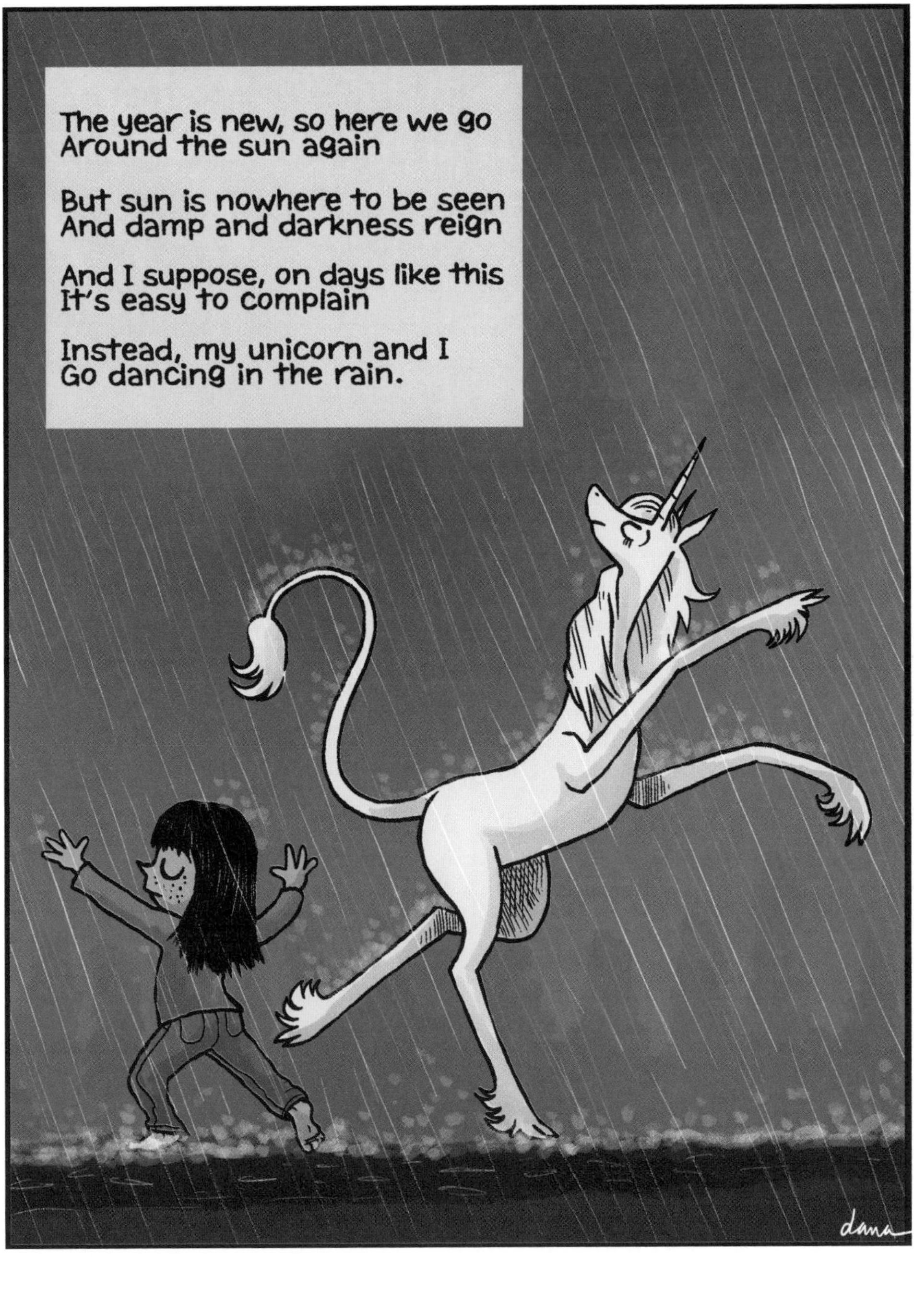
The year is new, so here we go
Around the sun again

But sun is nowhere to be seen
And damp and darkness reign

And I suppose, on days like this
It's easy to complain

Instead, my unicorn and I
Go dancing in the rain.
dana

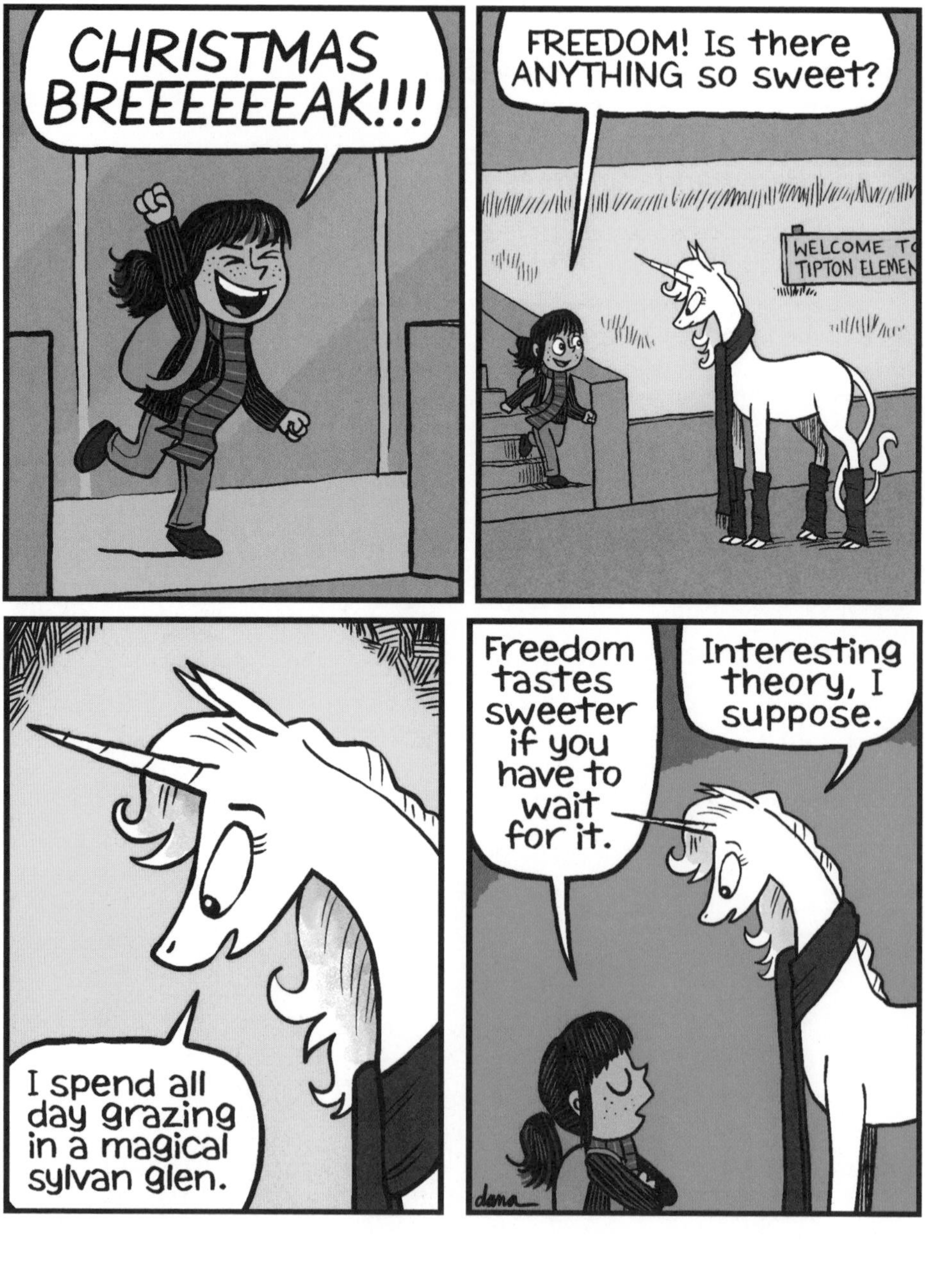
CHRISTMAS BREEEEEEAK!!!
FREEDOM! Is there ANYTHING so sweet?
WELCOME TO
TIPTON ELEMEN
I spend all day grazing in a magical sylvan glen.
Freedom tastes sweeter if you have to wait for it.
Interesting theory, I suppose.
dana

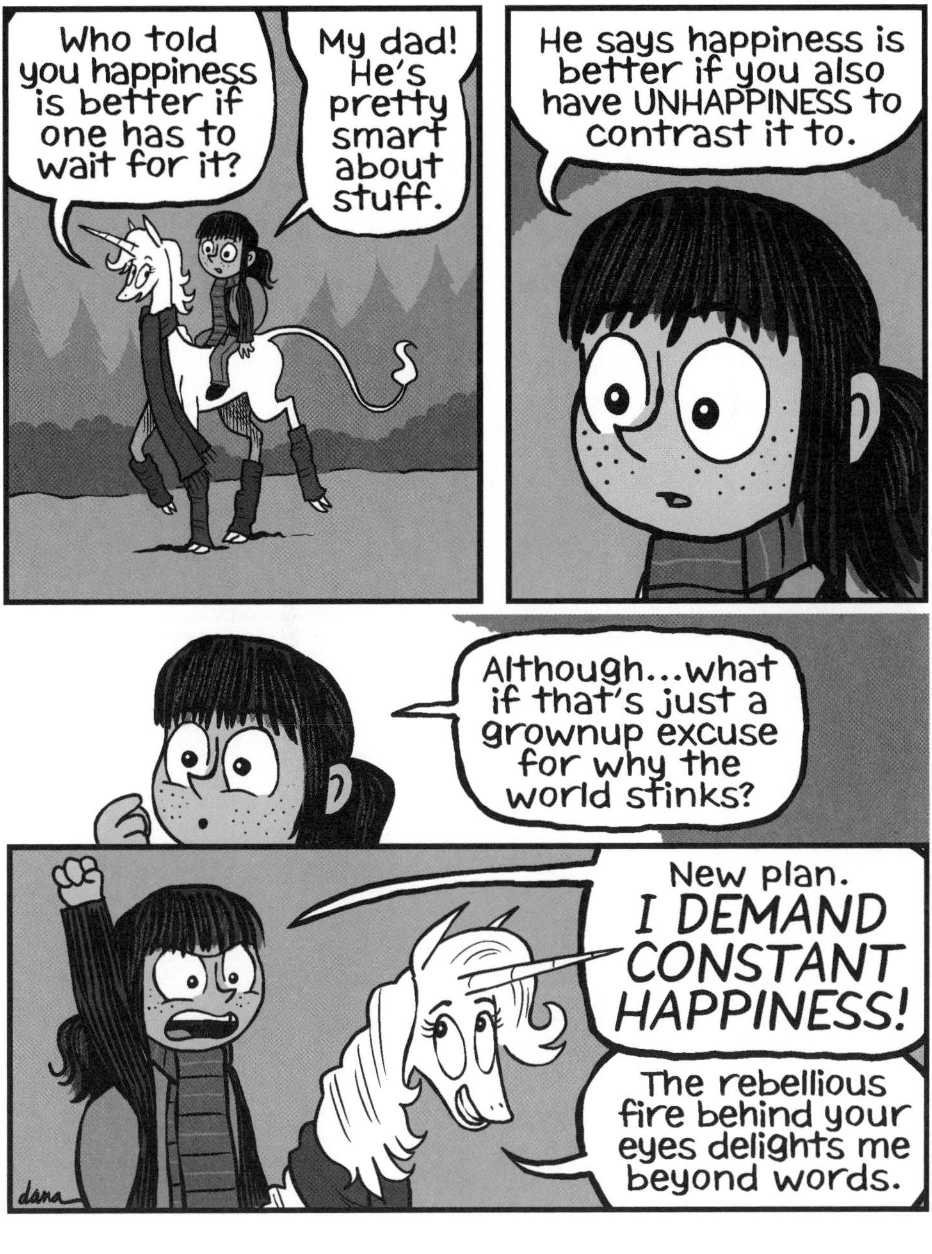
Who told you happiness is better if one has to wait for it?
My dad! He's pretty smart about stuff.
He says happiness is better if you also have UNHAPPINESS to contrast it to.
Although...what if that's just a grownup excuse for why the world stinks?
New plan. I DEMAND CONSTANT HAPPINESS!
The rebellious fire behind your eyes delights me beyond words.
dana

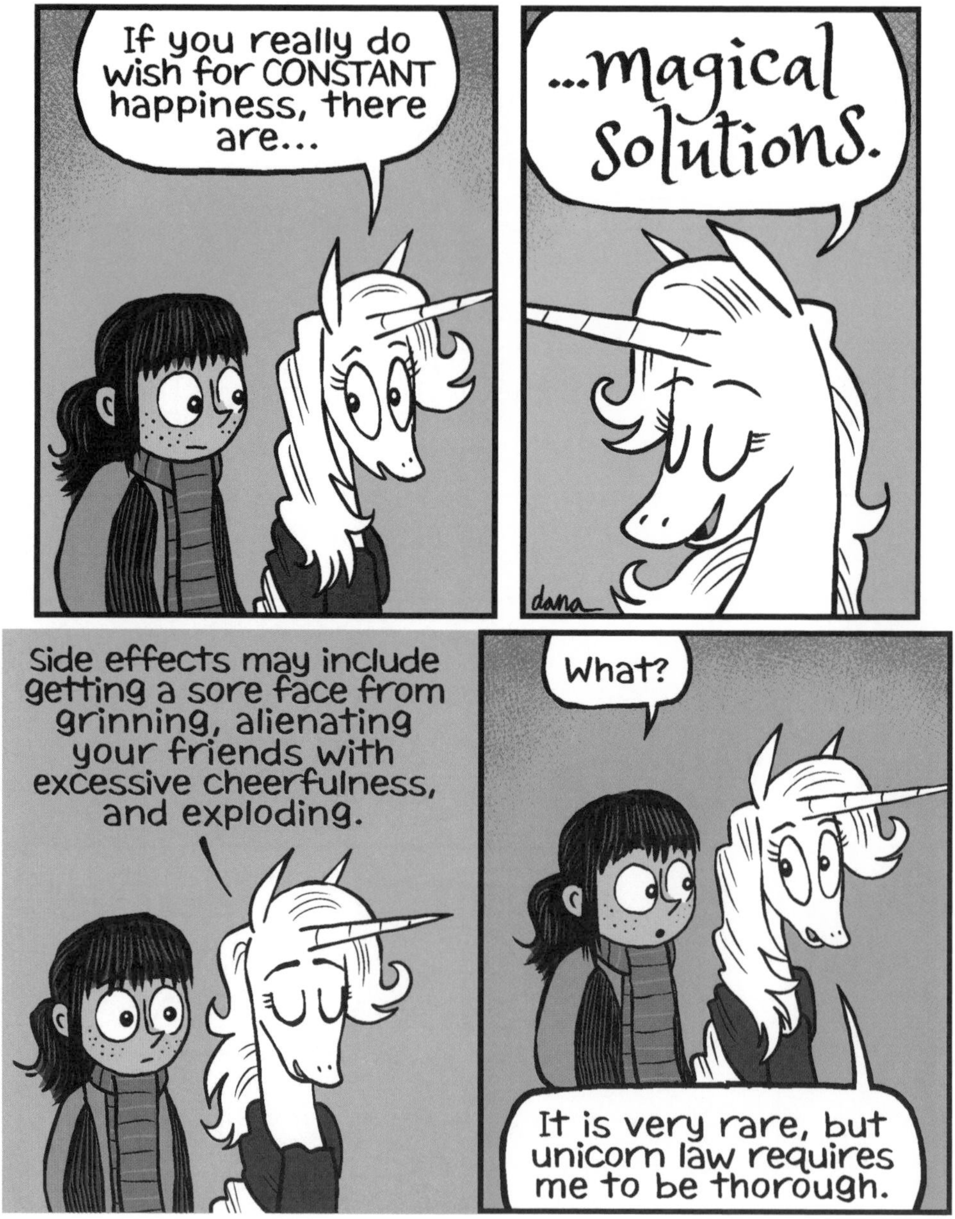
If you really do wish for CONSTANT happiness, there are...
...magical solutions.
Side effects may include getting a sore face from grinning, alienating your friends with excessive cheerfulness, and exploding.
What?
It is very rare, but unicorn law requires me to be thorough.

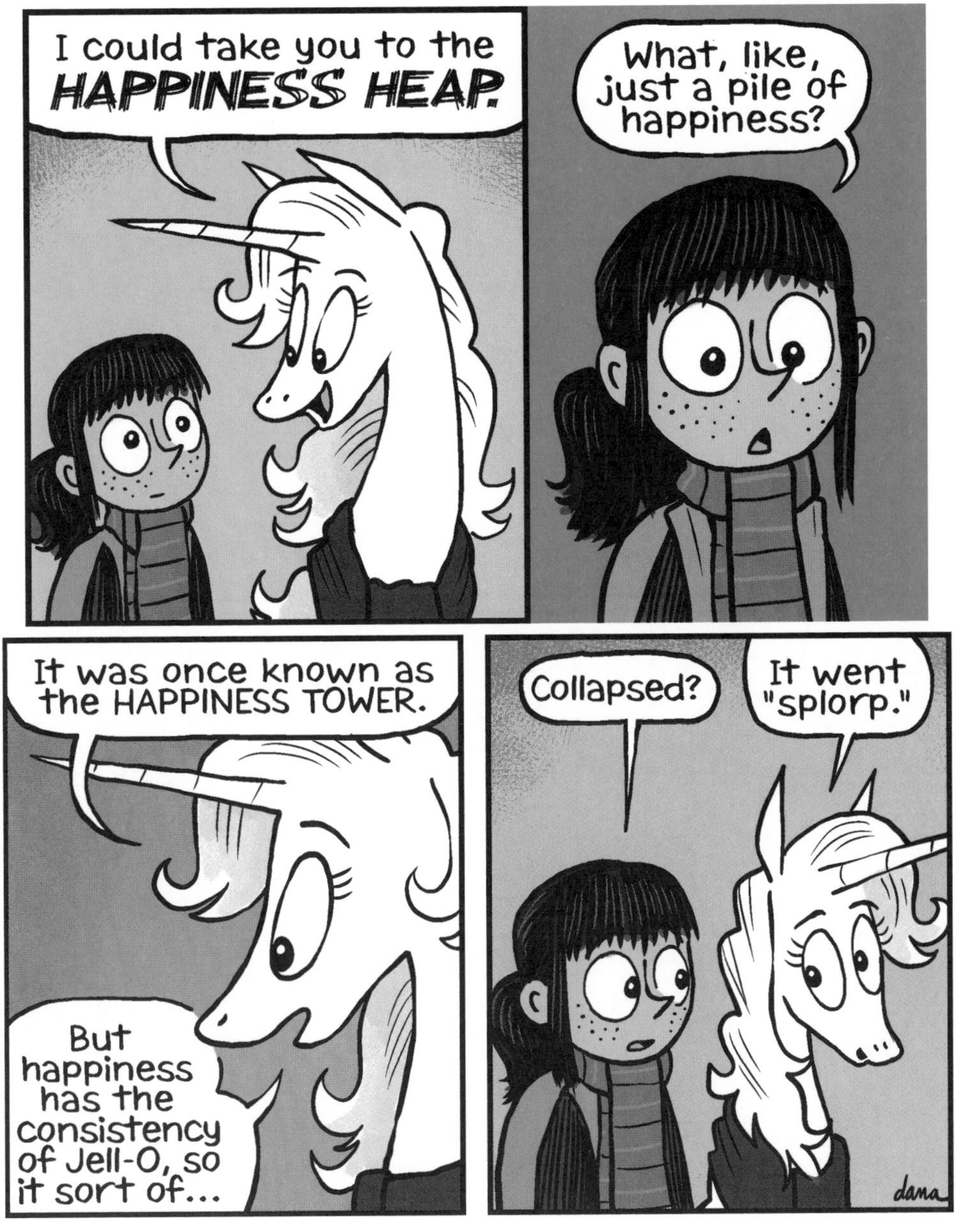
I could take you to the HAPPINESS HEAP.
What, like, just a pile of happiness?
It was once known as the HAPPINESS TOWER.
But happiness has the consistency of Jell-O, so it sort of...
Collapsed?
It went "splorp."
dana

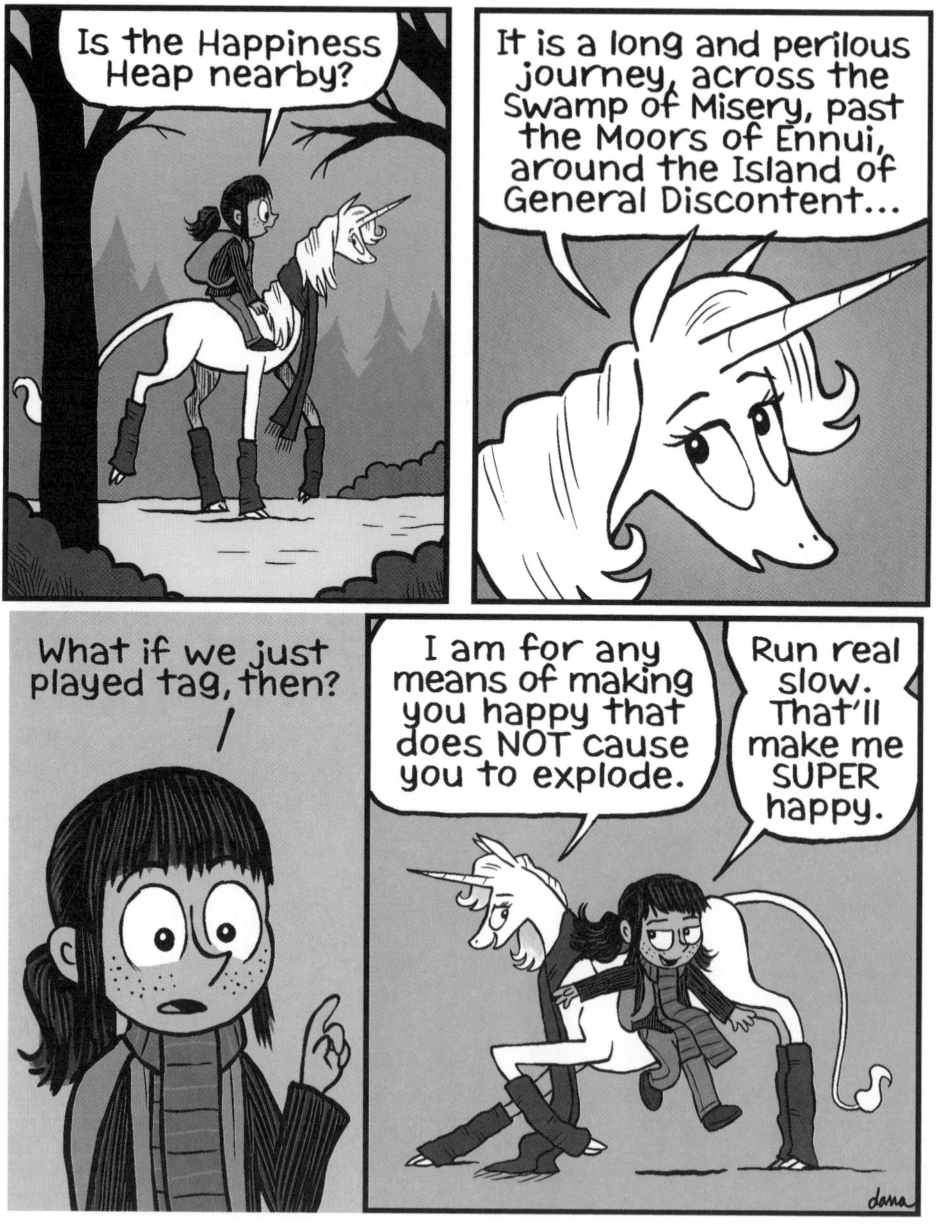
Is the Happiness Heap nearby?
It is a long and perilous journey, across the Swamp of Misery, past the Moors of Ennui, around the Island of General Discontent...
What if we just played tag, then?
I am for any means of making you happy that does NOT cause you to explode.
Run real slow. That'll make me SUPER happy.
dana

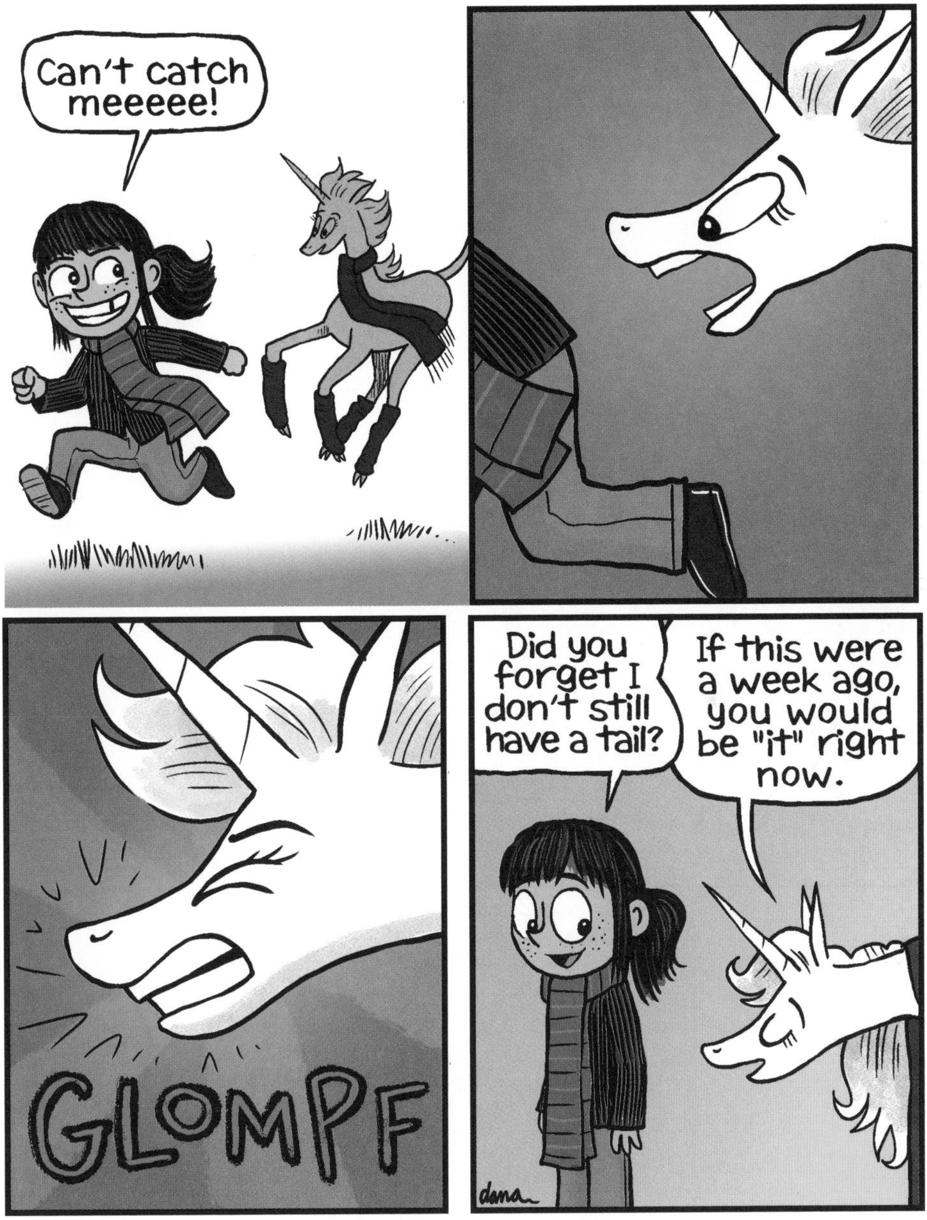
Can't catch meeeee!
GLOMPF
Did you forget I don't still have a tail?
If this were a week ago, you would be "it" right now.
dana

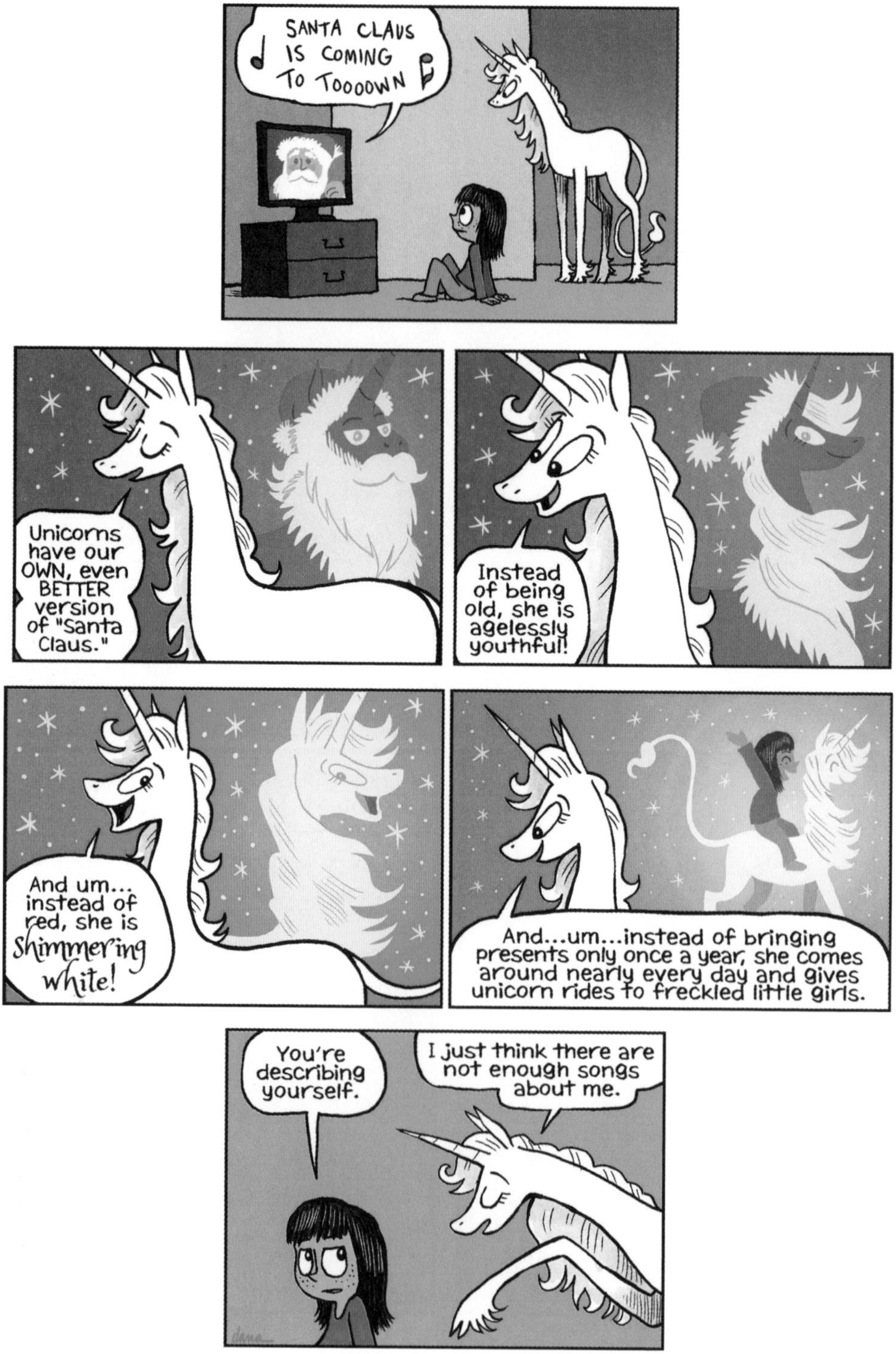
SANTA CLAUS IS COMING TO TOOOOWN
Unicorns have our OWN, even BETTER version of "Santa Claus."
Instead of being old, she is agelessly youthful!
And um... instead of red, she is Shimmering white!
And...um...instead of bringing presents only once a year, she comes around nearly every day and gives unicorn rides to freckled little girls.
You're describing yourself.
I just think there are not enough songs about me.

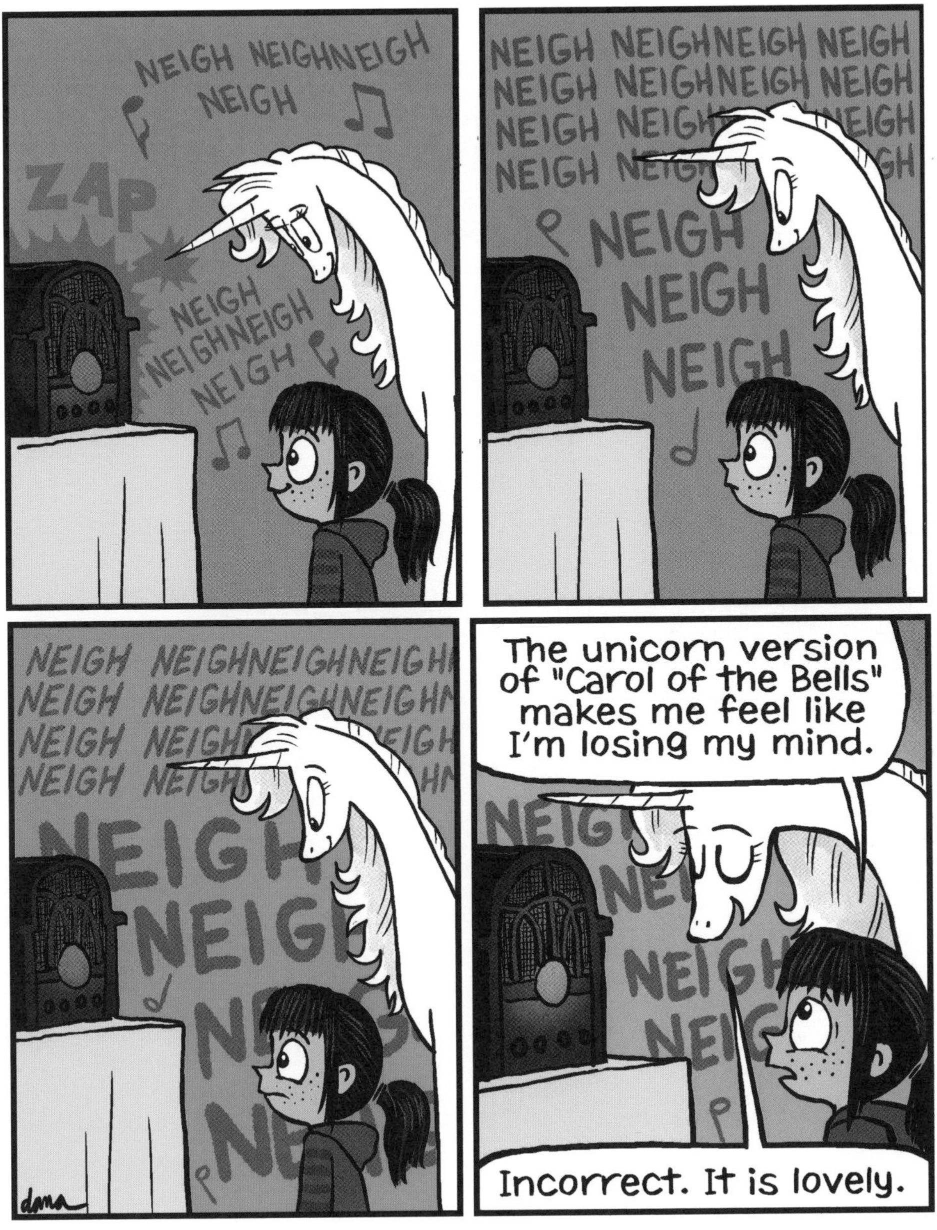
NEIGH NEIGHNEIGH
NEIGH
ZAP
NEIGH
NEIGHNEIGH
NEIGH
NEIGH NEIGHNEIGH NEIGH
NEIGH NEIGHNEIGH NEIGH
NEIGH
NEIGH
NEIGH
NEIGH NEIGHNEIGHNEIGH
NEIGH NEIGHNEIGHNEIGH
The unicorn version of "Carol of the Bells" makes me feel like I'm losing my mind.
Incorrect. It is lovely.

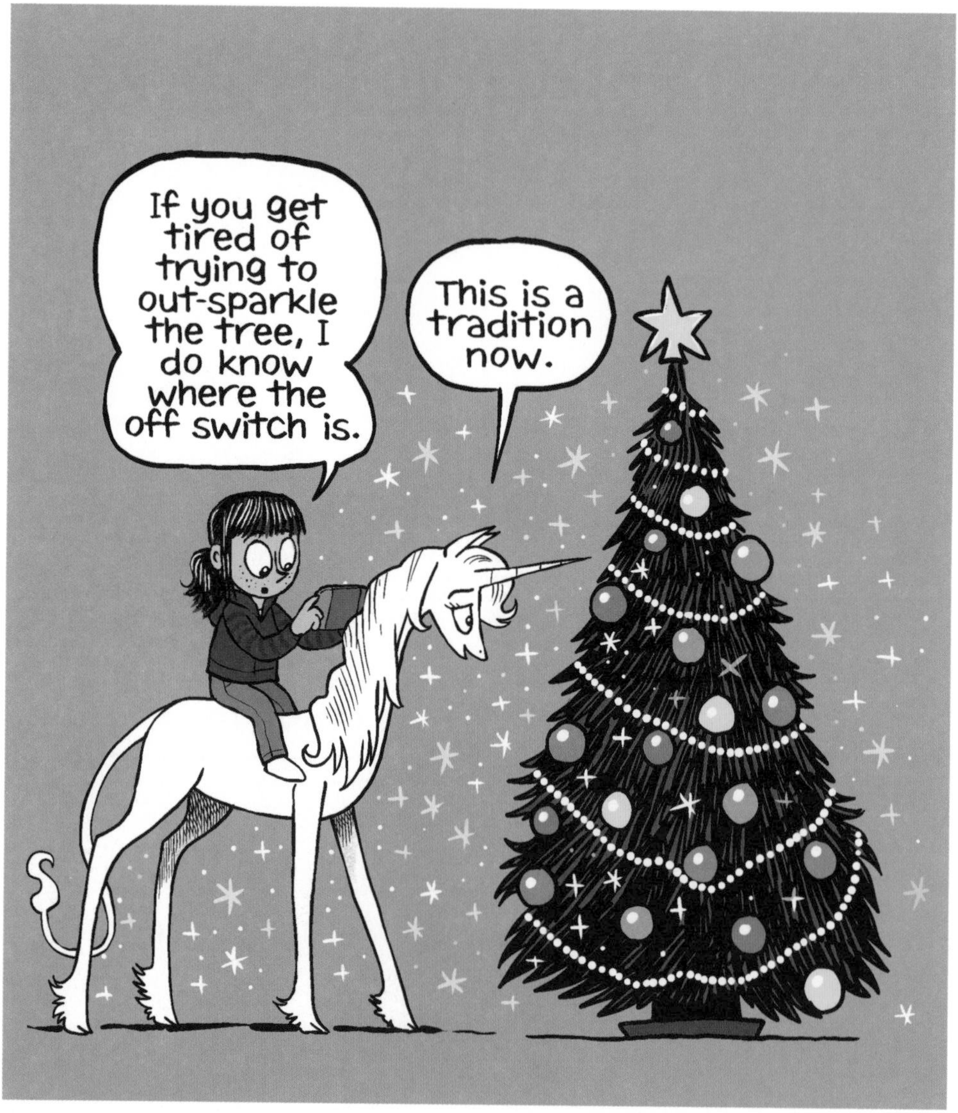
If you get tired of trying to out-sparkle the tree, I do know where the off switch is.
This is a tradition now.

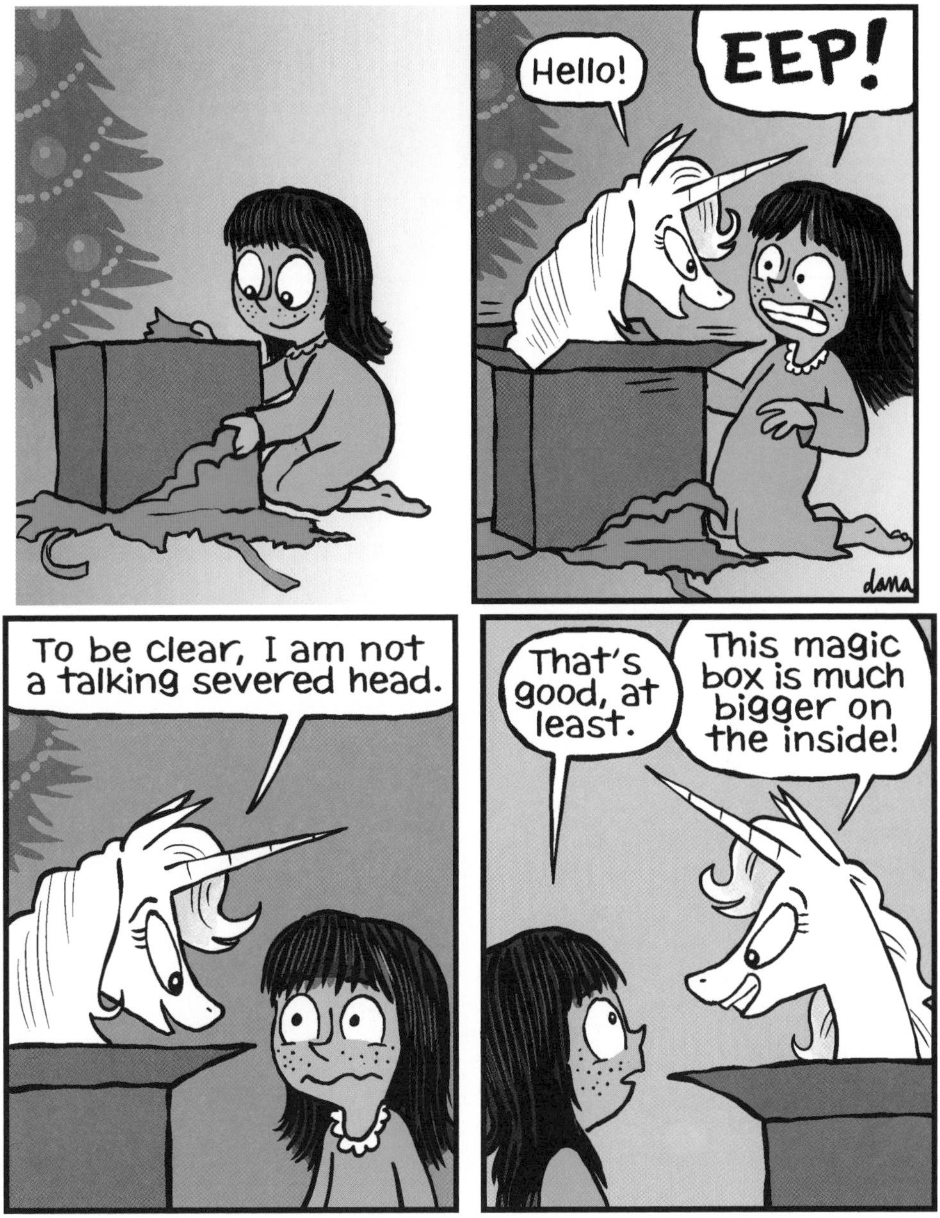
Hello!
EEP!
dana
To be clear, I am not a talking severed head.
That's good, at least.
This magic box is much bigger on the inside!

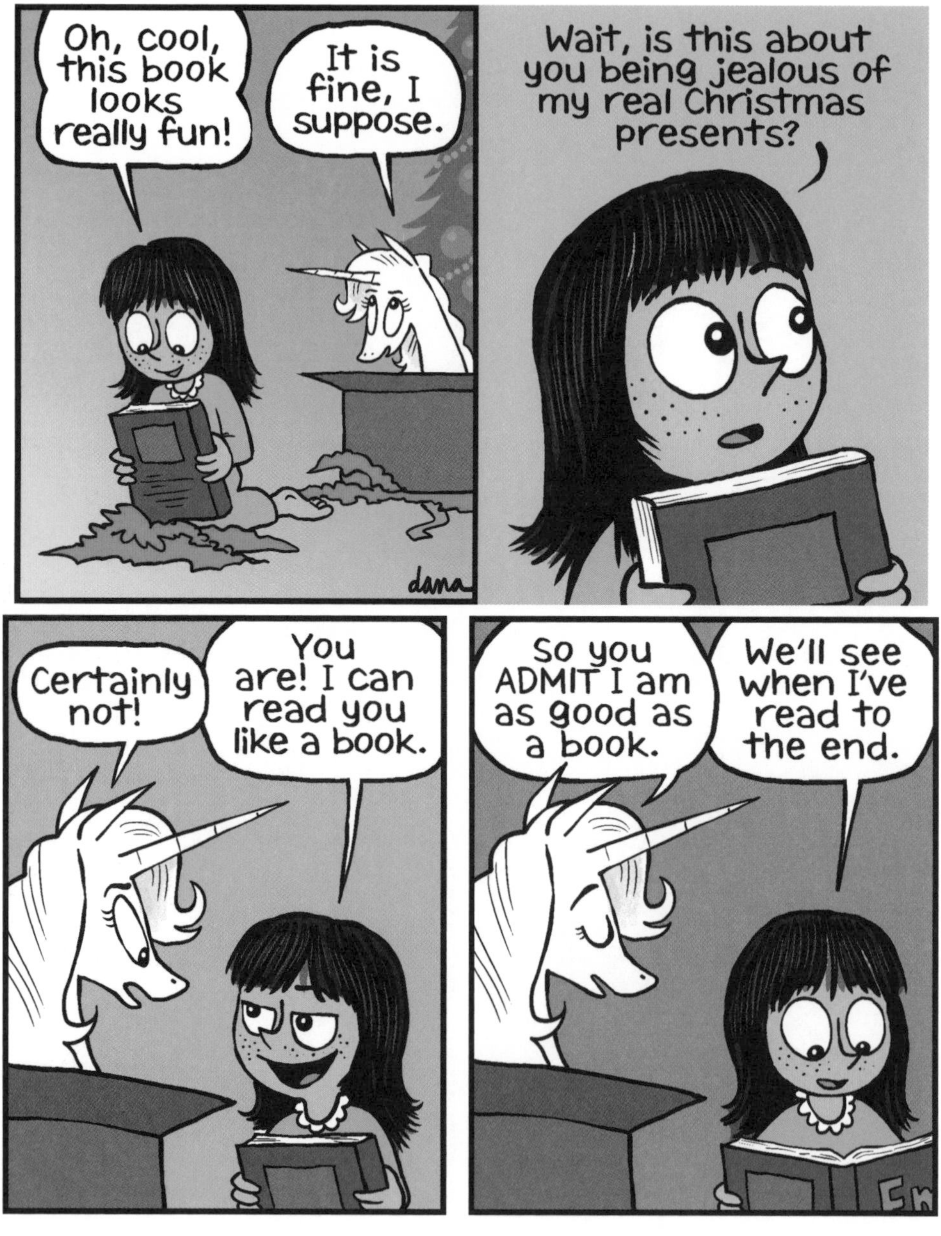
Oh, cool, this book looks really fun!
It is fine, I suppose.
dana
Wait, is this about you being jealous of my real Christmas presents?
Certainly not!
You are! I can read you like a book.
So you ADMIT I am as good as a book.
We'll see when I've read to the end.

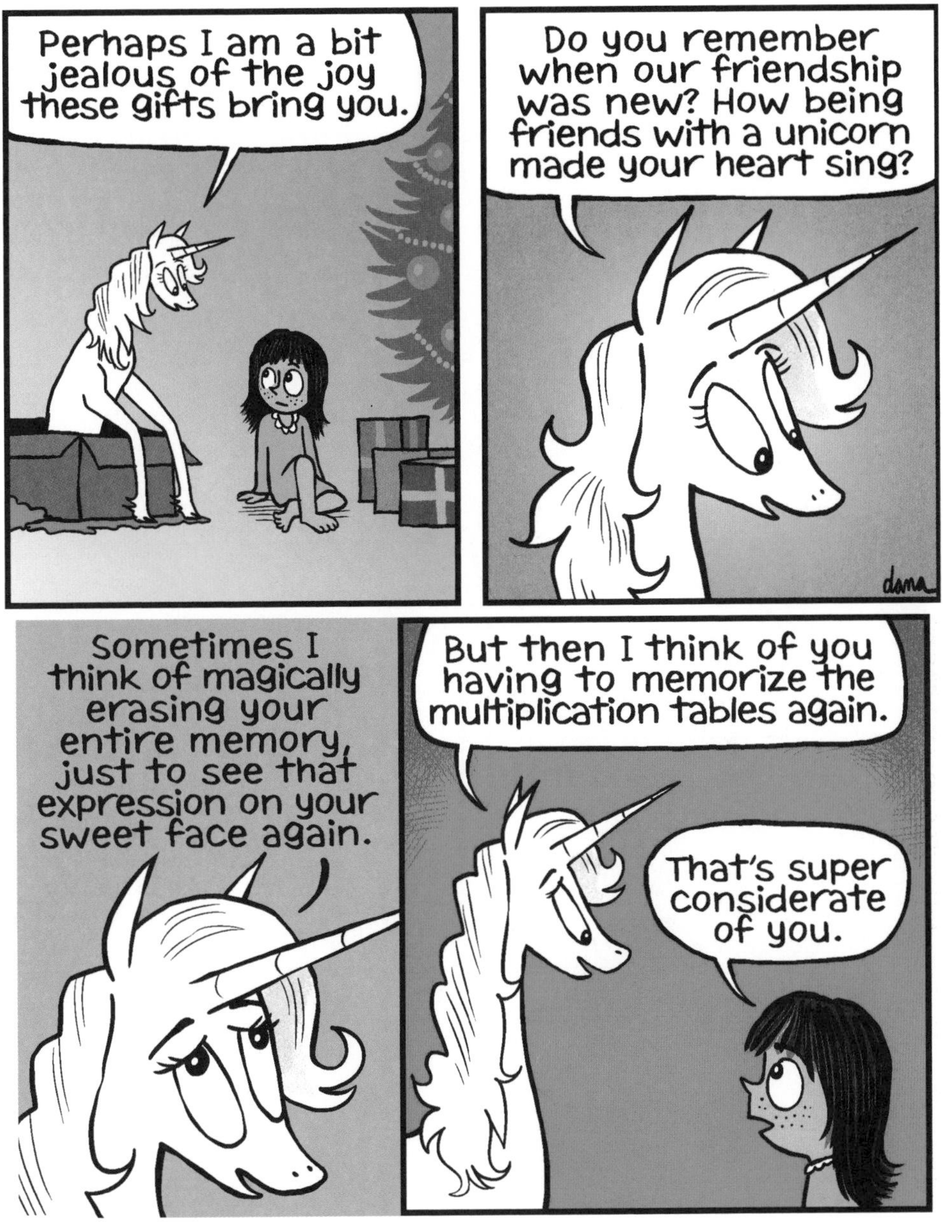
Perhaps I am a bit jealous of the joy these gifts bring you.
Do you remember when our friendship was new? How being friends with a unicorn made your heart sing?
dana
Sometimes I think of magically erasing your entire memory, just to see that expression on your sweet face again.
But then I think of you having to memorize the multiplication tables again.
That's super considerate of you.

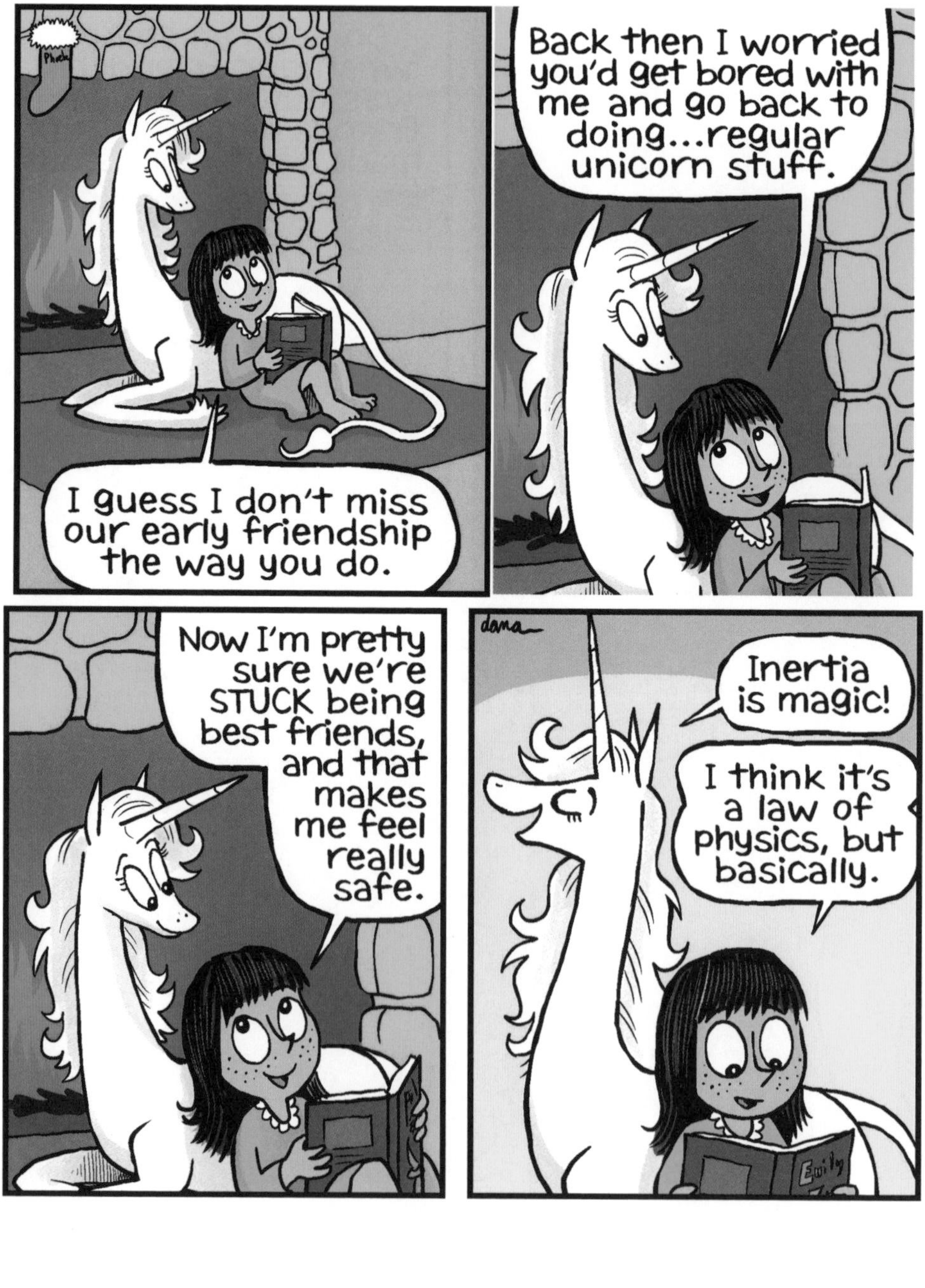
Phoebe
I guess I don't miss our early friendship the way you do.
Back then I worried you'd get bored with me and go back to doing...regular unicorn stuff.
Now I'm pretty sure we're STUCK being best friends, and that makes me feel really safe.
dana
Inertia is magic!
I think it's a law of physics, but basically.

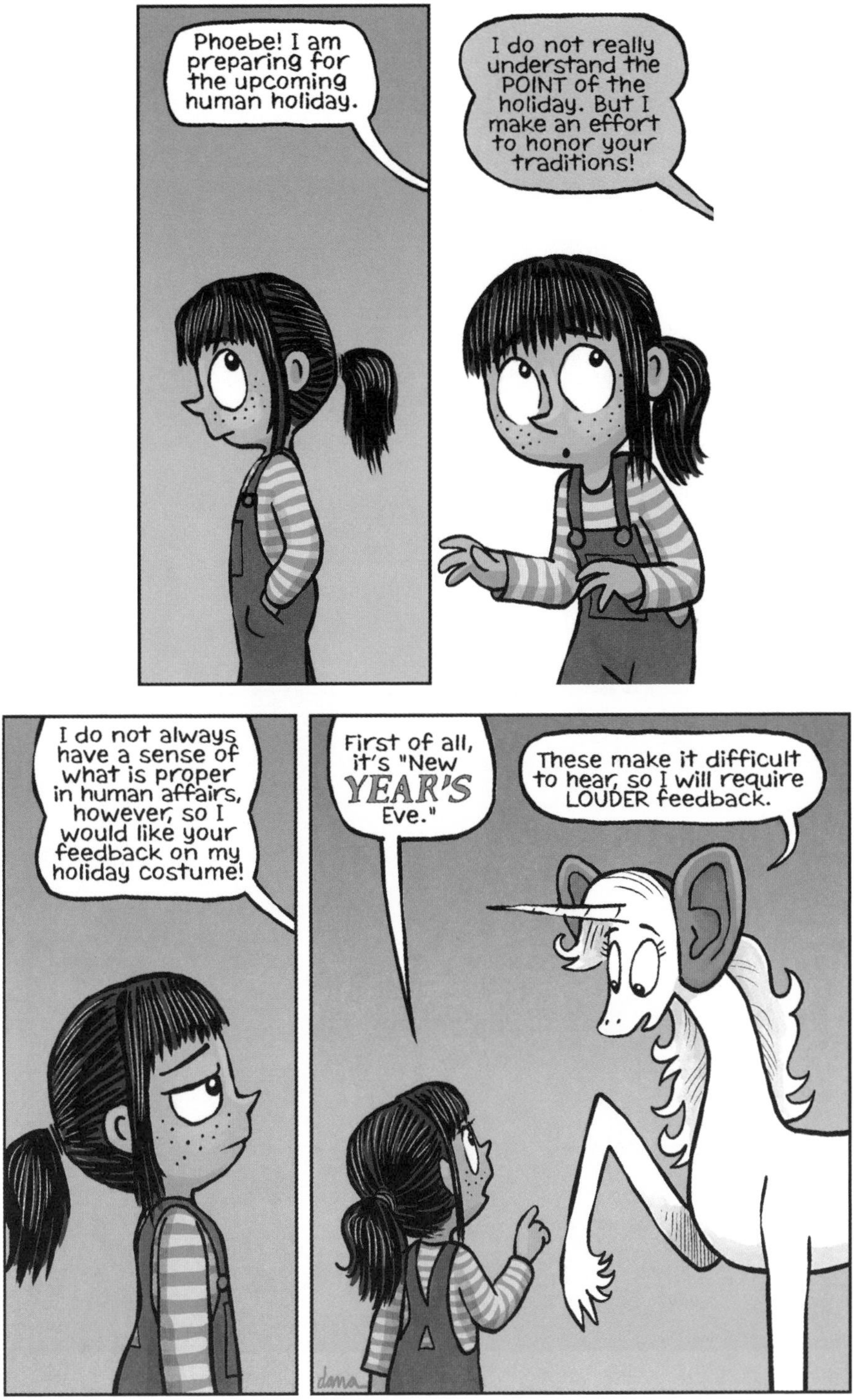
Phoebe! I am preparing for the upcoming human holiday.
I do not really understand the POINT of the holiday. But I make an effort to honor your traditions!
I do not always have a sense of what is proper in human affairs, however, so I would like your feedback on my holiday costume!
First of all, it's "New YEAR'S Eve."
These make it difficult to hear, so I will require LOUDER feedback.

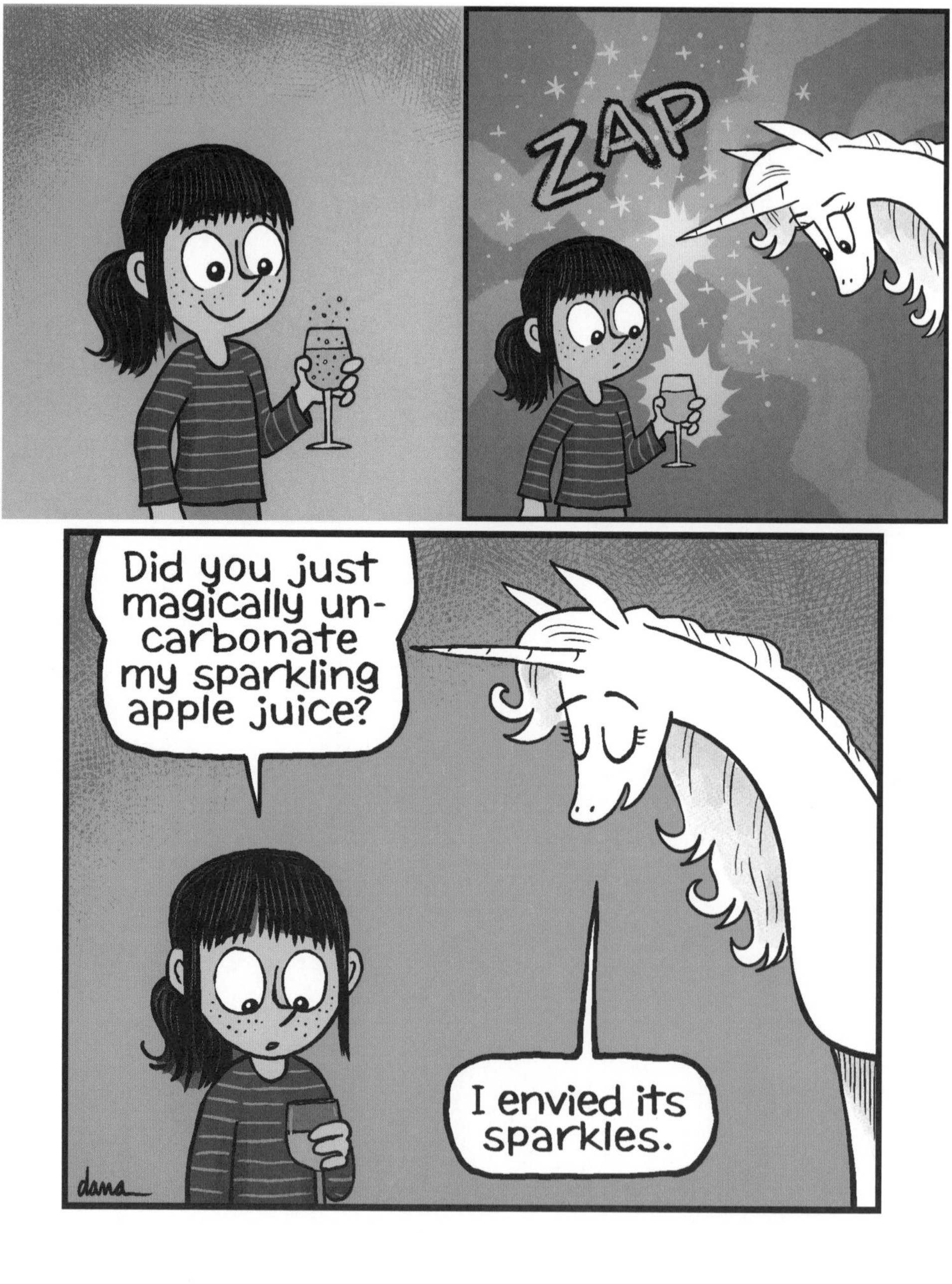
ZAP
Did you just magically un-carbonate my sparkling apple juice?
I envied its sparkles.
dana

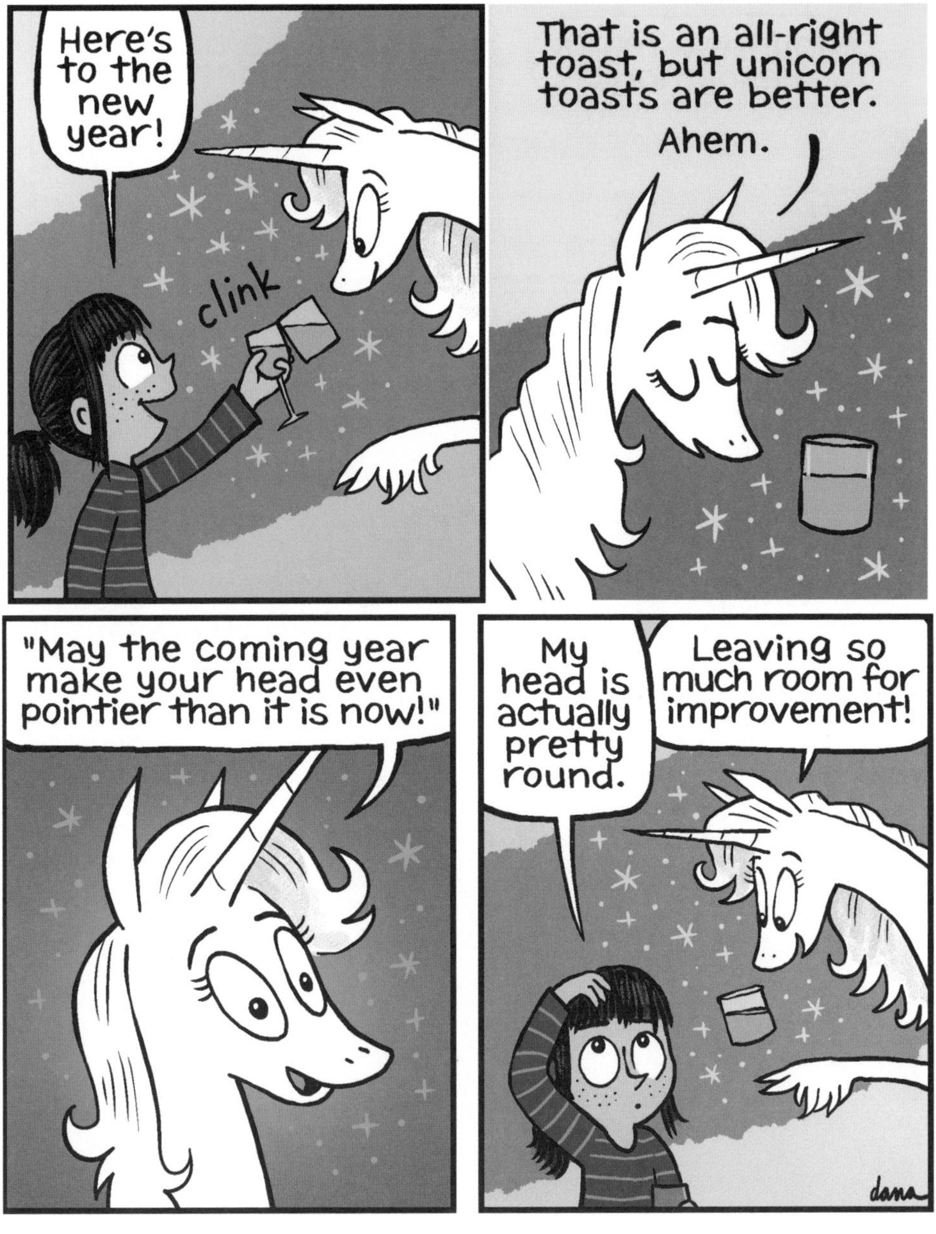
Here's to the new year!
clink
That is an all-right toast, but unicorn toasts are better.
Ahem.
"May the coming year make your head even pointier than it is now!"
My head is actually pretty round.
Leaving so much room for improvement!
dana

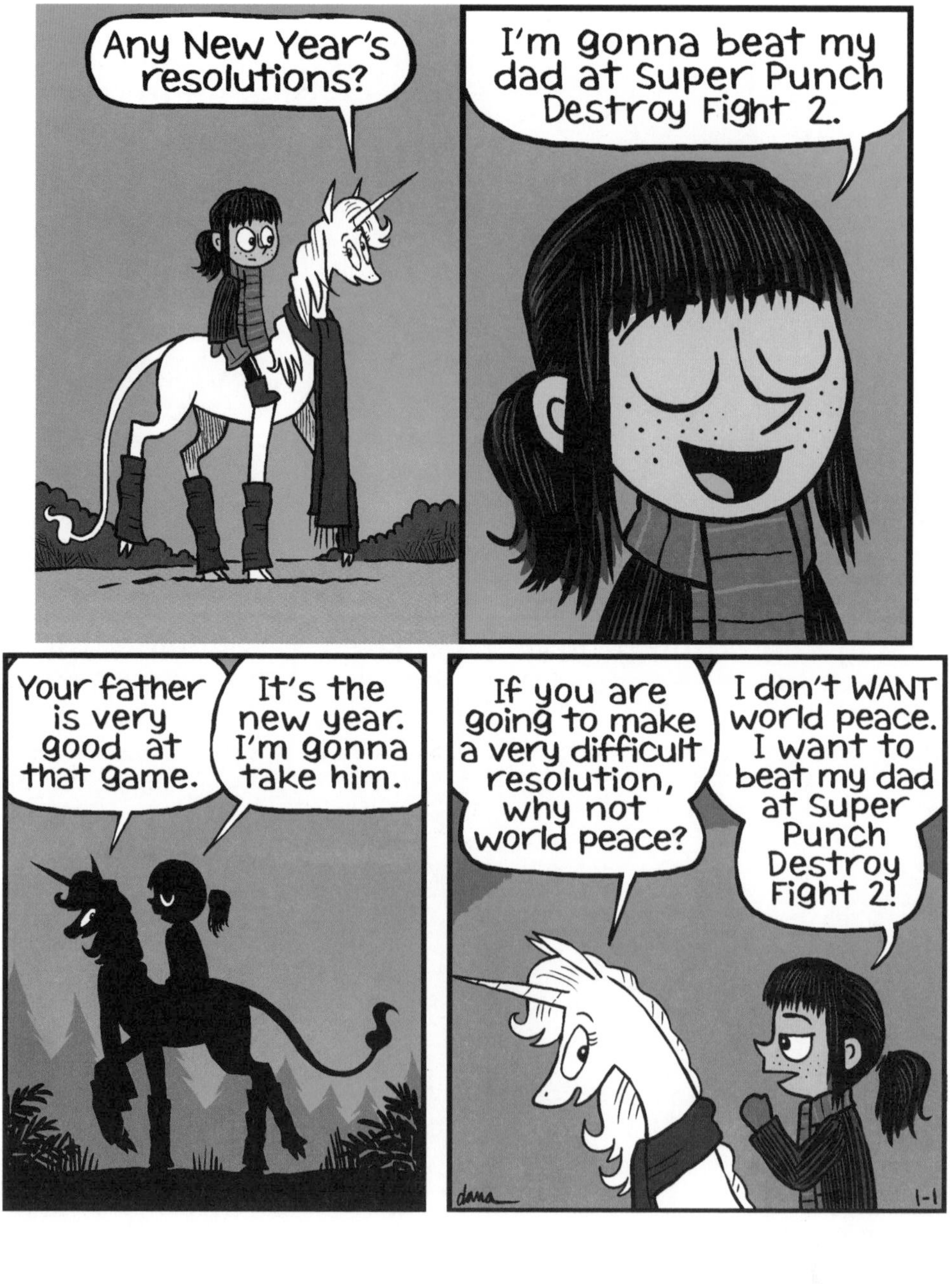
Any New Year's resolutions?
I'm gonna beat my dad at Super Punch Destroy Fight 2.
Your father is very good at that game.
It's the new year. I'm gonna take him.
If you are going to make a very difficult resolution, why not world peace?
I don't WANT world peace. I want to beat my dad at Super Punch Destroy Fight 2!
dana
1-1

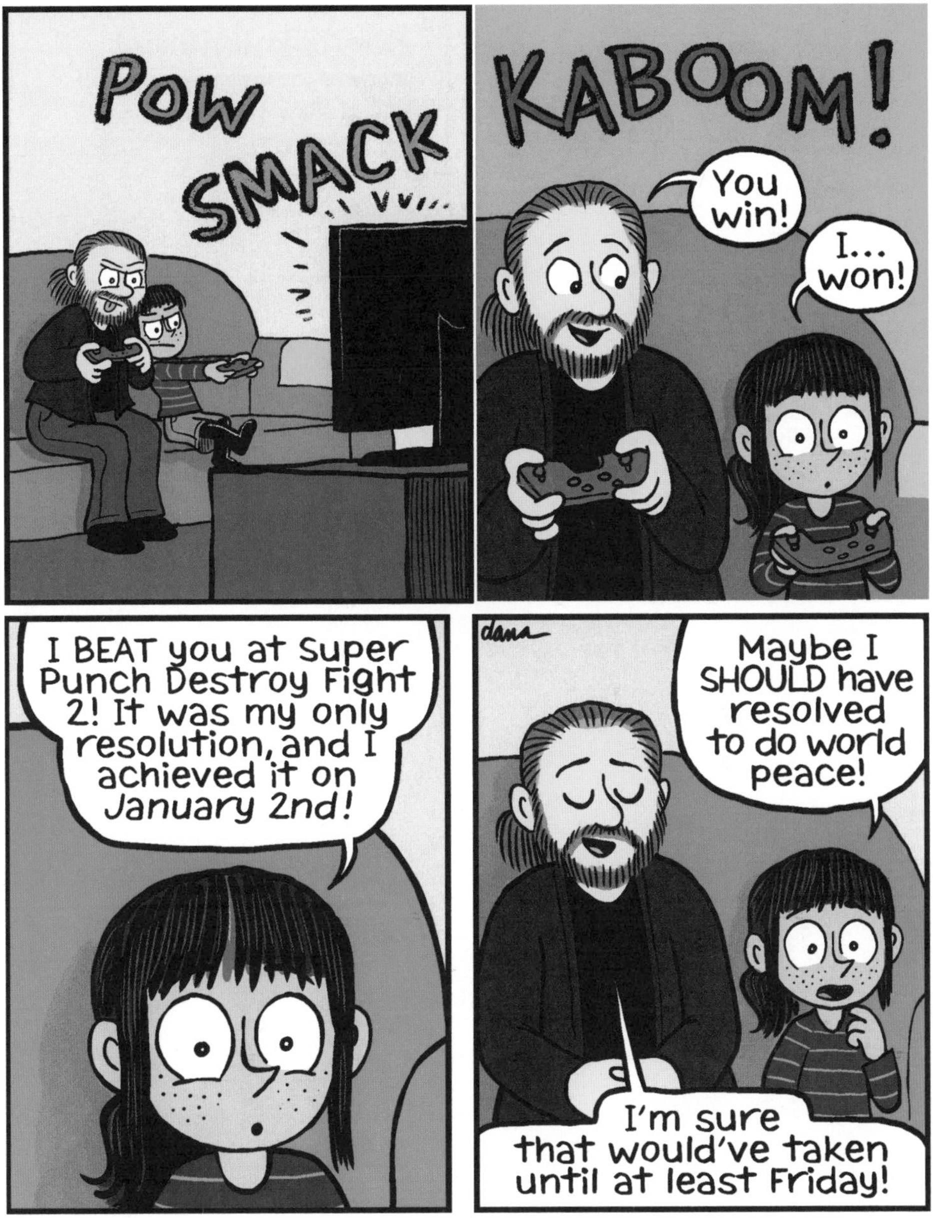
POW
SMACK
KABOOM!
You win!
I... won!
I BEAT you at Super Punch Destroy Fight 2! It was my only resolution, and I achieved it on January 2nd!
dana
Maybe I SHOULD have resolved to do world peace!
I'm sure that would've taken until at least Friday!

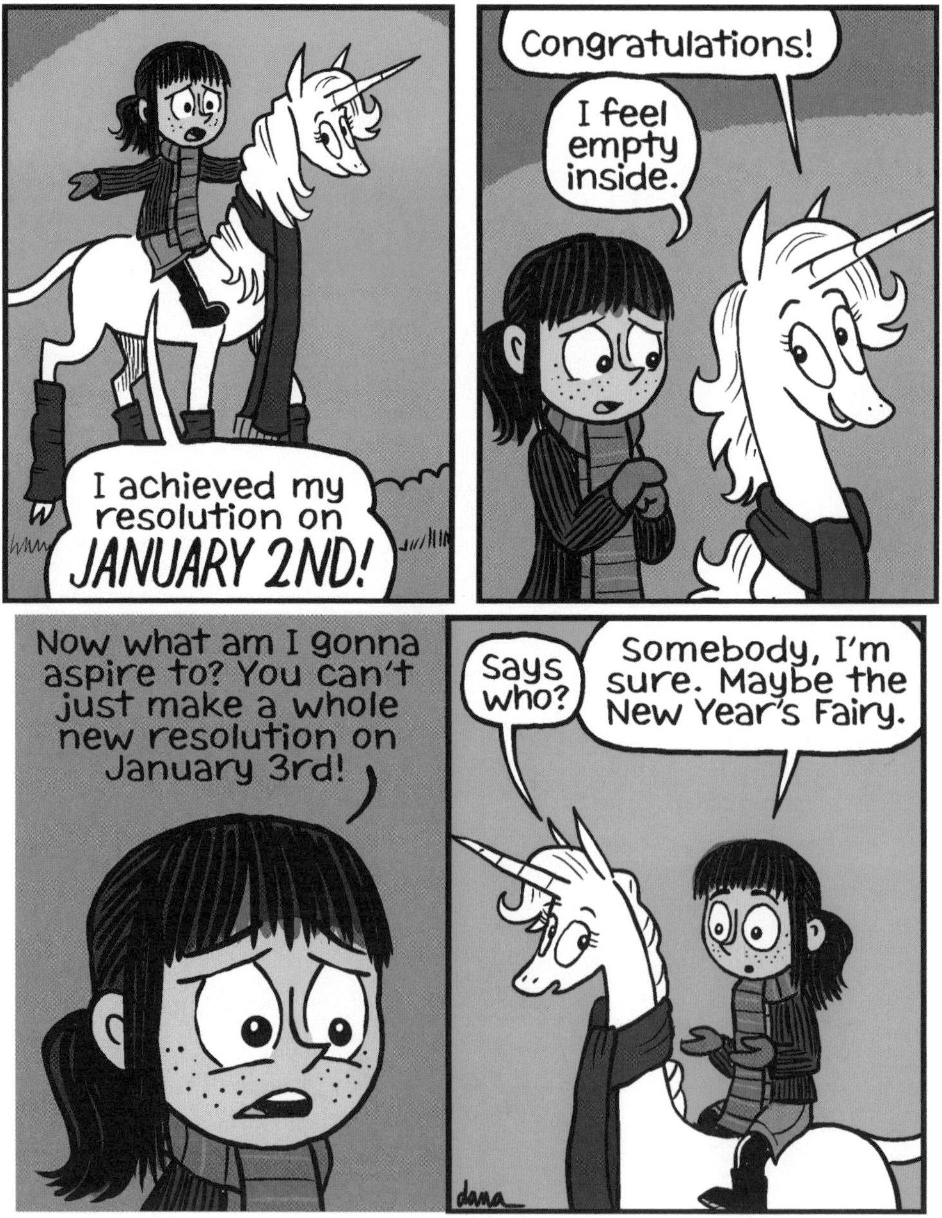
I achieved my resolution on JANUARY 2ND!
Congratulations!
I feel empty inside.
Now what am I gonna aspire to? You can't just make a whole new resolution on January 3rd!
Says who?
Somebody, I'm sure. Maybe the New Year's Fairy.
dana

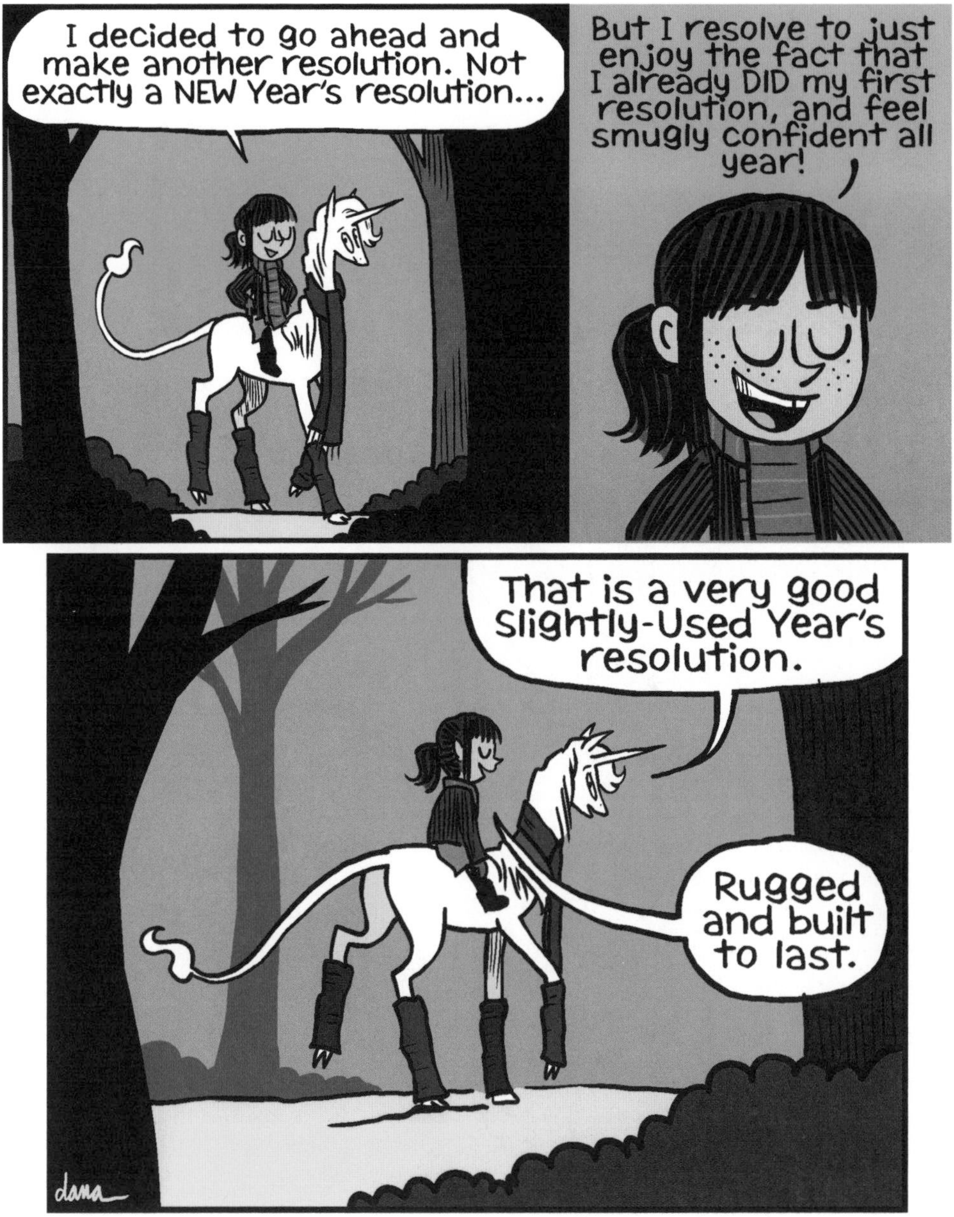
I decided to go ahead and make another resolution. Not exactly a NEW Year's resolution...
But I resolve to just enjoy the fact that I already DID my first resolution, and feel smugly confident all year!
That is a very good Slightly-Used Year's resolution.
Rugged and built to last.
dana

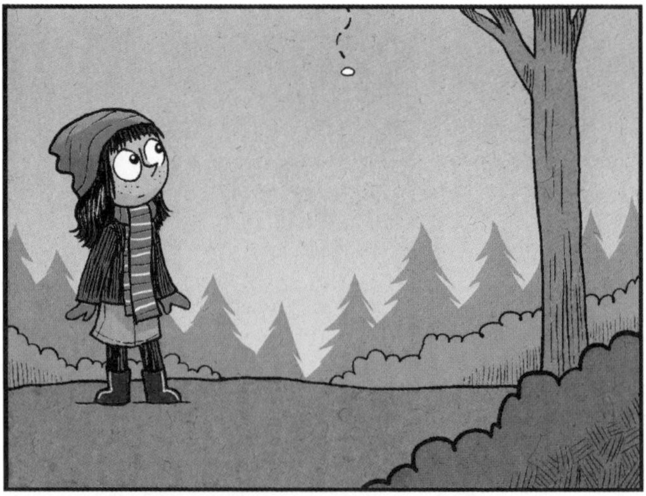

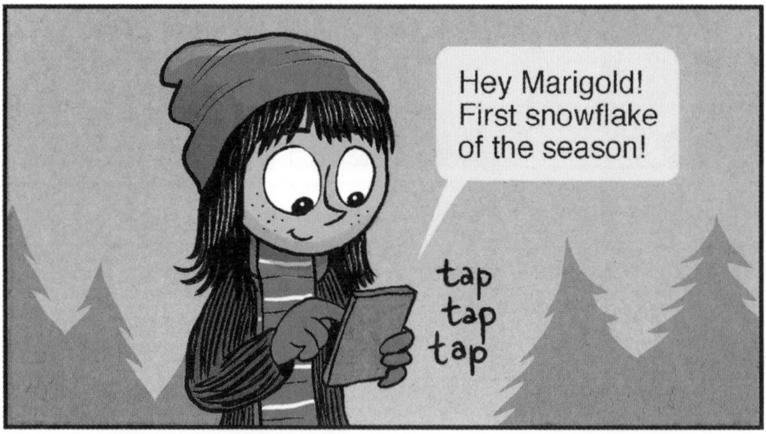
Hey Marigold! First snowflake of the season!
tap tap tap

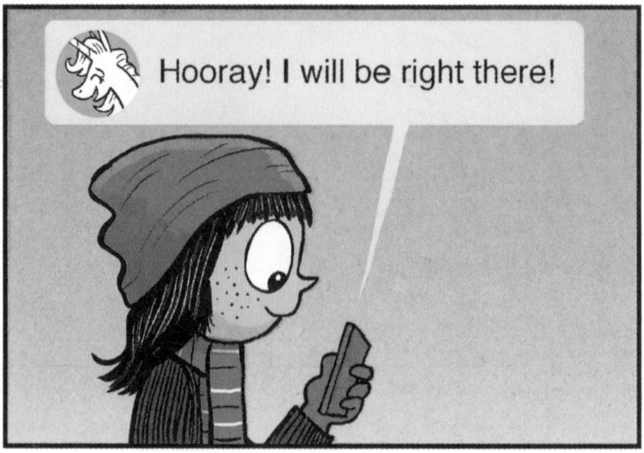
Hooray! I will be right there!

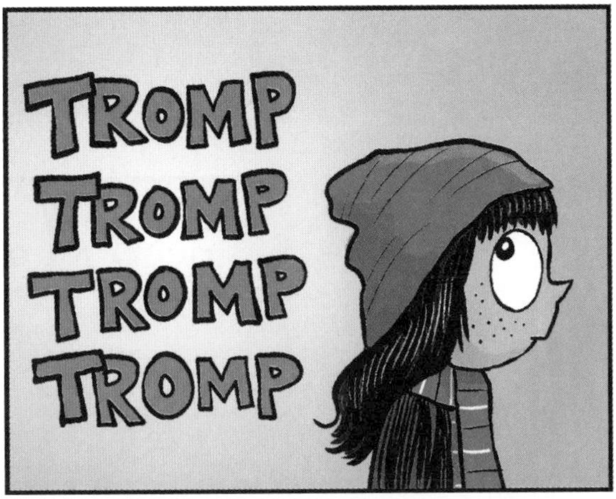
TROMP
TROMP
TROMP
TROMP

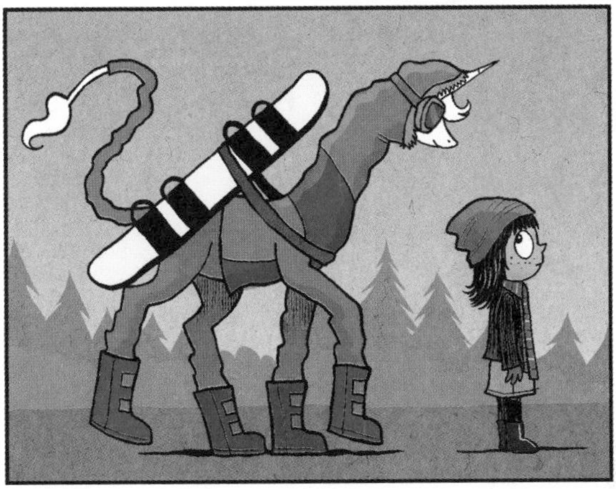

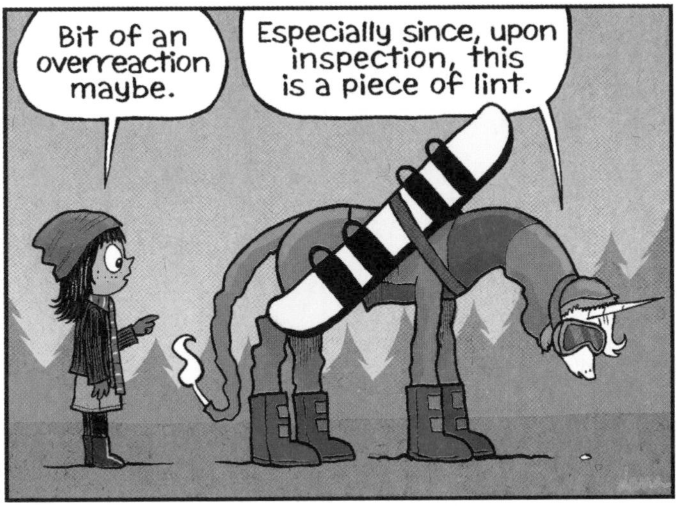
Bit of an overreaction maybe.
Especially since, upon inspection, this is a piece of lint.

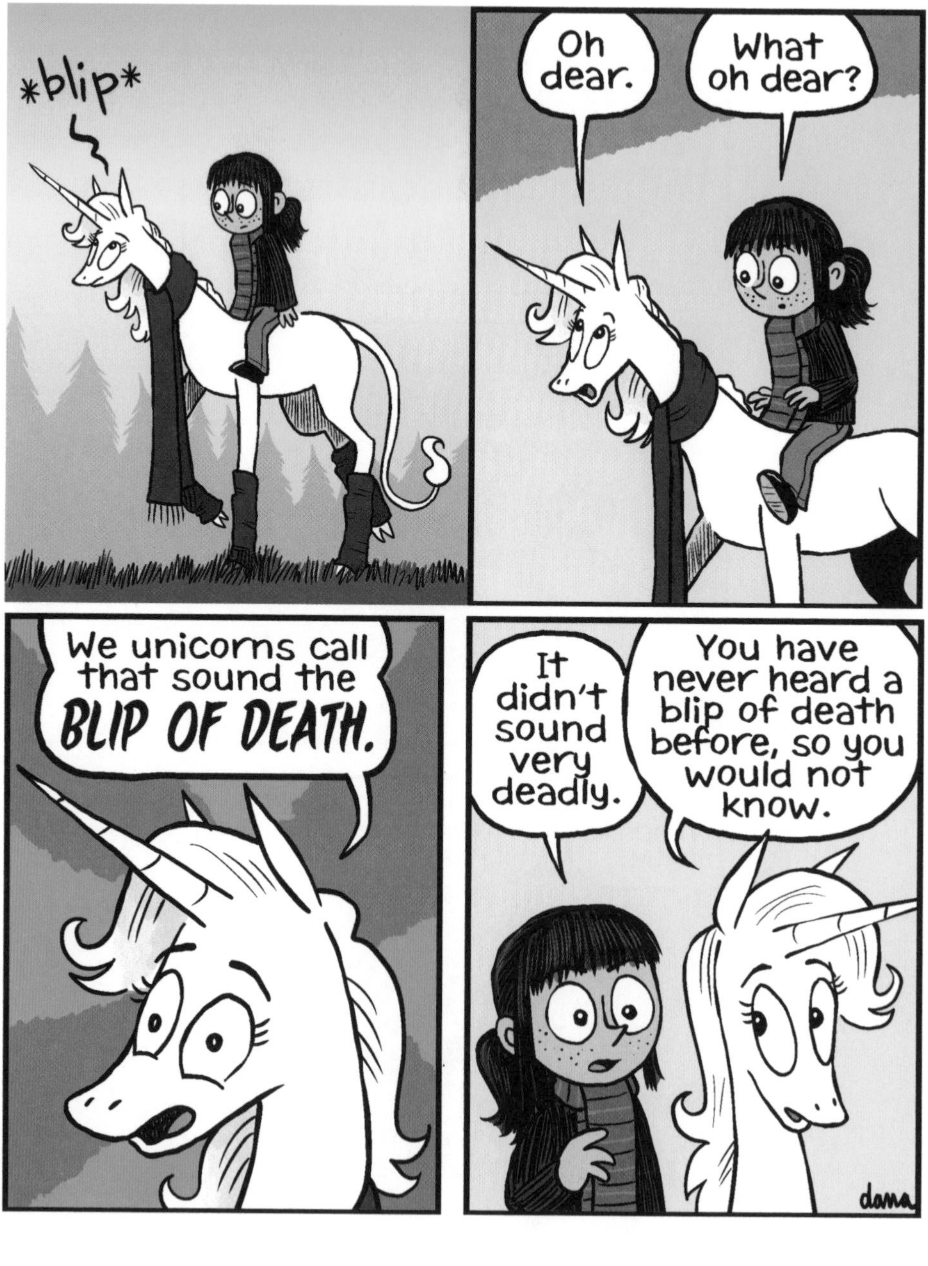
blip
Oh dear.
What oh dear?
We unicorns call that sound the BLIP OF DEATH.
It didn't sound very deadly.
You have never heard a blip of death before, so you would not know.
dana

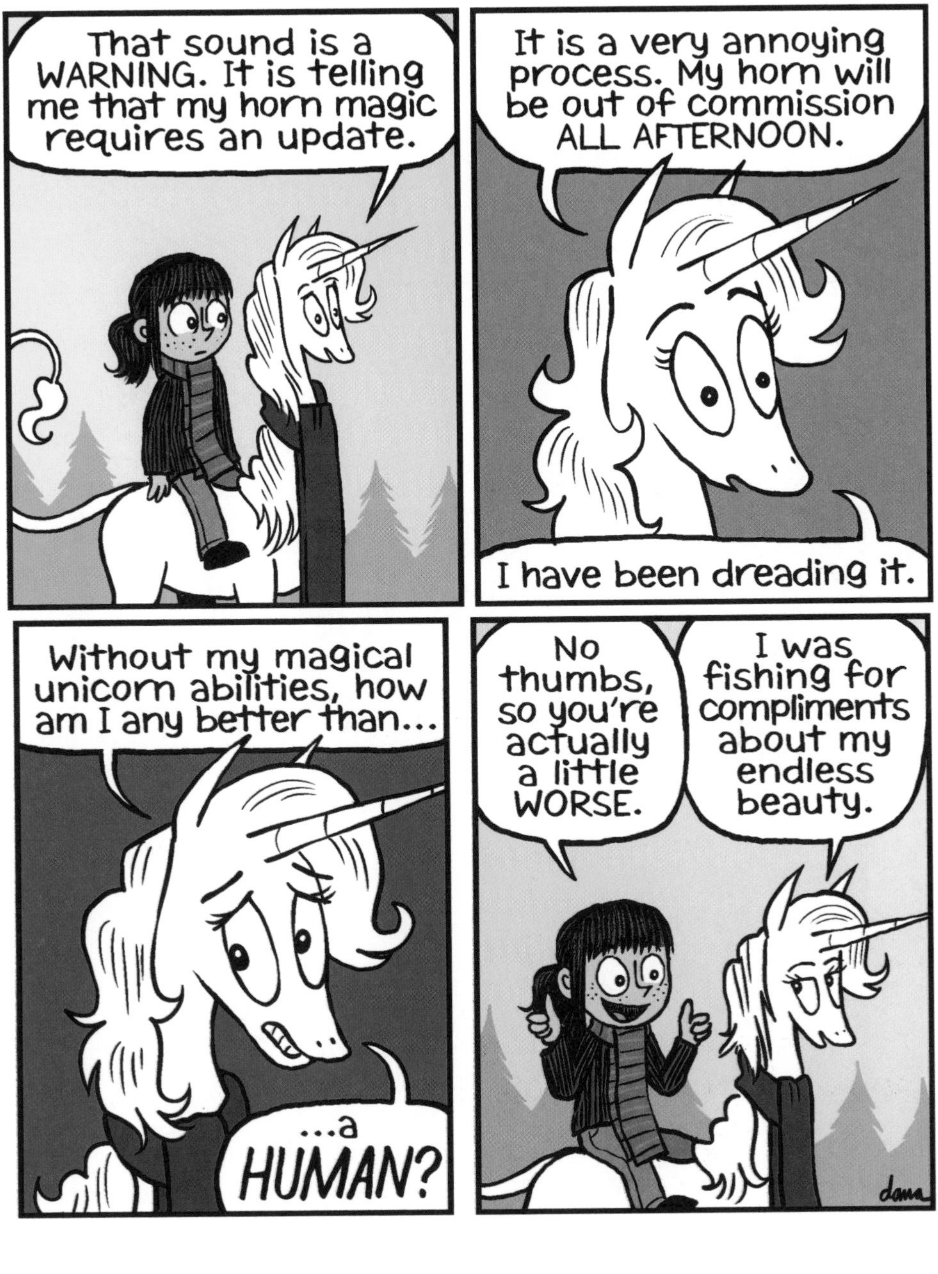
That sound is a WARNING. It is telling me that my horn magic requires an update.
It is a very annoying process. My horn will be out of commission ALL AFTERNOON.
I have been dreading it.
Without my magical unicorn abilities, how am I any better than...
...a HUMAN?
No thumbs, so you're actually a little WORSE.
I was fishing for compliments about my endless beauty.
dana

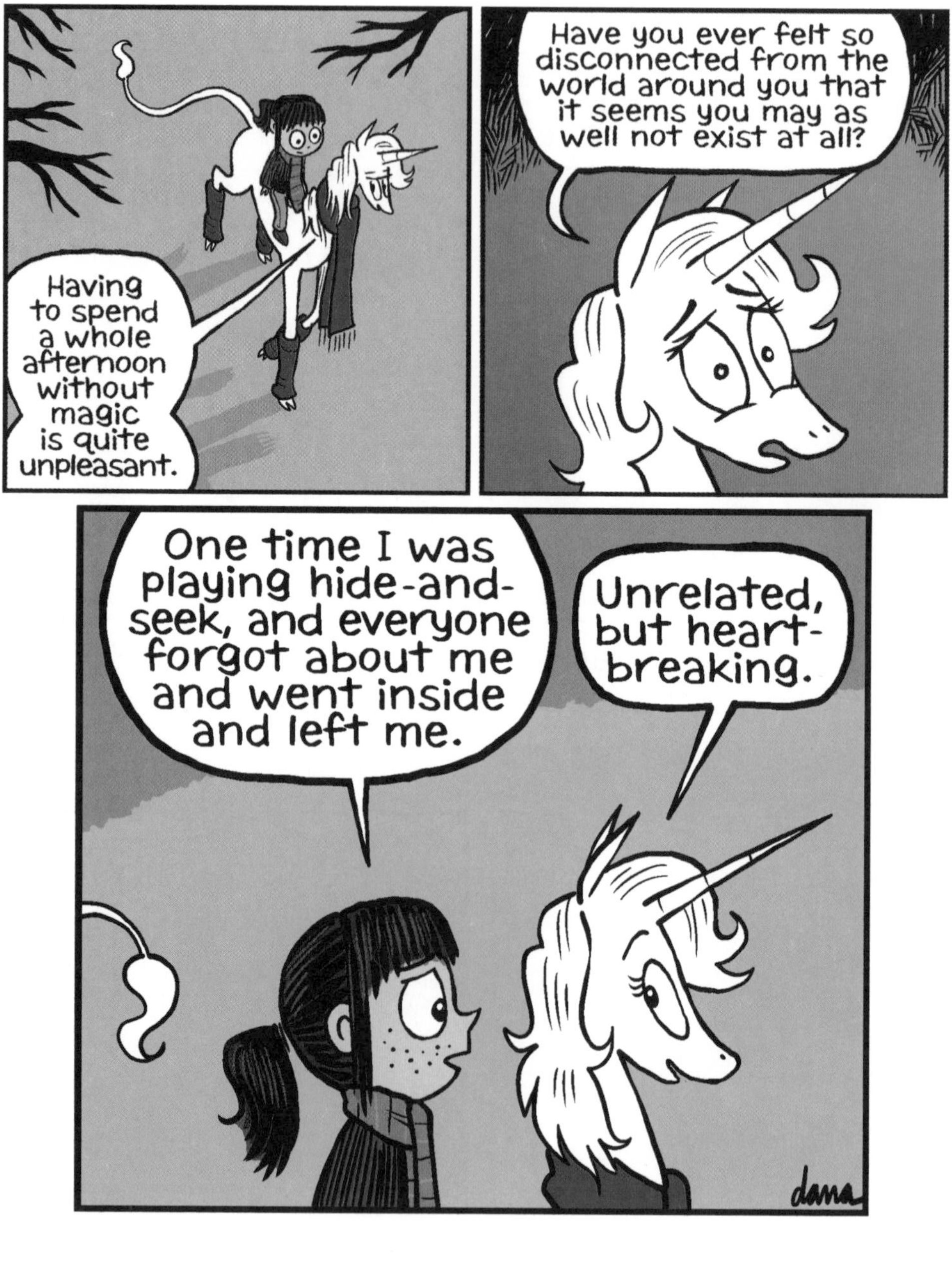
Having to spend a whole afternoon without magic is quite unpleasant.
Have you ever felt so disconnected from the world around you that it seems you may as well not exist at all?
One time I was playing hide-and-seek, and everyone forgot about me and went inside and left me.
Unrelated, but heart-breaking.
dana

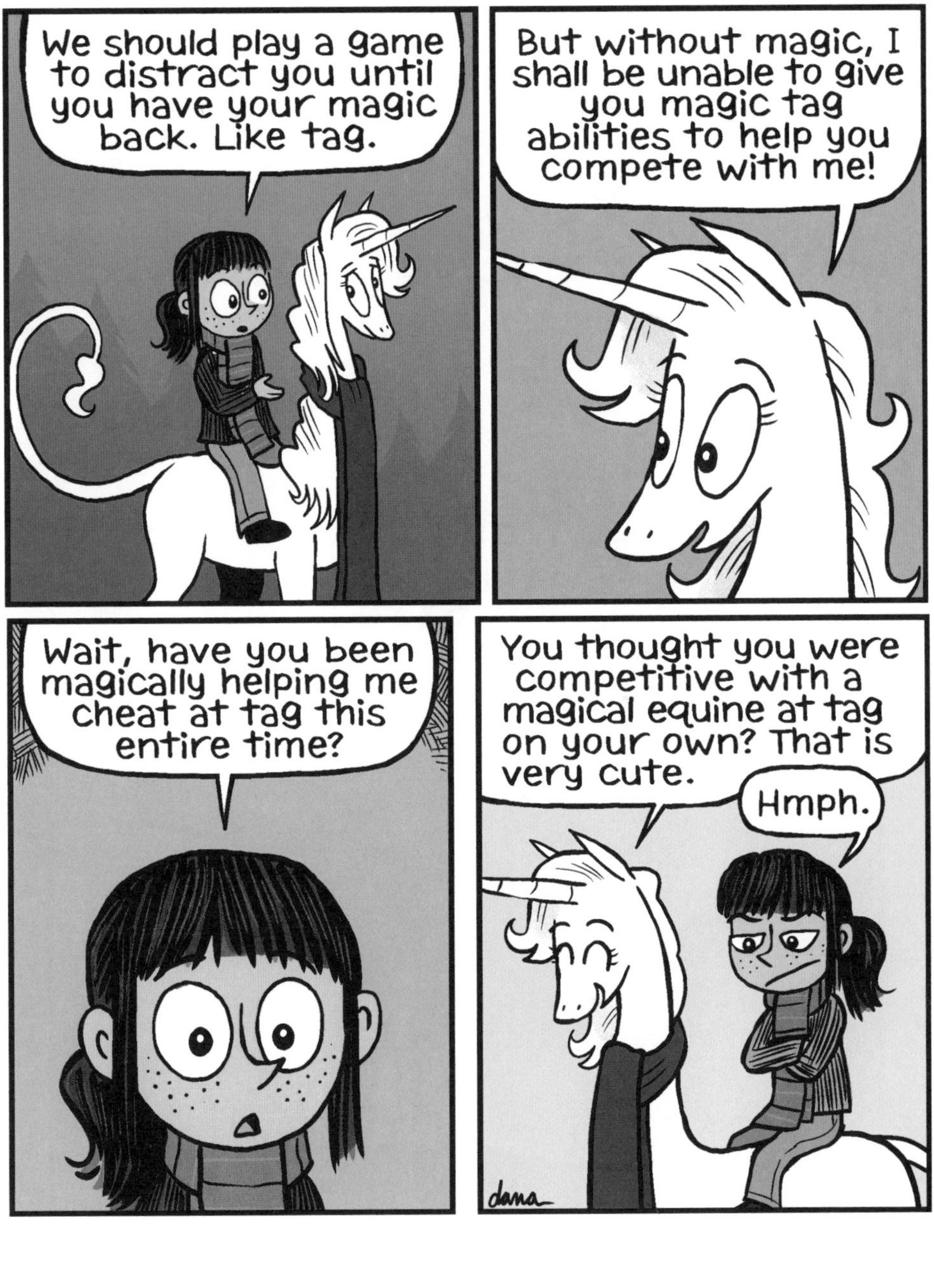
We should play a game to distract you until you have your magic back. Like tag.
But without magic, I shall be unable to give you magic tag abilities to help you compete with me!
Wait, have you been magically helping me cheat at tag this entire time?
You thought you were competitive with a magical equine at tag on your own? That is very cute.
Hmph.
dana

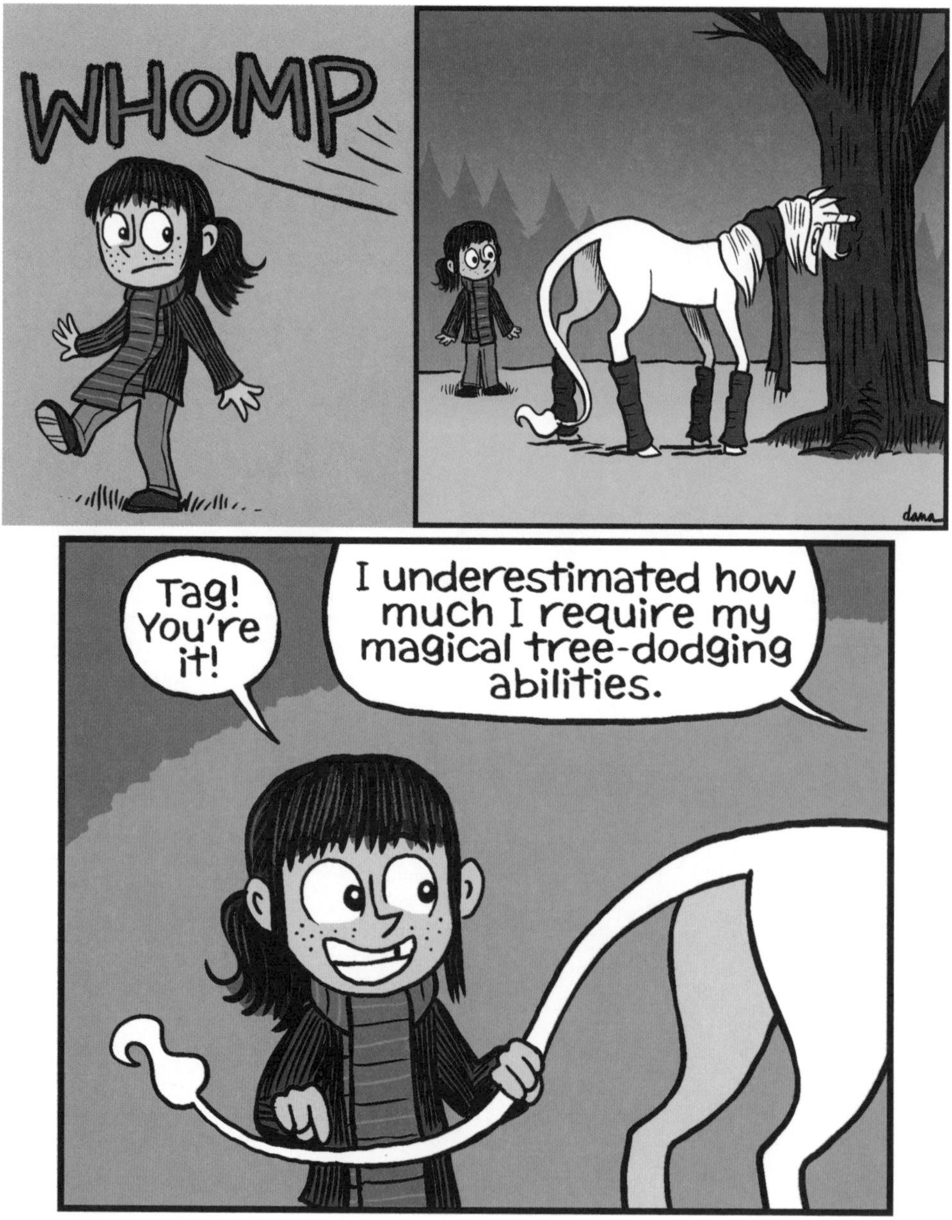
WHOMP
dana
Tag! You're it!
I underestimated how much I require my magical tree-dodging abilities.

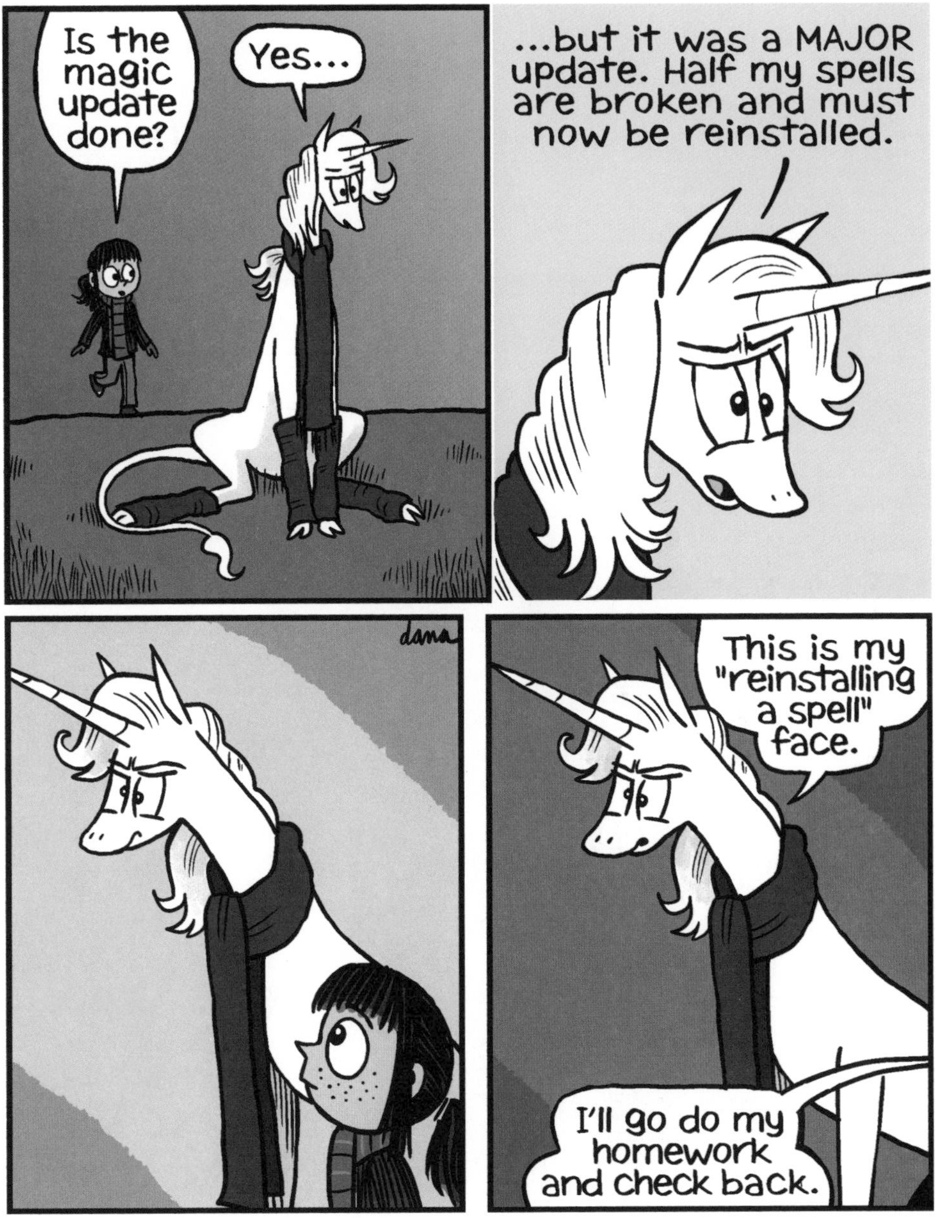
Is the magic update done?
Yes...
...but it was a MAJOR update. Half my spells are broken and must now be reinstalled.
dana
This is my "reinstalling a spell" face.
I'll go do my homework and check back.

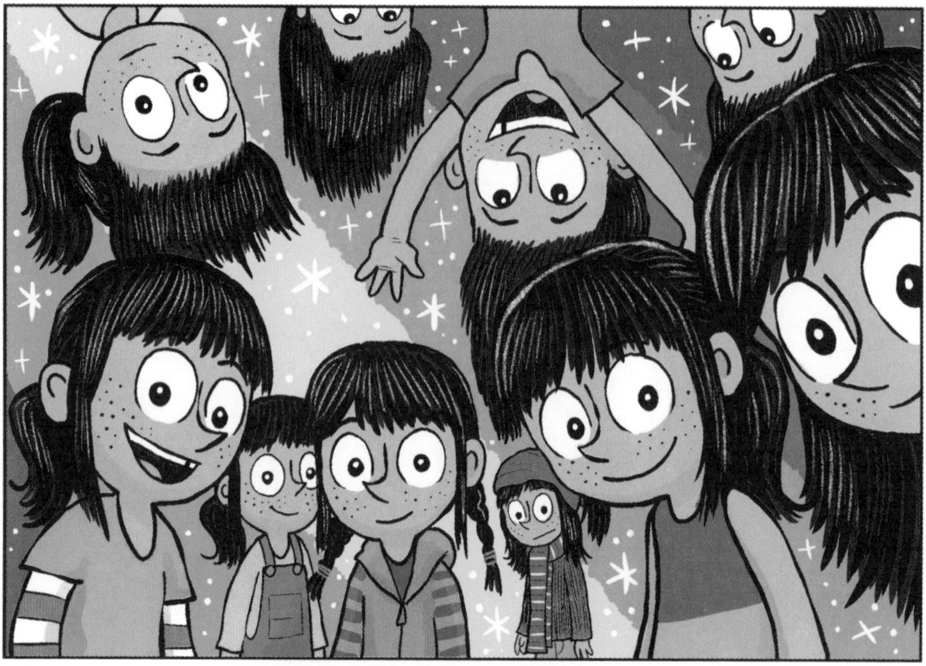

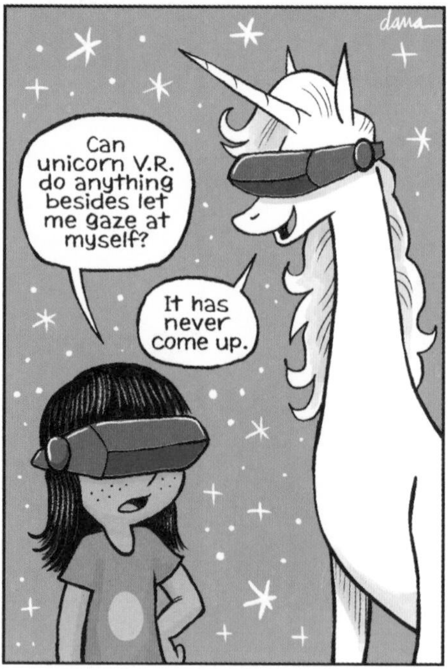
Can unicorn V.R. do anything besides let me gaze at myself?
It has never come up.

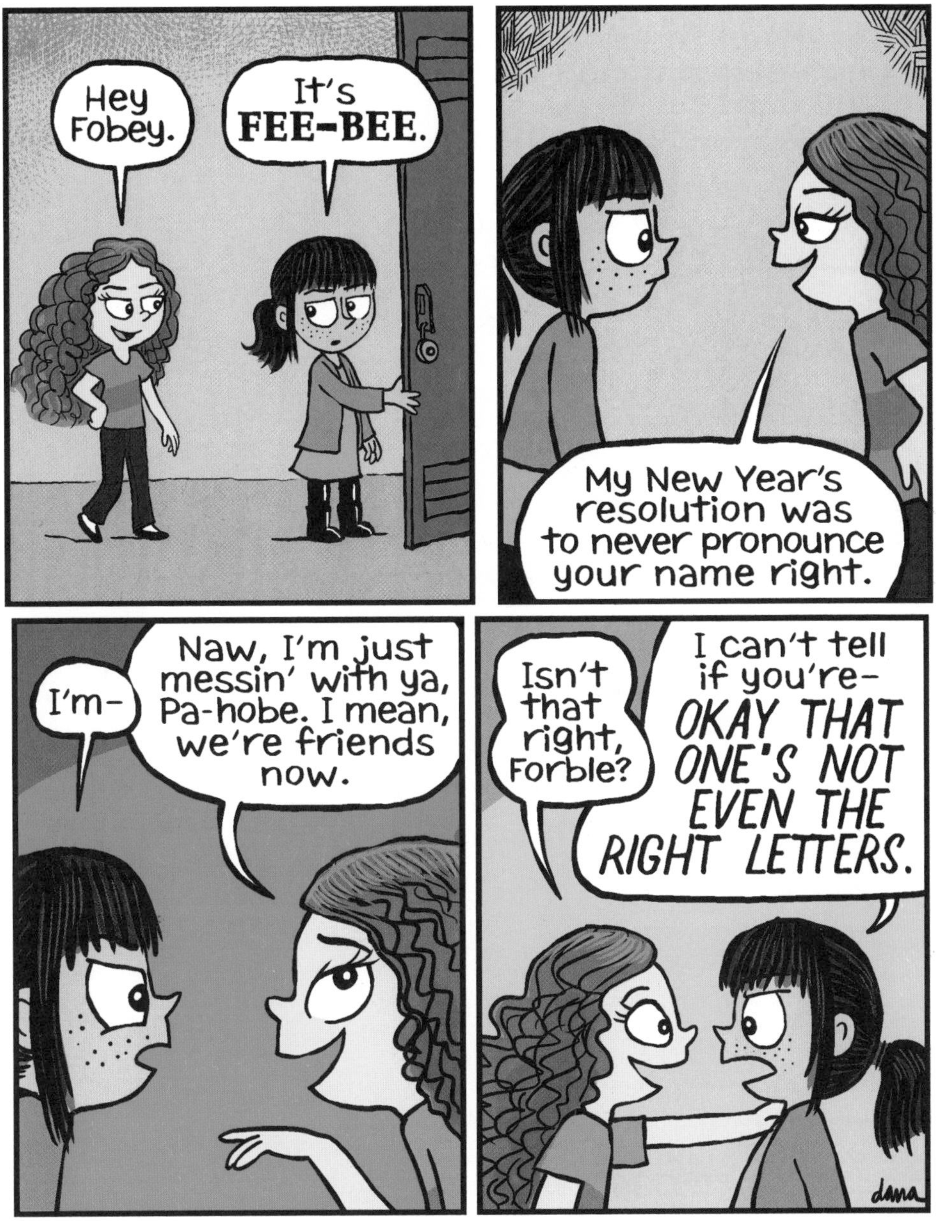
Hey Fobey.
It's **FEE-BEE**.
My New Year's resolution was to never pronounce your name right.
I'm-
Naw, I'm just messin' with ya, Pa-hobe. I mean, we're friends now.
Isn't that right, Forble?
I can't tell if you're- OKAY THAT ONE'S NOT EVEN THE RIGHT LETTERS.
dana

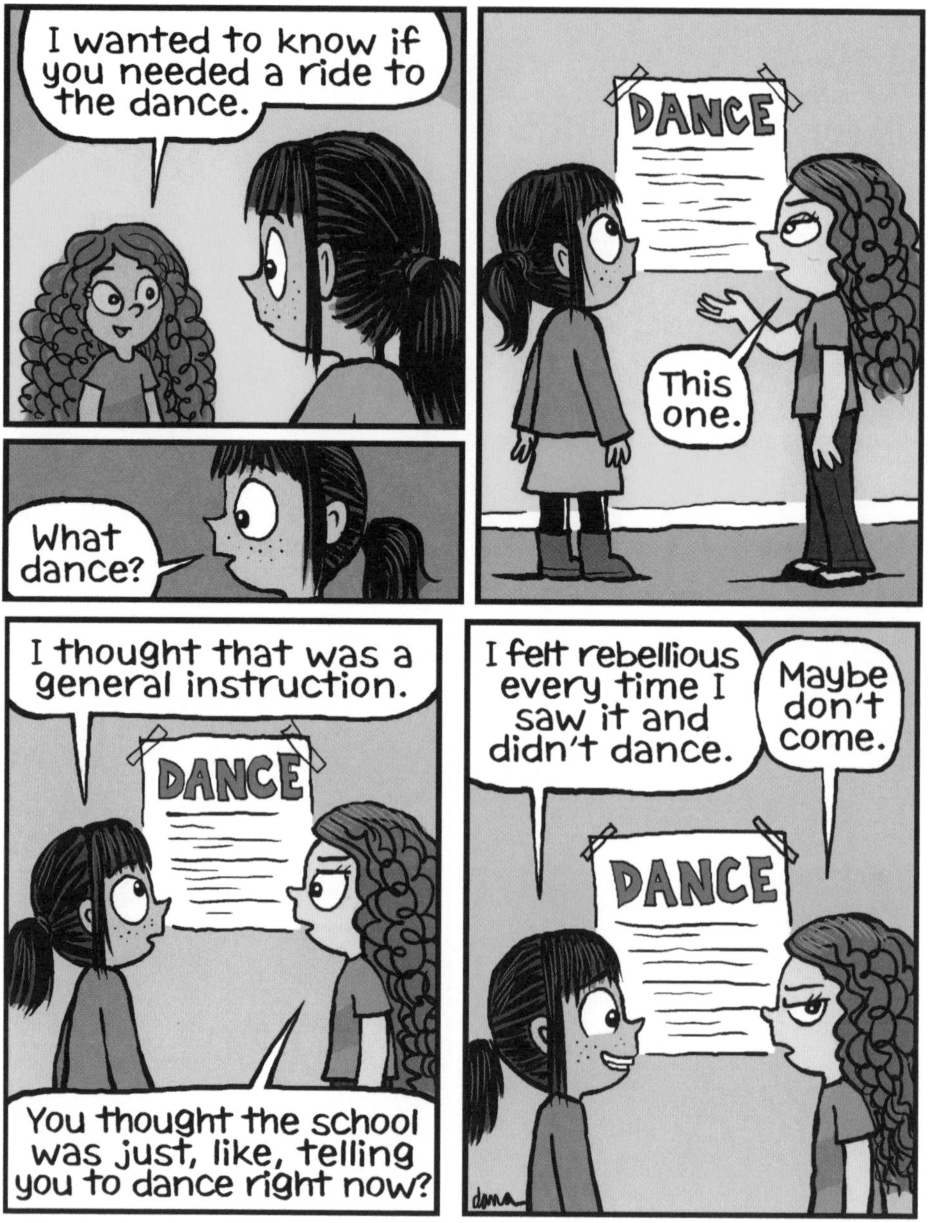
I wanted to know if you needed a ride to the dance.
What dance?
DANCE
This one.
I thought that was a general instruction.
DANCE
You thought the school was just, like, telling you to dance right now?
I felt rebellious every time I saw it and didn't dance.
Maybe don't come.
DANCE
dana

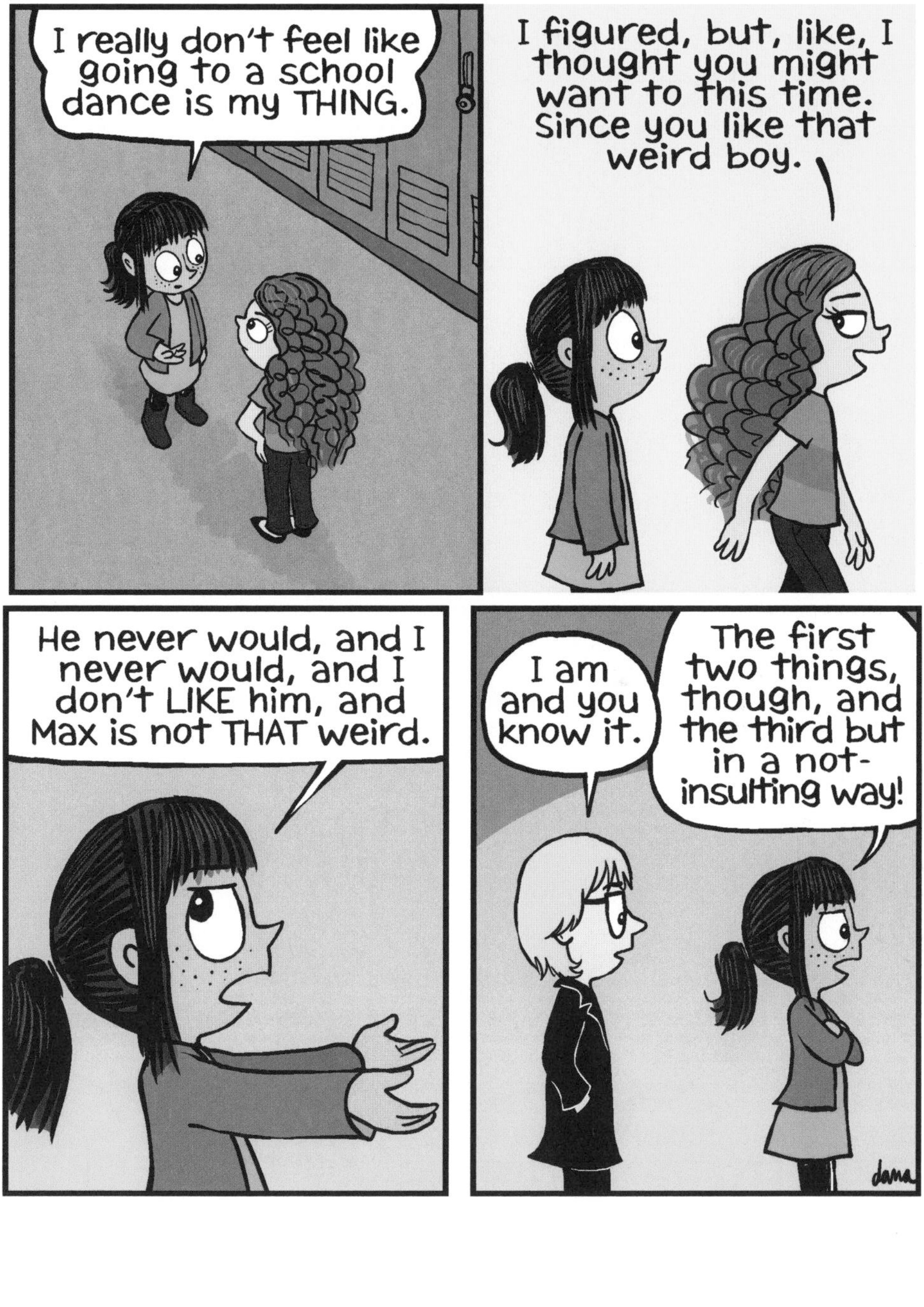
I really don't feel like going to a school dance is my THING.
I figured, but, like, I thought you might want to this time. Since you like that weird boy.
He never would, and I never would, and I don't LIKE him, and Max is not THAT weird.
I am and you know it.
The first two things, though, and the third but in a not-insulting way!
dana

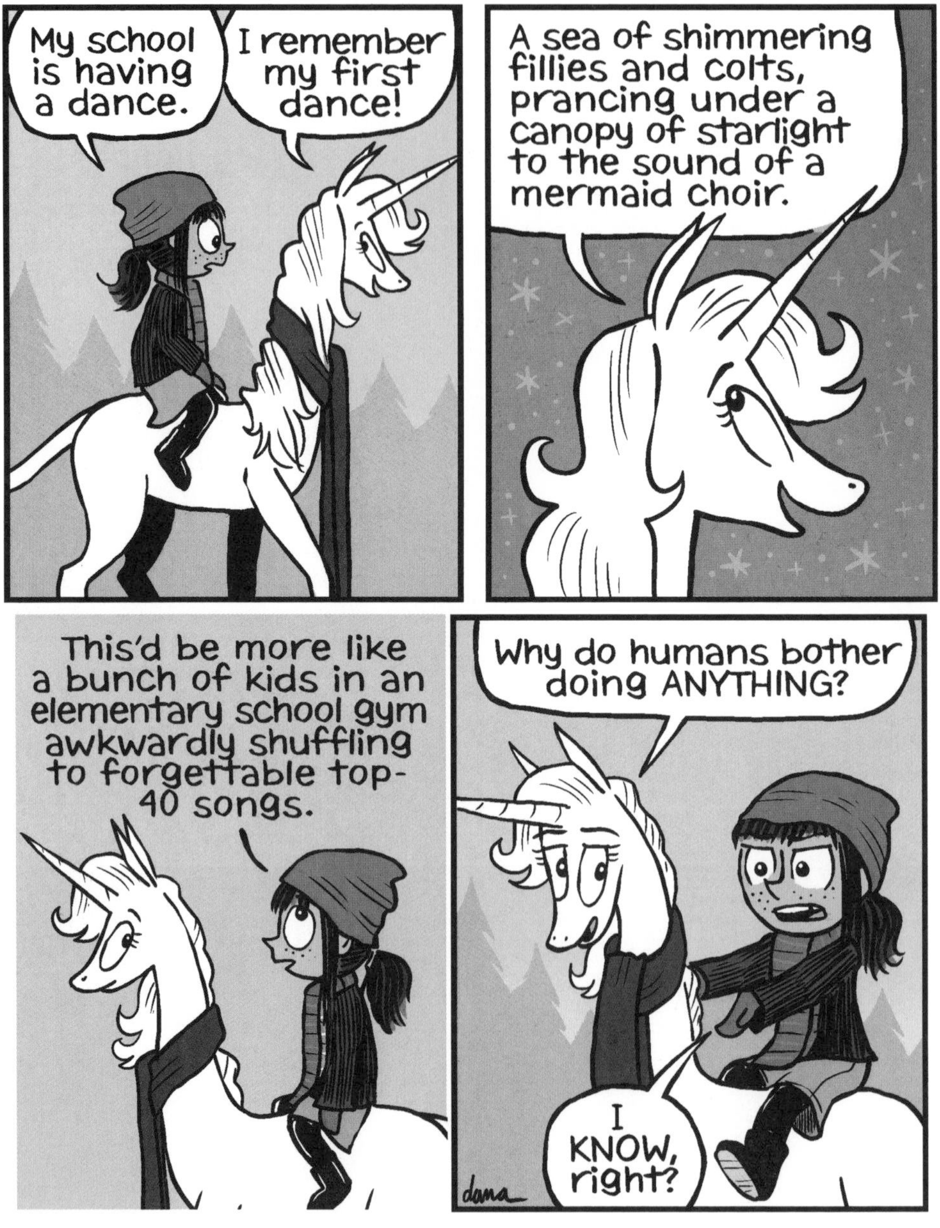
My school is having a dance.
I remember my first dance!
A sea of shimmering fillies and colts, prancing under a canopy of starlight to the sound of a mermaid choir.
This'd be more like a bunch of kids in an elementary school gym awkwardly shuffling to forgettable top-40 songs.
Why do humans bother doing ANYTHING?
I KNOW, right?
dana

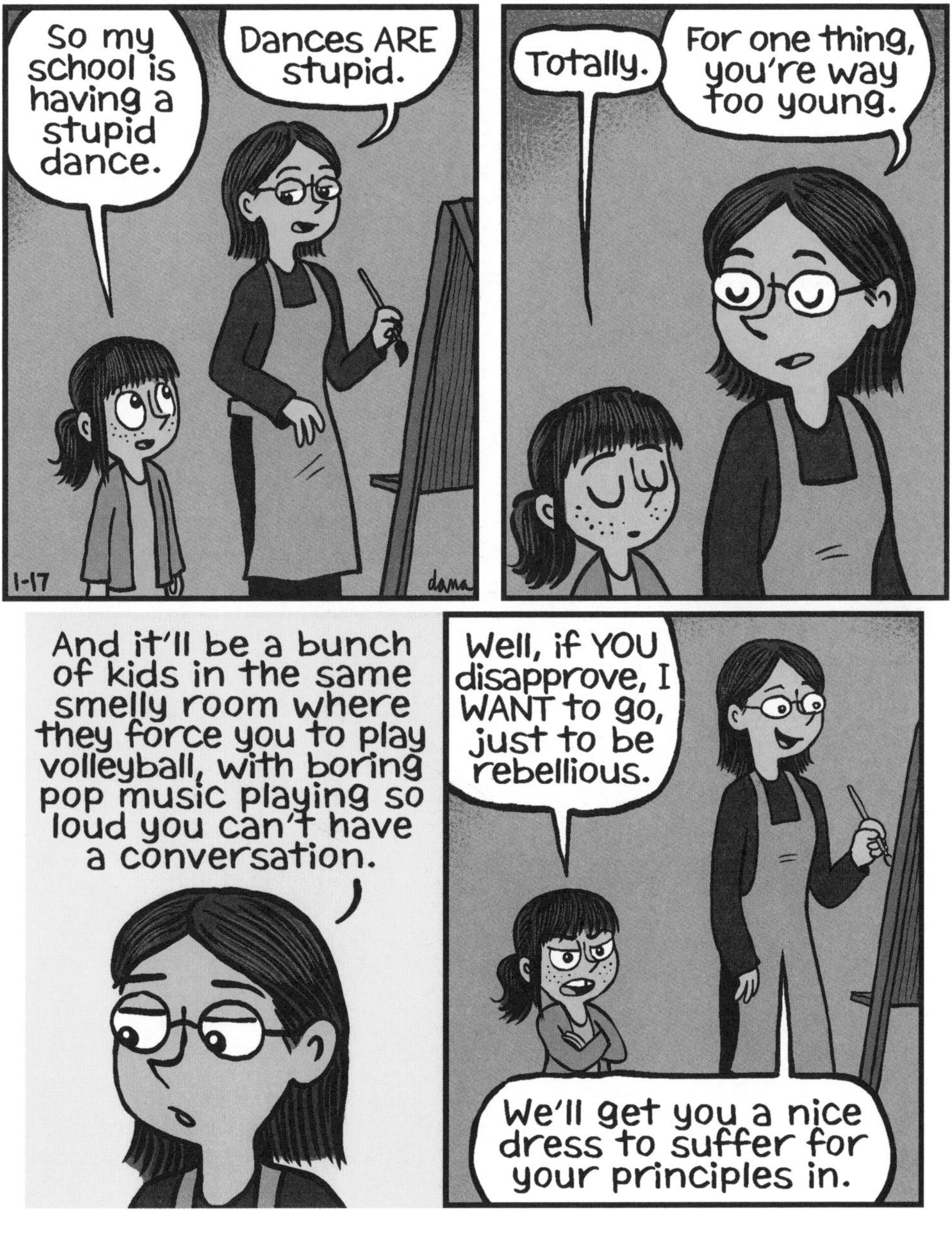
So my school is having a stupid dance.
Dances ARE stupid.
1-17
dama
Totally.
For one thing, you're way too young.
And it'll be a bunch of kids in the same smelly room where they force you to play volleyball, with boring pop music playing so loud you can't have a conversation.
Well, if YOU disapprove, I WANT to go, just to be rebellious.
We'll get you a nice dress to suffer for your principles in.

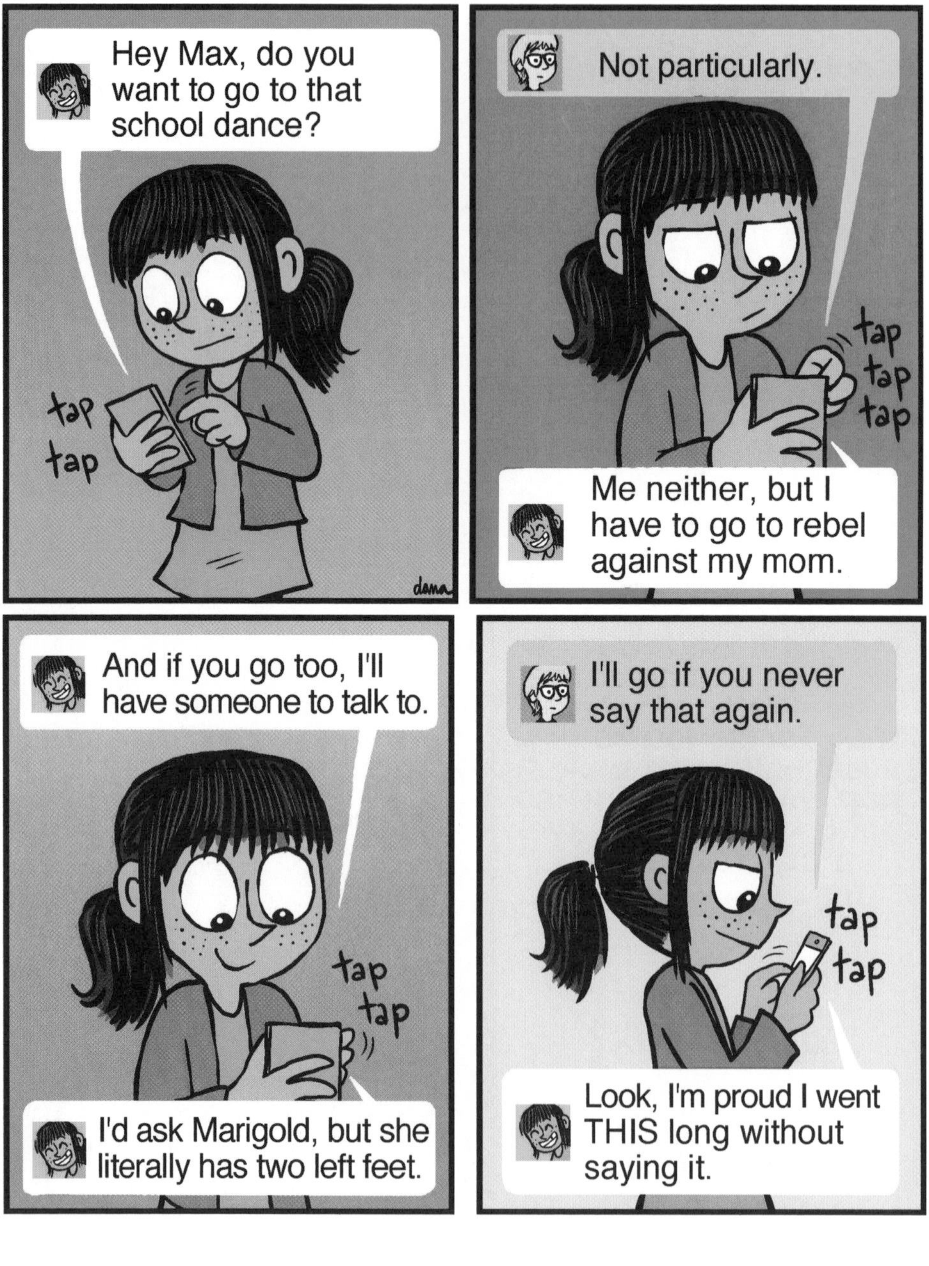
Hey Max, do you want to go to that school dance?
tap tap
dana
Not particularly.
tap tap tap
Me neither, but I have to go to rebel against my mom.
And if you go too, I'll have someone to talk to.
tap tap
I'd ask Marigold, but she literally has two left feet.
I'll go if you never say that again.
tap tap
Look, I'm proud I went THIS long without saying it.

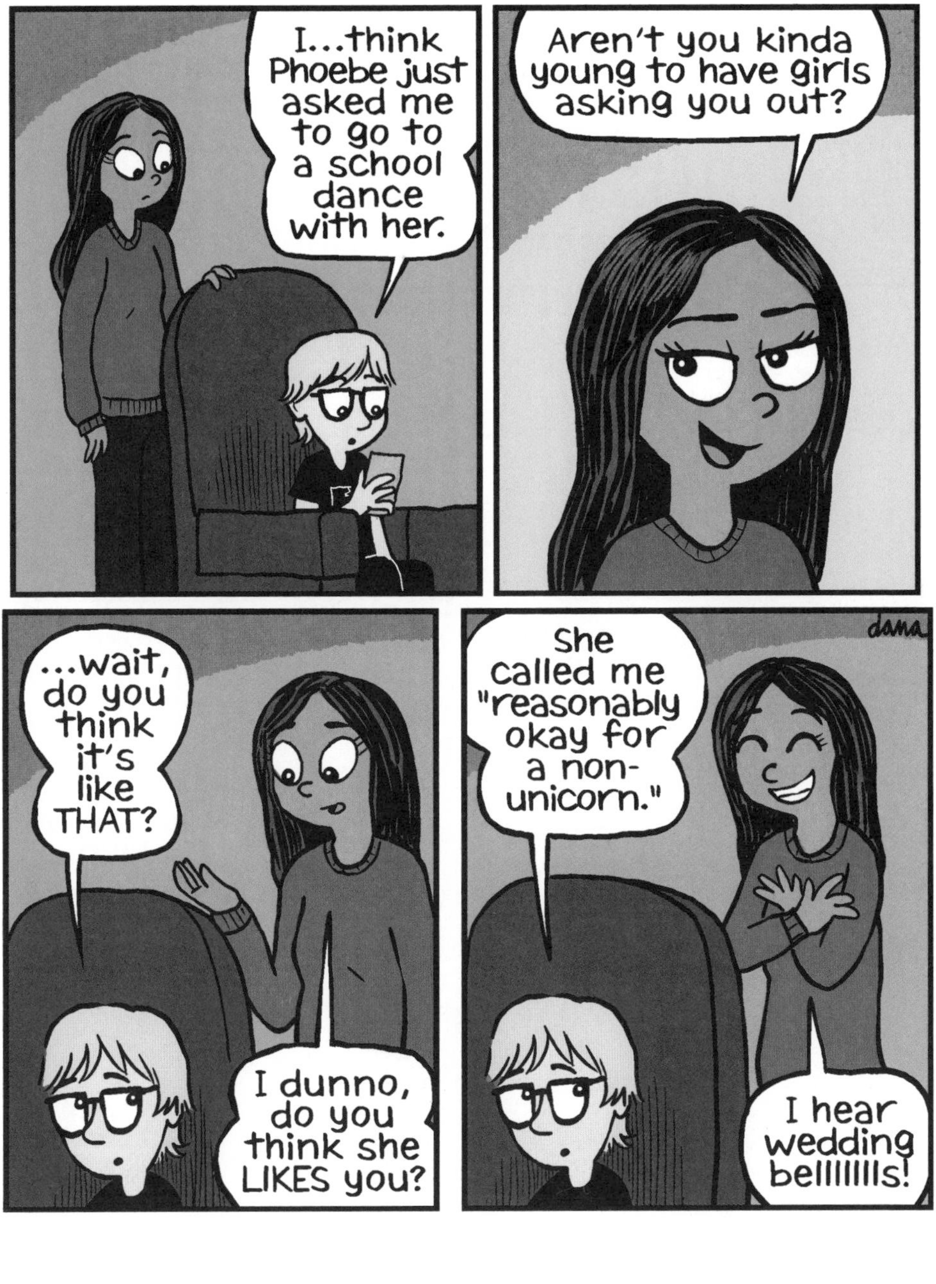
I...think Phoebe just asked me to go to a school dance with her.
Aren't you kinda young to have girls asking you out?
...wait, do you think it's like THAT?
I dunno, do you think she LIKES you?
She called me "reasonably okay for a non-unicorn."
I hear wedding bellllllls!
dana

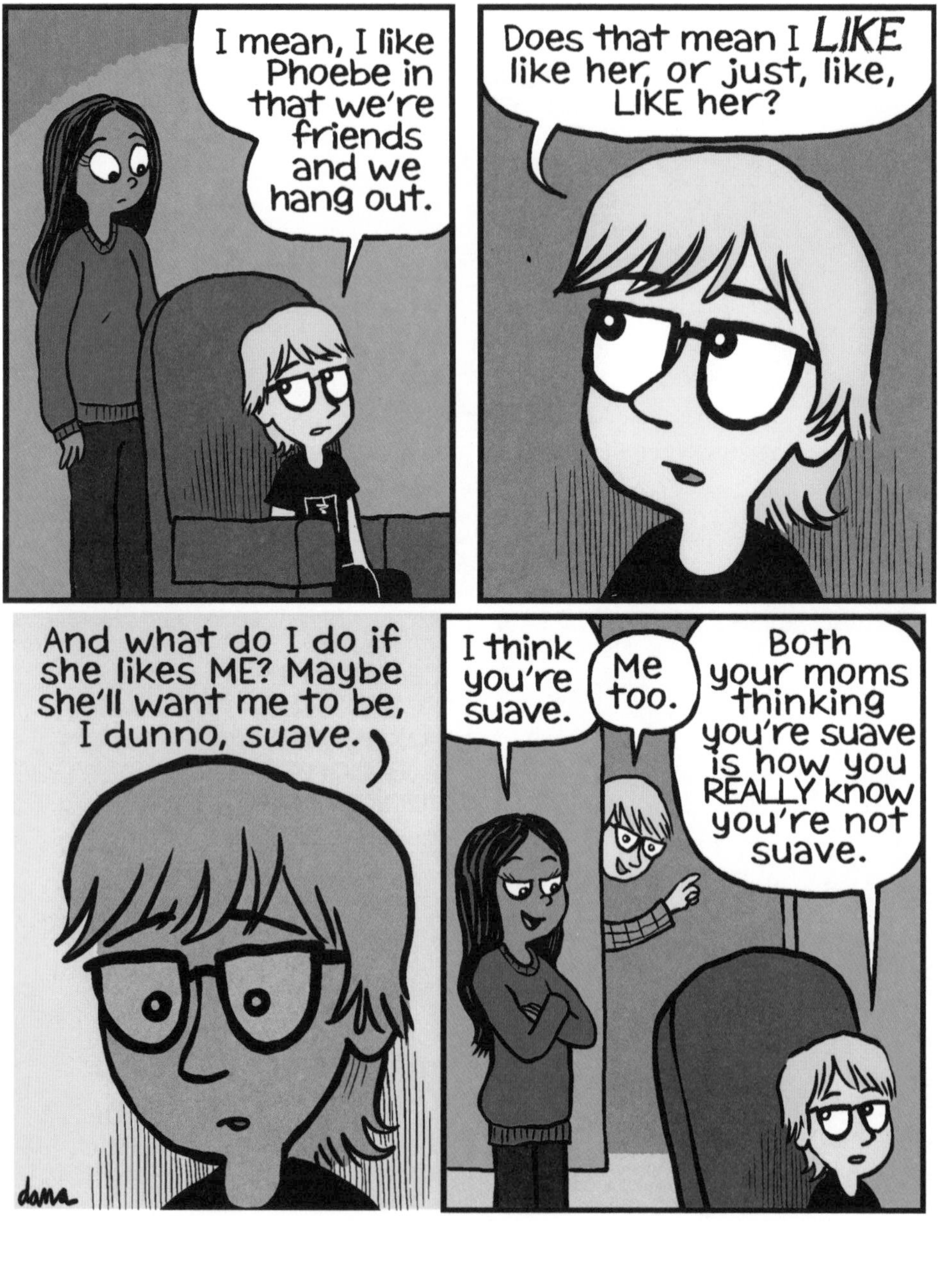
I mean, I like Phoebe in that we're friends and we hang out.
Does that mean I LIKE like her, or just, like, LIKE her?
And what do I do if she likes ME? Maybe she'll want me to be, I dunno, suave.
I think you're suave.
Me too.
Both your moms thinking you're suave is how you REALLY know you're not suave.
dana

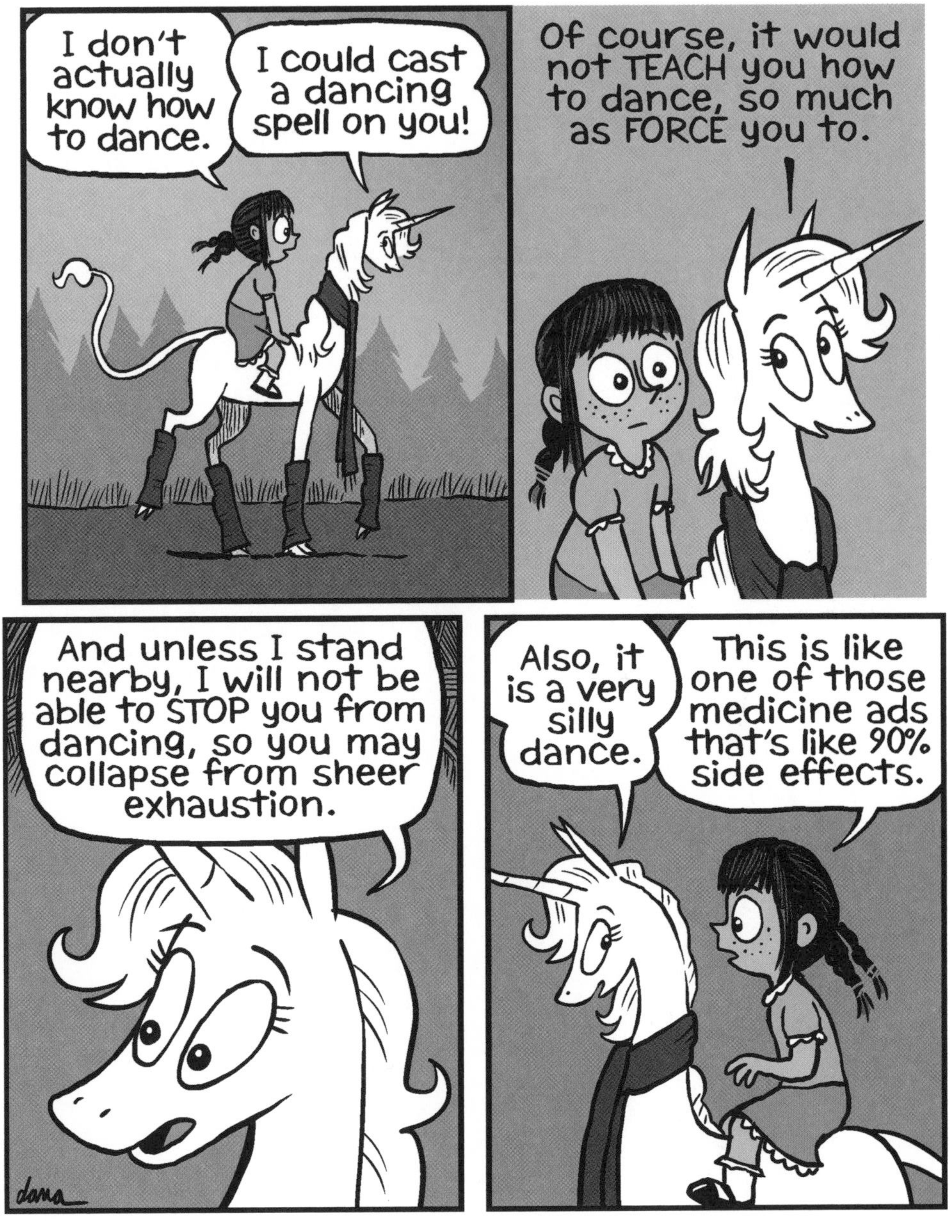
I don't actually know how to dance.
I could cast a dancing spell on you!
Of course, it would not TEACH you how to dance, so much as FORCE you to.
And unless I stand nearby, I will not be able to STOP you from dancing, so you may collapse from sheer exhaustion.
Also, it is a very silly dance.
This is like one of those medicine ads that's like 90% side effects.
dana

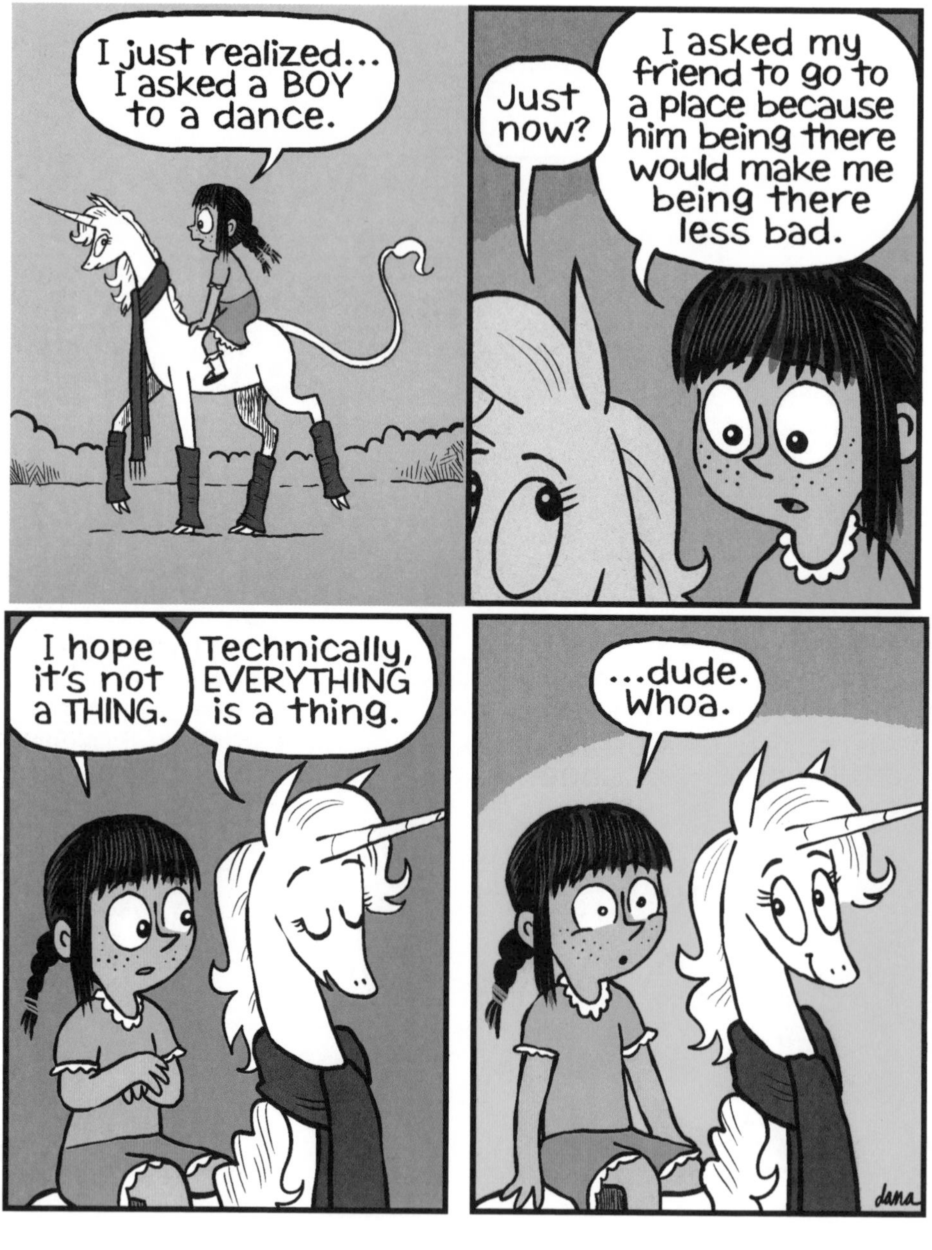
I just realized... I asked a BOY to a dance.
Just now?
I asked my friend to go to a place because him being there would make me being there less bad.
I hope it's not a THING.
Technically, EVERYTHING is a thing.
...dude. Whoa.
dana

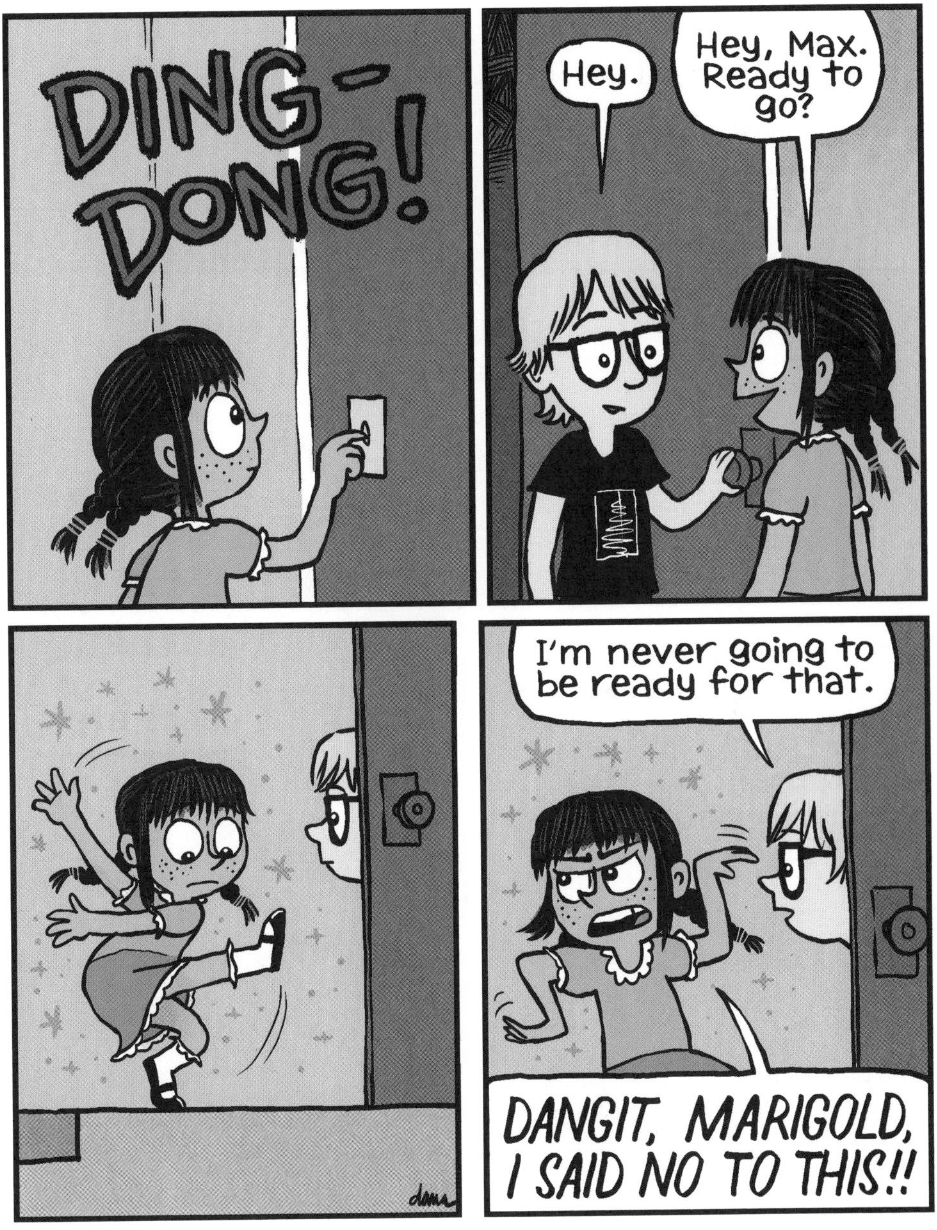
DING-DONG!
Hey.
Hey, Max. Ready to go?
I'm never going to be ready for that.
DANGIT, MARIGOLD, I SAID NO TO THIS!!

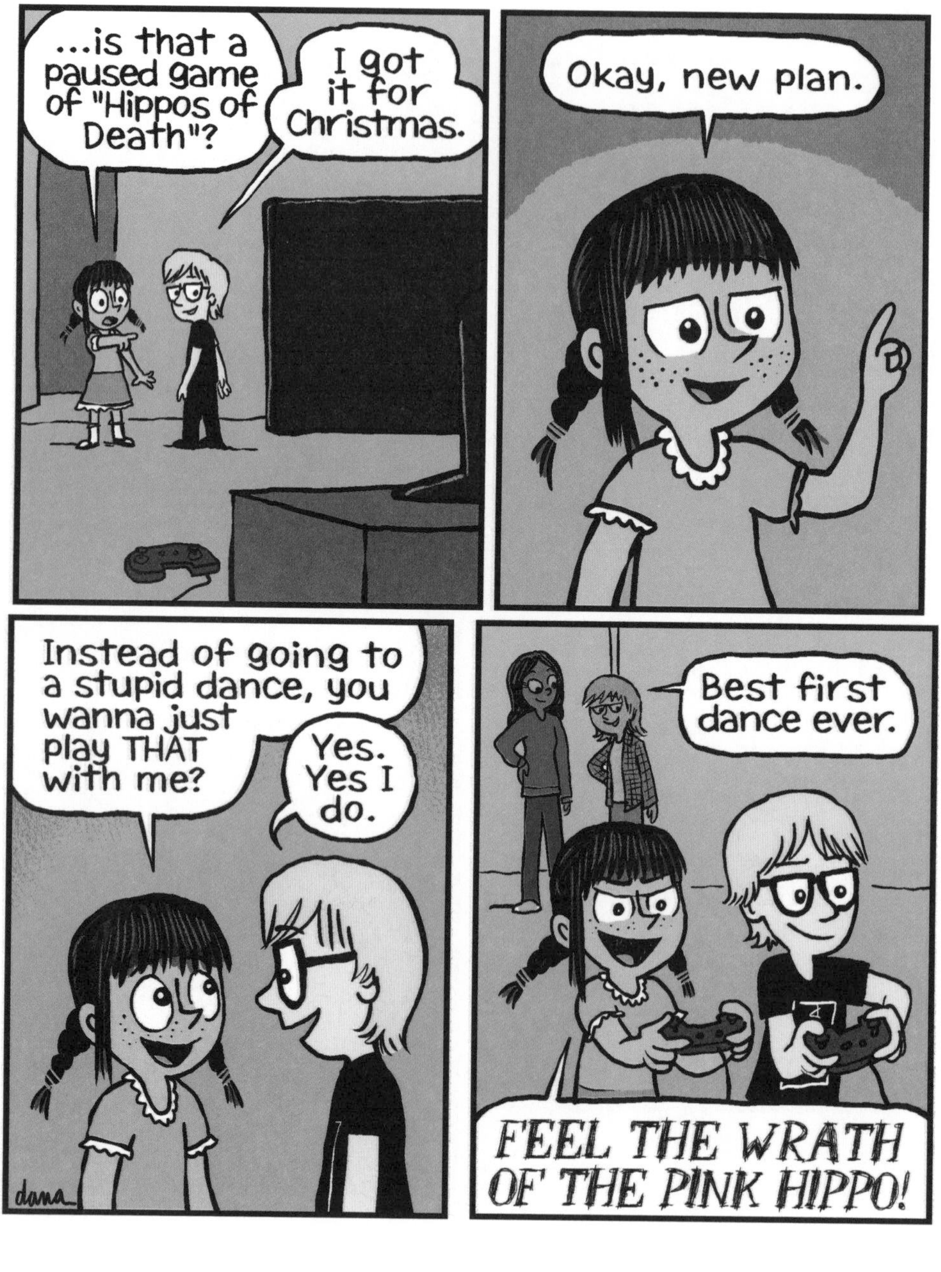
...is that a paused game of "Hippos of Death"?
I got it for Christmas.
Okay, new plan.
Instead of going to a stupid dance, you wanna just play THAT with me?
Yes. Yes I do.
dana
Best first dance ever.
FEEL THE WRATH OF THE PINK HIPPO!

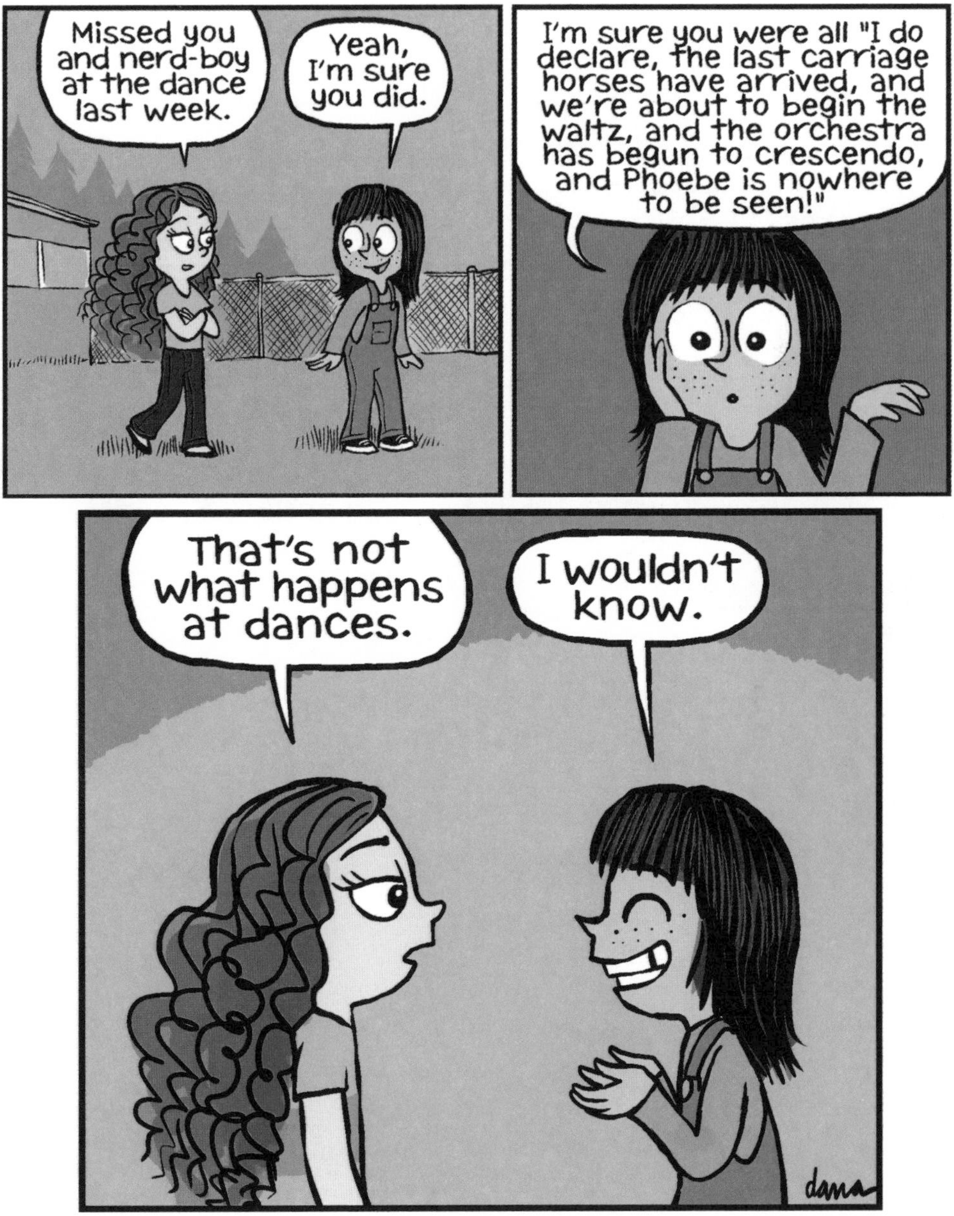
Missed you and nerd-boy at the dance last week.
Yeah, I'm sure you did.
I'm sure you were all "I do declare, the last carriage horses have arrived, and we're about to begin the waltz, and the orchestra has begun to crescendo, and Phoebe is nowhere to be seen!"
That's not what happens at dances.
I wouldn't know.
dana

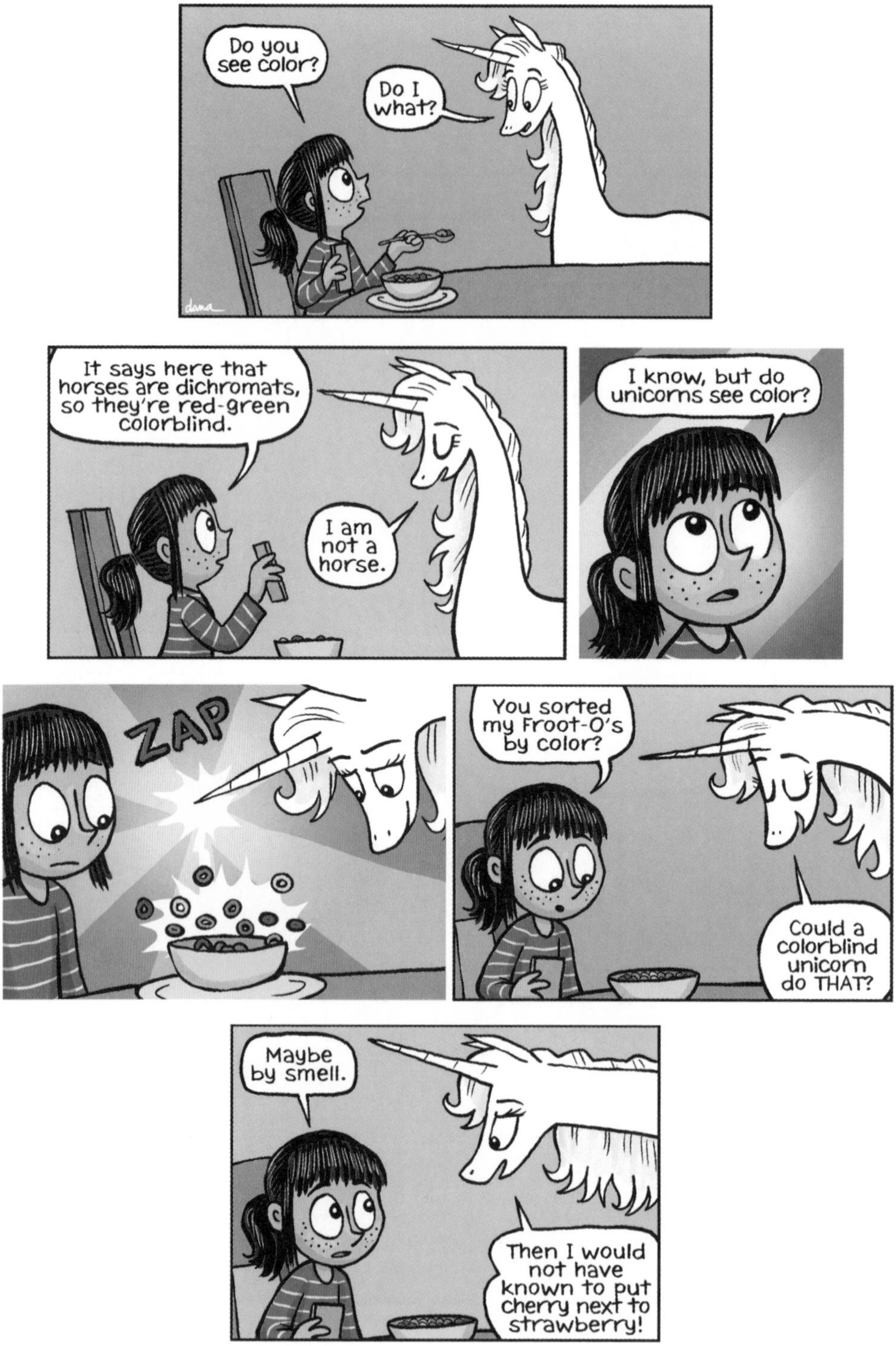
Do you see color?
Do I what?
It says here that horses are dichromats, so they're red-green colorblind.
I am not a horse.
I know, but do unicorns see color?
ZAP
You sorted my Froot-O's by color?
Could a colorblind unicorn do THAT?
Maybe by smell.
Then I would not have known to put cherry next to strawberry!

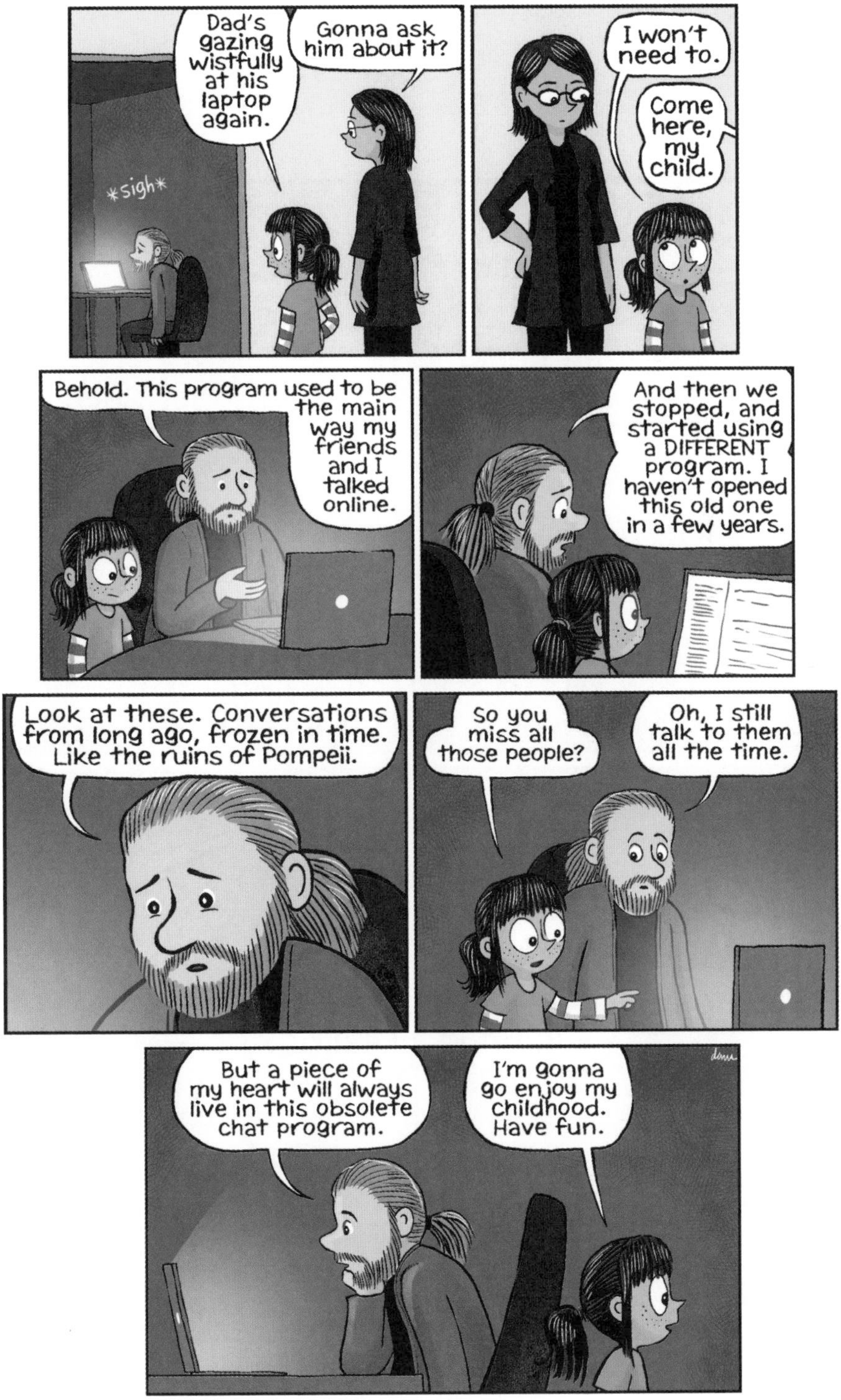
Dad's gazing wistfully at his laptop again.
Gonna ask him about it?
sigh
I won't need to.
Come here, my child.
Behold. This program used to be the main way my friends and I talked online.
And then we stopped, and started using a DIFFERENT program. I haven't opened this old one in a few years.
Look at these. Conversations from long ago, frozen in time. Like the ruins of Pompeii.
So you miss all those people?
Oh, I still talk to them all the time.
But a piece of my heart will always live in this obsolete chat program.
I'm gonna go enjoy my childhood. Have fun.

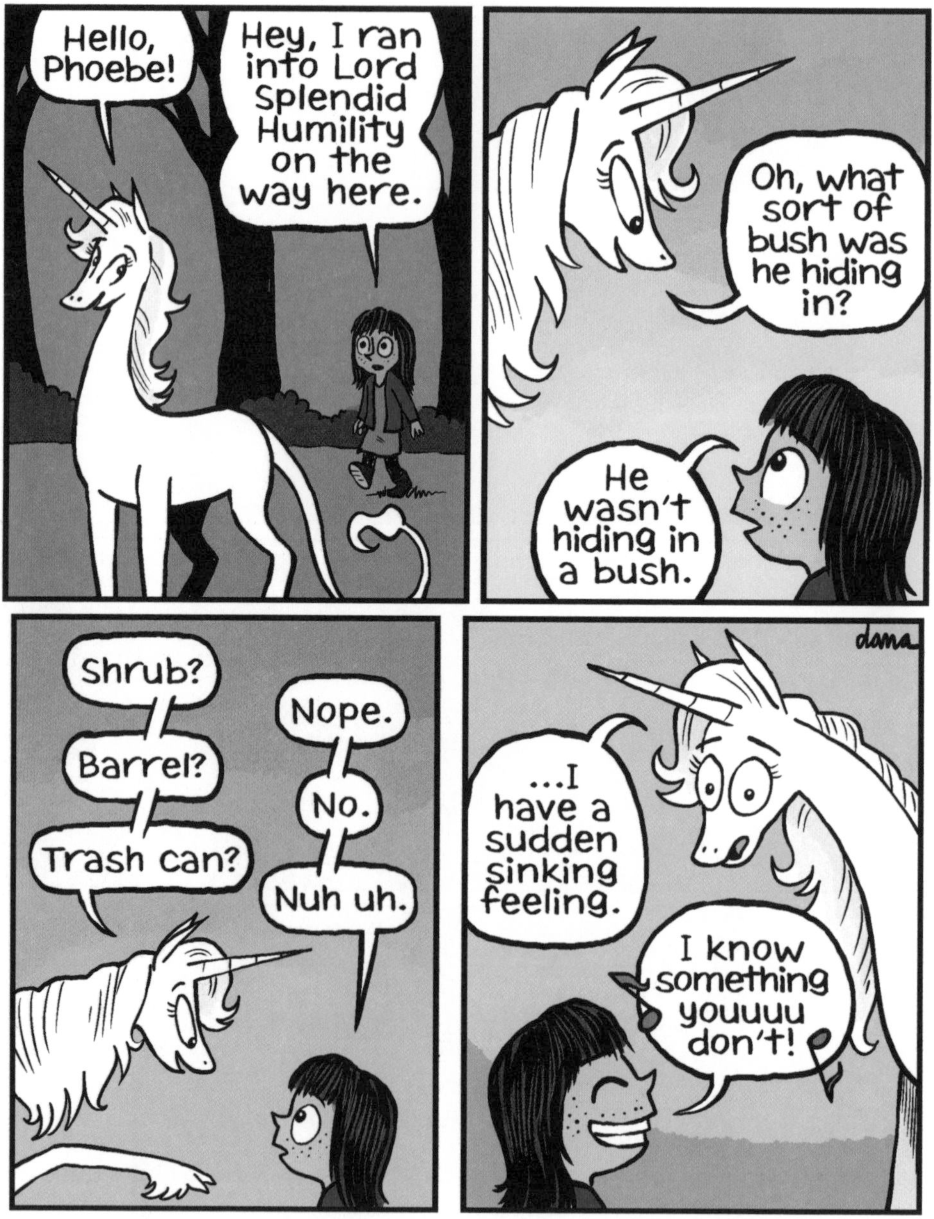
Hello, Phoebe!
Hey, I ran into Lord Splendid Humility on the way here.
Oh, what sort of bush was he hiding in?
He wasn't hiding in a bush.
Shrub?
Barrel?
Trash can?
Nope.
No.
Nuh uh.
...I have a sudden sinking feeling.
I know something youuuu don't!
dana

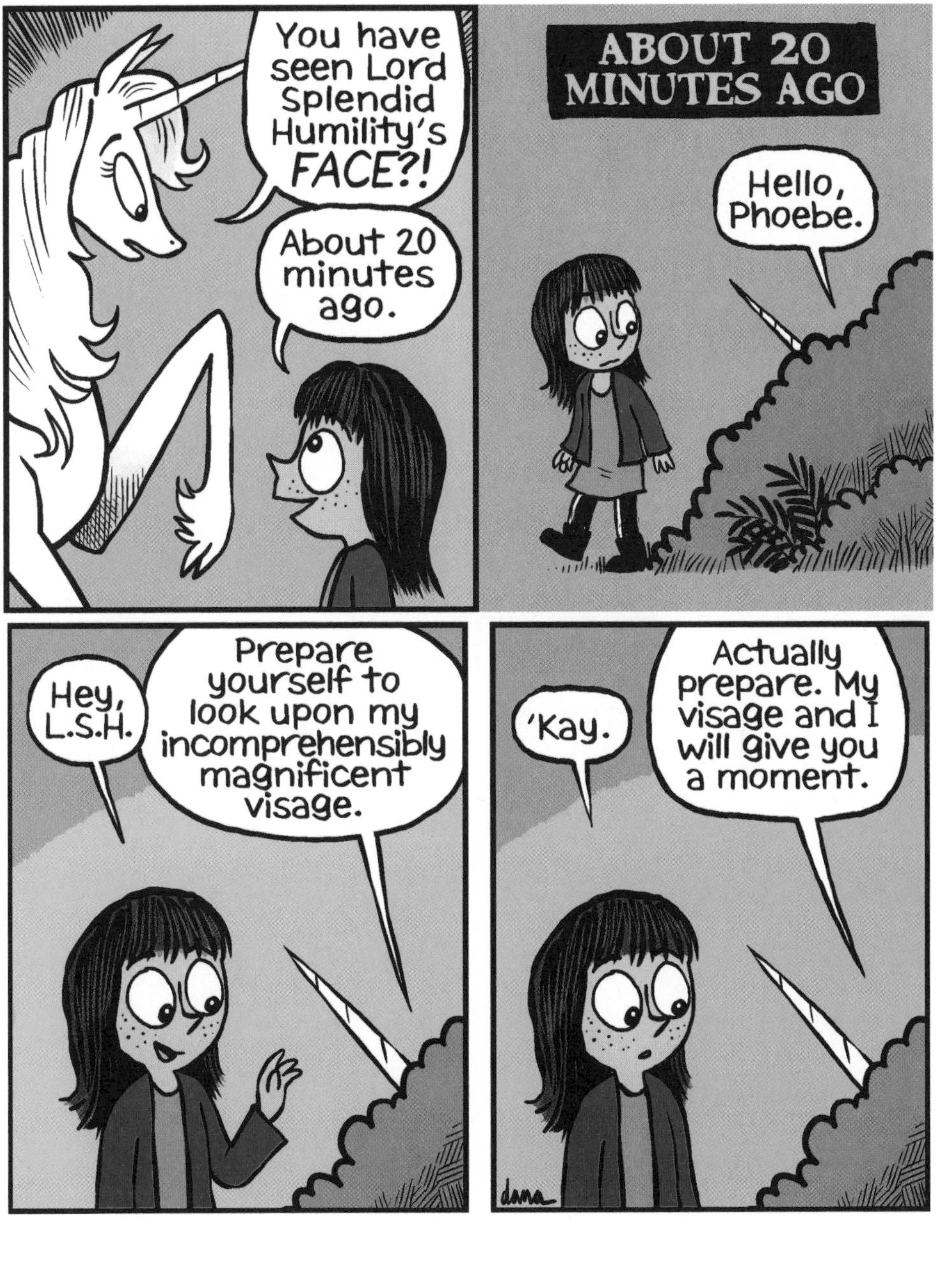
You have seen Lord Splendid Humility's *FACE?!*
About 20 minutes ago.
ABOUT 20 MINUTES AGO
Hello, Phoebe.
Hey, L.S.H.
Prepare yourself to look upon my incomprehensibly magnificent visage.
'Kay.
Actually prepare. My visage and I will give you a moment.
dana

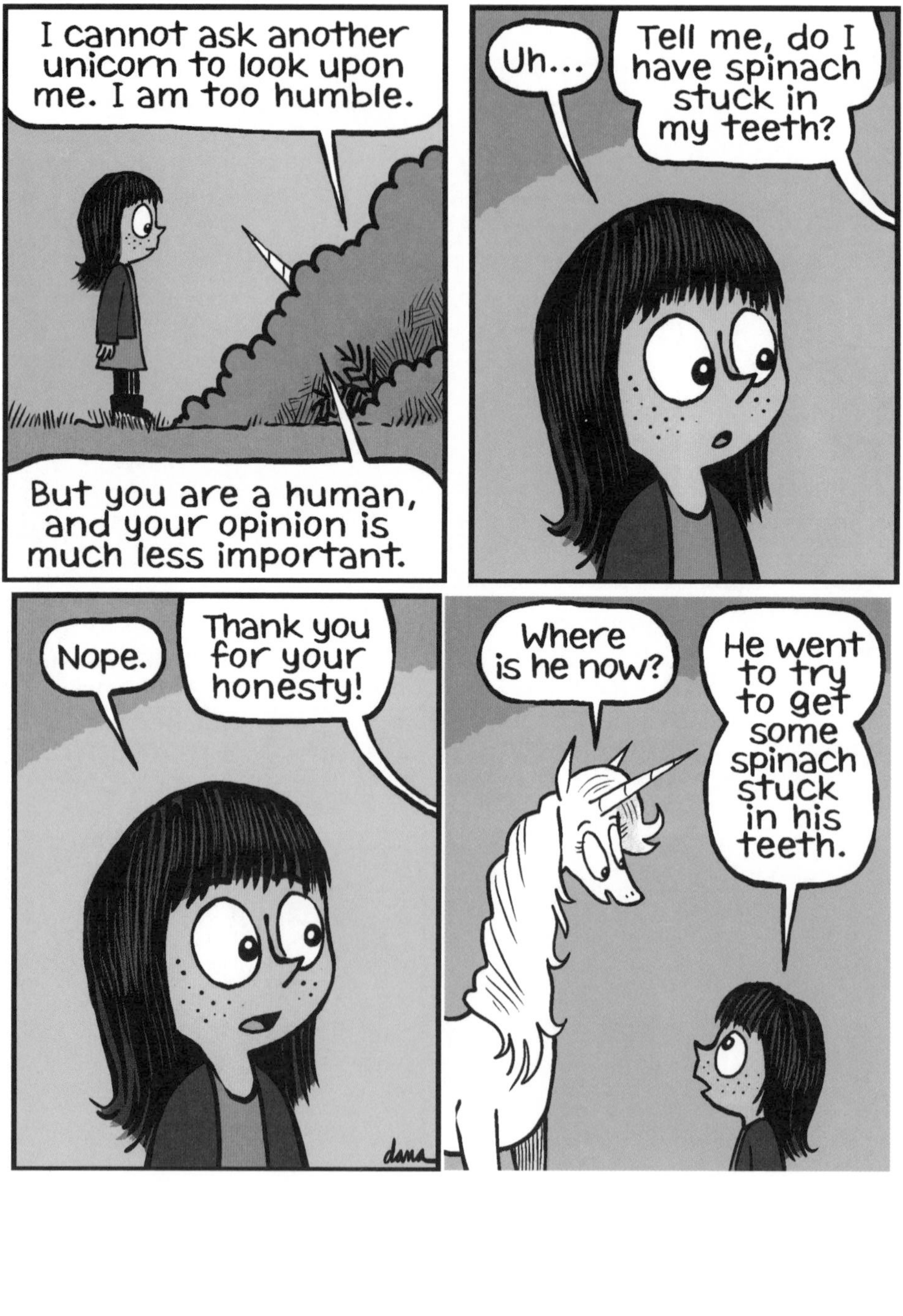
I cannot ask another unicorn to look upon me. I am too humble.
But you are a human, and your opinion is much less important.
Uh...
Tell me, do I have spinach stuck in my teeth?
Nope.
Thank you for your honesty!
Where is he now?
He went to try to get some spinach stuck in his teeth.
dana

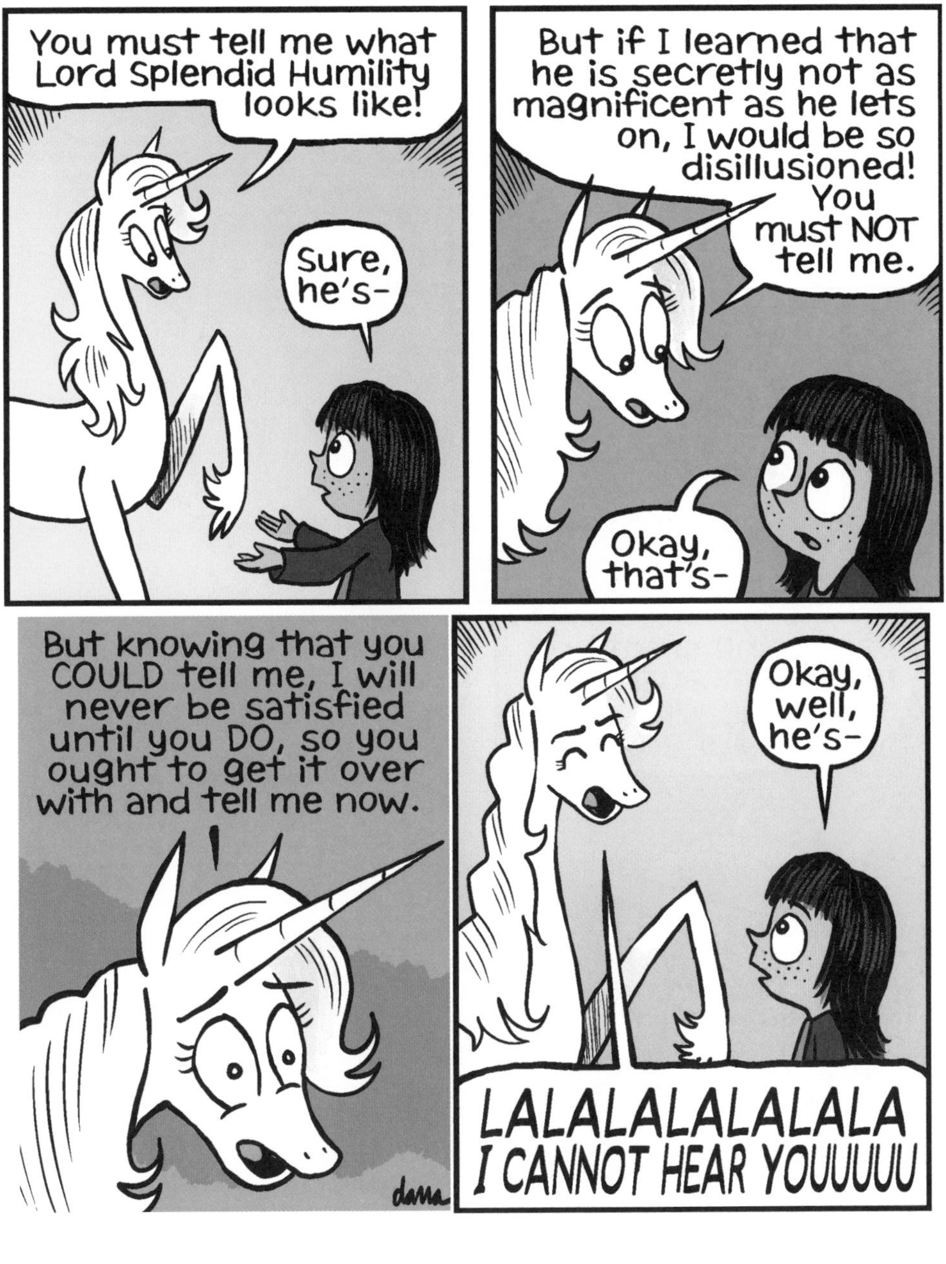
You must tell me what Lord Splendid Humility looks like!
Sure, he's-
But if I learned that he is secretly not as magnificent as he lets on, I would be so disillusioned! You must NOT tell me.
Okay, that's-
But knowing that you COULD tell me, I will never be satisfied until you DO, so you ought to get it over with and tell me now.
!
Okay, well, he's-
LALALALALALALA
I CANNOT HEAR YOUUUUU
dana

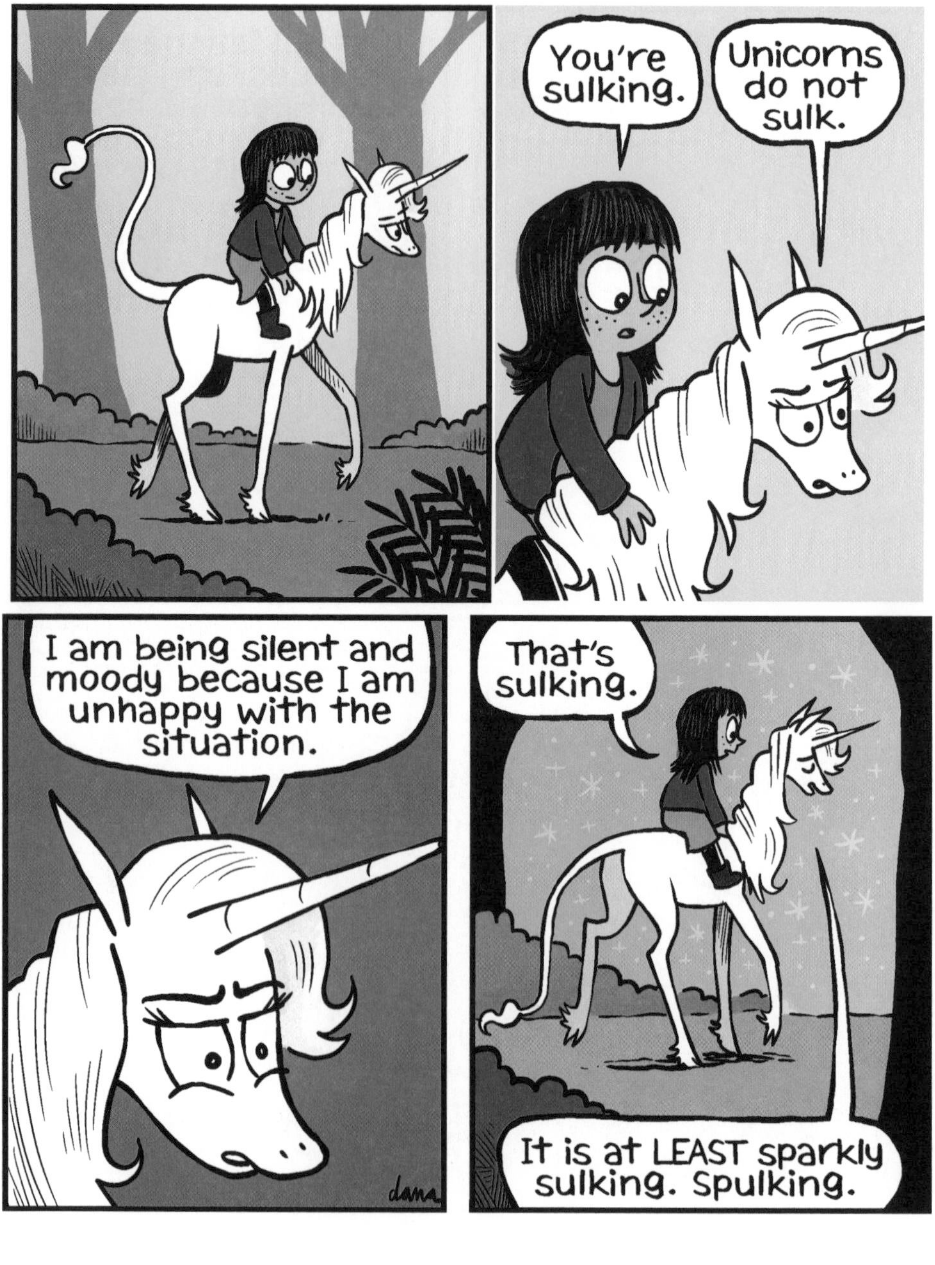
You're sulking.
Unicorns do not sulk.
I am being silent and moody because I am unhappy with the situation.
That's sulking.
It is at LEAST sparkly sulking. Spulking.
dana

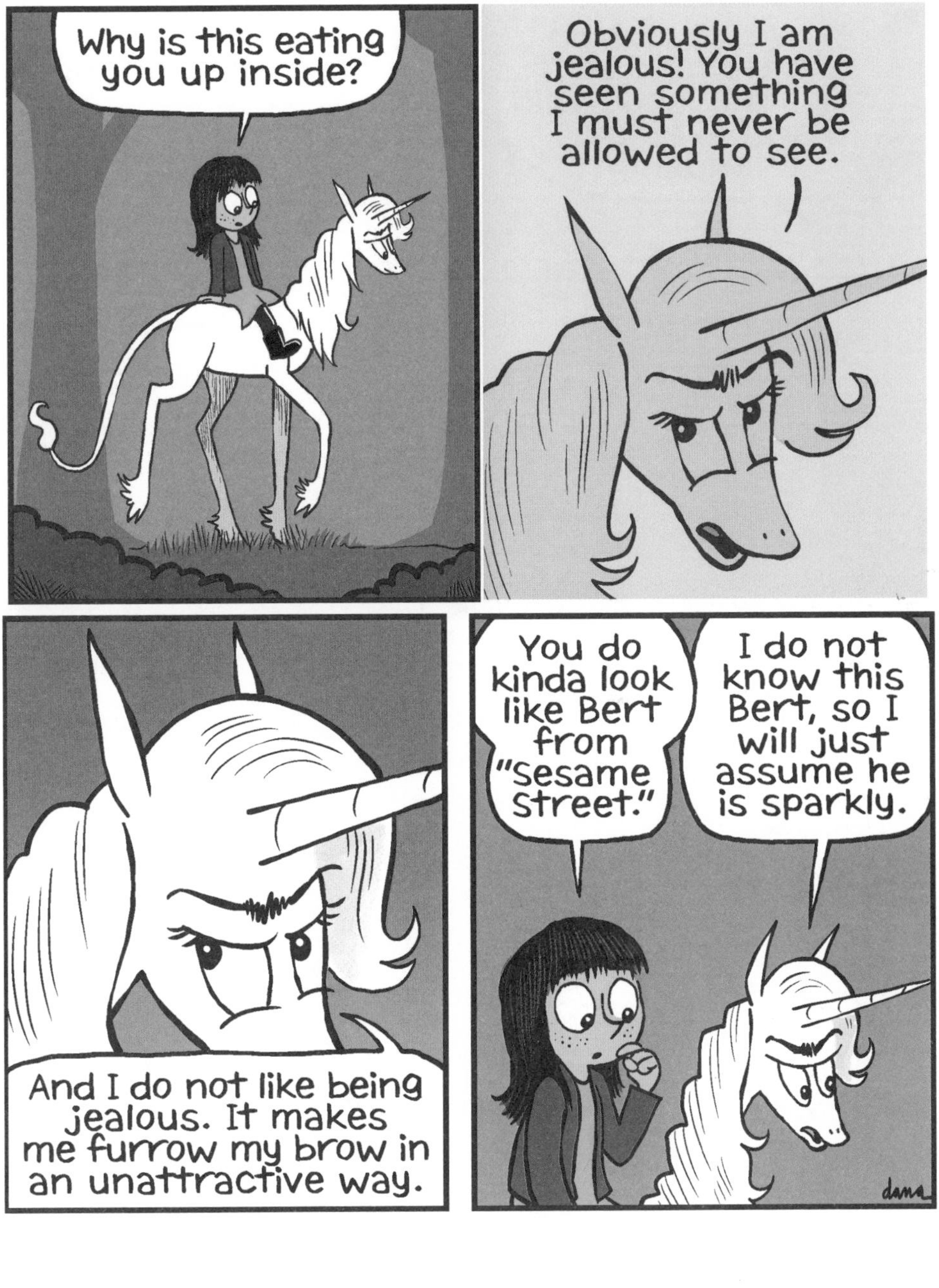

Why is this eating you up inside?
Obviously I am jealous! You have seen something I must never be allowed to see.
And I do not like being jealous. It makes me furrow my brow in an unattractive way.
You do kinda look like Bert from "Sesame Street."
I do not know this Bert, so I will just assume he is sparkly.
dana

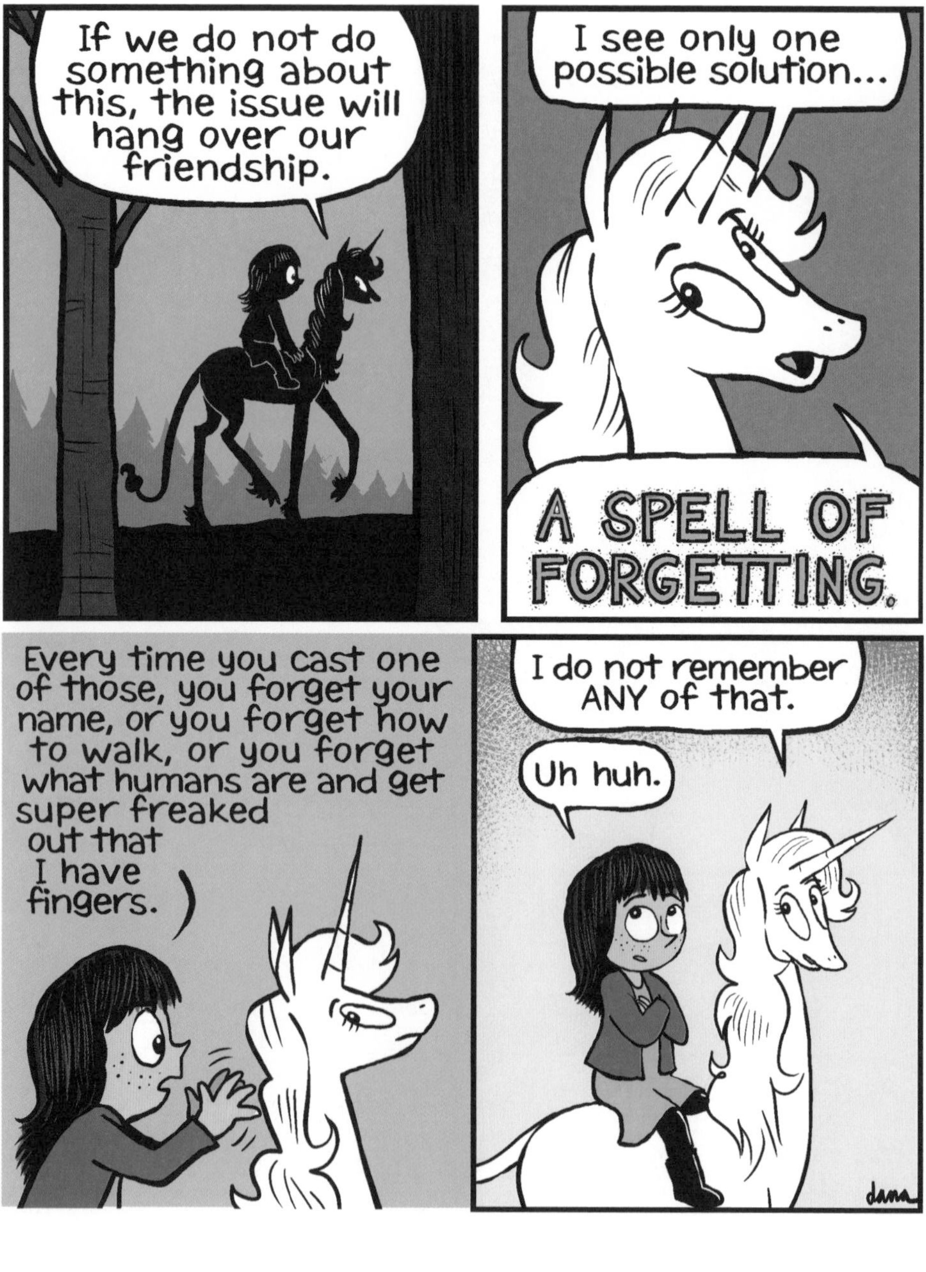
If we do not do something about this, the issue will hang over our friendship.
I see only one possible solution...
A SPELL OF FORGETTING.
Every time you cast one of those, you forget your name, or you forget how to walk, or you forget what humans are and get super freaked out that I have fingers.
I do not remember ANY of that.
Uh huh.
dana

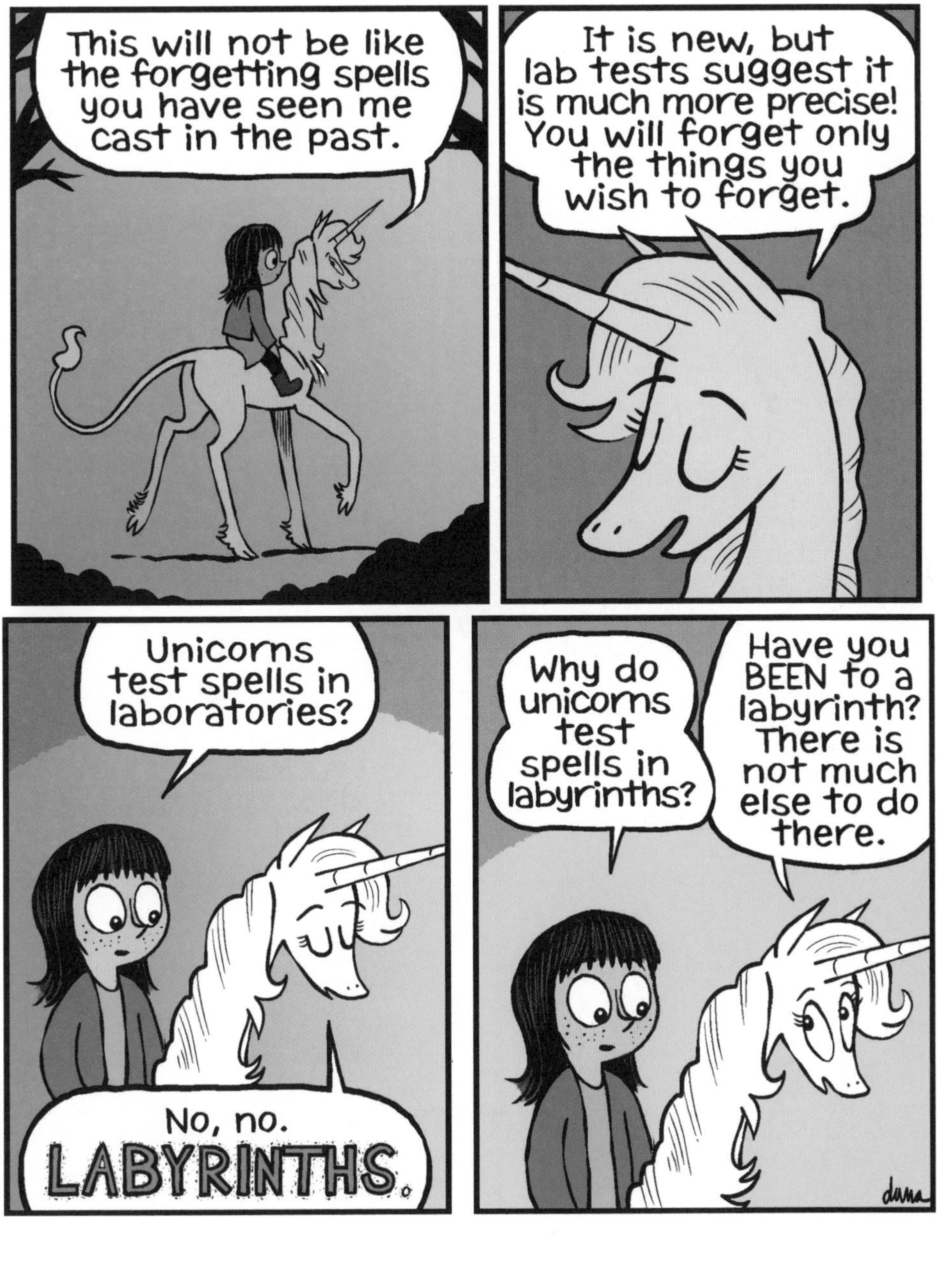
This will not be like the forgetting spells you have seen me cast in the past.
It is new, but lab tests suggest it is much more precise! You will forget only the things you wish to forget.
Unicorns test spells in laboratories?
No, no. LABYRINTHS.
Why do unicorns test spells in labyrinths?
Have you BEEN to a labyrinth? There is not much else to do there.
dana

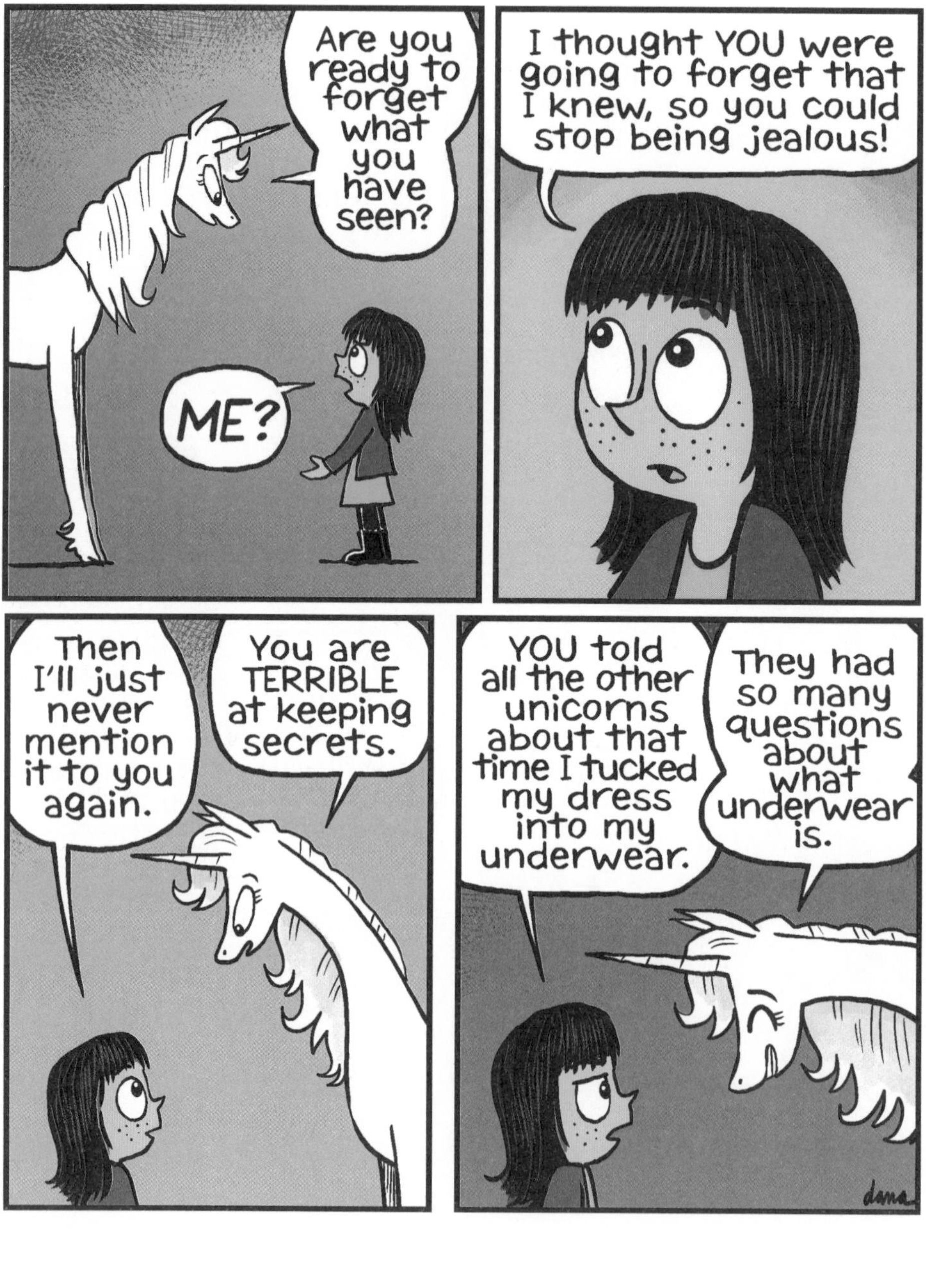
Are you ready to forget what you have seen?
ME?
I thought YOU were going to forget that I knew, so you could stop being jealous!
Then I'll just never mention it to you again.
You are TERRIBLE at keeping secrets.
YOU told all the other unicorns about that time I tucked my dress into my underwear.
They had so many questions about what underwear is.
dana

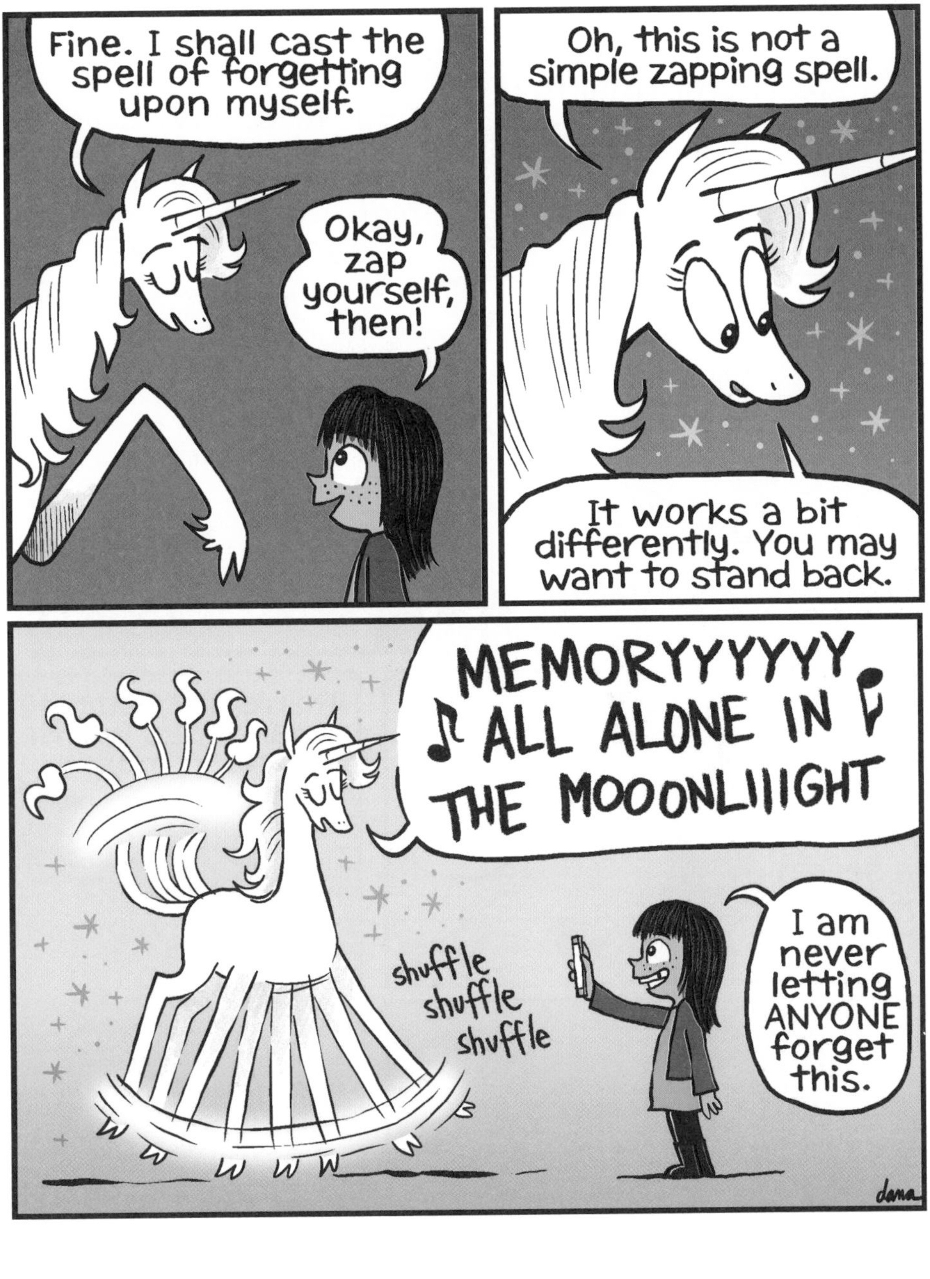

Fine. I shall cast the spell of forgetting upon myself.
Okay, zap yourself, then!
Oh, this is not a simple zapping spell.
It works a bit differently. You may want to stand back.
MEMORYYYYYY ALL ALONE IN THE MOOONLIIIGHT
shuffle shuffle shuffle
I am never letting ANYONE forget this.
dana

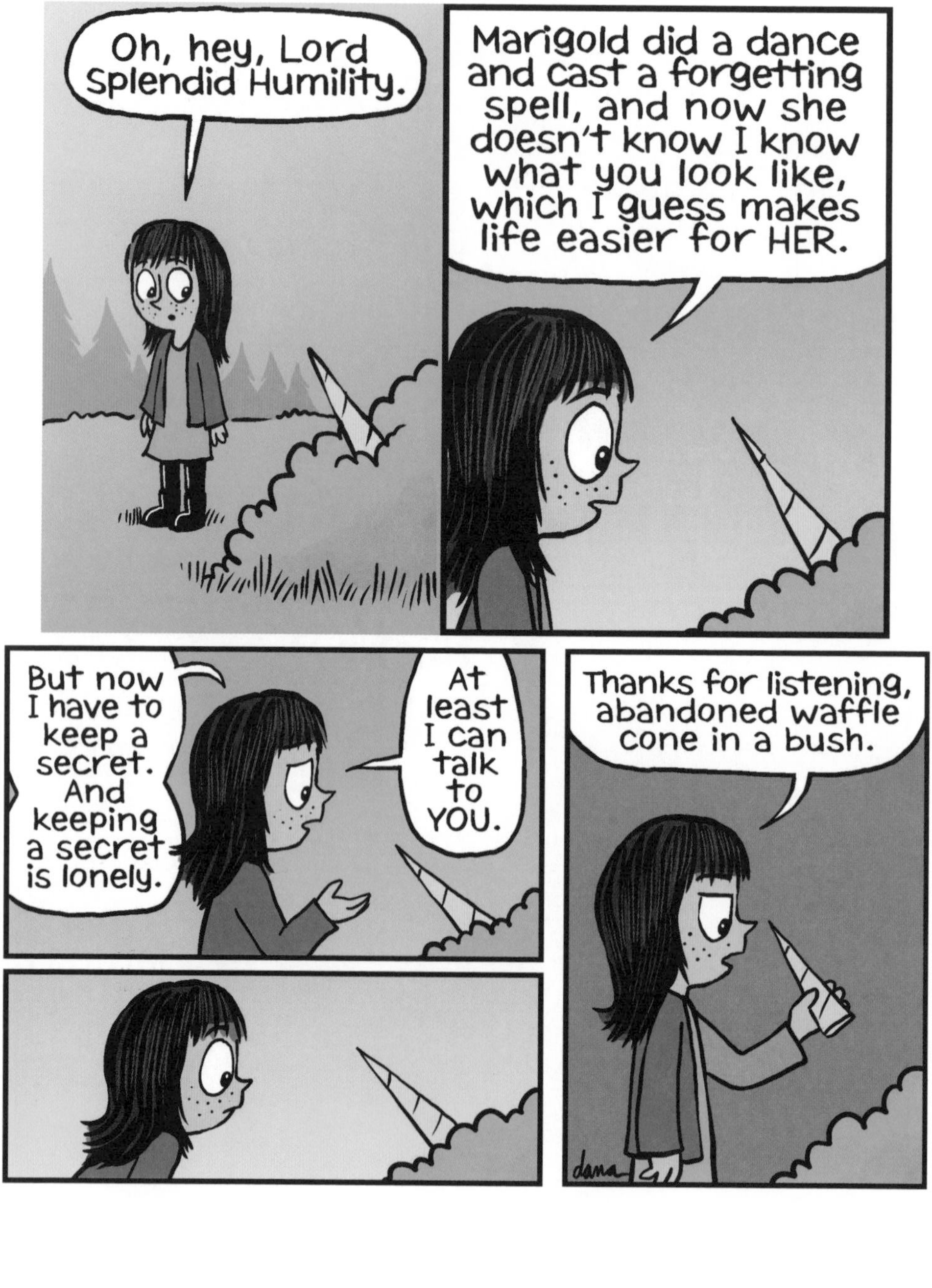
Oh, hey, Lord Splendid Humility.
Marigold did a dance and cast a forgetting spell, and now she doesn't know I know what you look like, which I guess makes life easier for HER.
But now I have to keep a secret. And keeping a secret is lonely.
At least I can talk to YOU.
Thanks for listening, abandoned waffle cone in a bush.
dana

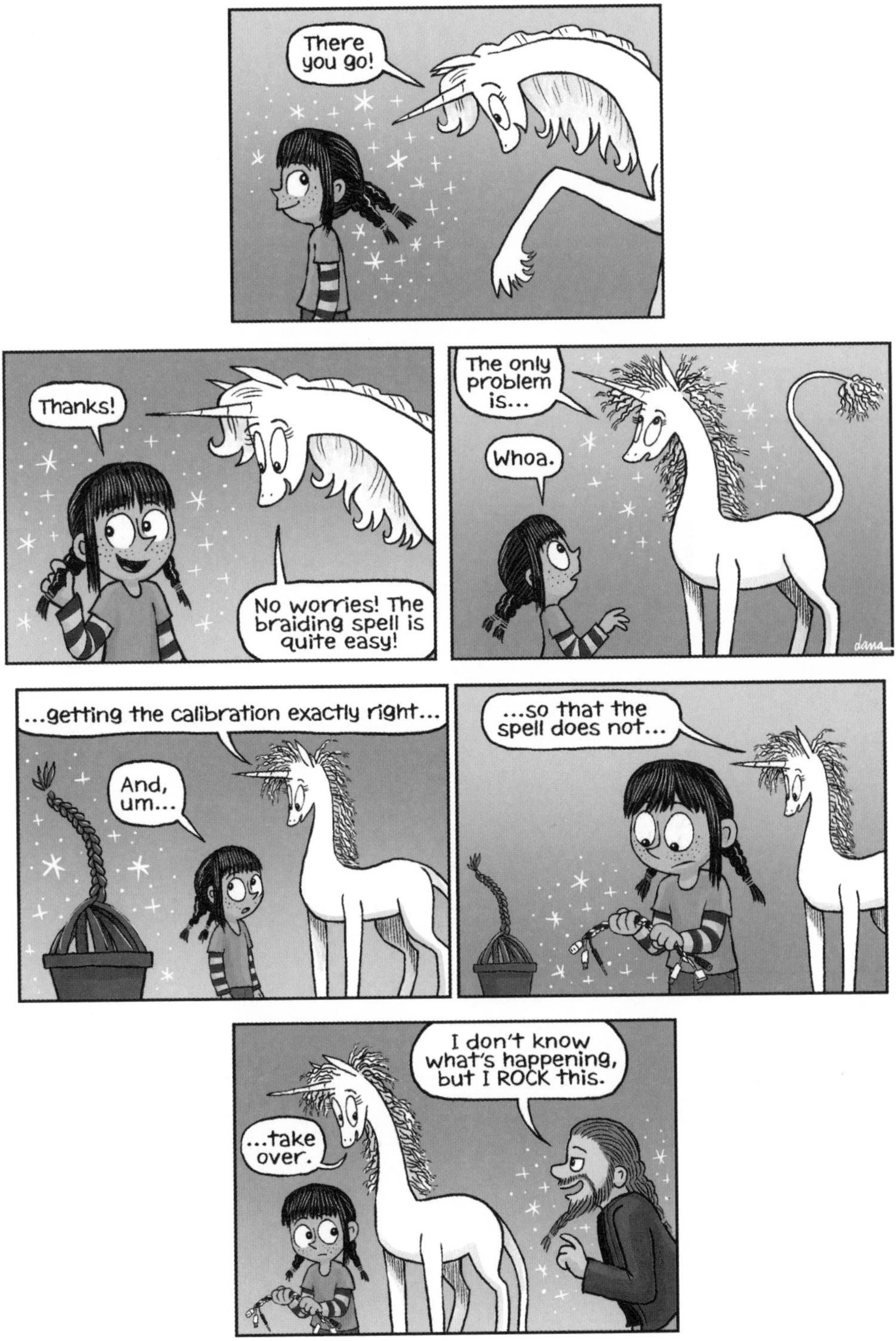
There you go!
Thanks!
No worries! The braiding spell is quite easy!
The only problem is...
Whoa.
dana
...getting the calibration exactly right...
And, um...
...so that the spell does not...
...take over.
I don't know what's happening, but I ROCK this.

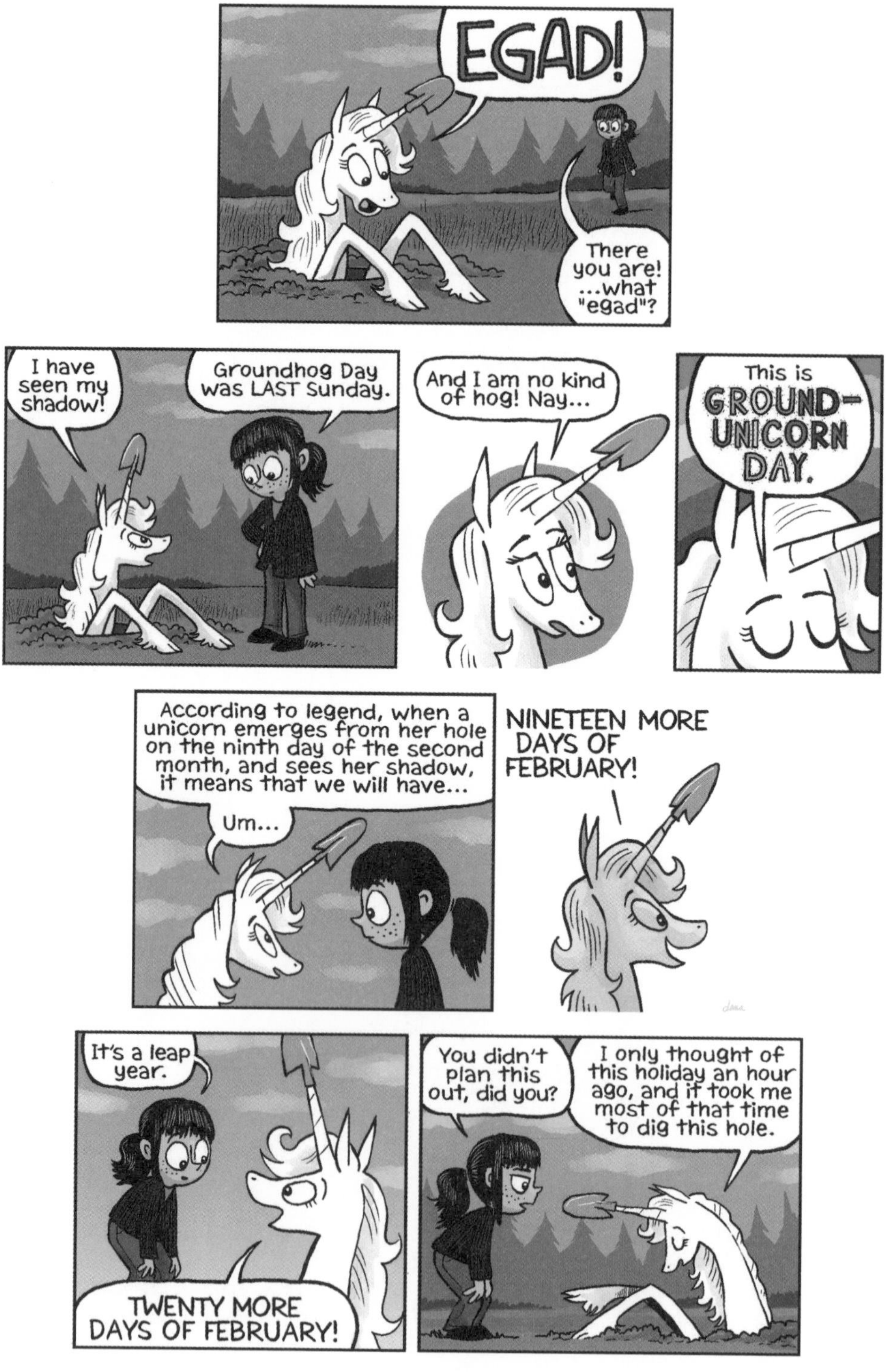
EGAD!
There you are! ...what "egad"?
I have seen my shadow!
Groundhog Day was LAST Sunday.
And I am no kind of hog! Nay...
This is GROUND-UNICORN DAY.
According to legend, when a unicorn emerges from her hole on the ninth day of the second month, and sees her shadow, it means that we will have...
NINETEEN MORE DAYS OF FEBRUARY!
Um...
It's a leap year.
TWENTY MORE DAYS OF FEBRUARY!
You didn't plan this out, did you?
I only thought of this holiday an hour ago, and it took me most of that time to dig this hole.

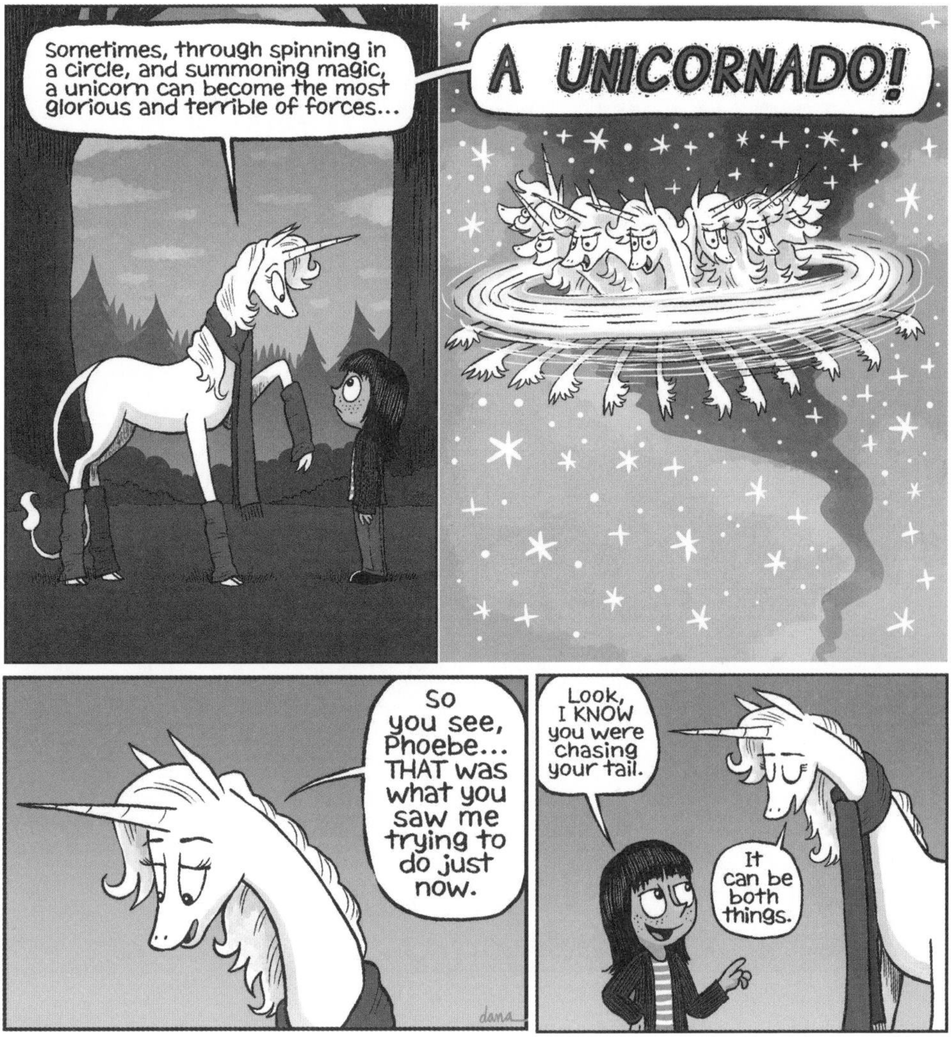
Sometimes, through spinning in a circle, and summoning magic, a unicorn can become the most glorious and terrible of forces...
A UNICORNADO!
So you see, Phoebe... THAT was what you saw me trying to do just now.
Look, I KNOW you were chasing your tail.
It can be both things.

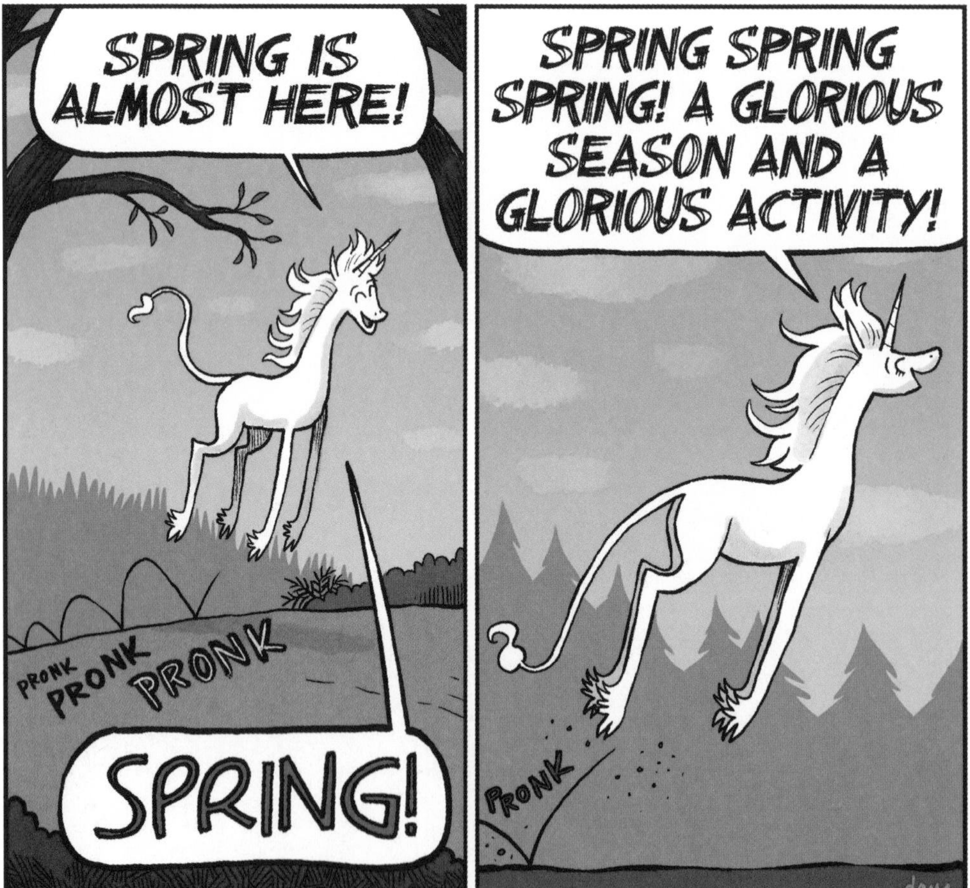
SPRING IS ALMOST HERE!
PRONK PRONK PRONK
SPRING!
SPRING SPRING SPRING! A GLORIOUS SEASON AND A GLORIOUS ACTIVITY!
PRONK
dana

PRONK   PRONK

THUNK

You sprung too hard.

"Sprang" is the more widely accepted past tense form of the verb "to spring," even if "sprung" is also sometimes accepted.

GLOSSARY

Abandoning (uh-ban-done-ing): pg. 29 – verb / to leave something so it contains nothing; empty

Alienating (ay-lee-un-ate-ing): pg. 114 – verb / causing isolation or inspiring disloyalty

Amnesia (am-nee-zhah): pg. 50 – noun / moderate to severe case of memory loss due to injury, illness, or other factors

Aspire (uh-spy-er): pg. 130 – verb / to have high hopes or goals

Assumption (uh-sump-shun): pg. 61 – noun / something that is believed to be true

Cabal (kuh-ball): pg. 42 – noun / a small group of people working together in secret for political purposes

Coincidence (koh-win-suh-dense): pg. 41 – noun / an event or multiple events occurring at the same time by chance

Compassionate (kom-pa-shun-it): pg. 94 – adjective / feeling sorrow or concern for another person's suffering

Consistency (kun-sis-tun-see): pg. 115 – noun / the thickness or firmness of a substance, usually a liquid

Conspiracy (kun-speer-uh-see): pg. 23 – noun / a secret plot or plan

Cranial (crane-ee-ull): pg. 78 – adjective / having to do with the skull

Crystalline (kris-tull-een): pg. 8 – adjective / an object with a similar structure to, or made up of, crystals

Disillusioned (diss-ill-loo-zhund): pg. 159 – adjective / to have lost faith in something once thought of as good

Disputes (di-spyoots): pg. 73 – verb / a heated argument or disagreement

Edifying (edd-if-eye-ing): pg. 17 – adjective / offering of emotional, moral, or intellectual instruction

Emit (e-mitt): pg. 108 – verb / to produce or give off, radiate

Equine (ek-wine): pg. 137 – adjective / relating to or resembling a horse

Fascinated (fa-sin-ate-ed): pg. 86 – adjective / to be very interested

Fescue grass (fess-kew): pg. 37 – noun / a type of grass that grows in cool weather and is native to Europe

Gallivanting (gal-uh-vant-ing): pg. 7 – verb / to move about in an enjoyable way

Honorary (on-eh-rare-ee): pg. 28 – adjective / in recognition of honor

Impasse (im-pass): pg. 36 – noun / a circumstance or situation that seems difficult to escape

Incomprehensible (in-comp-ree-henz-uh-bowl): pg. 157 – adjective / difficult to make sense of

Instilling (in-still-ing): pg. 58 – verb / to gradually put something in someone else's mind

Maneuver (muh-noo-ver): pg. 45 – noun / a careful movement involving skill

Meddle (meh-dull): pg. 79 – verb / to insert oneself in a matter that does not involve them

Ornamentation (orn-uh-men-tay-shun): pg. 110 – noun / decorated or adorned

Preconceived (pree-kun-seeved): pg. 61 – verb / forming an opinion about something before knowing the facts

Proposition (prop-uh-zih-shun): pg. 53 – verb / a suggestion or offer to be considered

Resolution (rez-uh-loo-shun): pg. 129 – noun / a new goal, often made at the beginning of a new year

Roughage (ruff-age): pg. 46 – noun / fiber; fibrous material in food

Sensible (sen-si-bull): pg. 86 – adjective / something that is practical

Sneer (snuh-ear): pg. 80 – verb / to mock or show anger or disgust in tone

Solidarity (saw-li-dair-uh-tee): pg. 39 – noun / to be in agreement with and show commitment to a group of people

Sphinx (s-fink-s): pg. 16 – noun / a creature with the body of a lion and the head of a human found in ancient Egyptian and Greek mythology

Sylvan (sill-vun): pg. 8 – adjective / having to do with the woods or forest

Underestimated (uhn-der-est-uh-mate-ed): pg. 138 – verb / to place a low value on someone or something

Visage (vy-suj): pg. 157 – noun / someone's face or facial expression

Wistfully (wist-full-ee): pg. 155 – adjective / a feeling of longing or regret

Withering (with-ur-ing): pg. 80 – adjective / becoming shriveled or dried of moisture

Phoebe and Her Unicorn is distributed internationally by Andrews McMeel Syndication.

Unicornado! copyright © 2022 by Dana Simpson. All rights reserved. Printed in China. No part of this book may be used or reproduced in any manner whatsoever without written permission except in the case of reprints in the context of reviews.

Andrews McMeel Publishing
a division of Andrews McMeel Universal
1130 Walnut Street, Kansas City, Missouri 64106

www.andrewsmcmeel.com

22 23 24 25 26 SDB 10 9 8 7 6 5 4 3 2 1

ISBN: 978-1-5248-7556-5

Library of Congress Control Number: 2022932535

Made by:
King Yip (Dongguan) Printing & Packaging Factory Ltd.
Address and location of manufacturer:
Daning Administrative District, Humen Town
Dongguan Guangdong, China 523930
1st Printing—6/13/22

ATTENTION: SCHOOLS AND BUSINESSES

Andrews McMeel books are available at quantity discounts with bulk purchase for educational, business, or sales promotional use. For information, please e-mail the Andrews McMeel Publishing Special Sales Department:
specialsales@amuniversal.com

Look for these books!

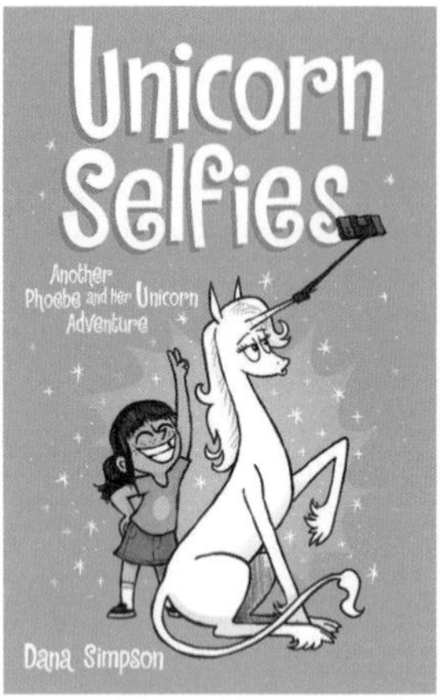
Unicorn Selfies
Another Phoebe and her Unicorn Adventure
Dana Simpson

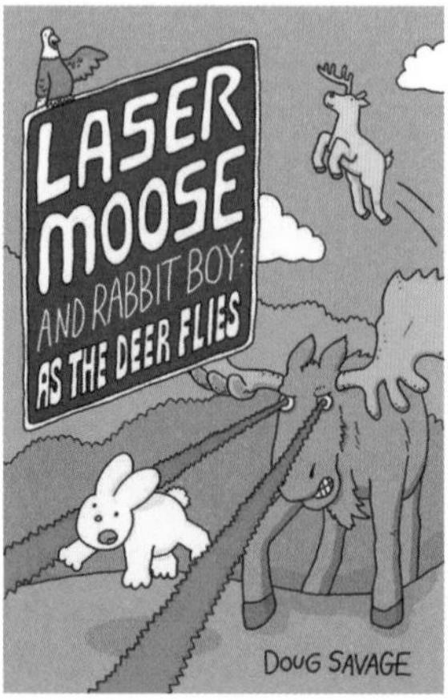
LASER MOOSE AND RABBIT BOY: AS THE DEER FLIES
DOUG SAVAGE

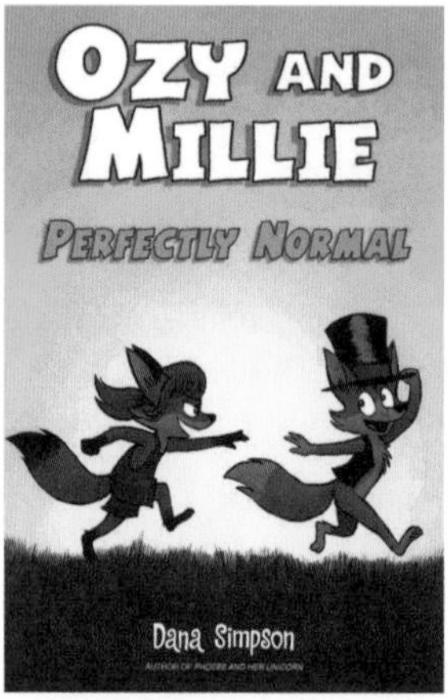
OZY AND MILLIE
PERFECTLY NORMAL
Dana Simpson

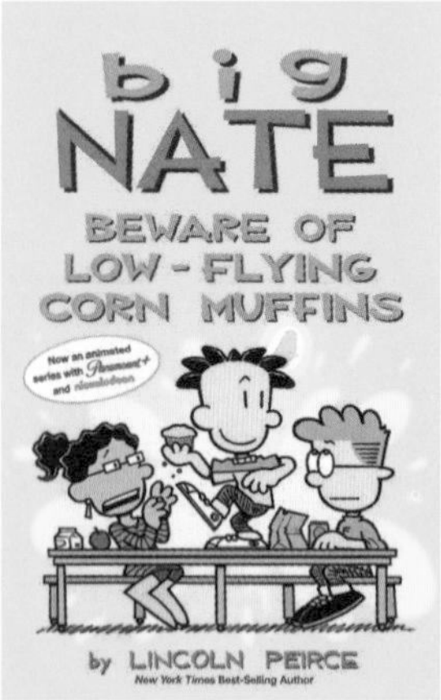
big NATE
BEWARE OF LOW-FLYING CORN MUFFINS
by LINCOLN PEIRCE
New York Times Best-Selling Author

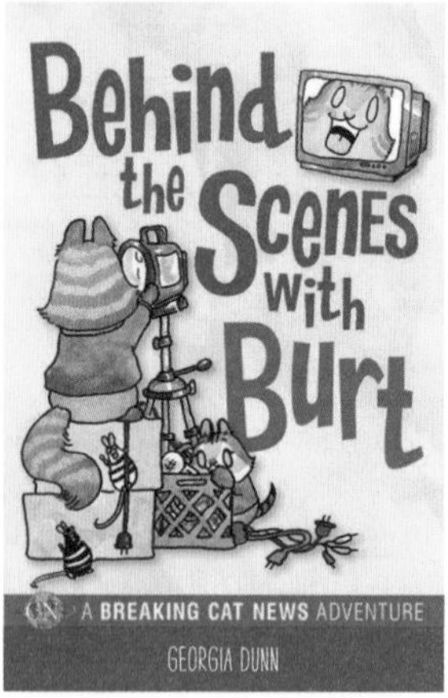
Behind the Scenes with Burt
A BREAKING CAT NEWS ADVENTURE
GEORGIA DUNN

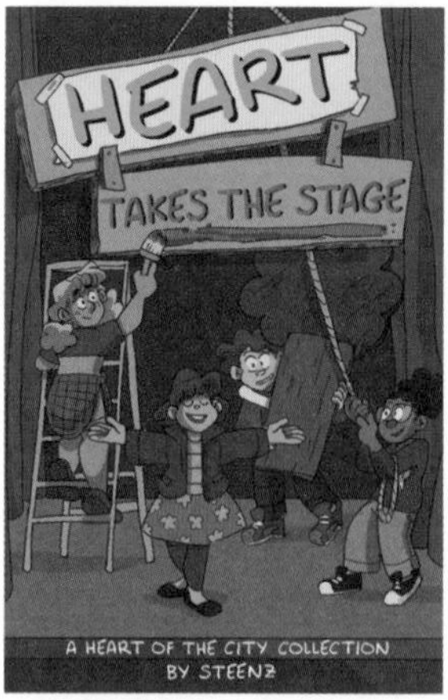
HEART
TAKES THE STAGE
A HEART OF THE CITY COLLECTION
BY STEENZ

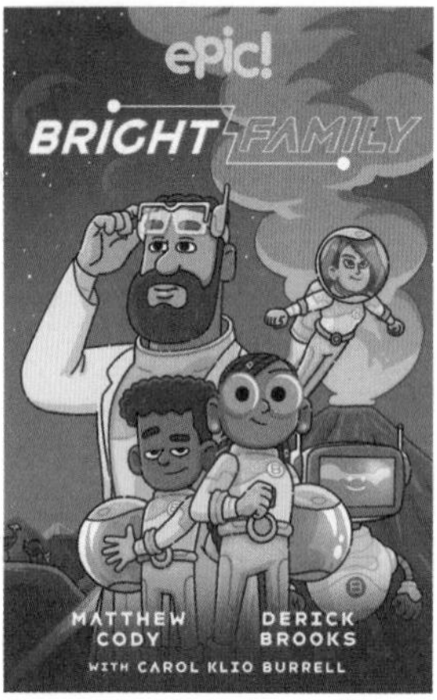
epic!
BRIGHT FAMILY
MATTHEW CODY
DERICK BROOKS
WITH CAROL KLIO BURRELL

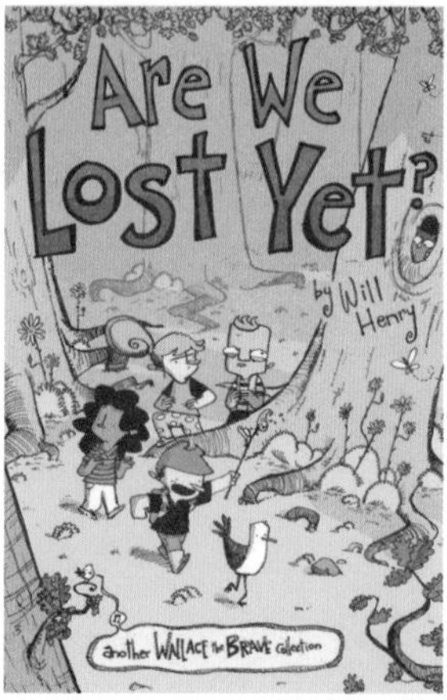
Are We Lost Yet?
by Will Henry
another WALLACE the BRAVE collection

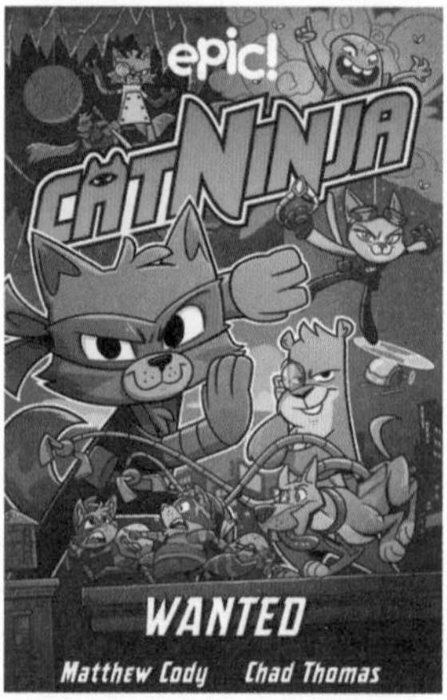
epic!
CATNINJA
WANTED
Matthew Cody
Chad Thomas